air

a novel

book two in the elemental journey series

caroline allen

Winner Of The 2016 Independent Publishers
Silver Medal For Visionary Fiction

Cover Design by Greg Simanson
Edited by Caroline Clouse
Layout by Deena Rae @ E-BookBuilders
Author Photo by Adrien Bisson

This is a work of fiction. Names, characters, places, brands, media and incidents are either the product of the author's imagination or are used fictiously. Any resemblance to similarly named places or to persons living or deceased is unintentional.

PRINT ISBN: 978-0-9975824-2-0
EPUB ISBN: 978-0-9975824-3-7
Library of Congress Control Number: 2015916178

|||

acknowledgments

HEARTFELT GRATITUDE TO editor Caroline Clouse for her genius and the depth of her engagement in the soul of the work, and to writer Polly Buckingham for her dimensional assistance in honing and aligning the story. When another person enters and lives inside your story, when they engage with your personal mythology, it transforms you. Thank you isn't a strong enough phrase for how much I value Polly's and Caroline's contributions to this novel.

For the delicious cover, I am indebted to designer Greg Simanson. It is rare to meet an artist who is capable of transforming your vision into such vivid reality. My sister, Cathy Allen, read an early copy of *Air* and asked all the right questions. I am also appreciative of the support Sheila Altishin provided so that I would have the time to write.

Much thanks to those who worked on the first book in the series, *Earth*, for they helped fan the spark for the second novel. Book manager Ensley Eikenberg helped in the initial stages to promote the series. Luanne Brown opened the floodgates, and has always been there when I needed her. Thank you, my friend.

I must always express thanks to the writers I coach in my business, Art of Storytelling. Through them, I am exposed again and again to the power of an individual's story. Exposing the poetry of our personal truth changes our lives and transforms the world. I am so grateful to be doing this sacred work in the world.

air

Finally, to Spirit or the Muse, by whatever name you wish to be known, I bow to the fact that the core message of *Air* came from something much bigger than me. I am honored (and intimidated) to be a creative channel for this book, and for the others to follow.

*This book is dedicated to Spirit,
from the Latin spirare,
"to breathe".*

VII

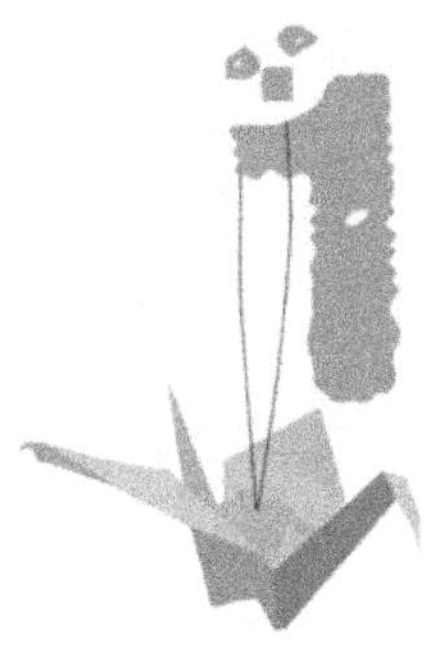

THE 737 HIT a pocket of bad air and the plane jolted. I felt as if I were falling off some cliff.

"Your first time flying?" the wiry man next to me asked, calmly, as if irate winds had nothing whatsoever to do with him. Miles below, the earth bucked and jarred, a gyrating patchwork of inlets and winding paths etched like frantic pencil drawings. The receding land bent in supplication, wailed a song of loss.

I yanked myself back from the visual precipice. "No," I croaked. "Not my first time." The first time I flew, I'd jumped out of the plane. "It is my first time," I panted, plane plunging, me clenching, "on a commercial jet."

"It takes some getting used to, flying," the man replied, working his jaw as if something was caught in his teeth, his face all bone and angle, whiskers gone awry.

A Baptist women's choir was on board, sixteen blooming women filling and refilling the six rows in front of us. They began a whispered *Amazing Grace. Through many dangers, toils and snares, I have already...*

A thump, a jolt. "Turbulence," the man said. A bit of something was wedged in his whiskers. "It's getting worse, you know." We jerked again. "Where you headed?"

"I'm moving to Tokyo." We bucked and buckled.

That saved a wretch like me. I once was lost but now...

air

"That'll take some getting used to, too." He hacked an involuntary cough. The plane joggled again.

My seat began to dissolve. I slipped through the bottom of the plane. My soul was not used to staying inside. That year of skydiving was my first ritual in the uselessness of flesh, my first lesson in the consequences of defying roots. Ever since I'd jumped out of that plane, I found that sometimes materials dissolved when I touched them. I'd be walking up stairs, in an elevator or on an escalator and the metal would dissipate, the wood dissolve, as if the state of matter was solid only if you believed it was so. Like jumping out of that Cessna had broken something in me that separated earth from air. As the plane seat crumbled from beneath me, I flew in the space between two worlds. I floated outside. I slipped into sky.

The plane jerked. I came back inside. It plummeted again, righted itself, jerked again, a collective whimpering filling the cabin.

When we've been there ten thousand years, bright shining…

"So, what's your story?" the man asked. "Talk. It'll help if you talk."

Something was rumbling up from the depths. I clenched the armrests harder. Dear God, not now.

"I know. I know," the man said, patting my clenched fist. "Talk and maybe it'll take your mind off the turbulence."

He didn't understand. This wasn't about turbulence. All my life I'd lived between worlds. This physical world with tray tables and seat cushions, and that other world, that other reality that I did everything in my power to avoid, ignore. Smash down.

The plane joggled again and the nose veered downward. "We gonna die! We all gonna die!" one of the Baptist women screamed.

"Sorry, folks, freak winds." The pilot's voice. "We're doing the best we can. Stay in your seats and keep your seatbelts fastened."

Unexpected air pockets. Inexplicable winds. Unfathomable air.

Again the plane chunked hard left, down, right. Then we fell down, way down. There was no doubt now that the nose was aimed not skyward but earthward. Everything went in slow motion. Seatbelts strained against flesh. An overhead compartment exploded, spewing roller luggage, coats and handbags. The smell of vomit rode in oceanic waves from nose to tail. My hand came down hard on top of the wiry man's, clenched and twisted, knuckles and nails.

Oh, to come this far, to have left that landlocked place, to have sold everything that connected me to that gnarly patch of earth, to have kicked and fought my way into flight, to suddenly go down in that spit, that whistle of fire, water and earth.

"I don't wanna die!" a Baptist woman yelled.

Another harmonized. "Lord, please, please, take me gently."

And another, "Heaven make a place for me."

The leveling was abrupt. The plane went horizontal. A mass holding of breath. The balance held. An eruption of applause. Oh the relief. My jaw was so tight I could hardly take in air, and made little gasps like a panting Lady Luck. That dog.

"Did you hear that?" the man whispered. "Freak winds." I still held his hand on the armrest. "I was an air traffic controller." He extracted his hand. "I…" He punched a thumb in his chest. "…was…an…air…traffic…controller." I felt as if I was going to vomit. "Do you hear me? Are you listening to me?" He looked left and right, twitched in his seat. "I told them it was getting worse."

The Baptist women began humming, low and rhythmic.

"Oh, I used to be like you." He said it bitterly and pointed to my lap. I'd forgotten about the poetry book now smashed between my thighs. I had an intention to move my arm to grab it, but my white-knuckled hands wouldn't leave the armrests.

"I used to believe in things like poetry and music…and hope. I used to think air had poetry." He spat out the last word. "When I was a kid, and some teacher said the Greeks used to think wind was the earth breathing in and out, I got hooked." He tried to snap his fingers, but couldn't. He reeked of ham hock and beans left cold on the stove. "Years I studied it, westerlies, trade winds, air pressure." He said "air pressure" slow and hard as if the phrase would make his head explode.

The Baptist women flowered into a low song. *Go tell it on the mountain, over the hills and everywhere; go tell it on the mountain…*

air

"I saw it changing. I saw it. Nobody would listen."

We were interrupted by the stewardess handing out water. I still couldn't move my hands, and the guy grabbed the cup for me and pulled down my tray table. He put his face near mine. His mouth stretched over distraught teeth. I could feel my skin stretched, too, the fleshy consequence of troubled winds. Another stewardess, green in face, held a garbage bag, and people were throwing in their vomit bags. The smell of it bled up into my face.

"What is it you do for a living?"

"Journalist," I managed. I hadn't actually worked as a journalist yet, just earned my degree. I didn't want to talk to this man. He was disturbing me almost as much as the turbulence. I turned my head to the window and pretended to watch the sky. The sight of all that defiant air sickened me, so I had to turn back.

"Don't even try to write about this, these winds. Hear me? I tried. I started saying there's something wrong, and nobody listened. At first. Then they said I was crazy, and it was the stress, and they fired me. They will think you are crazy." Sweat dripped from his forehead. "Well?"

"Okay." I pried my hand loose from the armrest, used the claw to grab at my water, spilling it on the way to my mouth. "Okay, I promise." I dribbled from the corners of my mouth like a handicapped child. "I won't ever discuss the wind."

WHEN THE WHEELS hit the tarmac in Seattle, the cabin broke into applause. We'd had more turbulence, sudden thumps, splashing sodas and fraying nerves. As the Baptist women entered the messy aisles to disembark, they began clapping. *When the saints…go marching in…When the saints go marching in…* From our seats the crazy wind guy and I joined in. He laughed and patted my wrist on the armrest. I patted him back.

I was a blob of scalding butter in a cast-iron skillet in the concourse. Nothing had edges. On the departure board, lime dots aglow in a black background, a strange universe of twinkling stars. Everything was color, shadow and light. Maybe the insane flight had befuddled me. Maybe leaving home forever. Maybe that man talking about the winds. Maybe my "condition" was about to rear its ugly head.

Passengers from the plane moved into the arms of loved ones waiting at the gate. The hugging, the smiling. A mother and daughter clung to each other. I watched coldly. Disconnected. There wasn't much hugging in Missouri to start with, and now it would be a long time before anyone would be meeting me at a gate. This was a journey I had to embark on alone. It'd already been such an exhausting life.

Slowly, the departure board came into focus. Up and down, all the flights were delayed, including mine. A tall, skinny woman beside me said, "They can't fly because of high winds."

air

What was I doing? Who did I think I was? Father used to say that. *Who do you think you are?* A mantra for a lifetime. Being myself boiled his blood. A fist, a nervy shadow, a scream. When being yourself drew up that much bile, you started to think you were cursed. You began to think you were special.

Who *did* I think I was? Some redneck. The farthest anyone in my family had ever been was Arkansas—if you didn't count Meghan. No one ever counted Meghan. The women in my family were infinitely dismissible.

I was moving to Japan? With no job? No friends? No Japanese? No money? What kind of idiot makes that kind of decision?

A bank of pay phones. I had to call Jason. I had to get back to Missouri.

"What do you want from me?" My oversharing seatmate was at one of the phones, his back to me. He was yelling into the receiver, loud and booming, echoes bouncing off the polished floor. "There's going to be bad weather if I stay put, bad weather if I get up and go. I'm not giving up my work because of weather!" He turned and looked straight at me, but his eyes were far away and he didn't seem to see me. "You can't ask that of me after all I've been through. I gotta do what I gotta do, and let the damned winds huff and puff."

I huddled my back to him, picked up the receiver and dialed the operator. I had to go back. Jason would come get me, take me home, and then, somehow, I would be safe.

I sat at the gate, hard-edged chairs, bright lights; rushing nervousness, televisions in monotone, news and more news of horror around the globe. It was hours before the plane was scheduled to leave. People slumping, slouching, shifting. How you can feel so alone even with hundreds, even with thousands, of people around you.

For the first ninety minutes, I could just make out the singing of the Baptist choir echoing from a nearby gate, but that stopped a long time ago. How many hours had passed? Waiting became a lifestyle.

Jason. When I left him at Lambert in St. Louis, I wished I'd never let him drive me to the airport. I would've preferred a stranger or no one at all. Him with his angles, that red hair as if his head were on fire, the stuttered length of him like the sassafras in the clearing.

"Pearl, what do you hope to accomplish by flying halfway around the world, when you don't know anybody and you don't have a job and…" He didn't say *and with that damned condition?* He didn't say, *Are you crazy?* Although I was sure we both thought I was.

I gritted my teeth. I hated when he called what I had a "condition." That was what the doctors had called it, what my stepfather, Jack, thought it was. I didn't like my visions, either, but I knew they weren't some kind of illness. Everyone was always trying to convey me as sick, or crazy.

And no, I didn't know why I was going to Japan. I just had to get out of that place of cow shit and severed chicken heads. I had to find out where I belonged. I had to fit somewhere, right?

He bent and hugged me, the smell of him like a drug, my father's boots on his feet, paint spatters on top of decades of animal blood from butchering. I'd given him the boots after my father died; I turned Jason the boy into my father. It wasn't fair. I often wasn't fair to Jason.

He was hugging me too long. I didn't like this hugging business. I didn't even like to be touched; Jason knew this, but I guess my leaving forever gave him permission to break the rules. We had not been lovers for years, and now there Jason was pulling this business. I clucked my tongue and fussed away from him.

air

"I'll miss your hair." He reached over and took a great handful at the top of my head. "Fuzzy wuzzy."

I didn't know what he was doing, making me feel all these things. I took my suitcase from his hand and walked to the gate, not caring which group had been called.

"Okay then, I guess it was nice knowing you," Jason yelled after me.

I turned. I shouldn't have. The smell still on me. It was as if he reached down my throat, grabbed the roots of me and tore them from my flesh. I couldn't cry. I didn't have enough of me left. Jason's face screwed up too, but he caught himself, did an arc with his hand at his waist and bowed low. My last sight of him was the top of his flaming red head. In my mind, I put my cheek against that hair, flesh of my flesh, blood of my blood.

Something at the gate smelled. Something was rotting. Something had the reek of fear. I sniffed around—beside my chair, my luggage. A few seats down, a hippie was stretched out over three seats; dreadlocks, a threadbare flowered shirt, flip-flops. The hippie stank. In mid-Missouri, we didn't have much use for hippies. There was too much work and not enough time.

The hippie got up and moved. He looked at me oddly as he passed. I noticed other people had moved too. I smelled my pits and reared back. It wasn't the hippie, after all. It was me. Fear was stinking through my pores.

In the bathroom, I squirted soap onto a paper towel and used it between my tits, on my pits and in my crotch.

Back at the gate, I waited again. Minutes became hours. I floated into the past. Since the decision to leave, the past was haunting me worse than ever.

They had to pry my fingers loose the first time I flew. I refused to embrace the sky with ease. My body was rooted to the ways of the earth, bound to its flesh. Accepting the sky felt like a death, a profound upending. Who in their right mind would embrace such root death with open arms? From earth to air, a leap of faith was required, and I had long been short on faith.

Hunkered on the Cessna's metal floor, the rumble of engine conducted through ass and spine. Beside me, the door was open to so much sky, prying wide the eyes and the heart. The jumpmaster yelled over the howl of wind and engine, "Get your feet out and stop!" The other jumpers in the belly of the beast glared at me.

I swung my legs out the side of the plane. In the movies, you just stood and jumped. Here you had to climb the strut to the end and fly with the plane before letting go. Leaping into air wasn't a matter of holding the nose and diving in. It required something of you, an open-eyed decision, physical dexterity, will.

My boots made a *rat-a-tat-tat* on the plane's metal side. I finally got purchase on the tiny step. Below me, air. So much air.

"Get all the way out," the jumpmaster yelled. I palmed the side of the plane, ran my hand down its cold and indifferent metal. I swung my ass out until I was squatting on the tiny step and holding the strut in my hands. The force of the wind played games with the face. I was meant to climb the strut, hand over fist, then let go of my foothold and dangle from beneath the wing, fly with the plane until the jumpmaster mouthed from his safe perch, "Go!"

It was a story I'd told often now, a tale that had joined the pantheon of my personal mythology. How I wrapped my arms and legs around the strut where it met the plane. How I lost myself. How I clung to the scarred and chipped metal as if it were a security blanket. How the tiny plane flew around and around with me attached

air

to its wing, a raptor with its prey. How I refused to let go. How I clung. How I clung.

"Pearl Swinton?" A woman in a navy skirt suit and red scarf walked toward me. The waiting area was empty. The hippie was gone. It was deathly quiet. "We've boarded. Are you Pearl Swinton?" The boarding pass was wadded up in my hand. She reached down and took it. "We've been calling your name. Didn't you hear? Is there a problem?" Flight personnel by the boarding door glared at me.

"I don't know." I was so lost in the past. I couldn't shake it.

Someone yelled, "Dominique! We have to close the doors."

She looked at me doubtfully. "If you're in no condition to fly, we…"

"Help me," I said.

"Dominique!" the guy waiting at the door yelled.

She sighed, extended her hands palm up, tapered nails, a smell of peaches. I put my cold palm onto hers. The stench of fear was still on me. She lifted me up. "There you go. One step. Yes. Good. No, leave your bag. I'll get someone else to bring it, just do the walking." We edged forward in a strange procession. Slowly, step by painful step, we made it to the gate door and down the gangway. As we went along the aisle, the other passengers stared at me with annoyance.

The pilot came on the overhead speakers. "Welcome to flight eighteen forty-two to Tokyo. Sorry for the delay; these winds have a mind of their own. We're in for some bumpy weather. Sorry, folks. We'll try to make this as painless as possible."

When I'd called Jason on the payphone, he did the opposite of what I'd expected. He talked me into going. He held his ground. I *had* to go. Jason, who not only had to let me go, but who now had to keep helping me leave. He was right. I didn't know what this other life in a strange country would hold, but I knew for sure what that old life in Missouri held. When I hung up, I saw a white feather on the polished floor, no longer than my index finger. I picked it up, opened the leather pouch around my neck, and put it inside.

"Your first time flying?" the young woman next to me asked. I turned, sweat making my skin itch.

"No," I said. "The first time I went up in a plane I jumped out of it."

She barked a laugh. The Japanese man next to her winced. She was a big-boned bear of a girl, broad shoulders, flourishing hips. Her body was American, but her face was Japanese; blue-black straight hair, a flat nose, almond-shaped eyes. Her English was American. I wanted to fall against her, to rest there.

She kept smiling at me as if I were the most interesting person in the world. "It was a Cessna," I whispered. "I jumped out of it twelve times." I was never much of a talker; in Missouri it just wasn't done. You kept your mouth shut and got to work. But now I couldn't seem to stop talking. "When you get to the twelfth time, they fly really high, and you jump out with the clouds *below* you, and then your body goes horizontal and you fly for a while before you pull your chute. If you so much as flick your finger, your body spins out of control, and then there's a chance when you pull the chute it'll get tangled and you'll die. On that twelfth time, my belly to the wind, I knew I would do something wrong up there. I just knew if I did it one more time I'd die. I've always had a knee-jerk reaction when something goes wrong; I'd do the opposite of what you're supposed to. So I quit skydiving. Cold turkey."

"Different rules up in the air, I'm sure," the woman said.

I looked at her surprised. She understood. Few people understood. "Exactly. Exactly."

I told her about how when I boarded the flight that day from St. Louis to Seattle, I couldn't find my seat, how one stewardess yelled to another that I was lost, and how the whole cabin looked at me. I didn't know where they put the numbers.

air

She laughed, a barrel laugh. "You don't know any of the rules. You're like a baby, a baby let loose into the sky." Her voice was booming. The man beside her was scowling.

"Since I jumped out of that Cessna, since my legs dangled uselessly, I don't believe in solid ground anymore. Can you understand? I keep imagining all the time that matter becomes dust and I'm flying or falling or both."

She nodded, blurted a laugh. She held out her beefy fingers. "Yuriko." Her broad hand swallowed up mine.

"Pearl." I realized I was being rude, speaking only about myself. On the farm, they didn't teach you social graces. "So, why are you going to Tokyo?"

"I'm going in search of my roots," she whispered as if it was a secret, tears springing. I could see a battle behind her eyes, a conflict in the flesh that left her exhausted. I knew that look. I had my own battles.

"You?" she asked.

"I'm going to Japan to get as far away from my roots as possible," I whispered back.

I COULDN'T FIND my keys. Like a frantic pilgrim begging for alms, I hunched over my purse, digging for something that did not exist. My handbag was stuffed with receipts, slips of paper, a wad of rubber bands—chaos in the depths. Somehow I'd become like my mother, whose purse was always on the verge of spilling its guts.

In the middle of Narita Airport, I felt unable to move until I found my keys. That hard-edged comfort in my palm—nothing made me feel more homeless, more rootless, than this lack. No truck key. No house key. No work keys. I'd sold the orange truck to Jason. I'd moved out of his house. I knew it was hopeless, but still I searched.

Narita Airport was a Japanese version of a retro heaven. Overhead spotlights glittered like stars on the glistening floor. Objects and people echoed in stark relief, sharp, acutely shadowed. My hair had gone wild, flying around my head like wildly flapping starlings alighting in a black bush. I'd let it grow, mostly because when it was longer I got less attention from men. When it was short, when my face was exposed, men flew at me like hawks.

The rabbit fur coat I thought was cool in Missouri weighed on me like a dead rat. A white polyester blouse with yellow polka dots, a yellow skirt with white buttons, and white patent leather pumps. I was the white rabbit in a forest of wolves dressed in black.

In my suitcase were clothes I'd sewn on an old foot-pump sewing machine that I'd found in the back of Jason's mom's closet: two trousers, two skirts, two blouses. Besides that, a pair of sneakers, a college sweatshirt, running shorts, one bra, five pairs of underwear, a hairbrush, Cover Girl makeup. These were all my worldly possessions.

When I got off the plane with Yuriko, somebody was holding up a sign for her. I was sad to see her go. On the plane, she'd been crazy and loud and drunk. I was from mid-Missouri and familiar with crazy and loud and drunk. I had grown to like her in those ten hours. When we said goodbye, she seized me in a bear hug, lifted me inches off the floor and planted a wet one right on my lips.

I didn't know how to leave the airport, how to get to the place where I was staying. I hadn't thought that far ahead. I thought the signs would be in English, but the script was so foreign, even a phrase book—if I'd had one—wouldn't have helped.

I started to walk. I'd left Jason's house in Missouri twenty-nine hours earlier and hadn't slept since. I went in circles around the airport. Metal posts with massive numbers rose at intervals like a modern Stonehenge. People swarmed from all directions—men in head scarves, women with only their eyes visible, girls in shorts and flip-flops, businessmen in suits. A cacophony of sounds. Air leaving lips, over tongue, through teeth. Breath channeled into consonants and syllables. Babel.

Every surface so clean, lights rebounding in confusing constellations. Men in lime-green jumpsuits pushed yellow buckets and mops. They cleaned the already spotless tiles near the bathrooms. Each time I passed, I didn't know if it was the same janitor or a new one.

A lifetime of roaming, centuries of circling. It wasn't heaven at all, but purgatory, and I didn't know how long I'd been sentenced to this no-man's land.

Finally, I glimpsed through a window a group of people in a line. I wandered outside. The group was an assembly line being deposited into taxis. The outside of the airport looked like Lambert in St. Louis, except for the people. There were hordes. I always thought St. Louis was crazy full after living in rural Missouri, but even Lambert was a backwater compared to this. Honking, calling, grappling, lugging, jostling. You couldn't stand in one place for long because people would push you from all directions, brush you from all sides.

The cars and taxis were tiny, their horns like tinny squeaks. I'd only known big cars and monster trucks; here the vehicles looked like Tinkertoys. And then there was the air itself, heavy and thick, billowing exhaust into flesh, nose and mouth. The crazy wind slapped at my rabbit fur, blew my bushy hair in great arcs above my head.

Frightened the stress would spark the "condition," I clamped down hard and got into the taxi line. I stared at a spot on the concrete six inches ahead, forcing myself not to look farther, not to look behind me, not to look up, or down, or around. All I had to do was make it six inches. Take one step, another. Another step. One more. My first lesson in survival in this new world—live in small blinkered movements.

At the front of the line, I opened the pouch at my neck and took out the slip of paper. I'd only taken a taxi once in my life, when I was five and had broken my arm.

The taxi driver spoke in Japanese. My hands shook as I handed him the paper.

"*Hai,*" he nodded vigorously. He got out, put my luggage in the trunk, and opened the back door. "*Douzo.*" He pointed to the backseat.

As we drove, the window threw back my reflection. I was sunk low in the seat, weighted with exhaustion, not just for what I'd left, but for what I was about to know. Lime eyes, dark circles, primal hair. Outside the window, buildings were stacked on top of each other, Lego houses with tiny balconies jutting out over the street. Every once in a while, a pagoda-style roof rose above the skyline, but mostly the structures were modern, concrete and glass. Japanese hieroglyphics splashed across massive billboards. The roads were narrow and car after car passed inches from my door.

Again that overwhelming feeling of too much stimulation. I brought my focus back inside, took out the copy of Father Dennis' letter and worried it, rubbing it like a genie's lamp. The paper glowed

air

in the darkened cab. I studied the symbols on the envelope, the crossings and huggings. I began merging with the letters, riding the strokes, galloping on the calligraphy, dancing each symbol.

Three months before leaving Missouri, I went to church. I never went to church. I guess I was seeking meaning, or permission, or absolution for everything I was about to abandon.

In the courtyard after Mass, I heard my name. "Pearl!" I looked around. The priest who'd given the service was calling me. How did he even know my name? He came toward me. After eighteen years of priests and nuns cramming religion down my throat, I was wary of them all.

"Pearl Swinton, a little bird told me you're moving to Japan." He was out of breath, put his hand on my shoulder as if he was holding himself up.

He was skinny and tall. A long forehead, a wisp of hair combed over a growing bald spot, bright eyes. I hadn't expected his eyes to be so full of light.

"I've got something for you," he said. Then I realized who he was. Father Dennis. He'd given me face-to-face confession once and cried on the back of my hands. I was a lost lamb, a wayward soul. He tried to say more, but kept getting pulled away by the older respectable churchgoers who jostled for his holy attention. "Wait for me. I'll meet you in the church after all the parishioners are gone." All I wanted was to make a quick escape. "Wait for me," he repeated, skewering me with that light.

I turned reluctantly and went back into the church. It was a filthy hot day, the church dark with shadows, my footsteps echoing in the emptiness. I sat on a hard pew, grabbed a hymnal. The pages smelled like incense. I belched up last night's Bud. I used to love church, desperately, passionately, stories told in stained glass, incense wafting, censers glittering gold, the ritual of it. I used to stand tiptoe on the kneeler and sing God's praises. At ten, I taught myself to play guitar, stood at the sanctuary every other Sunday and sang John Denver songs, loud and proud to elderly churchgoers hunched in the pews.

Now the church felt heavy shouldered. I had cultivated a loathing. The place made me feel homeless, drew up gasses from my gut. Too much had happened. Between me and that church now a deep crevasse, a gaping maw.

Father Dennis startled me. "Follow," he said, gesturing a finger, vestments flowing. Queasy, I loped after him down the aisle, up the stairs, past the altar, back through a narrow hall to the sacristy. He went to a desk against one wall, a disaster of loose papers and old coffee cups with hairy green mold floating in black liquid. He shuffled papers with long, bony fingers. "I've got it here somewhere. Somewhere." He pulled a stained leather address book from deep in the pile. Small receipts floated from it like dandruff.

"Here it is." He picked up a broken pencil and wrote on the back of a receipt. He made Japanese characters as if he knew the language. No one here knew anything so intelligent, and I stared at his slumped shoulders, confused.

"I met this fellow Usui at a Jesuit conference on global spirituality. He runs a mission in Tokyo. I'm sure he'll put you up. I'll write him a letter meanwhile. When are you going?" I told him the date. "I'll have a letter of recommendation for you by next Sunday, but you have to come to Mass to get it. No showing up just as the service is ending. You'll have to come to Mass."

I tried to smile, but my face was shaking. Few adults had ever helped me. Maybe two in my entire life.

He handed me the receipt. "Well, put it somewhere so you don't lose it." I folded it neatly and untied the pouch at my neck. "Don't lose it."

As he walked toward the door, he put his hand on my shoulder. "Many are called," he whispered. He patted my shoulder. "You are blessed."

air

My body started shaking. It was as if he cursed me. It vibrated for weeks afterward. If this was what it meant to be blessed, God help me, and God help the human race.

In the taxi, I folded Father Dennis' letter, put it away and stared at the black vinyl of the back of the driver's seat. I would have to be careful here. There were so many ways I could be triggered, so many means by which I could lose myself, so many modes upon which I could lose my connection with the present.

The driver appeared to be lost. He drove in confused circles, whispering to the windshield. We were in a suburb. It was past midnight, and there were fewer cars now. On both sides craggy branches snaked out over walls. The breeze whipped them into a frenzy, made monster shadows on pavement and wall.

The wind took the miniature taxicab and rocked it now and then like a crib. The driver wrestled with the steering wheel against sudden gusts. He slowed at every corner, trying to read signs that I could not see.

We wound through the same narrow streets over and over, the driver growing agitated, then frantic. On all sides, house after house. There was more room here, small courtyards instead of slivers of balconies, but still I'd never seen so many houses so crowded together. I couldn't breathe.

The driver stopped and turned around in his seat. He had a squished face, liver spots at his right temple, crooked teeth and kind eyes. He spoke nonsensical words. He opened his door and got out and a rush of frigid air hit me in the face. The wind billowed his coat, sent strands of hair flying heavenward from his nearly bald head. An old man stood in the shadows against a wall, and the driver went up to him and gestured. It wasn't an old man at all, but a bent old woman. She kept her head down and nodded, lifting one gnarly hand from the depths of her coat and pointing.

He came back to the cab, stood at my window, threw his dark head back, laughed and pointed to a house that towered above the rest, with oriental eaves and shimmering roof tiles that echoed points of light from nearby street lamps. The wind blew the driver's jacket back like the cape of a villain. He was puffed up and seemed epic to me, teeth bared, like some primeval driver of a horse-drawn carriage braving the wilds, as if I were a passenger in an ancient play.

He parked the car. He got out again, went to the trunk, took out my suitcase, bowed and nodded at my window, opened the door and took me by the arm. It was darkly cold, and we had to fight the wind as we trudged forward.

We passed through a metal gate into a courtyard, with the black arms of trees twisting out, dancing madly in the bluster. At a thick wooden door with rivets, he reached up, clanged an iron-ball knocker and bowed low. As the door opened, he sang toward his feet, *"Usui-san?"*

"Hai," the man answered.

The driver chanted a string of Japanese words toward the sidewalk. I bowed too, but couldn't keep my eyes down. The man at the door wore a loose kimono. He had a shock of thick black hair, high cheekbones, narrow eyes. He was tall for a Japanese man. I felt an airy sense that I knew him, as if our souls had danced in some other place. The driver handed my suitcase to him, took a business card from his pocket, bowed, his eyes toward the ground, and spoke rapidly while handing him the card with both hands.

Trying to imitate him, I bowed with my eyes lowered and with both hands handed him the letter from Father Dennis. A copy had already been sent in the international mail.

I peeked up at him as he took it. He rubbed it between thumb and forefinger as if he were searching for something in the texture of the plain paper. He opened and read it.

"Yes," the man said. "This is correct house. Please to enter."

air

The driver looked at me, bowed and spoke, but I did not understand. He spoke again, and I looked at him blankly. He looked down with an ashamed expression.

The man at the door said, "You must pay." His voice pulled like the current of a rapid river.

"Oh." I fumbled in my fanny pack, took out a stack of blue and beige bills. I'd ordered yen from our local bank before I left, and it took thirty days for the bills to arrive. I held up the wad to the driver, who bowed, and with meaty fingers, pulled and tugged. He kept taking bills. He pulled out nearly half of them, the equivalent of one hundred and twenty dollars. I lost my breath. I had less than a hundred fifty left.

The driver bowed repeatedly and walked backward toward the gate, even taking the steps to the front door backward while bowing. I turned to find the man at the door staring at me. His gaze traveled my body, and I wanted to fold into him. As if he knew how I might bend, and he would help me curl if I would just let him. His gaze went to the pouch around my neck. My hand grasped it instinctively. I didn't know what was normal for this culture, so I didn't speak or move.

"Please," he said, gesturing toward the open door.

He led me into a foyer and motioned for me to take off my shoes. As I put my white pumps in a rack, I noticed holes in my leggings. Sweat and stress gassed up, rode the air to my nose. The stench of me. My face flushed.

"I am Usui," he said, bending toward me. Behind my own smell, his aroma was a faint incense, not the heavy smoky kind the priests used at Holy Cross, but something softer, greener. I stared at his wrist peeking out of the kimono, delicate and graceful, and thought how subtle he was. Most of the men in Missouri were burly and square with fat fingers. Even Jason was burlier than Usui. A delicate man like this was a different species to me. In Missouri he would've been beaten up.

"You are Purr."

I said, "Yes, thank you."

"You are tired. I take you." He started down the hall.

"Yes, thank you."

We went past doors made of thinnest wood and paper. It was all so desperately slight; a harsh gale could crush the whole structure. Feeling ponderous and smelly, I tried to walk on my toes. We went down a staircase so narrow we had to turn sideways to descend. It was pitch black until the bottom, where there was a faint glow. We came out in a basement with concrete block walls and dozens of single beds, metal frames covered in thin mattresses and green blankets. The blankets were so perfectly fitted it looked as if they were painted on.

Usui smiled, bowed and put down my suitcase. "Welcome," he said. From his kimono, he took out a small wrapped package. He bowed, offered it to me using both hands. I took it. I looked into his black eyes. He broke the gaze.

"Sleeping is necessary," he said, turning quickly and going back up the stairs.

I chose a bed against the wall at the far side of the low room. The gift was a small square tied in string, wrapped in a leaf. I opened it. It was some sort of food. I took a bite. Rice. Another bite, a sweet pasty bean. I devoured it, eating through to the palm, licking up the grains. I'd eaten on the plane, two or three meals. There was no reason to be this hungry. I was ravenous. Insatiable.

My orange truck had been stolen. I knew I'd left something on the stained front seat and had to find it. I flew over the forest by our barn, to the clearing, but the truck was nowhere to be found. But of course I'd sold the truck to Jason. I glided over Jason's house, but still I couldn't find the Ford. I became obsessed and flew in frantic circles. The thing I'd left in that truck, I was desperate for it. I needed it like blood.

I awoke on top the covers, still fully clothed. It was dark; I must've been asleep no more than three hours. I was both wide awake and exhausted. Jet lag. The energy hollowed and frazzled me, the flesh's rebellion against flight. I thought about a shower, but didn't know where it was, and if it would wake up the household if I took one.

I'd always had vivid dreams, always had to maneuver the two worlds of waking and dreaming. I envied people who only lived in normal reality. For me, there were so many realities. Keeping them sorted, that was the problem.

My soul was lost in a dream place, forgotten somewhere over the Pacific, left behind in Missouri. I heard movement upstairs and remembered. Usui.

A small object floated white on the next bed. I reached for it. The iridescent paper felt silky and woven like cloth. It was an origami crane, folded into angular wings, slivered head and sharp tail. It could've been there the night before. I wouldn't have noticed. We'd made origami at school, but this wasn't like our childish attempts. It pulsed with energy, a thing with a soul. Art. A piece of folded poetry.

Outside, crazy winds whistled at the deep basement windows. A loose board bashed and clanged at the side of the building like someone desperate to get in, like something desperate to get out.

S LOW AND PAINFUL slivers of light through the high narrow basement windows. Feeling jittery, some heavy-bodied part of me was still in Missouri, trying to catch up. I forced myself off the thin mattress, opened the latch of my suitcase, dragged on a purple University of Missouri sweatshirt, white jogging shorts, white socks, white tennis shoes with a hole in the toe.

On a hook near a back door hung a skeleton key. I clenched it in my palm until it left a mark there. It was ancient-looking, bulky and substantial. How an object can tell the story of decades or centuries. How an object can pulse with the desires of so many hearts, past, present, future. I felt the flesh of many on that key.

Crooked streets, steep and narrow. Houses stacked and crammed, craggy cherry blossom fingers tipping over fences from miniscule courtyards. Red signs covered in slash marks. Paper lanterns. The reek of fish and other strange scents I could not yet name. People everywhere. So many people. I had to duck and stutter and weave and halt, so many arms and legs and heads and feet. Everyone marched forward, the sound of dozens, of hundreds, of thousands, of marching feet, echoing across the city. I was not used to people. Mid-Missouri was open land, the population more animal and vegetable than human. Life was full of filth, and grit.

Here, everything was so clean. Every third door, a woman was brandishing a handmade straw broom like a weapon. The wind had left debris. The wind had dismembered trees and flown entities onto

air

the road. The broom women dragged limbs and other detritus down long alleyways.

My hair frizzled out behind me like black smoke. Small restaurants and tiny shops emitted aromas that were deep, raw and fishy. Miniature cars zipped and honked up narrow streets. I ran in an ever-increasing circle around the mission so I wouldn't lose sight of it. The roads were not on any sort of grid, each street hunched like the protective arms of a wizened hag.

I'd gotten off the booze and quit smoking. My health went in phases—the anorexic Pearl, the hard-drinking Pearl, the pack-a-day Pearl. For now, I was the jogging, healthy Pearl. For now.

I took in great lungsful of air. The atmosphere was thicker here. Heavier. It left a scum across sweaty cheeks, and filled the lungs darkly. Running forced a person to breathe. It forced a person to stop holding their breath. But breathing here could have serious consequences.

I'd been out jogging near Holy Cross when I saw Father Dennis coming out of the church. He walked to the parking lot and got into his Ford Fiesta. I'd hoped he'd just drive off, but he saw me. Usually, I avoided people. I didn't like people. People were not to be trusted.

He rolled down his window and motioned me over.

"Pearl, your departure date is fast approaching," he'd said.

"Yeah." I ran in place to keep the rhythm.

"You know, I used to be a runner, too. Do you know that the word *yahweh* stands for breathing? *Yah* is the sound of inhaling. *Yah*," he said, breathing in.

A line of sweat rolled down my forehead, and I swiped at it.

"*Weh* is the sound of breathing out." He pushed air out between his lips. How he could be Catholic and still have that light in his eyes, I couldn't figure out. Somehow, the whole system hadn't crushed it out of him. "*Yah...weh.*" He breathed in and out. "You see?"

I nodded. Sweat got in my eyes. I rubbed at them, and the priest became a blur.

"Well, I must be off. I wish you luck on your journey. Say hello to Usui for me. Very few people undertake what you're about to do. It won't be easy, I assure you, but it is necessary."

I backed up. He rolled up his window and drove off. I waved at the blurry image of his retreating car.

Thanks to Father Dennis, as I ran the Tokyo streets, with every intake *yah* popped into my head, and with every exhale *weh*. *Yah*, left foot, *weh*, right foot. *Yah*, breath in, *weh*, breath out. I chanted it against my will as I did more dodging than running. People, *yah*, cars, *weh*, lamp posts, *yah*, curbs, *weh*, placards.

In front of a butcher shop, scrawny chickens hung by their necks. Next to a convenience store, I stopped and reached down to get cash out of my fanny pack to buy a bottle of water. The fanny pack wasn't there. I'd forgotten to wear it.

I felt sudden panic. I had no passport on me, no money. I needed to go back. I looked around. Where was the mission? The address was in the fanny pack. I pressed the skeleton key hard into the palm.

I jogged back to an intersection. Dozens of people veered around me as I spun in a circle, trying to figure out where I was. Had I turned left? Right? I'd been heading vaguely west, but nothing was on a grid.

Panic flew up my spine. The base of my skull buzzed. My condition. Dear Lord, not here. Not here! I bore down on it.

air

Up and down the street I paced, trying to figure it out. I'd turn down one side road, go a block, then panic and run back to the road I'd just left.

I heard a noise and looked to my right, down a long back alley. Some sort of creature was lurking there. I shook my head. It was a bear, black and burly. A bear in the middle of Tokyo? I forced myself to be rational. There could not be a bear in the center of Tokyo. I often saw something that was there that nobody else saw. I often knew what somebody was going to say before they said it. It was a way of seeing that made it hard to live in the real world.

The bear dug through the trash. I shook myself. Still my skull buzzed, threatening. I couldn't seem to move.

The bear started to walk toward me. He grew closer. When he was a few feet away, I could see it wasn't a bear, but a man. A homeless man, knotted black hair down to his knees, a ratty black overcoat, threadbare with strands of it sticking out like fur, his face covered in grime. He came to me. I tittered with anxiety.

He smelled of shit and urine, and something sweet like incense. I put my hand to my throat. The hordes of Japanese people around me crossed the street to avoid walking by him. His fat smudged cheeks twitched as he stared straight into me. The buzzing. The terror of it happening here, now.

He put sooty palms out toward me. I stared at them transfixed. My body started to arc with the force of my condition. I groaned and tried to control it. He put his hands toward my belly. He moved his fingers as if he were pulling something from my guts. He pulled invisible strands like weeds from my insides, flung the imaginary debris to the sidewalk. Someone shouted behind me in Japanese, but I didn't turn around, couldn't turn around. Someone else shouted. He pulled strand by strand until all panic left me, until my body relaxed, my feet came back down to concrete. Somehow, he'd yanked the condition right out of me.

The bear man stumbled backward. I felt as if he'd been holding me by the front of my sweatshirt, and I stumbled, too. His face looked exhausted. He didn't look me in the eye. He turned, lumbered back down the alley. In his receding back, I felt his sadness—as big as the earth. I'd miss him, even though I didn't know him. What had just happened? I looked around at the people passing me. A few looked at me distraught. A woman in a shop doorway was yelling something at me in Japanese. Passersby had their hands up next to their faces to hide themselves from me, or him.

The homeless man turned a corner at the far end of the alley. A voice said, *He has done this all of his life. Despite himself, he's compelled to take away the pain of others. What a gift that man has, what a curse.* I wanted to go after him.

He is your people, the voice said. I reeled backward as if I'd been slapped.

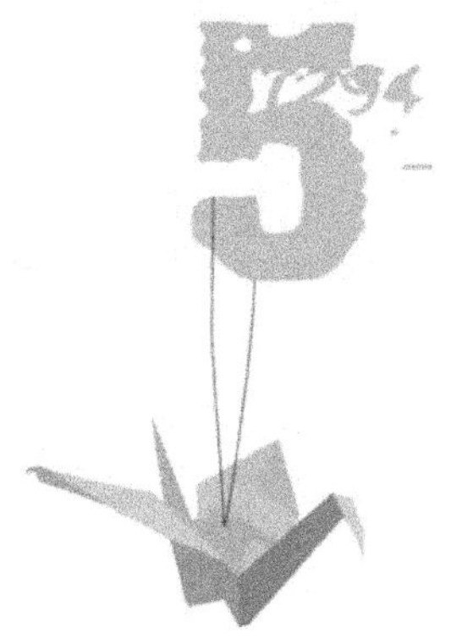

P ACING IN CIRCLES. Lost. I walked up the block and back, up and back. Sweat mixed with the cold air, and my body went into spasms of shivers. I couldn't remember the name of the neighborhood where Usui lived. Up the block, back. How could I have been so stupid? Was this what it meant to travel? Real danger in one small act of forgetting?

I noticed people staring at my butt and looked over my shoulder to see that somehow I'd kicked mud onto the left cheek of my white sorts. I stumbled into a small restaurant that had pictures of noodles and rice taped to the windows. "Restroom?" I asked. "Where is restroom?"

"Toilet?" asked an older man in a white chef's coat.

"Toilet," I repeated.

He pointed toward the kitchen. The restaurant was tiny with two stools at a counter and two tall tables where people stood to eat. I held a hand over the back of my shorts. The restroom was a closet near the kitchen's stainless-steel sink. Once inside, you could barely turn around. I didn't know how I was going to fit my big Missouri self into the small Tokyo spaces. I tried to wash the mud off my bottom, but in the end, half of my shorts were soaked and still brown from the muck.

When I came out of the restaurant, a freezing rain had started to fall. The wind pushed it with horizontal force. I roamed, bone frozen. I stopped random people, neat and tidy beneath their

air

umbrellas, repeating a soaked "Usui? Usui?" They waved their hands in front of their faces and moved around me. Icy wind turned my thighs mottled and numb. I slumped against an apartment building, seeking warmth in the concrete, making fists to ward off the cold.

I slipped into a convenience store, trying not to be noticed, but it was impossible. Even at five-foot-five I was too tall, and although I had dark hair, I was too foreign to go unnoticed. Narrow aisles, coolers of tall beers, packages of rice snacks. The woman shop owner was small and chubby. She smiled openly at me, bowed repeatedly. I tried not to breathe. If I took air too deeply into me, I knew what would happen. I went to the back corner of the store to get out of her sight. She followed me, put a warm hand on my wet sweatshirt, and said something in Japanese. She looked up at me, smiling, and waiting.

"Usui?" I asked, trembling like an alcoholic in detox.

"*Hai*, Usui-*san*," she said, nodding and pointing.

"You know Usui?"

"Usui-*san*," she replied, stressing the san.

I nodded. "Sorry. Usui-*san*."

She pointed out the window, speaking rapidly. She didn't look in my eyes, focused instead on my chin. I started crying. She said something in English, but I could only make out two words—broken children.

"Broken children?" I asked.

"He help for broken children," she said. I looked at her confused, but she turned and started pulling me toward the door.

Even as we came around a corner, and she nodded vigorously toward a house, I didn't recognize the mission. I'd been two blocks away from it for the past few hours. We went to the front. As Usui opened the door, the woman spoke to him in Japanese.

The world faded, shifted into slow motion. I'd fought it for hours, on the plane, with the homeless bear man. Now, it grabbed me by both shoulders like a wild beast and shook me. A force entered through the top of my head, forced my body rigid. I reached out to

Usui, heard the shop owner gasp, and then I was completely and hopelessly lost to this world.

When I opened my eyes, I was lying on the ground, Usui holding me. I had no idea how long the vision had lasted. I looked up at the woman. Her eyes lolled in her head as if what she'd just seen reminded her of something from her own past, as if what she had seen might just make her go utterly mad.

The next time I awakened, I was on a futon on the floor, beneath a comforter warmer than anything I'd ever experienced. I could've stayed there forever. I didn't know how long I'd slept. A vision always left me spent. Sometimes it took more than twenty-four hours to come back. I tried not to think of what I'd seen. I tried to block it.

I was in one of the rooms I'd passed the night before. Besides the futon, there was no other furniture. The floor was made of straw mats. On the walls, just one simple scroll, the words written in calligraphy.

Usui was sitting on his knees with his back to me, facing some kind of shrine in a closet. Incense filled the space, low and musky. The slow curve of smoke rolled and retreated. Usui turned. "So, Purr-*san*, you awake."

I started to get up, but he motioned me down, and although he didn't touch me, I felt the warmth of his hand on my shoulder, pushing me back. His face was in shadow, and soft light reflected off his crimson kimono.

I peeked beneath the comforter. I wore a casual kimono of deep green silk speckled in lighter green leaves. It lay against my body like a caress. I wore nothing beneath it. My fanny pack sat next to the futon, but my clothes were gone. I thought of Usui taking off my

air

soaking, filthy shorts, sweaty socks and purple sweatshirt. The stench and the filth of it. I blushed hard.

"Not to have worry," he said. "Ami-*san* help." When I looked confused, he said, "Shop woman."

He came to the futon and knelt. His robe slipped open, exposing a smooth, hairless chest. Nobody ever knelt in Missouri and no one wore silk robes, outside of church. He took something out of the pocket of his robe and handed it to me. The pouch I wore around my neck.

"Thank you." I felt the familiar worn leather in my palm like a comfort. I untied the string and dumped the contents onto the futon. Freshwater pearl. Arrowhead. Feather. "My most prized possessions."

He nodded. I put the items back into the pouch and tied it around my neck. He picked up a pewter teapot and emptied it into a small cup, the water tinkling like a fountain. "It is empty. And perhaps cold." He handed the cup to me.

"I'm so sorry to put you through such trouble. I got lost. Sorry, I'm an idiot." My voice came out whiny like a little girl's.

"It is permissible to get lost. Getting lost is sometimes of importance. There are things worse." He looked at me, as if he wanted to say something, then stopped himself and held up the teapot. "I must to go for water." He stood and left the room.

I sat up, dizzy, and tried to see the shrine he'd been kneeling at. On a shelf in the closet, a small Japanese gateway painted red, an origami bird like the one on the pillow last night, a ceramic incense holder, and behind it two large framed photos, one that looked like grandparents, and the other of two boys.

Usui walked in. "Is that you?" I asked, pointing at the picture of the two boys.

He knelt and placed a tray with the teapot on it on the floor. "It is me, yes, and it is brother."

He said, "He is not boy, of course, now. He is Ideko. He is salariman. Do you know salariman?"

I vaguely remembered reading about it in Missouri. I'd done some research on the country I was moving to, but not much, because every time I tried I nearly had a panic attack.

Usui went to the shrine. I'd almost drifted off to sleep again when he spoke. "Salariman. Salary man. Ideko works for corporation. He works one hundred hours week. It is Japan idea of success. I was supposed to go this way. I made parents very angry. It seemed too terrible to me. Jesuit seemed far away from salariman." He turned, his face clouded over with emotion. "Go for other side of it, but cannot escape.

"Before the war, we did not have salariman. My parents think it is good money to work for corporation. It is one big family. They think it helps Japan. I believe it is whole world going the wrong direction." He went up to the altar and picked up the picture.

A wave of exhaustion. I didn't know if it was the jet lag, or the vision, or Usui's words. I sighed.

"I tell you too much. You tired. Sleep."

"How long did I sleep?"

He looked at a small alarm clock on the closet shelf. "Twenty hours, fifteen minutes."

"Oh no. I'll go." I sat up quickly, my head spun, and I fell backward.

He came over, knelt and put his hand on me to stop me from getting up again. "Please." He fussed with the futon cover. "Do you have medication for problem? I am sorry, looked in suitcase. Cannot find."

"Medication?"

"Yes, for problem," he said, nodding his head toward me. "Yes, problem?"

Finally I understood. My condition. I looked at his brown eyes, at the angle of them. Usually I hid the truth from new people, but with Usui I felt like telling him everything, like absolving myself and dissolving into him.

And so I told him. How it wasn't an illness, how I'd had visions since I was thirteen. How I was a kid in the garden with my mom,

air

and my head buzzed like a million crazy bees. I looked up quickly at him, felt as if I was revealing too much, as if I were showing him my naked body. His eyes were cast down, toward folded hands.

I told him about how the garden had shifted and morphed, how a Native American woman came on the air and wanted something from me. How when I came to, lying in the dirt, my mother said, *Not again*, as if I'd had visions before. I could not remember having such a vision before. You'd think I'd remember something like that.

"I had visions every few months after that. They were telling me to do something, but I couldn't figure out what. I didn't know which was worse, the visions or the anxiety of not knowing what they wanted."

"What is vision you have just now?" Usui asked.

I sighed again. "I was in a Japanese town. It was still, this eerie emptiness, like a nothingness. Then there was this sucking sound, like a massive inhaling. Sometimes there are voices with the visions, giving me messages, and there was this voice that said, *You are not us. You are different than us. We are not the same.* And I knew they weren't talking to me, but to the people of the town.

"Then a fireball scorched the town, burned everything. The fireball sucked upward into the air, and it pulled the earth with it, rocks, twigs, whole trees. The air was on fire, and it was pulsing out in shock waves. There was this high-pitched wail, mine or everyone else's or it came from the air. And that voice again, *You are not us. We are not you. We are not the same.*"

Usui leaned backward, looking ill. "You must tell me about all of these visions. You must…"

I put up my hand. I was already too tired from this one recounting. "I can't…"

"Purr-*san*…"

"I can't." I lay back. Everyone wanted an explanation. As if I were channeling some holy message. As if I brought back some answers from another realm. As if the visions gave me wisdom to pass down to the masses, when all they really left me with was pulsing despair.

"You must have ideas on meaning—"

I interrupted him. "I don't have an explanation. I don't have understanding. The visions take me like a rapist and leave me for dead." I heard the despair in my own voice. "I refuse to engage them. I ignore them. Even telling you this story has me worried I'm upsetting some force that I won't be able to push back down." I tried to calm the beast thrashing in my chest.

Usui stood and went to his altar. I could smell the gritty scent of freshly lit incense. I was hollowed out by the telling. The last few years in Missouri, especially when I was in journalism school at university, I told no one about the visions. Even if they witnessed me having one, I would not speak of them. That side of me just needed to go away. I would pretend it didn't exist. I would make it go away.

Usui said with his back to me, "Please answer me, one question."

"What?" I grunted warily.

"You know this vision is a Japan vision. It is, of course, atomic bombing of my country by your country."

"Oh," I said. Of course it was, but no, I hadn't realized it.

"Did you have Japan visions in Misery?"

I almost laughed at his pronunciation, but decided not to correct him. "No," I said. "In Missouri, I had visions of Missouri."

"So…" He nodded. "When you have vision, it is about feeling land where you live, true? You pick up place where you are?"

"Oh, I guess so." I hadn't thought about it that way. This was the first vision I'd had outside where I grew up. I thought about the Osage woman who kept coming to me in Missouri, how she was of the land I'd grown up on. What Usui had just said was the first real clue I'd ever had as to the nature of my visions. I actually felt excitement, a deep throbbing in my groin, a passion about this new knowledge and even about the vision.

"No," I said. I closed my right fist against the excitement. "No." Usui turned to look at me. "I do not want to go here, okay?"

"Okay, Purr-*san*. It is okay."

air

We were quiet. Usui hunched forward at his altar, as if he was praying. He lit an incense and seemed to be moving it over his body, covering his limbs and torso with the gritty smoke. He came back and knelt by my futon and moved the incense over my prone body. "We are not protected from darkness. You have darkness, Purr. I have. So many in darkness."

I didn't want to hear about darkness. My family was full of blackness, a weighted gloom. It went back generations. How many of my ancestors had put a bullet through their heads to stop the darkness?

He reached out and touched the leather pouch around my neck and looked about to say something, but instead he released a small breath. His breath entered through my mouth, and his touch went through the pouch and tingled my vocal chords.

I closed my eyes and arched myself toward him. I felt the heat of him leaning in, waited for his breath on my lips. Suddenly, I felt him jerk and pull away. I opened my eyes.

He was standing. "Must leave."

"Usui-*san*." He headed toward the door. I said, "No, I'll go. I'll go." I scrambled up from the futon. My head went dizzy, and I veered wildly like a drunken person. The door opened. He was gone.

"Please, I'll go!" I cried after him, my feet caught in the futon sheets. Twisted up, I fell headlong to the floor.

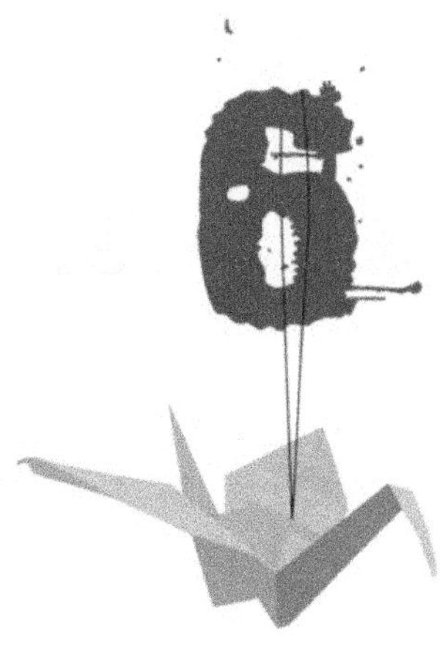

I WAS A giant running across the Missouri landscape. Vast leaps, boom, boom, boom. My head touched the clouds; one foot was wider than a farmhouse. I was so big, leaping the Missouri River, jumping the Mississippi. Filled with the glory of the land, I bellowed, heady, giddy. Farther and farther I flew, over parceled fields, beyond the hills and flatlands, beneath black bulbous skies, farther, over barren deserts and rocky mountains. I swam oceans to foreign lands. I went so far. I could see so far.

I was standing on the hill behind the house, icy wind numbing cheeks. Father had just been buried. I stood up there a lot. It was my favorite place, a good vantage point. It gave a person perspective— the two-story house, brambly forest; down a rutted road I could just make out the red tint of the barn and the barbed-wire fields for the cows, the chicken coop. It was rough, wild and dirty. Smelly and filthy. Dozens of neighbor kids ran around, wild and whooping, a screaming pack of beasts. Mid-Missouri was a vast place; the people fisted it up, but the earth itself was infinite.

It was a fraught time after Father died. It was hard enough when a good father died, but a bad father rattled the already loose foundations. I was not eating. I was slowly disappearing.

As I stood on that frigid hill, I felt the vision coming and did not stop it. Me as a giant, running across the land, the big, wild soul of it all. Afterward, I fell to my knees, my forehead on hoarfrost, my body bowing to this earth I loved so much.

air

I sat downstairs on my bunk in the basement of the mission, listening for Usui's footsteps. I wanted to run up and apologize. I wanted to burst through the door and tell him, *Not all the visions are bad, Usui! Not everything I see is bad.* I wanted to apologize. Mostly, I wanted to say I was sorry.

I smelled the stench of me and went to the far end of the basement to figure out the bath. I wasn't a big taker of showers. It used to drive Mother crazy. I thought natural smells were best, but at this point even I couldn't take my own scent.

The toilet was in a closet. The bath was in a separate room. This was my first time really looking at it. It was a big space, tiled from floor to ceiling, two shower heads, a narrow deep bath in the center, plastic stools and buckets all around. I used a square of soap I found in a small tray. You had to hold the shower head. I cleaned myself the best I could. I used the soap on my hair. Afterward it dried into a ratty fro.

Muffled light through the rice paper; the house was dark, except for that glow. It was the next morning. I had come to beg for forgiveness. I'd been up half the night, remembering, touching his face, flipping between elation and shame. I assumed Jesuit missionaries were celibate like Catholic priests.

His door was cracked. He sat on a cushion in a pale blue robe. The futon was gone. His head down, he focused on something in his hands. The light was dim from the paper lamp in the corner. How could he see anything? He seemed to be folding something. His fingers moved along a piece of paper as if it were a musical instrument. He made the folds with such speed. He was singing to it, or breathing on it.

"Purr-*san*, do not stand like thief. Please." I jumped with the sound of his voice, then slid the door and stood at the entryway.

"I had a dream of it many nights ago," he said, "a vision of many birds." He kept working, his fingers folding a complicated tune. Again he leaned to breathe on the figure. "My parents wanted for me to be mathematician. Then wanted origami master. In Japan, we do what is expected." Not just in Japan, I thought. "Today, I only want to have crane come to life, just one bird." He was quiet while he worked. I felt so relaxed watching his hands. It'd been a long time since I'd felt this calm.

"You think you control paper, but it is other way. Learn humility. Paper speaks language. I must listen. I have to be humble to paper. I have conversation with it."

I couldn't seem to stop myself from imagining his fingers on my flesh. "How can you work in this light?"

He didn't look up. "In Japan, we call '*ke*.' Low light. It is feeling of home, of soul. Deeper feeling, not harsh and bright. Magic lives in low light. Do you understand?" He looked up and laughed. "Maybe this is not so much the American way."

I blushed. It was my cue to apologize. Ugly, horny American. I was a brute from some rural, uneducated, peasant stock. I stood there mute, needing to say the words, but my mouth was clenched.

Usui held up the finished crane. In the dim light the iridescent paper looked like a bird you'd see in a dusky vista, radiant in the distance, a spot of enchantment on a darkening night.

He placed the crane on the tatami, and stood. "I have technical skill for folding," he said with his back to me, "but it is not only good to be technical. We must see crane, feel flight, to know heart."

"I can see it flying."

He shook his head. "No, it is useless. As Buddha said, 'Way is not in sky. Way is in heart.'"

He slid open one of the closet doors. Inside was a tall, clear plastic set of drawers full of hundreds of what looked like the same origami crane he'd just made, the sudden glow of so many of them like a spray of heat lightning.

I stumbled into the room toward the drawers of birds. As I stepped forward, my foot landed on something. I looked down. I'd crushed the crane.

Usui turned. A white wing protruded from beneath my big toe. I stood, teeth clenched, unable to move my foot. When I was a kid, something like this would've ended in a beating.

He came over and touched my arm. I flinched. He leaned, lifted my ankle, and pulled out the smashed crane. He studied the flattened figure and laughed. "You cannot take life unless it first has life!"

"I'll go now," I croaked. When I was already out the door, he called after me. "It is not apology, Purr. It is a humility. Do you understand? Humility is way, not speech."

I blushed, not knowing for sure what he was talking about. He walked toward me. The energy of him immobilized me.

"Come," he said.

I followed him as he walked down the hall and out the front door. We stood at the front garden. I'd seen it in the dark with the taxi driver and after I'd gotten lost, but both times I hadn't really noticed it. It was stunning, a miniature universe of tree, bridge, pond. I couldn't seem to close my mouth.

He looked at me and laughed, went to a metal container and pulled out a large handful of incense. "There is no room for garden in back, which is tradition."

Surrounding the garden was a white stucco wall about five feet high that kept the rest of the world out. A large traditional wooden gate with oriental curves was built over the metal gate. A symbolic entryway.

We walked a stone path through the garden. A single red-leafed maple was complemented by low-growing grey foliage. Here and there, airy plumes of switchgrass. The ankle-high fencing along the path was made of bamboo tied at the joints with twine. We came to a sea of white pebbles raked in thin lines, and rising from the small pallid stones were large blackened boulders.

Usui said, "We rake stones in curves, like flow of ocean, the black rock like islands coming out of sea."

We continued on the path to the pond. The varied smells of the vegetation—here the scent of lemon, there wafting lavender—were sudden and striking. We walked over an arched wooden bridge, and on the other side stood a fountain, a single piece of bamboo as a spout and below it a moss-covered stone with a top worn to a smooth bowl. He lit the incense in his hand with a long match and then placed it in a metal fire pit beside the fountain.

In the fog of sweet smoke, I took in the garden. After the hardscrabble of the land where I was born—the clutch of blackberry thorns, the shifty burrs catching clothes and hair—this polishing of the land was a curiosity, some marriage of man and soil and poetry I wasn't used to. Growing up, people may have grown a rose bush or two, or planted some flowers in front of the house, but I'd never seen anything both so natural and so man-made.

I followed Usui to the side of the house. A group of bonsai trees were arranged on a wrought-iron table. I kept my distance, worried I'd mangle something as I had the crane. This big galoot feeling was not new for me. The visions made me feel monstrous, too big and too much. How was I going to live in a place as delicate as this country?

"Please to come," Usui said. I picked my way carefully to him. The bonsai trees were in pots that were thick and earthy, misshapen in purposeful ways. The branches of the small trees reached out like arms. There were perhaps two dozen, each with its own personality, each speaking to the other. It was a miniature fantastical world, a minute play with trees as the main characters. Usui looked old and wise and young and fragile all at the same time. He could've been twenty-five or sixty.

"In Missouri," I said, "we have overgrown forests, rough, hard, twisted. I love it. Loved it. I never liked manicured yards. I never liked anything where they took the wild out. But I like this."

At that moment, a motorcycle raged down the street. I flinched. Usui cringed. We couldn't see it, but the sound was like a knife to the

air

heart. And even after it passed, you could still feel the assault of its engine vibrating in the flesh.

"How to keep that out of this place?" He pointed his sheers toward the noisy street. "Don't know." He shook his head and a darkness seemed to flood his face. "Do not know."

We were going back into the house when Usui turned to me, and said, "I ask you come with me today, Purr-*san*. We take train in fifty minutes. Please."

Of course I would go with him. I would go with him anywhere. That was the problem.

T

HIS WAS THE way you massacred a quail. This was the way you scaled a catfish, decapitated a chicken, disemboweled a deer. Shut up and watch. Learn it. Learn it good. Don't be asking any questions. Shoot. Slice. Gut. Chop. Fry. Missouri survival poetry, the cadence of subsistence.

Mother and Father. They showed you once, and you'd better figure it out from there. There was a violence to it. I will give them credit, though. Their way taught me to learn things at lightning speed; helped me take on things most coddled people would not even dream of. I could watch anyone do anything and repeat it perfectly. It was a twisted superpower, a hyper vigilant, crazy gift.

Left at the shop with rows of woven flip-flops, left again at the clothes store with the manikin with one arm. Where I was from, stores had aisles, Walmart and JCPenney and such. Here the shops were walk-in closets. Six blocks and take a right at the building covered in blue tarp. Concrete and glass, the buildings all looked alike to me.

I watched Usui. He wore a normal black jacket and black trousers. After the kimonos, he looked diminished, like a human and not some mystical man from another era. As we walked to the train station, I also studied the Japanese, their bodies as they moved, mouths as they talked, eyes as they lowered. Different rules for men and women. Their attire, their hand movements, their hair.

Right at an open-air bizarre. In the distance, a temple.

air

"Sensoji," Usui said, pointing. "Buddhist Temple. Oldest in Japan. I show you."

Flags and banners in a flying script. Music, arcades, bullhorns, noise spewing from so many sources. So many people you couldn't walk in a straight line. We were brushed, jostled, stopped, diverted. For sale around us cheap kimonos, paper fans, scraggly batches of incense, skewered dumplings. On tables along the sidewalk, men in white chefs' hats grilled meat, slabs of raw animal flesh on trays. Next to that a small shrine. The smell of blood and incense.

Usui took me down a side alley to a shop that sold incense. He purchased a large bunch of dark sticks tied with twine. Next to the stop was an old potter's, in the window a collection of tea pots just like Usui's. I stopped to look, crooked gems. I wanted to go inside, to touch them.

"Yes, favorite pottery. Buy many teapots here. But, Purr-*san*, we must go. No time."

Reluctantly, I followed him back to the main road. We traversed the courtyard. The temple was supported by four immense red columns, the paint chipped in fantastic patterns. From lavishly carved eaves hung massive red lanterns nearly one story high. Into the depths, I could make out shimmering tiled floors and in the corners large statues of violet, cobalt and gold gods.

Usui stopped at the front at a blackened cauldron where several large batches of incense burned, the smoke fogging the light from the hanging lanterns. He took out a lighter and lit the batch he held, waved his hand to put out the flames. He placed it in the cauldron with the others. Nearby was a large metal box. He threw a coin into it. He bowed, bent his head, prayed. I folded my hands beside him.

The ritual at the pond. The ritual here. I felt filled up with it. I used to love the rituals at Holy Cross, the incense, light refracting through stained glass. That church was the only place in that practical Midwest place of boiled chicken feet and stringy deer guts that had any mystery. I'd stand on the kneeler on tiptoe and sing high and mighty.

I followed Usui to the side of the courtyard to stone statues of children. They were the same size as normal children, the stone blackened as if very old. Their faces were shocking, the eyes and mouths carved to look like old men, weathered and weary. Around the base were gifts of origami, oranges, flowers.

Someone had crocheted crimson hats for their heads, a loose red scarf. Usui reached into his pocket and extracted the wounded origami crane, the one I'd crushed, and put it with the rest of the gifts. He touched one of the child's heads.

We stepped just inside the temple, but Usui held back. In the shadowy corners, I could just make out the statues—colored stone flesh, blustery hair, squally faces. They seemed to be carrying otherworldly objects.

"We must go," Usui said. "I am not to be here. It pulls me too deep. I forget myself." He inhaled deeply. "I have given myself to Jesuit cause. I forget myself." He pulled at my arm. "Please."

I followed him back outside into the chaos. "I have another thing to show you," he said.

The train station was called Minami-Asagaya. The letters were not in English, and I had Usui write it for me in a notebook I carried in my fanny pack. I had a subway map, but panicked when I looked at it, so many lines and intersections. Names of places I couldn't pronounce. My only experience of trains was sitting on a hill and counting the cars as freight trains labored across the landscape.

Usui dropped yen into a machine and purchased our tickets. He showed me how to insert the ticket at the turnstile and push a metal bar to get through. I observed. I echoed. I absorbed.

The train was a small older contraption, swaying and clunking over old tracks. I was thought of as small and even skinny back home, but here I felt huge and bumbling next to the petite women. In the Midwest things were big and heavy and you could slam your whole body and not break them. But here, even a wayward step could ruin everything.

Father would bring a quartered cow into the kitchen and put it on the long counter. I'd have to hold this half-rump, thigh and leg by

air

the ankle with both hands while he sawed the joints. My little girl body would jerk back and forth with the grind of saw against bone and gristle. The carcass would slide around in its own blood. That was how I grew up. That was what I knew.

As we sat on the train, Usui remained silent. A group of older women got on, stopped to chat with him. I watched their eyes light up to see him. A faint jealousy. I was not the only one privy to the charm that was Usui.

We disembarked at a place surrounded by grass and trees. I took a deep breath. The air was clean. I didn't realize until that moment how the toxic air of Tokyo had been affecting me. Every day, when I blew my nose, the snot came out black. It was my first experience with pollution.

Usui led the way down a narrow metal staircase to a car lot. We walked three blocks past old wooden Japanese structures until we came to a newer concrete and glass building. We entered, passing a reception desk and rooms full of beds. Everything was white, clean, in order. It was some kind of hospital. We went down the stairs to the basement and all the way through to the rooms at the very back of the building.

Usui opened a door. A guttural cry rose, like a pen of blue tic hounds. Kids rushed at Usui. He laughed and touched their heads.

The kids were mentally handicapped. There were some who were more disabled, who couldn't walk, scattered on tatami mats, held by young Japanese women in white lab coats who were exercising the children's limbs. There weren't enough helpers, and some of the kids were left to loll on their own. These children were broken so fully in body and only had control of their eyes.

Broken children. The phrase came to me suddenly. That's what the woman at the retail shop had said. What did Usui say her name was? Ami-*san?* These were Usui's broken children.

Sweat dripped between my shoulder blades. I'd always been scared of the handicapped. It was irrational and unfair, and I knew it. Any sort of handicap made me want to run screaming down the middle of the street. Usui looked over and smiled. I tried to turn my fear into a smile, but was not sure I succeeded.

"Keiko, *konnichiwa*." A little girl's voice. I felt a small damp hand grasp mine and looked down. Flattened features and heavy eyes. She smiled up at me.

"Keiko, *konnichiwa*." When I didn't answer, she repeated over and over, "Keiko, *konnichiwa*. Keiko, *konnichiwa*. Keiko, *konnichiwa*." I wanted to yank my hand away, but stood still and let her squeeze my fingers.

Usui motioned for me to follow him. As he walked across the room, kids attached to both legs, both arms, one around his neck. He trudged like a twelve-headed monster, gut cries, wheezy cackles, wordless happy groans. We came to a door toward the back of the room. Usui laughingly extricated himself from the throng. A helper came up and led the children away. He opened a door, and I followed.

A woman in plain clothes stood immediately and spoke to him, wringing her hands. A severely handicapped child lay on mats on the floor. By the far wall, an upright piano with a Japanese teenager on the bench. There was a folding chair in the corner, and I went and sat in it. Otherwise, the room was empty. No other furniture, curtains or pictures.

Usui led the woman to a corner and urged her to sit on the tatami. He went to the child. The kid looked about four, but it was hard to tell his age because he was so severely handicapped. He didn't seem to be able to move any part of his body but his eyes. He was on his back, his body moving spastically. He made squealing, high-pitched noises. His eyes were clear, though, as if he could see everything, as if he understood everything.

Usui spoke to the teen at the piano. The boy started playing, a lilting tune.

Usui put one hand behind the child's back, another held his ankle loosely. For several minutes, nothing happened. He held the child, waiting, as the music filled the room.

I'd tried all my life to avoid being around the handicapped, but they always found me. It kept happening. I felt helpless, small and disgusted with myself, but mostly helpless.

As a kid, I delivered newspapers on a six-mile route. The Hobson's farm was about a mile up the road, and they had a mentally handicapped son. I'd ride my bike up the long dirt path to deliver the paper. It was a large yard, and I could throw well, but the mother wanted the paper put inside the door. I had to get off to walk it up. Every day the handicapped boy would shoot out the screen door and sidle up and walk with me to the house and back. He had this way of rubbing his hands. I'd smile and nod, teeth rattling. As I tried to leave, he'd grab my jacket. I'd have to yank myself free, and I'd bike as fast as I could to get out of there.

When I was fifteen, I was smoking and waiting for the bus. It was so rural, the buses didn't come often, and when they did, you spent hours going from farm to farm just to turn back and go the twelve miles toward town. When the driver finally pulled up, I started fumbling for change with a cigarette in my hand. I dropped my keys and wallet and had to scramble in the gravel to pick them up, then dropped them again. Change spewed into the dirt.

The door opened, and the driver yelled for me to put out the cigarette. I was still scrambling for my change. Three people got off the bus. I looked up and saw they all had Down syndrome. One took the cigarette out of my mouth and then stomped it. Another picked up my coins, along with some dirt, and deposited them in my hand. The third grabbed my arm, helped me get on the bus and showed me how to insert the money. I didn't know what was happening. I let myself be led. Then I saw that the entire bus was filled with people who had Down syndrome. My three new friends took me to a seat and sat around me as if they were protecting me. For one hour, I sat with jaws clenched, sweating palms and pits. The handicapped people acted as if I were the wrecked one, as if I were the one with problems.

Then in college, a journalism professor kept assigning me stories on the mentally handicapped, human interest pieces about halfway houses, and work programs, policy debates. I went to a factory, an old dark warehouse with a single conveyer belt. A group of handicapped men and women filled boxes with bags of balloons. The walls, the floors, the windows, everything was dark and ugly. I was expected to ask questions and write a story. I stood there dumbly, staring, thinking I'd never seen such a depressing place in my whole life.

There was some bigger reason I was forced to engage with handicapped people. I could see that. It had something to do with being so scared. My reaction wasn't something I was proud of, but I could never seem to get past it.

Movement on the floor. Usui was moving the boy's leg as if he were dancing it to the music. Then the other leg. He lifted the child's head and swayed it. The pianist reached a crescendo, and Usui got to his knees, picked the child up off the floor, danced the body of the child. He swooped, sashayed and swayed. He swung, swiveled and shimmied.

Something in my soul stirred. The child was not fussing anymore, but laughing a throaty gurgle. His body remained limp in Usui's hands, but his face was alight with fire. I caught sight of the mother. The need in her pupils and jowls was palpable. As if she didn't know how to take the soaring soul of her child, as if she was desperate for someone to dance her like that. My mother worked herself ragged on the farm, but even my mother's exhaustion was nowhere near what I saw on that woman's face.

air

The dance ended. Usui gave the child to the mother and spoke in soft tones. I didn't know what I'd just witnessed, but my heart beat fast. I didn't know what this man was doing to me, but more had moved in me in the past few days than had been stirred since I was five years old. That was not true. A lot of ugly had been stirred up. But this was different. I leaned against Usui as we left the room. His body stiffened, and I pulled myself back.

He went to speak to some of the staff. I walked up to a large window. Someone had planted fresh bamboo in front of a fence and turned a dark and ugly view into something beautiful. I put my hands flat on the glass and stared out at the green shoots. The girl, Keiko, came up beside me and put her hands flat on the glass, echoing me. I looked down and saw drool dripping from her open mouth. I saw myself there. I saw myself in that little girl. It scared me. I pulled back as if the glass had grown blistering hot. I had to get out of that room. I rushed out and sat on the back stairwell.

When Usui came out twenty minutes later, he was glowing.

"What were you doing with the music?" I asked as we made our way to the exit.

"It is new therapy. I thought, if child cannot move, let me try to feel how child would like to move. I thought, music will help to move. I sit and feel in hands where urge is, move for him.

"Results good. Child cannot see it is separate from mother because mother does everything. Mother is arms, legs of child. Now, child maybe sees he is person, different person from mother. Happy, not so much crying. But now mother not so happy. She not know how to act. She see boy is changing. She only knows old trapped boy, not new dancing boy."

"Maybe you can have a session where you dance the mother."

"Yes." Usui laughed. "Yes. Okay." He looked at me. We were at the bottom of the stairs leading up to the train platform. An elderly couple had to maneuver awkwardly around us.

"But I feel so horrible for them," I said. "What a rotten life."

"It is karma of child. It is desire of soul to develop. This is not Jesuit belief, but my belief. Purr, it is arrogance to pity. Pity is violence. Do you understand?"

I wasn't sure I did.

"We are all broken children." Usui's eyes were hooded. "We are afraid of our own inside broken child." He squinted at me. "We are afraid of inside. Inside." He stabbed himself in the heart with his fingers.

On the rickety train ride home, we didn't speak. So much of what Usui said and did swirled around in my head. When we got to the mission, I turned to him and touched his arm. I wanted desperately to go sit in his room with him, drink tea, talk.

He bowed. The darkness from earlier seemed to be creeping over him. "I must attend to business, Purr-*san*. Thank you."

I wanted more of him. "Thank you," I whispered to his retreating back.

THERE WERE DEGREES of separation. Layer by layer, you were torn from what you loved. Starting young, you were educated in a peeling back, step by step until you could abandon almost anything without batting an eye.

When I was a girl, I could not discern myself from other living beings. Rain storms bled through veins; lightning seared the nervous system. Every dandelion stem made crooked by heavy winds became my childish body, leaning. When I was little, the world was a multihued palette. The mystery set my belly aglow, tingled my spine.

Mother often said, *Pearl, you've got to toughen up. You ain't gonna survive feeling so soft about the world.*

Toughen up. They taught me well, leathered my soul, and callused the spirit. Growing up, everybody's vision of the earth was so mean. Each day of my life, each year was a study in distancing. The world gave lessons in learning not to love, learning how to leave, deciphering how to steal and horde and, in the end, how to ignore the earth altogether. I turned my face away from the land and hoped the feelings would die inside me.

These were early preparations. These were the first separations. There were to be many more.

air

I didn't see Usui for weeks. He was avoiding me, and I couldn't understand why. I listened to the pad of his feet overhead, to the sliding *shoji* door to his room, to his muffled voice on the phone. I knew when he left the mission, knew when he came home. What sort of work did a Jesuit missionary do? Where did he go when he left? I didn't know.

No other visitors showed up to sleep in the dozens of beds. I didn't mind it that way. I was always better alone than with other people.

I had to get a job, was nearly out of money, but the world outside the mission hit like a hot wind. Train whistles, car horns, jostling, jabbing, soot, smog, clanking, clunking, jarring. The babbling, the bowing, the bustle—everything so different. How was I supposed to conduct myself in this place? Every time I left the mission, I rushed to get back. Once I boarded the wrong train and spent all day zigzagging around the city, lost. Another time, I ordered food at a stall, and instead of tempura, the cook gave me a raw egg floating on top noodle soup. Without the words to return it, I gagged on every spoonful.

How do you maneuver a world that gave you no reflection of yourself? I could barely handle life before, but at least at home the woods were there to embrace you, to hide you. Here, every sound invaded the flesh and jarred the psyche until I was so filled up I couldn't function. I came here to get as far away as I could, and now I desperately needed some semblance of home.

When I decided to leave, I knew nowhere in the U.S. would be far enough. I had to go abroad, but I didn't know how I would be able to work. I thought about Europe, and went to the library to check out some books, but couldn't find anything to help me get a job there.

Jason told me about a friend of a friend whose brother had just gotten back from Tokyo. He agreed to meet me at the McDonald's on the boulevard. He wore pressed trousers and a thin scarf. You didn't see that much. It was easy to find jobs teaching English, he told me. The Monday *Japan Times* had listings. He'd saved forty thousand bucks in three years. He fidgeted in his orange plastic seat, talked about getting a job in New York and seemed eager to get out of there, out of the McDonald's and out of the state.

In the corner of the mission basement, I fed coins into the payphone and called listing after listing from the *Japan Times*. I wasn't getting offers, kept blurting out the wrong thing at the wrong time, screwing up the interviews. Somewhere, I knew as long as I didn't have a job, I could stay at the mission. If I got a job, I'd have to find an apartment. I'd have to leave Usui. I'd have to say goodbye to origami gifts on pillows, scratchy incense, mottled teapots, thick stunted bonsai. I'd have to go live in the "real" world. Home wasn't just Usui. It was the energy of the mission. Even the basement with its rows of beds seemed to hold a tenderness my soul so desperately needed. Did the building itself harbor a spirit? Was it the aura of the garden? Or simply the mystery of the man upstairs, who for some reason just kept avoiding me?

My life became centered around listening for Usui. Once he passed close to the basement stairs, and I held my breath, but he did not come down. I was used to a moody father. It would pass. I just had to wait it out. I went up once and met an older Japanese woman who came in to cook and clean, but she ran and hid in some back room. Other times when I tried to find him, he was out, or his door was tightly closed. The lamp glow through the paper door was a beacon, a fire in a bitterly cold life, but I was not invited in to warm my hands.

One day, I spent an hour in the front garden on the vague hope I'd run into him. The conk of bamboo wind chimes, gritty sweet incense, a caw, a chirp, a coo, the flush of windy maple leaves. The lick of sun on the waters of the pond. Behind it all, a raging hum, the roaring, explosive, engorged city.

I went in to see if I could make myself a cup of tea. I didn't usually do this. I would go out and get what I wanted, but I could only afford two small meals a day and I was hungry.

The kitchen was down a long hallway. The cook wasn't there. Stepping down into the low room, I entered another era, a sanctuary from a hundred, a thousand, years ago. Half the kitchen was basic and modern with a tiled floor, and the other half came from another century altogether.

I went over to a primitive stove, a three-foot-high rough rectangle of clay and sand. A carved hole in the front led to a hollow interior with ashes and the remains of firewood. On top were two openings like the burners on a stovetop, and in one of them a cauldron whose base fit neatly into the opening, so that a fire underneath would lick its bottom. The cauldron was rough and hand beaten and had been used thousands of times. The floor here was hard-packed dirt.

I leaned and touched the earth. I felt myself being pulled down, like in the garden when I was a child, like when my visions began, where I was the crumbling dirt, a whole world beneath the earth beckoning me. I yanked my hand back as if I'd been stung. But it was too late. The vision came. I couldn't have stopped it if I tried.

A Japanese woman in a kimono knelt at the stove, poking the fire with a stick. At a wooden table stood a tiny bent grandmother, peppered hair pulled back from a surprisingly unlined face. What was the light source? A radiance pulsed in from a hole cut directly in the wall. Every object around glowed with it. Smoke misted up the vision, and for a moment, the beauty was lost in fog.

At a low table, a little girl of about seven squatted, arranging fish on an earthen platter. The smell was of ash, rice and fish guts. The three generations of women spoke only single words or short phrases. They lived their lives in shorthand. I could understand the Japanese. They had been in this kitchen hundreds of times in this forever moment.

A man came in. The middle-aged woman bowed low and went to him. He wore a kimono. She helped him with his shoes, took his cloak. A boy ran in from another room. He barked an order. In a little boy's voice, a dark child's voice, he demanded tea. The women bowed and served them both.

I entered the mother's flesh. I became the mother, felt the heaviness in her. I was overworked and anxious. I thought about the husband, about sex, about his weight, the thickness of his middle, his stick-thin legs, the repetition of him. I was apprehensive for the day that was just over and for the day that was to come, and for the many days after that until I could finally lay my head down and die. I was scared for my daughter, for the life of drudgery before her, and for my granddaughter who was yet to be born.

The boy threw an insult. He spat the word stupid. *I had been thinking of the husband and sex and was staring at the hard-packed earth, and the boy called me stupid because I wasn't paying attention to his every whim. I was stupid because I was thinking about something else.*

At the moment of the insult, I was forcefully thrown out of her body. I was so suddenly back in the present, I knocked a jar off a table. It fell and broke and spilled dry beans onto the floor.

The cleaning woman came in. I was holding myself up, using the table for support. She looked at the broken jar. I apologized in Japanese. She grabbed a broom and fussed around my feet. I tried to leave, but I wore only socks, and there was glass. She stopped me from moving.

When she was done, she took my arm, helped me down the hall and the stairs. I had no idea what she was thinking. Another dirty foreigner on drugs? But her energy was kind, and I let myself be led to the bed, let myself be tucked in.

They were right, my parents. I'd never survive in this world. The present for me was not just the present. It was the past and future. When folks said to leave the past behind, it never made sense

air

to me. The past was everywhere, and the future, too. How could you leave the past behind? It was right there. And right there. And right there.

A week later, I was barely able to afford one meal a day. It was too quiet upstairs. It'd been too quiet for several days. There was something wrong with the silence, like a breath being held too long. I slipped up the stairs. A light glowed through the paper in Usui's door. I tapped on the wood frame. Nothing. I tapped again. I could hear movement. I slid open the door.

What hit me hardest was the smell—yeast and sweat and something like despair. The futon on the floor was a mess of crumpled blankets. It was just after six p.m. and the futon was always stored in the closet until bedtime. Usui was a stickler about it.

I took two steps into the room and realized the futon was not empty. Pale fingers slid from beneath the comforter and gripped the edge of the mattress.

"Usui-*san*?" I whispered. He moaned. "What is it? Are you sick?" Again a moan. I went up and pulled the cover from his face. He was gritting his teeth. His chin was covered in stubble. How long had he been like this? The white of the fingers, the pallor of the neck, the lustrous pain on the face glowed in that room like a painting of a ghost. There was something epic about him. Even around his despair, I could breathe more freely than anywhere else in the world.

Was the cleaning lady around? Should I go find her? "What can I do for you?" I knelt on the *tatami*. He moaned and turned his head away. "Are you in physical pain?" He shook his head, wild like a coyote caught in trap. An avalanche of books lay in one corner of the room. Glowing origami birds spilled from the cupboard. A pile of kimonos were crumpled in the corner. These disturbed me most. Usui would never crumple anything.

He spoke with a low growl. "Purr. Leave."

"I'm not leaving you like this."

"You insult with your presence. Please to leave."

"No." I sounded more confident than I felt.

"Not up to you to decide what best," he said.

"Not up to *you* to decide what is best," I repeated.

He grunted and turned on the futon so he was facing away from me. I knelt and stared at his back. After a while, I said, "I'll go make us some tea."

I knew this kind of depression. I was familiar with it.

I went down the hall to the kitchen. The cleaning lady wasn't there.

In one corner stood a massive cherry wood cupboard with straw slats for doors, five feet high, six feet wide with beams through the middle that extended out each side like handles. It looked like the Ark of the Covenant. Dozens of teapots were lined up on top, an exotic array. I grabbed one.

They weren't like any teapots I'd ever seen. Back home, kitchen items were utilitarian. Banged-up pot for fish guts, blackened pan to boil the chicken feet that Father liked to snack on. The nicest dishes we had came from green stamps, the flowers scratched from so much scrubbing.

Textured bronze, rough pewter, smooth glazed ceramic. One had a square base with etched images of dragonflies. Another was squat and round, the handle a strip of hardened leather. There were more than a dozen. The heft of the teapots in my palms, beauty against skin.

When I was ten, a bunch of poor cousins came to visit, Mother's people. They only came once. We had these two lamps in the living room, the belly of them like tie-dyed glass. They were old and fiercely ugly. They gave me shivers; I hated them so much. One of my cousins ran her palm over the glass, over and over. When I asked what she was doing, she said, "You all have such perty things." We were dirt poor. We had nothing. I understood then that my

air

mother's family had less than nothing. I understood what my mother had clawed her way out of.

I felt like that cousin as I touched the teapots. Such perty things. Something in me ached for this beauty. I couldn't believe there were people who lived daily with such delicacy.

I chose a cast-iron teapot, green and etched with slashes like pine needles, and two matching cups. At the ancient stove, I leaned down and touched the earth. I pulled my hand back quickly as I felt myself again being pulled backward in time. Usui was right—it was as if the land itself held the memories. I heard him groan from the other room and knew I wasn't the only one picking up the messages of the earth.

There was an electric kettle near the sink. I made the tea quickly, found a tray, rushed back down the hall.

"Purr-*san*," Usui barked from the futon as I came into the room. "No. No. Please."

"I've made us tea." I put the tray on the *tatami*.

He shook his sweaty head. "Usui-*san*, just tell me what's going on." He shook his head again, strands of his hair sticking to his temple. "Tell me so I can feel all right about leaving you."

How could I tell him I didn't think his despair was bad? Some of the best people I knew had depression. It wasn't just personal grief, this kind of sadness. I knew this even as a little girl. It was a barometer of how the whole world was doing. Isn't that what Sister Alice had taught me? She was the only person in the psych ward who'd made any sense. I wanted to listen to what Usui's grief had to say, just as he wanted to hear about my visions.

He opened his eyes and looked at me with so much pain I almost gasped. Currents of electricity, jagged electrical fissures, buzzed in the room. He spat a single word in Japanese, his voice like thunder. He brought his hands from under the covers and put them both over his face. Blue veins snaked up slender fingers, tiny black hairs, square nails, small purple half-circles at the base. I reached out and touched his hands. They were hot. They were on fire.

"Sometimes I have darkness." He hissed when he inhaled. "World darkness in my blood. Sometimes black dog comes, warns me something bad will happen. I do not want."

I was on the *tatami* with my legs tucked beside me. My feet and calves grew heavy like metal. I couldn't seem to move them. Sometimes this happened; I'd pick up someone else's darkness and it would invade my body like tar.

What could one girl's presence do? One witness? "What can I do, Usui-*san*?"

He turned his face into the pillow. "There is nothing. It is nothing. It is black hole. No light. No God." He tried to laugh, but it came out like a gagging.

He turned his face and spoke into his pillow in Japanese, words I couldn't understand. I moved his tea cup, edged closer to the futon and pulled back the covers. He wore a T-shirt and boxers. Again the smell. I used to have to scoop out the guts of dead animals. Even that was fresher than this.

"Purr," Usui gasped, but it was a weak protest.

Fully clothed, I climbed into the futon with him. He turned sideways to make room. I put my head on his damp pillow. He pulsed with heat. He was a raging inferno. His shirt was wet with sweat, his body limp. His pallid flesh glowed us both. I put my hand flat between his shoulder blades, between his wings. When I was little, my sister and I used to play a game where we'd trace letters into each other's flesh and guess the words. Simple things like bike or sun.

Other than that game, I'd never learned to touch. In Misery it wasn't done. Touch was a slap, a smack, a shove. The touch between human and wildlife was a slashing, a ripping, a gutting. I'd done more touching with Jason and Yuriko and their airport hugs, and now here with Usui, than I'd done much of my life.

I didn't trust my hands. When all you witnessed was the power of fists to punch and dismember, you grew up not trusting your own fingers and palms, not knowing how to balance the power. Worrying that your hands might suddenly let loose of their own accord and start punching thighs and neighbors, and goats and plaster.

air

Usui let out a weak moan. I felt something in the center of my palms, as if I were pulling the darkness out of him. He let go and sank deeper into the futon. I thought of the Bear Man in the alley. I thought of an earlier memory, a foggy half-forgotten event, with me, Jason and a damaged bird in my palms.

The atmosphere of his agony invaded my bones. It was a dangerous slope, this gloom. I could be pulled down into Usui's whirring hurricane. I could help or I could be swallowed. Or both. My hand pulsed against his back. His temperature broke. Soon, his breathing grew rhythmic. He'd fallen asleep. I was dog-tired. I didn't know where the darkness had gone when it left him, and hoped it hadn't entered me.

Usui was my home. The thought pacified me and scared the shit out of me. I hadn't felt at home since I was a little girl on the farm and the whole natural world moved in orchestral harmony. The whole blessed earth was my cradle then. I moved closer to Usui, wanting to burrow into him, to stay curled up with him, and finally to rest. I was suddenly shattered, utterly, bottomlessly wiped out. I fell fast into a hard sleep.

When I woke up I was alone. I staggered up and looked out the window. I couldn't tell if it was dusk or dawn. How long had I slept? All night and day? Whatever happened when I put my hands on Usui had left me spent.

I sat on the futon, feeling as if I'd been hit by a semi. The room had been cleared of all objects of the night before, teapot and cups, books and papers, crumpled kimonos. I had slept through it all.

On the floor was a white piece of paper, its folds purposeful and distinct. At first, I thought it was another origami crane. I picked it up. It was a note.

Pearl-san, it read in delicate calligraphy. *I am sorry for my responsibility of last night. You must not remember it.*

With respect, you must leave mission. Today. I feel sorry. He'd marked out three words before he settled on the word "sorry."

I think you must understand staying here is not possible.

He crossed out a sentence after this, thick black impenetrable hash marks. He signed it, *Respectfully, Usui Genji.*

I reread the note. I read it at least a dozen times. I kept thinking I was reading it wrong. I couldn't leave. I had nowhere to go.

There was a knock at the door. "Usui-*san*?" I called. The door slid back—the cleaning woman. She saw me, uttered a cry, and nearly dropped a tea tray.

She said something in distraught Japanese and started bowing, but then stopped and looked at me. She cried words I could not understand. How many levels of trouble had I gotten Usui into? I tried to speak, to apologize, to stand, but every move I made flustered her more. She backed out of the room, slid the door closed so gently it was like a curse.

I got up quickly and ran out, flung myself down the stairs.

My clothes were strewn across one of the beds. My paltry possessions. I took the ugly suitcase out from under my bed, stuffed everything inside. Small bottle of shampoo and hand towel from the shower. I put the origami crane I'd found on the pillow the first night into the pouch around my neck. I packed as if I were underwater. It didn't take long; I owned so little. Everything I had was torn, misshapen and ugly. Everything was so ugly.

I put the skeleton key on its nail. The keys to the kingdom. I opened the door and turned to look back at the basement. The bunks were lined up, a home for lost and wayward souls. So many empty beds.

I stepped outside. The door shut with a clang and locked behind me.

A fine drizzle fell, coating me in Tokyo soot. There was a cigarette butt on the back landing. I stood and stared at it. I stared and stared.

air

The story of my life. Tossed from Eden. Always, perpetually, thrown out.

A IR SUCKED THROUGH fire. The feeling was simmering and familiar. The vapor fogged my lips, fevered my gums, licked my lungs. Smoke signals exhaled into the humid night. I was high, dizzy and nauseous. Next to me on the bench, a copy of the *Japan Times*, a circled job listing, and a nearly empty pack of Marlboro Lights. I'd spent almost all my remaining money on the pack. When was the last time I'd had a cigarette?

I'd sat up all night on the bench. Was it just yesterday that Usui had thrown me out? It seemed like a lifetime. All night I'd stared at a nondescript sign on the building in front of me. Setagaya School of English. The ad said they were looking for teachers of English as a second language. Immediate opening. I hoped they meant that.

After the sun set, I watched from the bench as Tokyo transformed itself. It became a different beast altogether, a homeless, outlying, marginalized, far-flung, pink-haired, black-lipped, naked creature. I sat straight and looked only a few inches ahead. Not too far forward, nor too far behind. I inhaled fire into my soul.

As dawn broke, the peripheral people disappeared, absorbed back into shadows. In their place flocked the black dressers. Women and men, old and young, black trousers, black skirts, black coats, black bags, black shoes. The *pat-a-pat-pat* of thousands of feet. The city awoke to the din and clatter of machinations and man. The thump and tap of footsteps, grumble of motorcycle and car, clang and clatter of a pachinko parlor, drone of Musak from trendy shops,

air

crying sirens, the smack of a single car door slamming and slamming again.

I went into the bathroom of a noodle shop to change. The space was so narrow, I barely had room to change into the outfit I'd worn on the plane. Canary-yellow skirt with big white buttons, white polyester blouse with big yellow polka dots. It was the only interview outfit I owned. I splashed water onto my face, brushed my crazy hair and practiced smiling into the mirror until it stopped looking as if I was grimacing.

The owner of the Setagaya School of English was a pale American woman named Mrs. Reinkemeyer. Her wrinkled gray suit hung onto her skinny frame. She sat hunched forward in an earnest fashion. Her desk was a metal monstrosity that took up a quarter of the room. The light was dusty, windows darkened by cigarette tar, the ceiling low, the fiberglass tiles yellowed.

She gave me the job. She was from Ohio. With her hair pulled back in a harsh bun, she reminded me of the nuns at Holy Cross. Maybe I reminded her of a dutiful Catholic student. Or maybe it was because we both came from Middle America. Or maybe it was a position no one else wanted.

I would be teaching English to salarimen. I stifled a giggle. Would Usui find this amusing? She handed me a photocopied pamphlet of school rules and lesson plans that was as thick as a phone book.

We'd begin with two weeks of training, she told me. The pamphlet contained everything I needed to know to teach English. Most Japanese learned English in primary school, but Mrs. Reinkemeyer said she liked to start with the basics. She opened the manual to show me one of the lessons. It was illustrated with cartoons.

Faint from lack of sleep and food, I nodded and smiled. *Yes, Mrs. Reinkemeyer. Of course, Mrs. Reinkemeyer. I'm going to pass out, Mrs. Reinkemeyer.*

Later, when she gave me a tour around the office and introduced me to the others, I noticed how slight she was, how a large wind could've blown her over. She looked at me over cat glasses. She had layers of puffed circles beneath her eyes and a dark deep look, and I thought, *There is more to this woman than meets the eye.*

She sent me to see Jerry in Human Resources to sign some paperwork. He sat behind a huge metal desk. The entire school was filled with these monstrous metal desks. I sat floppy, like a puppet. He was not much older than me, tall, gangly, with thin wispy hair so blond it was almost translucent. He told me he was from Oregon. He wore white socks that peeked out of too-short trousers. He was good looking in an accidental way. He twirled a long thin pen in his hand like a miniature baton.

Jerry handed me pages to sign. A bowl of tangerines on his desk glowed. I resisted the urge to bury my face in them, devour them one by one, peel and all.

After I finished with the signing, he looked through some paperwork. "I am so sorry," he said, looking up with desolate eyes. "All I have right now is this one other teacher who nobody can deal with. She works at our satellite office in Shinjuku."

I had no idea what he was talking about. When I said nothing, he went back to rifling through the papers. "That's really all I have." His eyes were a watery blue, like a hazy lake, the kind of blue that could put you into a pleasant sleep. "She's scared off two people already in just a few weeks."

"Scared them off?" I asked.

"Sorry," he said. "You're right. It's not fair to you. I'll find someplace else. I won't throw you to the wolves." He picked through sheet after sheet of paper. "I'll be honest, I really like her. But liking and living with are two different things."

"Living with?" I asked.

"Can you handle a difficult person?" he asked.

I snorted. I laughed and laughed. I couldn't seem to control myself. "Sorry," I said, wiping my nose. I couldn't stop. "Sorry." I was a master at dealing with the difficult. I grew up with Father. I'd dealt with my half-sister Meghan. I had a stepfather who despised me.

air

I wanted to say, *This should be on my resume, my ability to handle horrendous people.*

"I don't know what else I can do…" He thought my guffawing was a refusal. He held a wad of papers up in his fist.

"I'll take her!" I cried. I leaned forward and took his hand off the desk and brought it to my lips. I let go and the back of his hand was wet. Somewhere in there my laughing had become crying.

He blushed, dropped his pen and bent to pick it up. His hand shook as he wrote the address. He reached into his desk drawer and extracted a key, handed it with the paper to me without looking me in the eye.

"Thank you," I whispered, pocketing a tangerine.

"Don't thank me yet," he whispered. I picked up my suitcase and left the room.

Back on the bench, I studied the rail map for thirty minutes to find the address. The area was called Gyotoku, but I couldn't find it. The map was a woozy riddle—red lines spinning in circles, intersecting blue, crisscrossing yellow. Peach, pink, gray. The names of the stops were written in tiny sideways lettering—Ohtemachi, Nihombashi, Kayabacho.

Into the subway and onto a platform. I was so lost. I was so hungry. I held up the map and asked a Japanese man leaving one of the trains, "Gyotoku? Gyotoku?" He bowed three times, pointed to an incoming train, the train line he'd just gotten off, and waited with me until it came. When it arrived, I turned to thank him, but he ushered me forward and got on the train with me. I didn't know what to think, standing next to him, holding the overhead strap. He didn't seem to speak English. He broke into a sweat and had to loosen his tie. Several stops later, he motioned me off the train. I looked at him as we walked. I knew I could trust him. I knew he was not leading me for some evil purpose. After all that had happened to me, I still had a gut feeling for whom I could trust. I often thought it was this ability to trust that had saved my life.

He walked me through the tunnel system to another platform. It was rush hour, and we stood pressed up against each other; the smell of him was fabric softener and baby shampoo. He took the map, pointed to Gyotoku and counted the stops with his finger. *Ichi, ni, san, shi, go, roku, shichi, hachi, kyuu, juu, juuichi.*

Juuichi, he repeated. *Juuichi.* Eleven stops. I smiled and nodded. He had a chubby face and a cowlick that stuck up at the back of his head. When the train arrived, he bowed low. I bowed back. I crammed myself with the others into the over-packed train. He waved and laughed, his teeth crooked, his laugh high-pitched. I lost sight of him in the mass of people as the train doors closed. This tiny nervous man, this sudden angel.

I counted the stops, my suitcase smashed up against my knees. As businessmen and women pressed up against me on all sides, as we passed stop after stop, a fear welled up. I was moving so far away from the mission, so far away from Usui. It was like the dream I'd had the first night, that feeling that I'd forgotten something, that I was losing too much, misplacing too much, as if I was losing what little I had left to hold on to.

I awoke at two in the morning to the sounds of crashing and laughing. Someone turned on a radio and the Bangles were singing *Walk Like An Egyptian.* The walls were so thin it sounded like the radio was at the foot of my futon. I looked around the dark empty room and couldn't figure out where I was. Then the memories flooded back. This was my new home, a two-story concrete block apartment building painted a milky blue, trimmed in pasty white.

air

When I'd arrived the day before, no one answered the door, and I let myself in. The apartment was tiny. The door opened onto a kitchenette about six feet wide and nine feet long, a knee-high fridge, two-burner stove, miniature kitchen table with two chairs. The window over the sink had bars and overlooked the front walkway. Two doors led off the kitchen to two medium-sized bedrooms. Besides a bathroom, that was the entire apartment. I found left-over yakisoba in a carton in the mini-fridge and picked at it, my hunger having long ago devolved into numbness. I knew I should've felt relief. I knew that this was unbelievable luck, that I should've been grateful, but…

I'd left a note on the kitchen table, but wasn't sure my new roommate saw it. The thrashing and grunting seeped through paper-thin walls. It was as if they were fucking right next to me. So this was the girl no one wanted to live with. So this would be my life now. So that was it. They went at it until the sun came up, and only then did I fall into a fretful sleep.

Around ten, I got up. It was Saturday. I started work at the school on Monday. I found eggs in the refrigerator and put two on to boil. My note was on the floor.

The door to my new roommate's bedroom slid open. A skittish Japanese guy looked at me, his face morphing into mortification. He sheepishly bowed, apologized in Japanese, grabbed his shoes from the rack at the door and didn't stop to put them on as he continued bowing and fled out the door. I heard my roommate clear her throat and turned just as she walked into the kitchen. We stood staring at each other. She had a fleck of lipstick on a front tooth, eyeliner smeared down her left cheek. She wore a loose floral silk robe that barely covered her boobs.

I started laughing. She barked a laugh. I leaned over holding my stomach, laughing until I was crying.

"What the *fuck* are you doing here? What in the fuck?" It was Yuriko from the plane.

"I'm your new roommate. Apparently, we work at the same school."

She lunged toward me, threw her arms around me in a bear hug and lifted me off my feet with my arms pinned to my side. "Only in Tokyo! A big city, but a small world." She smelled of barley, tobacco and semen. I could feel her bare breasts pressing against my sweatshirt. "If it isn't the baby let loose upon the sky!" she said and laughed again. "You learn to fly yet?"

I let myself rest against her. "Not yet, I'm afraid," I answered, something like relief filtering up from the depths.

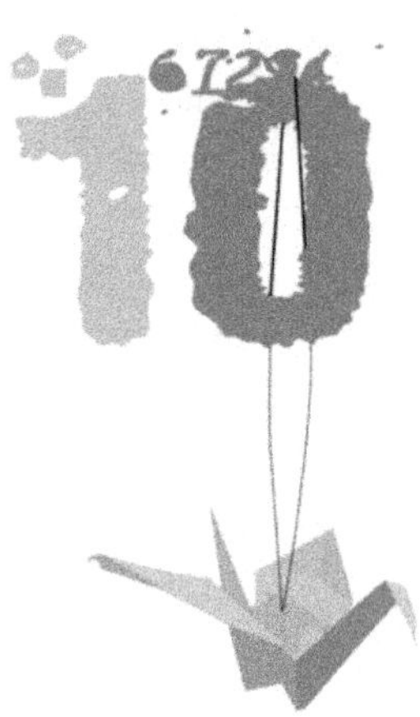

MOTHER AND I were in Father's truck, *yah*, driving home from Montgomery Ward department store, *weh*. In the bed was a new fan, *yah*. The humidity sucked a person flat, *weh*, left them damp and on their backs, *yah*, on the kitchen linoleum. The fan would've been a big expense, *weh*, for our poor family. A half-mile from home, Mother pulled the truck over, *yah*, on the side of the gravel road. She reached into the glove compartment, *weh*, and found a big black marker there. *Yah*, she got out of the truck, *weh*, and she took the black marker, *yah*, and scratched and scribbled all over the fan's box. *Weh*, she blacked the words *Made in Japan*, *yah*, on the side of the box, *weh*. Father hated the Japanese, *yah*, although he'd never been in World War II, *weh*. It was a generational or cultural hatred. Was that why I'd moved to Japan? As a rebellion? To prove them wrong?

Racing the thoughts, outrunning the recollections. *Yah...weh... Yah...weh... Yah...weh...*

Yuriko devoured the city, wolfed, engulfed, consumed. Restaurants, parties, men, booze. Yakisoba, sushi, tempura. Clubs. Dinner parties. Raves. Akira, Hiro, Juro. Yuriko was a hurricane, a tornado, a

air

tsunami, every moment an exaggeration. I let myself fall into her amplifications.

For a few weeks after leaving the mission, I tried to keep up the running, even though I'd have a cigarette here and there. I tried. But what was the use? Who cared, anyway? Days bled into nights bled into days. Clink of glass, grunt of men, hungover repetitions in white-walled classrooms. Months passed.

I'd always veered between health and wild debauchery. Over time with Yuriko, I regressed to drinking my calories, smoking a pack of Marlboro Lights a day. In Tokyo, you could smoke anywhere—at work, in the bank, at the post office. With all the smog and pollution, what difference did it make, anyway?

We roamed the city at night. Yuriko had an insatiable curiosity. It was a lesson in concrete, an education in glass and metal. Manmade light burst in sudden explosion, in doorways and windows, on cars, beaming from overhead, a thousand times a day, in a thousand ways. Blushes of neon reflecting on doorways. The streets teemed with moving cars, moving people. The ringing, shrilling, babbling. Trains, pachinko parlors, pubs—the whistle, the ting, the pat of thousands, millions of feet.

I hadn't known silence until it was no longer. I hadn't known clean air until it didn't exist. I hadn't known big sky until it became wisps and slivers caught in flashes between skyscrapers. Here weather happened in zips and dashes, from above, in short takes, in quick bursts. There, in that Midwest place, weather unfolded in waves, like a story rolling a beginning, surging through middle, climaxing an end. Here it flashed and clapped. There it labored onward, shadowing pastureland and texturing landscapes. No one paid attention to the seasons here, barely acknowledged the rhythm of day and night. The exhaustion of Tokyo was profound. The sun itself was shadowed into indifference.

My biggest challenge was fitting myself into tiny spaces. I was used to the wild flinging of body and soul over open fields. It wasn't just the miniscule restaurant tables, not just the bathrooms you couldn't turn around in. It was personal space, people so close one could read their flesh like braille. It was more than that, too. Fitting my wild self into a restricted package, a subtle package. I felt like a slab of meat on Styrofoam under suction plastic beneath fluorescent lighting, and often I couldn't breathe.

Then there were the endless days of teaching English to men squeezed too tightly into business suits, many of them reeking of late-night sake and despair. Me reeking of late-night beer and cigarettes. They were kind, called me *sensei*, and were hard workers. Mr. Tanaka, Mr. Suzuki, Mr. Ichikawa, Mr. Watanabe, Mr. Sato, Mr. Ito, Mr. Kato. Still, the mindless repetition of it. *This is a pen. These are pens. Your pen. My pen. That pen. Those pens.* These salarimen, all these Idekos. I often wondered what Usui would think of it all. *This is a pencil. These are pencils. Your pencil. My pencil. That pencil. Those pencils.* All of it illustrated by cartoons.

Our favorite haunt was an *izakaya* in Setagaya. Yuriko would take the train over from the satellite office in Shinjuku. The old pub was hidden down a long alley, a low, flat wood building, crimson lanterns dangling from the front. Most Tokyo pubs on the main streets were trendy, but this had been run by the same family for generations. Laborers sat close to the bar, and businessmen and passersby gathered around the six tables. Yuriko and I were almost always the only Westerners there. But Yuriko didn't look like a Westerner, and therein lay the rub.

The *izakaya* was low and dark. Cigarette smoke hung like smog. The old mama-*san* served deep-fried tofu, squid and vegetables on chipped mismatched plates. In Japan, you ordered a large bottle of beer and poured it into glasses. You never poured your own beer. Someone else at the table had to refill your glass. You held the glass up for the person while they poured. If you wanted to be really

air

respectful, you placed your fingers flat on the bottom of your glass. So many rules.

It was rude to allow a friend's glass to become empty. So, you'd take a few sips, and someone would refill the glass, and by the end of the night you had no idea how much beer you'd actually drunk.

Yuriko spoke too loud. The older Japanese guys gave her dark looks. She wasn't acting like a proper Japanese girl. She confused them. She loved confusing them.

But then there were the guys who found her irresistible, the ones she'd bring home two to three nights a week. They'd sidle up with sharp jaw and darting eyes. Yuriko would make room at our table, but I had a revulsion to them.

I attracted my own type of man, shy and languid types, but when they approached, I'd deflect them. I'd pretend they were interested in Yuriko. I'd usher them toward her. I'd learned that with Meghan. How to defer a man's interest, how to feed them to another woman, how to remain in the shadows.

Month after month, this life with Yuriko became my new reality. I left the spirit of the mission, the soul of Usui, for Sapporo, Marlboro Lights and mindless repetition. In one hand the beauty, in the other the grit. I didn't know how to square the two. My life had always been two realities, and I never knew how to balance the scales.

He was tall for a Japanese man, high cheekbones and long limbs, and longer still his fingers. Jiro or Juro? It was Yuriko's idea. After we'd been going to the *izakaya* for months, after I'd fed her man after man, she decided it was my turn.

She'd bought me a pair of black jeans and a turtleneck. "You've got a great rack, a tiny waist. You need to accentuate your assets, sister. You're always dressing like a clown or a beggar." Where I was from, no one had fashion. Journalism school, at least the newspaper classes I took, was full of radicals and few girls who dressed up. Fashion was a subject I knew nothing about.

At the *izakaya*, she'd kept thrusting Jiro or Juro toward me. I guided him to her, and she guided him back to me. Finally, I gave in. What was I holding out for? With the dim red lamps and the amber liquid in my veins, his eyes became fathomless. His eyes became Usui's.

We were in my bedroom. I tried not to think how much he looked like Usui. Tried not to think. Yuriko was crashing around with his friend in her bedroom. They started screaming, a mixture of Japanese and English, guttural and hard, and it was difficult not to imagine them into the futon with us.

Jiro or Juro ran his Usui hands the length of my thighs. Jiro or Juro on his knees desperate to go deeper. Screaming from the other room. It was not just Jiro or Juro and me, but Yuriko and her lover, all of us howling and thrashing like caged chickens.

Jiro or Juro grunting, his face in the nape of my neck. The sweat on his back sticky and dark. Bruising hip bones. I woke up for a moment and realized he wasn't Usui. He wasn't anyone I knew. A despair crept up, up and up, until it exploded in me.

I pushed him off me, pulled myself away so he fell out of me, just as he yelled in English, "I am going! I am going!" He came on the sheets like a dog desperately escaping a fenced-in pen.

Afterward, lying next to Jiro or Juro, I stared at his desolate profile. He looked nothing like Usui. I felt sticky and numb and groped for my Marlboro Lights. What was I doing? I was living in some floating place, some fantasyland, where I thought none of the normal rules applied.

I awoke hours later to Yuriko's radio. Jiro or Juro was gone. Sunlight pierced through the dirty sliding doors. I'd rigged a clothesline on the tiny balcony. The legs of my skinny jeans had gotten twisted in the wind and danced from the line like a wounded bird. I coughed up phlegm into a chipped teacup filled with remnants of scotch, found my Marlboro Lights beneath a pair of underwear and lit one.

air

Yuriko's music bled through the walls, Bon Jovi's *Living on a Prayer*. She never seemed to tire, had a well of energy that was insatiable. I staggered up, threw on a T-shirt, grabbed the cigarettes and ashtray. Her door was open. Her guy was gone, too. She stood at her easel, wearing a backward baseball cap, dungarees, and a black muscle shirt that read *Tokyo*, the red letters simulations of Chinese pagodas. Around her waist, a paint-encrusted apron. Strands of her hair were glued together with ultramarine blue. I tiptoed across tubes of paint and paintbrushes. She'd smeared more crimson and hansa yellow into the tightly woven *tatami*. I couldn't imagine what the landlord was going to think after we moved out.

I lay on her futon, reached up with one hand and tried to pat down my hair, which flew in frizzled static around my head like a ratty halo.

"So, I'm out getting milk," she began. She often launched into a conversation without a greeting, finished thoughts the next morning that had begun over beer the night before. She painted while she talked. "This old guy stops me and begins rambling in Japanese. I figure he's asking for directions. I'm like, man, I don't speak the language. He keeps blabbering on, pointing down the street, and I'm like I don't speak the language. I'm waving my arms like some kind of freakin' bird. No speak Japanese! No speak Japanese!"

I took a deep hit of the cigarette.

"It's like always the same. Where do I fit? Where do I fit?" Her black eyes widened, rounding up the slight slant at the edges. When she had that wild open expression, she looked most Japanese. Yuriko was beautiful. Disconcerting and beautiful. A hybrid of extreme delicacy and robust heartiness.

A photo of her parents hung over the futon. They stood in front of a low wooden house in misty fog, a trail of smoke from a fireplace. Her father, quintessential American, tall and weary, a protective arm around his wife. The woman, tiny and Japanese, in floral kimono, her expression both lost and stern. Yuriko had told me the story. Her mother was from Nagasaki, but had been in Tokyo when the bomb fell. Her father was an American GI who had seen the wreckage of the bomb, and he wanted to do something about all that death. He attached himself to a girl whose family had been destroyed. He wanted to save her.

"Yeah, where do *I* fit?" I asked, belching up last night's beer.

Yuriko grunted. "Oh, prease, Purr-*san*, you are ah American guhl," she said. "You are belle of Japanese ball. With your looks…" She looked me up and down on the futon as if I were an object, something to be observed. I could take the late-night sex sessions, her insatiable hunger, her incessant talking, but it was the staring that made me understand why so many girls had not wanted to be her roommate. It chilled you.

"Anyway, nobody here expects *you* to know the rules. You can stride up and look a Japanese man right in the face and he might think you're totally impertinent, but then he's like, well, she's a *gaijin*, no way *she's* going to know she's being rude, looking at me like we're *equals*. With me, they're like, how dare you not bow lower? How dare you not apologize more? I'm *so* sorry I *exist*, Mr. Tanaka. *Sumimasen*, Tanaka-san. *Gomennasai*, Tanaka-san."

We often had long conversations about our frustrations with Japanese culture. In Missouri, I couldn't find a woman I wanted to be, girls knocked up at seventeen, marrying a local guy and settling down into some sad duplex. I'd come to Japan looking for something different, but had gone from the skillet to bush fire. The Japanese women were cowed, as subservient as the women back home. It was a shock. I still hadn't come to terms with it. Yuriko often said, *The only thing more oppressed than a Japanese woman is her younger sister.*

"You get the foreign country you need, Yuriko," I said. "Not the foreign country you want." I didn't know why I said it. Didn't even know where it came from.

She came and stood over me, brandishing her dripping paint brush. "Hmm." She narrowed her eyes. "You got a lot more going on in that head than you show," she said.

I lit another cigarette and thought about what she'd said. We were silent for a while, the only sound the scratch of her brush on the canvas.

air

"So how'd it go with Juno? They both ran out of here this morning like the place was on fire." She laughed.

So Juno was his name. "Fine. Great." I didn't want to discuss my sex life with Yuriko; it was bad enough the walls were so thin we could hear each other's orgasms. I never asked her the details of her string of lovers and didn't see why I had to share mine. "What are you working on?"

Her easel was turned away, and she moved it to show me. I barked a laugh that shot pain into my head.

She'd painted the guy I'd met that first morning, months ago, his clothes askew, bowing and picking up his shoes. Yuriko in a mirror reflection in an open robe, smoking. Both were loosely painted, as if they had no edges, as if they'd lost their boundaries. She'd painted herself much uglier than she really was.

"That's progress from your swirls," I said. For weeks, Yuriko had only been painting spirals, thick, rich circles in fantastic colors. Against one wall were dozens of canvases covered in the circles like overlapping, spinning thoughts.

"So, you like?"

"Very much," I said.

"Good, because I have another one to show you." She pulled a canvas out of the closet. It was a painting of me sitting across from her at the *izakaya*. My face was red. The beer glass was red. Red lanterns hung in a string behind me. Around my head was a red glow. "I'm the devil."

"Either the devil or an old-world saint," she said. I made a face, and she said, "Hey, I don't decide what to paint. It decides me."

She leaned the painting against the wall facing me and went back to the easel. "You know, I have this theory about people who go to live in other countries. I think we choose countries, consciously or unconsciously, that take whatever our core issues are and project them onto this massive canvas." She dabbed a slur of crimson beneath the eye of the Japanese man in her painting.

"It doesn't matter if you're trying to run away from home, or you come to another country looking for a new home, or whatever the reason. The country you choose will take whatever you've got going on and expand it, blow it up, until it's so huge you can't ignore it." She nodded at the canvas. "It's actually quite profound."

"Anyway, I'm glad I've finally gotten past the swirls. That's all I had in my head for the first several months here. Swirls. It's been hell trying to find my voice in this place. The whole new culture thing… I don't think I know who I am anymore. Maybe I never knew who I was."

She dabbed paint on the edge of the canvas. "Speaking of voice," she said, "when am I ever going to get you to really open up?"

"What do you call what I'm doing right now?"

She rolled her eyes.

"Is there any coffee?" I asked.

She clicked her tongue and rolled her eyes again.

I dragged myself into the kitchenette, filled the electric kettle, threw instant coffee into two cups. She called from the other room, "Oh, that's right, Pearl never talks. I've told you everything about my depressive mother and my silent ever-suffering father, and I know almost nothing about you, except that you like jumping out of airplanes."

I poured the water, went back into her room and handed her one.

What could I say? It was a learned thing, this silence. Besides, a traumatic childhood did not make for normal conversation. When people shared stories, they told the basics of their lives, their parents, and their upbringing. If you had a dark story, nobody wanted to hear it. So I'd learned to keep my mouth shut. My father was dead. I hadn't seen my mother for years. She had a new family I'd never officially met. Just like with my ancestors, I let my throat close up, my voice go dry.

Yuriko took it personally, but I kept this silence with almost everyone I met. How could anyone possibly understand? How could I explain fists clenched tight around throat until you didn't even know *how* to speak anymore? And if someone tried to be understanding, if they tried to respond to my story, what they said annoyed me, was too easy. Or worse, they would pity me. When someone pitied me, I wanted to smack them hard across the face. *Pity is a violence. Do you understand?* Yes, Usui, finally I did understand.

"Okay, let's keep it simple. Just tell me how you ended up on that bench, before Jerry gave you my address." She laughed. We were always laughing about the serendipity of meeting each other again. She sat on the floor, squishing a tube of paint. "Okay, go."

If you grew up gagged, you didn't know how to tell a story. You had to teach yourself how not to leap from detail to detail, how not to rush to get the story out before you were threatened with a fist and told to shut up.

I told Yuriko how I found my way to the mission, about Usui's garden, the cranes, the handicapped kids. I didn't say much more. I felt protective.

"So, he's a Jesuit missionary?"

"Yeah, why?" Chunks of undissolved Nescafé floated in my coffee. I must have poured the water before the kettle boiled.

"He's got one hell of a job. Only one percent of Japanese are Christian. The whole Christian conversion thing has never worked with the Japanese. Oh, they'll pretend they're interested to be polite, but that's about it. My mother told me all about how they tried to convert her when she first moved to Seattle."

"I don't think Usui was really trying to convert anybody. I mean, he had a Shinto altar, books on Buddhism, Hinduism, Islam, and we went to this Shinto temple…"

"Oh, come on. He's a Jesuit missionary. His whole job is to convert people! Why would somebody put himself so at odds with his own culture like that? Especially if he didn't have to." She snorted. She was thinking of herself. How her entire body was at odds with two different cultures and she couldn't seem to do anything about it.

I didn't like Yuriko analyzing Usui, but before I could think of a way to get her off the subject, she asked, "So, why did you leave the mission so abruptly?"

I didn't want to, but I told her about Usui's depression and how I tried to comfort him.

Yuriko laughed. "You climbed into *bed* with him. Oh, my God. Oh, you act so innocent." She waved a paint brush at me and a yellow glob flew out and spattered the futon. "Oh, little Miss Goody-Goody."

"I wasn't trying to…" I shook my head, clamped my mouth shut. "I knew I shouldn't tell you."

"You have secrets. I knew there was a dark side there. I knew it."

"Listen, don't talk like you're the standard by which I should live my life, because you're not." The words came out with a force of rage I hadn't expected.

"Whoa, ouch."

I just had to stop talking. I didn't do the whole normal conversation well. I said too little, or too much, or slapped the person too hard with truth.

She scooted on her butt over to the futon, held her paint brush up like a wooden soup spoon. With her painted black hair, the wild spatters of color on clothes and forehead, she looked like the statue of an Asian goddess. "Look, you've been moping around here for months."

"I haven't been moping. I've been partying with you every damned night!"

She kept talking, as if I hadn't spoken. "All I'm trying to do is figure out what all the damned grief is about. Quit acting like such a victim, and go back to the mission and talk to him. For God's sake, don't throw the baby out with the bath water."

I was stunned. Go back to see Usui? But he'd thrown me out! Who was I to think he'd even let me in the door?

I rolled off the futon and went to my room. What Yuriko didn't understand was that I was the baby in the bath water. I was the one who was always being thrown out, and not the other way around.

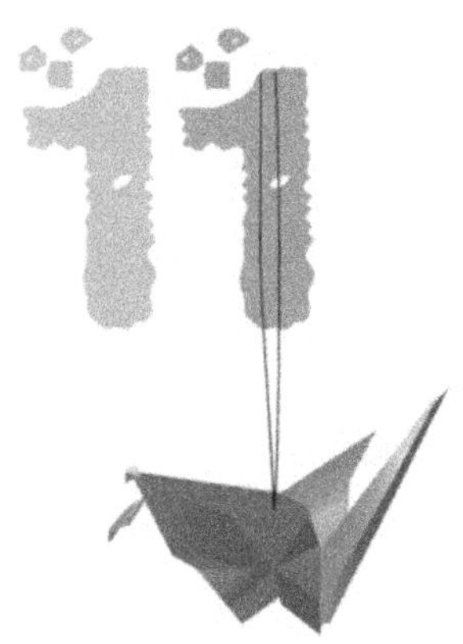

A T FIRST, I thought I'd entered the wrong metal gate. I thought I was at the wrong house. The garden was shriveled. I looked around, confused. The shrubbery around the pond was withering, straggly and unkempt, like a homeless old woman. I walked the path Usui and I had taken. In the raked white pebbles, some creature had dug a hole, left a black wound. Here and there the twine had broken and the short bamboo fencing tumbled like Pick Up Stix. No water flowed through the bamboo stalk at the fountain. In the metal pit, rain had mixed with burned incense and left a black, liquid mess. I shivered as if a cold wind blew through me. I ran to the bonsai forest and was relieved to see that most were still okay. They needed pruning, but they must have been of hardy stock.

A man called to me in Japanese. He stood at the open doorway to the mission.

"*Gomennasai,*" I said, *excuse me.* You learned right away in Japan how to apologize. It was a country where you were always apologizing. "Usui-*san?*" I asked and then bowed.

"Usui-*san?*" The man's eyes watered. He spoke in rapid Japanese, pointing at his face and bowing to me. He was short, stocky with cropped hair, his face sharp and hard.

I walked up to the front door, leaned sideways to see around him. "Usui-*san?*"

He looked back into the house. There was something about his left shoulder, some story lodged there, the way he held it rigid as he

air

moved. I could always see a person's story lodged in their flesh, beneath the left eye, just above the knee, a blockage to the belly. How our mythologies could embed in the flesh.

The man looked at me with dead eyes and shook his head. He said something in Japanese and I heard the name Genji several times and nodded vigorously. This went on, his Japanese, the name Genji, my nodding, until finally he shook his head and started to close the door.

"Please…" I said, holding the edge of the door. "I am Pearl," I pointed to my nose as I'd seen the Japanese do. "Pearl."

He bowed and kept closing the door. I looked around frantically. I had my fanny pack on. Since I'd gotten lost running that first day, I never went anywhere without it. I had the letter from Father Dennis to Usui. I dug for it and handed it through the crack in the door. I waited as I heard the rustle of paper.

He moved back and opened the door. "*Gomennasai.*" He bowed slightly.

I entered and slipped off my shoes. The man stood back and watched me absently. There was some profound grief bleeding off him.

The door to Usui's room was open. I peered in. Several boxes sat on the *tatami.* The closet doors stood open. The altar was gone, the origami. On the wall, the calligraphy print was missing. I turned back to go down the hall to the kitchen. I needed to check the teapots. If the teapots were still on the cupboard, all would be okay. It was crazy thinking, but I just wanted to see the teapots. The old man was there, and I couldn't get past him in the cramped hallway.

"Usui-*san?*" I asked.

He shook his head, pointed toward the basement stairs. He said, "*Douzo. Douzo.*"

"Usui-*san?*" I asked again, following him to the stairs.

He motioned me down. With him behind me, I had no choice but to descend. At the bottom, he pointed to one of the single beds. He took my backpack off and placed it on a bunk.

"You are welcome," he said with excruciating slowness. I was still holding Father Dennis's letter. The old man thought I'd just arrived and needed a place to stay. He walked over to the skeleton key on the nail and drew my attention to it. He pointed across the room. "Toilet, bath," he said in slow English.

He bowed and with bent body walked back up the stairs. Despair sweated off his back.

Something was wrong. Usui's possessions boxed up, the sadness emanating from the old man. Where was Usui? Fear brewed in my gut. I had to find a way to communicate with the old man. I sat for an hour, thinking. The footsteps overhead ceased, so I went quietly up the stairs, whispering, "Hello? Hello?" No answer. I went to the kitchen. The teapots were gone.

In Usui's room, I ripped open one of the boxes. Inside were his clothes. I frantically opened the other boxes. The Japanese scroll. The items on his altar. His pictures. A box of books. I found the teapots. But there was no sign of his origami birds.

A roll of tape lay on the *tatami* and I re-taped the boxes, wadded the old tape up and put it into my pocket. I went downstairs again, but was too agitated. I felt trapped in the basement. How many nights in Gyotoku had I desperately wanted to come back and live here? Now I only felt like a caged fowl.

I grabbed the skeleton key, made sure I had my fanny pack on, and let myself out the basement door. I needed to think. I needed air.

I walked aimlessly. My guts were in turmoil. Mindless roaming. I had no idea how late it was when I stopped and looked up. It'd grown dark without my noticing. I stood on the walkway leading up to the temple Usui had shown me. A smattering of the shops were still open; a few people lingered.

air

I purchased a bundle of incense. At the temple, I lit it, waved the fire out, put it in the cauldron. I bowed and prayed for Usui. Not praying exactly, more anxious thoughts. I didn't really believe in prayer; the nuns and priests at Holy Cross had slapped the faith right out of me.

At the statues of the children, there were two glowing white origami birds left at the base. I picked one up, studied it. It was one of Usui's. I was sure of it.

Hollow footsteps echoed on stone inside the temple. So few people about now. I found myself magnetized to a statue of a barrel-chested demon four times the size of a normal man. The creature was painted light blue, and the paint had chipped off shoulder, hand, chest—a mottled demon. His corpulent belly hung over an ornate loin cloth. His mouth stretched in an animal growl, teeth bared, ears pointy. He held a gilded tubular sack.

The sign in English beneath it read, *Fujin, God of Wind*.

How wild and imaginative these Shinto gods were. My days were white walls and white chairs inside glass and metal buildings. Around me, everyone dressed in black. This Fujin was dimension and color, wild and cracked, ferocious. So much bigger than this mundane life.

I needed this, something bigger, epic, mythological, something beyond the daily drudgery, something to give tint and drama to existence, even if it was a blue demon with sharp fangs, especially then. Our Christian God seemed too human, victimized, just too plain compared to this.

Hadn't I had this grand feeling when I was close to the earth? Hadn't I had it for the sky when I was little? For the mesh of the Milky Way in the night sky?

Smell of incense, pure eccentricities of statue, dark temple with shadows. I lost myself in Fujin. Entered and became him.

Fujin moved. His blue flesh writhed. His face and thick black hair blew away from his leering face. His mouth opened. The hands opened the bag on his shoulders. A great wind blew from the monster's mouth and from the depths of the bag.

It blew out a rage so great it toppled buildings. From Fujin's mouth poured volatile syllables in mythological exhales. His rage was monstrous. It uprooted concrete, wrought havoc on the temple, thrashed the dirt at its foundation, plagued every vendor in its path. From its blue-chipped belly and ornamental bag a bluster against all that was concrete and gray, against all that broke the soul, blanded the spirit.

Fujin's face became Usui's. Morphed into my face. Evolved into Father's. His rage, their rage, my rage. We all blew waves of anger, like shock waves, across the uniform landscape, until we lost ourselves, until there was nothing left of us but this blistering rage.

A white gloved hand on my arm. I was lying on the cold tiles of the temple floor. The face of an official-looking Japanese man in a blue uniform. Something was stuck in my throat. Something huge was lodged there. The man spoke to me. I could not understand the words.

He thinks I'm on drugs. Post-vision, I could read his thoughts. After a vision, the thoughts of those near me were too clear. His jaw worked in disgust and he tried to control it. *Another foreigner comes to our country to do their drugs. They pollute us with their behavior.*

He helped me up, held my arm and led me out. He was thin and light skinned, and sweated a dark smell due to his aversion to the task at hand. We walked through the nearly deserted market. My legs were wobbly and the going was slow.

My heightened senses turned noises into gunshots, a dropped pan, a jingling dog collar, a rustling paper bag. I twitched and jumped. I'd always had this reaction post-vision, but it was the first time I was really noticing the flavor and details of it. Slight smells became monstrous, the grease from a food stall like a thick coat down the back of the throat. I read the passersby's minds. A mother with a stroller did an abrupt one-eighty, terrified of the ghosts she saw spinning around the head of the crazy drunk *gaijin.* A man behind a newspaper looked up and wondered if I was a whore. The intensity of their thoughts made me nauseous.

air

The guard and I were heading toward a payphone. He was going to call the police. I knew they would come, and I would spend the night in jail.

At the phone, he let my arm go. I stood for a moment confused, but then I turned and ran. I stumbled and lurched across the temple courtyard. I fell against a couple, and the girl's gasp came out like a musical note. She was in love and even her fear escaped her like a tune. An elderly man with a dog looked at me with concern, as if he could see right into me, and he wanted to help. I avoided his gaze and kept running. As I was leaving the courtyard, I turned to see the officer gesturing and yelling into the phone.

I careened forward with what little strength I had left. Sometimes that was all a person could do. Sometimes all you could do was just get the hell out of there.

On a side street, I ducked into an alley. What did Japanese police do to foreigners they thought were addicts? *No, sir, I'm not on drugs. No, you see I have visions. I saw Fujin come alive.* Try translating that.

Amid the smell of fish entrails from a stack of wooden crates, beside a homeless man stretched out next to a garbage bin full of half-eaten restaurant food, to the sounds of a man sobbing from some far-up window, I crouched and waited.

I'd spent so many years trying to ignore the visions, trying to repress them. I couldn't understand why I couldn't have a normal life. Why did everyone else get to live an ordinary existence and not me? The homeless man behind me belched and farted. I trained my eyes toward a sliver of an opening between the buildings ahead of me, waiting for the police to come. I was wary of any authority when it came to my visions. They would banish me, jail me or call me crazy. They would do whatever they could to control me, dismiss me, demonize me, medicate me. They'd already tried. They'd put me in a psyche ward when I was a teenager. If it hadn't been for Sister Alice, I might not have survived.

The sobbing man above me suddenly ceased. A feral cat ran at me, and I jumped. Mother was right, Father, Jason—I would never survive this life if I didn't try to figure the visions out. But how?

All I knew at this stage was that the visions hit me whenever they damn well pleased, that they seemed to be born of place, that after they were over I could read minds, that my senses were heightened, and that I felt the hurt of the whole planet. But what then? What kind of life could I live? Whose idea of a joke was this?

The homeless man slurred something in Japanese. I reached into my fanny pack and found a couple bills. I was tired of hiding. I palmed the wall and pulled myself up. I handed the man the money, but he was too out of it to raise his arm to take it, so I leaned down and put it into his breast pocket.

I used walls for support as I labored out of the alley, through the dark and winding streets, vestiges of the vision wobbling my coordination. I tried not to look at the people turning to stare, tried not to read their minds. Neon signs threw shadows that grew faces.

Finally, I made it to the back landing of the mission. I used the skeleton key and pushed open the door.

It took a while to focus. Someone was there. Someone was sitting on my bunk. I made out my backpack—it had been moved to another bed. I tried to focus.

"Oh, you're the lass with whom I'm sharing this humble space." A shock of white hair that pointed in all directions, thick lips stretching from ear to ear, a curled-up thin body. His trousers hung low on his hipbones. He stuck out his hand. It glowed. I stared at it, confused. He put his hand down. I lurched inside.

"You pissed, then?"

I didn't know what he was saying. Walking carefully past him, I went to my backpack and pretended to look through it.

"Finn's the name." When I didn't answer, he continued. "I'm just off the boat from London."

"Pearl." I said it short so he wouldn't talk more. Post-vision, the guy was visceral. He was permeating my skin.

"Usui's been worried about you. He didn't know where you'd gone off to."

"Usui's here?" I made for the stairs.

"What are you on about? You met him. He told me about you."

air

Confused, I started climbing the stairs, but then stopped when I saw the old man descending. He was even more upset than before. Finn spoke to him in Japanese. How did some guy from London know Japanese? "Can you ask him if I can talk to Usui?" I interrupted.

Finn frowned. "Umm, he *is* Usui."

"What?"

Finn pointed to me and spoke in Japanese. The old man looked distraught as he replied.

Finn turned to me. "He's Mateo Usui. His son, the Jesuit missionary, is Genji Usui. His son has apparently gone missing."

"What do you mean exactly by missing?"

While he spoke to Usui's father, I observed the old man. So this was the conservative father Usui had told me about, the father who'd commanded one son to work for the corporation, the father who'd wanted Usui to follow suit. I thought about my own father and felt a pain in my gut.

"Well, I'm sorry to report that it's worse than just the fact that his son has gone missing. He has another son—"

"Ideko," I interrupted.

"Indeed, Ideko. Ideko has apparently died of *karoshi*."

I looked at him confused.

"I haven't a clue what this *karoshi* is either." He spoke to the older Usui.

"It's a Japanese term for dying at one's desk of overwork, a stroke or a heart attack or something. Oh yes, now I remember reading about this. They work the poor bastards like dogs, all night, holidays, seven days a week, no sleep, year after year after year. People die in their thirties, suddenly." He shook his head. "Well, where else would they die, right? If they live at work, they'll die at work."

"Where's Usui, um Genji then?" Poor Usui, *my* Usui, how horrible he must be feeling.

Finn turned to speak to the elder Usui, who was barely holding it together.

"A fellow missionary called the father here in Hokkaido and said his son hadn't been seen in a fortnight, since Ideko's death. His father filed a missing person report, but it's been a month. He's gone round to the neighbors, and no one has seen him. The mission leaders are bringing in a new bloke, so he's come to collect his son's things. I think this Genji fellow was probably going to be excommunicated or whatever it is they do to Jesuits who run away."

I slunk down onto one of the bunks and felt a rush of guilt. I should've come back sooner and checked in on him. I should've apologized.

Finn spoke again to the elder Usui. The older man bowed slightly and excused himself and walked slowly up the stairs.

Finn turned to me. "You don't look well, love. What's your connection to this Genji anyway?"

"Just a friend," I said. I didn't want to talk. I just wanted to sleep. It must've been well after midnight. "Maybe you're right. I'm not well. Maybe I'll just go to sleep."

I curled up on my side, cradling my backpack. For a moment, I worried about what kind of guy I was sleeping next to in this basement, but I didn't have the energy to move. Besides, this space was mine. This experience was mine. Usui was mine. This Londoner could just go home.

Where was Usui? I felt an intense need to find him, to make sure he was okay.

As I closed my eyes, I heard rustling, then the sounds of a flute. *Typical man, blowing his horn while others are trying to sleep.* Finn played a lullaby, hollow, haunting. I resisted it, but the hum wound around me, snaked into me, as if Finn were entering my flesh with his breath. It was as if Finn were singing me to sleep.

I awoke hours later to go to the bathroom. Street light from the basement window glowed around Finn as he lay languidly, his arms splayed out poetically. His forearms were thin, pale. I wanted to run my palm up his flesh. I shook myself at the thought. My gaze came to his face, and I noticed his eyes were open, and he was staring at me.

air

He didn't see me seeing him. His gaze traveled up my legs, to my waist and farther up. He stared long and hard. Before he could see me seeing him, I pulled my gaze away, went down the hall to the bathroom. I didn't look at him as I returned to my bed. I curled up with my back to him. I could feel his gaze.

He could see me too clearly. Post-vision, I understood how clearly he could see me, how clearly he could see everyone. It was not an easy gift to have. There was nowhere to hide. I hardly slept the rest of the night.

When the first signs of dawn showed through the narrow windows, I got up as quietly as I could, saw that Finn was sleeping, picked up my backpack, tiptoed up the stairs and let myself gingerly out the front door.

"Usui-*san*?" I asked Ami-*san* as she lifted the shutters on the front windows of her store. "Usui-*san*?" She laughed and pointed in the direction of the mission. She thought I was lost again. I followed her inside. The father hadn't found his son, but maybe he didn't know where to look.

"No. No. Usui-*san* is missing. Can you understand?" She wobbled her head. I told her the story in English, but she looked at me confused. I retold it as slowly as I could bear. As she put money into the register, she kept shaking her head and pointing in the mission's direction. It was obvious she didn't know where Usui was. I bowed. Thanked her. She bowed several times, offered me a bag of rice chips.

I stood outside and thought for a moment. Where would Usui go? I had no idea. I could only visit his old haunts. I felt so helpless. I rushed to the train station and took the beat-up old train to the handicapped clinic. I ignored the woman trying to speak to me at the front desk and went down to the basement. Dozens of children turned as I opened the door. The little girl, Keiko, rushed toward me.

"*Konnichiwa,* Keiko," she said, smiling. Two caregivers said something in Japanese, but I could only see the little girl.

"Usui-*san?*" I asked her. Her hair was freshly washed and was still wet in places. She smelled like medicated ointment.

She grabbed my hand. "*Usui wa arimasen.*" She put her free hand palm up as if to say, *All gone.*

One of the caregivers said in slow English. "We not know. Usui-*san* not come for much time."

When my face fell, Keiko must've felt it because she made a sad face and squeezed my hand. I wanted to pull away from her, but couldn't seem to manage the separation. We stood in the middle of the room holding hands, the faint sound of the piano playing close by.

How could Usui stay away from these kids? Even with the death of his brother, surely he would've come back here, of all places.

As I got back onto the old train, I thought of his tea pots. I knew the idea was ridiculous, but I didn't know what else to do. I remembered the pottery shop near the temple.

At the Minami-Asagaya station, I found the street. Most of Tokyo was modern, rebuilt again and again after the war and earthquakes. But hidden down side streets, you could still find the old Japan, ancient gullible places. Two-room wooden buildings crammed between modern structures could carry the stories of entire eras. Taverns, tiny shops, potters' studios.

There were new teapots in the window. A string of bamboo conked as I entered. The narrow space was full of vases, cups, saucers and teapots. I went up and said Usui's name to the balding man behind a pockmarked wooden counter. He moved his head from side to side. He had liver spots and a clay caked apron. I leaned over the counter and repeated Usui's name. He backed up.

I went to one of the aisles, ran my finger along the teapots, and waited. In the back of my ailing mind, I thought Usui might come by to purchase a teapot. I tried not to think about why or how he'd happen to come in to make this purchase at the very same time that I happened to be there waiting for him. When someone goes missing, your mind does all sorts of crazy logic. I couldn't even begin to imagine what his father had been going through.

Every time the bamboo on the door gave its hollow sound, I stared hopefully at the entering customer. After an hour, the man behind the counter stared at me with heavy eyes, so I bought a teapot. It was rust colored and cheap, the top caved in like an accident.

In my daily life, I began to see Usui everywhere. Unbidden, he appeared dozens of times a day, hundreds. On the cramped trains, in the eyes of salarimen, in the men at the *izakaya*. Every Japanese man was Usui. A man would find me staring wistfully full into his face and take it as something else, insolence or interest. It got me into trouble. Finn would crop up in my vision too sometimes and I'd push him away, guilty that he took my thoughts away from Usui.

When Meghan ran away, her body was gone, but her ghost lingered. She haunted her empty chair at the kitchen table, lurked behind her locked bedroom door, appeared folded forward at the living room window. She was etched in the hard frowns on Father's face. She floated in Mother's sighs. She whimpered in my whines.

Usui, too, remained. A whiff of grainy incense, the emerald edge of a kimono out of the corner of my eye, an origami bird found muddied on the sidewalk. He was everywhere. He was nowhere.

At the grocery, the anime magazine shop, department store, noodle stand, pachinko parlor, temple, I looked around for him, peered into the eyes of people passing on the sidewalk, studied hands that poked from sleeves, listened for a voice. I was looking for Usui, but I saw his brother. I searched for casual kimonos, dancing calligraphy, earthenware teapots, knotty origami, but found instead business suits and dead eyes. I found Ideko. A thousand Idekos, a million. Dressed in corporate uniforms, hair cropped, eyes cast toward concrete, white shirts, buttoned down.

I CAME HOME from work and went to bed—every night. It was too much loss. One loss, two, so many losses. The earth beneath my feet, Bonnie, Jason, Mother. Now Usui. Loss on top of loss.

I'd flown to a place where I could float above, a place where no stories embedded in the paper and wood of the tiny ramen shop, no memories at the noodle stand, no childhood stories in the cleaners with a kimono hanging in the window. A place where even language could not interfere.

I'd made the leap. I'd backed up to get a head start, flung myself up and out. Risk after risk. Leap after leap. What more did the gods want from me?

Where was my damned reward? More loss? More heartbreak? Was that all that I was ever going to get out of life?

Yuriko tried to lure me out of my futon, but I wouldn't be enticed.

I'd lay in the dark, ruminating on loss and my life. I didn't know if I was upset about Usui, or Missouri, or both.

When you grew up in a place, you could just take up where your parents left off. You could live whatever customs and rituals were already in place.

In Japan, I had to question everything. Who was I? What was I doing? I had no clue what my life could or should look like. I wasn't going to live the life of my ancestors, and I certainly wasn't going to

air

live the life of the average Japanese person. What life then should I live?

In these nights of dampened wails, I would hear Usui. *There is a reason, Purr-san.* The plaintive way he'd lean forward. His angular way of begging. *There is a reason Father Dennis sent you. There is a reason.* I held on to it. *Purr-san, a reason.*

It was the darkest night. I could barely lift my head on the walk home from the station. I fell onto my futon fully clothed, smashed my face into the pillow. An hour went by or two, I couldn't be sure. I heard my bedroom door slide open.

"What the hell is going on?" Yuriko asked. I turned my racked face away. "I was knocking and knocking. Didn't you hear?"

She sat on the *tatami*. I rolled over, turned my back on her. "Listen, I'm not good at this. But you have got to snap out of it. Every night this crying. It's freaking me out. You're like my frickin' mother."

"Just go, Yuriko. Leave me alone."

"This is just the crisis phase of being an expat. You know that, right? We've all gone through it. You're homesick. It's brutal, but you'll come out of it."

"Great. Thanks. That helps," I said deadpan. I was homesick for a home I knew I could never go back to. Great.

"Listen, my mother has phases like this. I call them bleeders. It's like something happens that triggers something deeper, and you're bleeding out. Who gives a shit where it comes from…"

I pulled at my hair. "Get out!"

"This isn't about Usui going missing. You know that. You've got to cap it. Staying like this, in this horrible dark place, will not help you. You have to cap the bleeder and get up and get on with your life."

"What life? *What life?*"

She put a hand on my back. "It's called living in the real world. The real world is getting out of bed. The real world is taking a bath." She moved strands of wet hair that were pasted to my cheek. "The real world is cleaning up this smelly shit." She picked up a coffee cup filled with phlegm. Around me were ashtrays, teacups full of hardened scotch, used tissues. The detritus surrounded me like the chalk outline of a dead person at a crime scene.

She leaned down and whispered into my ear. "Come on, Pearl. You're such a beautiful person."

I started sobbing. I couldn't stop. I went into a dark night of the soul, in and out of consciousness. A hard lump in my throat stuck like something inside me, wanting to get out. All night I tossed, a tsunami of the spirit. Yuriko came and went, putting wet towels on my forehead, cooing to me. My body was bowed by some force that was beyond my control. The grief was physical, from soles to gut to chin.

Somewhere toward morning, the storm broke. I crashed in exhaustion. It was afternoon when I awoke. Limbs ached. Shoulder throbbed. My body, a wilting. I'd lost my voice. I felt as if I'd been beaten by a baseball bat.

Describe the tabletop. Describe the speckles in the Formica. Describe the coffee cup. Describe the *I heart Tokyo* logo on the white cup. Describe the undissolved Nescafé crystals in the murky water. Describe the railings over the kitchen window above the sink. Describe the knee-high fridge. Describe the bland cupboards, the two-burner stove, the faded picture of Mt. Fuji above the table. Describe the flecks like shards of glass in the thick linoleum. Describe your feet in socks. Describe the big toe showing through a hole in the right sock. Describe your wrinkled sweatpants. Describe the cigarette hole in the arm of your sweatshirt. Describe the scrunch of your

air

frizzy hair. Describe the eggy smell of your unwashed armpits. Describe the flesh around your thumbs where you've picked the skin bloody.

This was the way I came back from a vision. This was the way I came back from a bleeder. The minutiae gave me something to grab on to. I stared at one object and then the next. I reached out to each particular switch, knob, handle, corner, edge, surface. I touched my way back to this world, this streamlined, mundane, brutalized humanity.

Maybe Mother was right; maybe I would never survive in this real world. But what else could I do? What other options were open to me? Survive or not survive, only these two.

Yuriko was sleeping. If nothing else, I would come back to this world for her, to stop myself from hurting her. She was right. There was no good in staying down. I'd been there before. Already over several lifetimes, I'd had to peel myself off the floor, stiffen myself up, force myself to move. One step, two, like walking bent over in a blistering headwind.

Saturday, a week later, I got dressed and then went down the street to the news agent and bought all the English-language newspapers. Yuriko had taken the train a few days earlier to Nagasaki, to the Atomic Bomb Museum. She'd asked me to go with her, but I just needed time by myself.

As I was walking back from the news agent with six English dailies, I thought I saw Usui out of the corner of my eye, but forced my face forward, forced myself not to look. I had to stop. Looking. I had to stop. Seeing.

I spread the newspapers in front of me on the tiny table in the kitchenette. I was going to get a journalism job. Journalism had saved me before, and it would save me again. It had taught me distancing, and it would teach me distancing again.

The Dow had a one-day drop of 508 points. They were calling it Black Monday. Each paper led with the story. Four of the dailies covered global population growth reaching five billion and the hole that kept growing in the ozone layer. The inside pages were filled with Japanese stories of robbery, murder, sexual assault. I made a list of the stories on a legal pad, then made a list of the editors named beneath the mastheads.

One thing I could always count on was my brain. I had a good brain. If it weren't for my unrelenting soul, I'd have been just fine.

In college, I did well in journalism school. They taught us to back up, to extricate ourselves from the world's story, to analyze details to refuse emotions. We learned to keep ourselves outside the world's story. They presented us with the gift of disconnection.

Also, I simply loved stories. I could spend hours thinking about a single person's tale. I didn't even have to know the person to love their particulars. If I dug deep enough, I would find some meaning. If I analyzed, poked and prodded *their* lives, I'd be able to get a handle on *my* life.

The professors had us read newspapers and study earthquakes, tornados, fires and floods. They sent us out to cover local disasters. I learned to interview the soaked and the scorched with ice-cold detachment. We moved on to global catastrophes, third-world mudslides, Asian hurricanes, Middle Eastern wars, tsunamis in Asia.

The trauma wasn't that far from my visions. It felt familiar. Maybe this was what I was called to do, to go out into the world and analyze the clutter, to clean up the messes…from a distance.

Yuriko burst through the door. I turned vacant eyes toward her. "You gotta see this shit," she said, hauling her pack off her back and plopping it onto the other kitchen chair. The pack was smeared with paint thumbprints. She had on red skin-tight trousers tucked into thigh-high boots, a short leather jacket with a half-dozen zippers. It just wasn't done to leave your shoes on in the house in Japan, but Yuriko rarely took hers off, her hard-to-remove, laced boots yet another rebellion.

"I thought you were gone until tomorrow," I said, unable to hide my disappointment at losing any scrap of time alone. She wore mirror sunglasses, and when I looked at her I saw a warped fun-house mirror version of my own face.

"I ran out of canvases, and I couldn't figure out how to buy them down there."

"When have you not been able to figure something out?"

"Okay, okay, I couldn't take it. The museum just freaked me out."

She opened the main zipper of her pack and extracted a long flat box. "They've got this center where the people tell the stories of what they were doing when the bomb dropped. And they were in English, so even I could read them." She opened the box. Inside were two canvases. She'd built a rack in the box that kept the canvases separate. The paintings were still wet. "If my mother could just open her mouth and talk like those people in the museum. Man, just talk, you know, not bury it.

"She goes on and on about how the past is the past. *Yuriko-*chan *purease leave the past in the back of the closet. Do not put it in center of house.* And I'm like, Ma, come on, the past creeps around this freakin' house all day wearing a Japanese robe and crying in the bathroom where she thinks I can't hear. The past is right here every day, all day. Why don't we just air it out? *Oh no, no, we cannot, Yuriko-*chan. *Silence,*

Yuriko-chan. And my father just stares at her with those sad puppy eyes."

I gaped at the paintings. Both were of a wasteland. The landscape was torn up; the big wind had come and blown the entire city to bits. She'd painted a couple walls that were still standing. Two people with melting flesh stood at the edge. One wall had a shadow of a human burned into it.

"Can you believe this?" she asked, pointing to the shadow. "The bomb actually did this, blew people into walls and disintegrated them and left their silhouette behind, like a permanent shadow. I'm calling this series 'Fat Man.' That's what the Americans called the Nagasaki bomb, Fat Man. Fat Man and Little Boy. Ugh, right?"

The paintings swelled until they took up my vision. I felt my back arch painfully.

The roaring, the wicked explosion of light, crashing, bashing, sucking, but then utter quiet. A wind so intense it blew apart everything in its path. I'll huff and puff and blow your house down. I saw the blue and terrifying Fujin, that wind monster, hovering over all of it, roaring with rage.

It was the same vision I'd had with Usui, but this one didn't stop at the explosion. *The landscape became a sea of fire. Layers of corpses, bones, hair, twisted metal, rubber tires—a city turned into a layered, fleshy junkyard. A goo dripping from the sky, sticky rain that burned the skin. On the outskirts, where people weren't completely turned to ash, they walked around with flesh dripping like strands of a burst balloon. I put my hand to my cheek, felt my own flesh melting. I reached to Yuriko's face and felt the flesh like liquid slipping through my fingers.*

"We're killing ourselves! We're so enraged we're murdering ourselves!" I screamed.

Yuriko's hands beneath my armpit, lifting me as if I were a rag doll. "My God, Pearl, Pearl! Where are you? Come back. Come home. Dear God, you're losing so much weight! You're light as air." She hauled me onto a chair.

I put my elbows on the table, and rested my face against my palms. Once I had a dream that I was sitting with my head in my hands, and when I sat back up, it didn't come with me. Throughout the dream, I carried my head under my arm like a sack of potatoes. I felt like that now; even if I was able to sit up straight, my skull was so heavy, it wouldn't come with me.

"What the fuck was that?" Yuriko yelled, her voice a drill grinding into the center of my ear. She got a glass of water from the tap, and smacked it in front of me. "Okay, sister, what the fuck?"

I groaned.

"You gotta be kidding if you think I'm going to just let that go without an explanation." When I still wouldn't or couldn't speak, she sat across from me and waited. I held on to my head. I was so damned tired.

Finally, she said, "Fuck, you really, truly are as bad as my mother. Things get tough and you just shut the fuck down. I'm sick of it." She shoved her chair back and slammed open her door.

"Okay, okay," I croaked.

She sat back down. And so, I told her. I spoke through my fingers to the Formica tabletop, a muffled story, a voice that sounded old and small, like an ancient child's. I told her about the first vision in the garden, about the one with Usui, the one I'd just had.

"You've had these visions all your life and you aren't studying them to see what they're trying to tell you? I don't understand."

"Get off me. I know I need to figure them out."

"I mean from watching you…despite the physical theatrics, this must be some kind of a gift, right? Maybe it's tied to the depression, too. Did you ever think of that?"

"Why can't I have the luxury of living my life like a fucking normal person?"

Yuriko snorted a laugh. "Yeah, maybe you could get married and have 2.5 children. Sure. Live in the suburbs…"

I gave her a hangdog look. Yuriko's eyes were far away. Her voice went soft. "You know, maybe it's like how I feel when I'm in a zone with a painting. Sometimes I dream the painting like it's real. I can spend days *inside* the painting. Maybe it's like that, and you can use some of this energy for something. Maybe you're this unrealized genius."

"The people who call what I have genius should have to spend one month living my life."

I stood, and on shaky legs, headed for my room. "The unrealized genius has just lost a whole day because a certain vision has just wiped all the life out of her." At my door, I turned. "Before I forget." I pointed at her paintings. "You need to add more fire." She looked from me to the canvases. "More fire, more flames. A sea of fire, a raging inferno."

A day or two later, when I'd recovered, I sat again at the table with the stack of newspapers. No matter how many times my turbulent soul knocked me down, I was just going to have to get up again. I'd learned it early, this knocking down, this getting up again.

Yuriko had gone out to a park to do plein air painting. Finally, some peace. She'd been unrelenting since the vision, wanting to hear everything, to process it all. She wanted to take me to this psychic she knew. I'd scoffed and shook my head and left the room, but she followed me, as tenacious as a dog with a bone.

"So deny who you really are then. That's the plan?" she'd asked.

"Are the visions who I really am?" I'd cried.

"Hmmph." She'd put her hands on her hips.

"They're not!" I'd screamed, louder and more desperately than I'd meant to.

"Okay, okay, don't kill the messenger."

I'd run to my bedroom and discovered it was nearly impossible to slam a Japanese sliding door.

I sat at the table now in peace and quiet. I was going to use my good brain, some had called it a great brain, and I was going to get a proper job, and I was going to be fine. Just fine. I would show them "normal."

air

I called every editor from every one of the English papers. Each told me there were no openings. I kept being pulled backward by flashes of the Nagasaki bombing, a sudden blinding radiance, the dark wind hollowing soil and soul, the eerie quiet afterward. I thrust the mental images away. Hard. I raised my fist and punched the visions in the face. I told them all to go to hell.

Maybe a vision was like a child screaming for attention, and if I just ignored it, if I locked the child away in some dark closet, the crying would stop. Let me set up a normal life, then I would study the visions. That was the plan.

I was still teaching English. *Where is the library? Where is the post office? Where is the supermarket? Where is the restroom? Where is the insane asylum?* Most days, I imagined poking my eyes out with a pencil. I imagined throwing myself in front of a train. Mother used to say, *Pearl can take almost anything, but she just can't take being bored.*

I redoubled my efforts, haranguing the editors every few days from a payphone at the school. Finally, some of them gave me interviews. After each interview, they swore there were no jobs, but they'd keep me on file. I called them back after that twice, three times a week. The squeaky wheel got the grease, and I made myself shrill.

Finally, Mr. Jameson, one of the editors at the *Daily Kaze*, called. They had an opening for a "rewriter." He told me I wasn't the first on the waiting list. I read between the lines that he was giving me a job because he was sick of my incessant phone calls.

With great glee, I presented my notice to Mrs. Reinkemeyer. Over the top of her cat eyeglasses she looked crestfallen. She shook her head and told me I was a great teacher. I didn't say, *A monkey could teach that curriculum.*

On the final day, I came into the classroom and the chairs were arranged in rows. One of the students, Mr. Tanaka, directed me to sit in the front. Mrs. Reinkemeyer, Jerry the HR guy, the secretary, the financial guy and a few other teachers were already there. Jerry leaned over and said that he'd miss me. "I'm glad you're still with Yuriko," he added. "She needs someone like you. You're good for her." Jerry was always saying the strangest things.

Mr. Tanaka, Mr. Suzuki, Mr. Ichikawa, Mr. Watanabe, Mr. Sato, Mr. Ito and Mr. Kato had prepared a goodbye skit. They created a mock classroom. Each took a turn pretending to be the teacher—that is, me—while the rest sat with glued-on mock smiles. Apparently, I used my hands a lot at the side of my face, jazz hands waving by my ears. The men took their thinning hair and tried to muss it upward so it stuck out in all directions. When it was Mr. Sato's turn, he wore a long, black wig and used hairspray to make it frizzy and wild. My hair always did have a mind of its own, a beastly mane. Jazz hands, wild hair, a lilting singsong way of speaking. They walked around imitating me, moving their bodies like a young woman, exaggerating a sexy walk. Did I look like that?

When it was Mr. Ichikawa's turn, he jazz handed his way over to the bookshelf, pulled a large novelty pencil from behind the shelf. "*Ah, so desu ne.* This is a pencil." I laughed so hard I choked on my coffee.

He passed the pencil around to his students in the mock classroom. "No," said Mr. Ito. "*This* is a pencil." He pulled from beneath the table an even bigger pencil. And so it went until Mr. Kato ended it with a pencil taller than himself.

The audience applauded and cat called. After their choreographed group bow, they invited me to the front. Mr. Watanabe offered me a package wrapped with a delicate pink tissue. He presented it with both hands and a blush. He was the boss of the team, and everyone deferred to him. I'd watched as they were doing the skits, and he was quietly directing the whole thing. I opened the gift. It was a handmade journal, its spine made of brown string, translucent blue beads sewn onto the cover.

Mrs. Reinkemeyer came to the front. She handed me a box with a blue ribbon. Inside was an azure teapot covered in faint flowers. It was a piece of art. Usui would've loved it.

She rushed to say, "I saw that you had a teapot once from a place in Asakusa and went there myself. We'll really miss you, Pearl."

As a child, I had not been given gifts often, and went cold. If you didn't know me, you would think I was upset or didn't like it, but

air

truly I'd never learned the art of receiving. I had much confusion in my heart. She looked at me, and I saw my mother there in her eyes, or maybe it was the universal mother. Something in me broke open, and I had to rush from the room.

Later as I sat on the bench to wait for Yuriko, I nestled the journal and teapot in my lap. I did not know how to process that goodbye. I'd hated the job. I traced a flower on the teapot, opened the journal and felt a single page between thumb and forefinger. I'd only learned in my life how to run away, how to save myself. I'd only been taught how to escape. This was something new, this celebratory goodbye. I picked up the teapot and hugged it to my raging chest.

Yuriko and I went to the *izakaya* to celebrate. We drank a beer, another beer, another. I smoked one cigarette, another, another. The fisticuffs in my chest quieted. Booze always helped. Boys and men saddled up to the table, but Yuriko dismissed them. This was our night.

She raised her glass. "A toast."

I raised mine.

"I'm not sure being in a newsroom around all those stories of death and dismemberment is the best thing for someone who has apocalyptic visions, but cheers!" she said and then took a deep drink.

I smiled and drank. I didn't tell her that she need not worry about me. Journalism was going to save me. Now everything would be normal, and I'd go on to live a fulfilled and successful life. My parents had been dirt poor, and I was raised with nothing, but here I was with a fancy degree, an international life and now a proper job. The visions could be dealt with later.

I drank. Smiled. Nodded. The person I really wanted to tell was Usui. *See, Usui-*san, *I'm going to change the world. Can you see?*

IT WAS A twenty-five-minute train ride from the apartment to Ohtemachi, the business district where the *Daily Kaze* was located. That morning I'd put on my airplane outfit, the one with the polka dots, but Yuriko reacted crazy about my "canary suit" and demanded I wear the black jeans and turtleneck.

On the train, I kept pulling on the top. It clung to my figure and showed too much; a lot of the Japanese men kept looking at my chest. I was curvy, but I kept my body hidden. I'd learned early that being curvy and attractive was a dangerous thing.

The business district seemed to be abandoned. Even with all the businessmen on the sidewalk, still the area was eerily dead. Empty. Soulless. The modern drab low-rises were covered in soot, doused in a film of ash.

I took the elevator to the third floor, stood in the doorway and surveyed the newsroom. A cloud of cigarette smoke hung low like morning fog. It was an open-plan room about two hundred feet long by eighty feet wide. The smell of the place was hard, sour and scratchy. At the south end, a bank of young Japanese men sat at computers. I saw one Japanese woman in the group. At the other end were the Westerners, the English speakers. Men in suits spoke into telephones or paced around within glassed-off offices in one corner.

A man in his forties walked toward me. He was skinny and short, balding on top with a ponytail down his back. "Can I help you?"

air

"I'm Pearl Swinton. It's my first day."

"Hold on." He went to the corner of the room and talked to a middle-aged, overweight man in his sixties. They looked as if they were arguing. He came back shaking his head.

"Sorry, nobody tells me anything. It's like Vietnam all over again. That was Mr. Jameson." He waved from the other side of the room, and I waved back. "I'm Michael." He put out his hand. His fingers were shaking. I shook his hand. He had pockmarks on his face that were so deep you could fit your pinkie into them. At the corner of his large lips was a white gooey substance that he kept licking. "Follow me."

He led me to the other side of the room to the tinted windows that covered one wall. He leaned back against the windows and crossed his arms over his chest. "Those are the rewriters. That's where you'll be sitting." He pointed to a group of six Westerners at computer terminals. He spoke in a whisper, and I had to stand close to hear. I touched the glass on one of the windows and it was sticky. It wasn't tinted; it was covered in a film of black cigarette tar. I looked around and about eighty percent of the people were smoking.

"The Japanese reporters come back from reporting and write up the articles." He flipped his ponytail. His voice was gravely from cigarette smoke. "It's the rewriter's job to rework the copy, slap on a headline and send it to the editor's desk. My desk." He pointed over to it. It was covered in crumpled papers. A coffee cup had spilled, and he hadn't bothered to clean up the mess. In the middle of the desk was an ashtray heaped with cigarette butts. "The editor edits it, finds images, sends it to paste-up." He pointed to a walled-off area toward the back of the offices. I could just make out a bunch of older men in orange jumpsuits. "That's the paste-up crew." Somebody dropped something, and the noise made Michael jump so hard his hand hit the window. It was some kind of post-traumatic reaction.

His hands were shaking as he led me over and introduced me to the other rewriters—a quiet, curly-haired Canadian boy, a strapping Australian woman, a blonde American girl, a burly guy from New

Zealand, a young male English lit graduate from New England, and a Chinese woman who was screaming into the phone.

"Since this is your first day, we'll go easy on you," Michael said, but it was hard to hear him over the screaming woman. "Just one story today. Let you get the hang of it." He put his hand on my shoulder, and I flinched. It stayed there like the weight of a dead fish. "In a week, you'll need to be rewriting at least six stories a day."

I sat at the desk, happy to get away from his hand. He leaned over me to pull the story up on the old computer terminal. He smelled like something rotting.

The article was hard to see. I put my finger up and ran it over the screen and it came back covered in tar. I grabbed a napkin from the floor and rubbed a small spot on the screen. The keyboard, too, was sticky like glue. Michael still stood there.

"I think I've got it. Thanks," I said. He was reluctant to leave, but finally Mr. Jameson yelled his name, and he was gone.

The article was written in difficult English, and it took a while to understand. It was about a teacher who'd kicked a child in the head. The teacher had accused a student of dyeing her hair red. The student denied it, saying she was born with red hair. The teacher went to the student's home for an apology, and while the child prostrated herself, kicked the girl repeatedly. The more I looked at it, the more confused I became.

I went to the corner of the room where the Japanese reporters lived. The rewriters seemed to watch me suspiciously. The reporters were across the room, but they might as well have been across an ocean. In the time I'd been in Japan, I'd come across this divide again and again. You'd meet Americans who only hung out with other Americans. Sometimes, the U.S. group would have one token British guy, or even a token Japanese girl, but it was like going to any American party in the U.S. I hated these events. Why not just stay in the States? But still, I wasn't that much different. Yuriko was American, and right now, she was my entire social life.

It wasn't that most Westerners didn't want to get to know the Japanese; it was there were just so many rules. It was too easy to

air

deeply offend our hosts without knowing why. Every day, I felt as if I had insulted a half-dozen people without the slightest notion why. The social etiquette was complex, based on social status, age, gender; and even within these groups there were rules. Trying to figure out how to act so as not to offend could make you a nervous wreck. It felt as if many of the Japanese didn't want us inside their world. They held each other so close it was hard to wedge in.

Someone on the Japanese side must have mopped the floor, because I left brown floor tiles and stepped onto beige. The reporters bent forward toward clunky computer screens, or murmured softly to each other. Across the room, the English speakers were apes in a zoo, screaming from desk to desk, cursing, running.

I asked the girl reporter, "Where can I find Shinji Kurosawa?" She pointed two desks down without looking at me.

When I stood in front of his desk, he looked up startled. He was maybe twenty-five, but looked younger, like a lanky teenager, with soft pale skin and a constellation of miniature moles across the left side of his mouth. "Shinji-*san*, on your story here." I leaned over with a hard copy for him to see. "I don't get it. Why is the teacher so angry?"

"Japanese girl with red hair, teacher thinks she puts the color." He widened his narrow eyes again and again as if he was trying to take in something. He reminded me of Usui, and I leaned closer. He said, "Sometimes, Japanese born with red hair, we think they have Korean blood. Not so good for some Japanese people. They want purity." He said the word purity as *pooeety*. "Sometimes Japanese people dye hair black to keep from trouble."

I was beginning to understand. If the girl had natural red tints, some wicked ancestor must've slept with a dirty Korean. I was used to racism; woe to anyone who was black or Asian or gay in that rural neck of the woods where I grew up. I thought living in a big international city would mean sophisticated people who weren't racist or sexist. I guess I was wrong.

The teacher was being brought up on charges, and I could sense in the story that even the official complaint was unusual, that the situation would usually be hushed up. I asked Shinji.

"Teacher facing charges," he said. He smelled like cherry Lip Smackers. "Here." He tapped the paper in my hand. "Police involved."

"The teacher kicked her in the head," I said.

"No." He nodded. In Japan, a nod didn't necessarily mean yes. "In past, no police."

"So the teacher didn't kick her in the head?"

"No. Sorry. Yes. I mean, yes, teacher kick her. Yes, police called. In past, no police."

"So they usually ignore it? This stuff happens a lot?"

"Yes. To women. Girl."

The Japanese woman reporter looked up from her desk. Her forehead was heavy, her face flat and expressionless. I felt as if I recognized her, or recognized the pain on her face. Her eyes were unfocused as if she was remembering something.

Michael came over from the editor's desk. "I know you only have one story today, but you do have a deadline," he said, putting a protective arm around me. Again, that creepy feeling. What was he protecting me from, anyway? Shinji?

I rewrote the story and submitted it well before deadline. I simply polished the English. I couldn't and didn't elaborate on the situation with the teacher. I had a profound lack of context. How could I do a good job without any cultural context?

As the days went by, as I went from rewriting one story to rewriting six, I promised myself I'd learn the context as I went and add it where I could. The Japanese had brutal notions about work and expected employees to put in ridiculous hours. As I sat there day after day, staring at the green letters on the murky computer screen, I couldn't help but think of Usui's brother dying at his desk. I worked six days a week, twelve hours a day, but the Japanese reporters and editors worked much longer. The intensity of it entered my bones, defined my marrow.

I liked most of the stories. They were eclectic. Eccentric. I rewrote a feature about a Chinese fashion show in Tokyo and led it with "From Mao to Wow." There was a piece about a Korean thief caught at a restaurant eating spaghetti carbonara. I asked and asked, but was never able to figure out why his choice of food was important to the story. My favorite was an article titled, "A Man Today Found a Finger in His Bum." A guy had apparently found the tip of a finger in a pastry. The Japanese reporter thought "bun" was "bum." At the rewriters' desk, the harder we English speakers laughed, the redder the Japanese reporters' faces became. It was rude, but we couldn't help ourselves.

When two Japanese tourists in Spain were hurt in a train fire, I came up with the perfect newspaper headline haiku.

A Train

In Flames

Causes Pain

In Spain

It fit the column width specs perfectly. I sent it to Mr. Jameson for a laugh. Of course I knew we couldn't use it. He called me over as soon as he saw it. "We do not make fun of those who are suffering, Miss Swinton."

"Come on, Jameson, it's a goof," I said, pushing his shoulder. I liked him. He was awkward, goofy, shy. He wore polyester suits and bottle-thick glasses and had a comb-over.

"We don't goof here, Miss Swinton," he said, but I could see him smiling. He didn't look like a guy who had much fun. If our hours were brutal, his must've been extreme.

I was fast. I'd always been a fast reader, a fast writer. A quick study. I was up to editing eight stories a day by the second week. I turned to see the strapping Australian rewriter timing me once with a stopwatch. "One hundred ten words a minute!" she'd called out to the others. The problem with being fast was the more I did, the more I was given to do. *Bring me your rapes, your murders, your arsons, your mudslides.* I would save the world one trauma at a time. Overall I was happy, although I rarely saw Yuriko. I'd climb out of the futon and rush to work. Get home and climb back into bed.

One day at the *Kaze*, I went looking for the lunch room on one of the upper floors. I'd heard about the place, but had been eating at my desk. I took the elevator from floor to floor, but couldn't find it. I worked for the English version of the *Kaze*, and the staff of the Japanese version worked on the upper floors of the building. The Japanese version had the largest circulation in the country. The company even owned a baseball team. There were other companies in the building, too, renting space.

On the fifth floor, I peered through a circular window into a room that looked like a gym. Next to workout equipment sat plastic picnic tables, but no one was eating at them. I wondered if this was supposed to be the cafeteria. I went in and sat at one of the tables. Several Japanese businessmen slept on the workout benches, stretched out on their backs in suits. I wondered if they simply couldn't get home after the long work hours and the notorious drinking sessions required of salarimen after work, or they were catching up on their sleep during lunch hour. I wanted to tell Usui about this, about the half-dozen Idekos stretched out on the workout equipment, snoring.

I had a bento box. The *Kaze* bought everyone a bento box for lunch every day. Inside were pickled vegetables, rice, a deep-fried chicken cutlet with brown sauce.

I ate a sliver of chicken, then moved the bento box aside and lit a cigarette. I often skipped lunch. Sometimes I would have to stop and think when the last time was that I'd eaten. Someone brushed my arm. It was a Westerner, and he walked up to a bulletin board on the wall. I watched as he tacked up a poster. It took a while for me to register the white-blond hair, the tall, thin, lanky form.

"It's you," I blurted before I could stop myself.

air

He turned. He looked startled, too. "Well, if it isn't the mysterious girl from the mission." With that shock of white hair and his tall languid body, Finn would have stood out anywhere, but there, surrounded by these sleeping bodies, he was like a white-haired god.

"What are you doing here?" I asked.

"I work here actually."

He looked me up and down. His gaze lingered on my tight turtleneck. I folded my arms across my chest. "I work here, too," I said.

"Fancy that." He came over, put one leg over the bench and sat facing me. I could smell the dark musk of marijuana on his clothes.

"I'm in marketing," he said. "You?"

"In the newsroom, a rewriter."

"You say it with such pride." He wore a loose-knit light blue sweater with a small hole at the elbow. His brown trousers were loose and wrinkled. On his feet were surprisingly shiny black shoes, what we'd call "church shoes" back home. "You ran out on me at the mission," he said.

"I had someplace to be."

"Sure, love, don't we all. By the way, I've come up with a nickname for you. It came to me in a dream that night we slept together at the mission."

I shook my head. "We didn't…"

"Queenie. I've named you Queenie." He leaned over and touched the pouch at my neck. It was as if his fingers traveled through the leather and entered my throat. I sucked in a raspy breath. He let go, took a cigarette from my pack, lit it and leaned back. His mouth stretched over stained teeth that pointed in different directions. His teeth turned me on. His teeth were so un-American.

"Queenie was the name of a crazy cow we had on the farm," I said. "My mother used to say, 'Queenie got the crazy eye. Watch out for Queenie.'"

"Splendid. Perfect," he said, blowing a jagged waft of cigarette smoke.

His nose was Romanesque, his ears too big for his head. He was a combination of frightfully ugly and shockingly gorgeous. "Did Usui ever come back?" I asked.

"You mean the son? No, love, not as far as I know. When the old fellow left, I had to leave. I wrote a song about the bloke when I was at the mission. It came to me while I was sleeping."

"Everybody just gave up looking for Usui?"

He blew a smoke ring. "What about you? Have you given up?"

I shrugged.

"What if everybody just left the poor bloke alone?" His words came out fierce. "He's probably taking a break. We all need a break from our fucked-up cultures. Just leave the poor sod alone!"

Before I could respond, there was a tinny sound, small beeps. A man sleeping on a bench next to us sat up. He had black circles beneath his eyes and his skin looked sallow. He leaned heavily over to the floor and hit the button on the travel alarm.

"Poor bloody bastard," Finn said. I didn't know if he was talking about the waking man or Usui or himself. He stamped out the cigarette. "Break's over." He got up and headed for the door "Ta for now, Queenie." He pointed toward the poster. "Why don't you pop round to see the band Saturday? I'll be playing the Usui song."

After he left, I walked up to the bulletin board. The band's name was The Emperor's New Clothes. It was "a fusion of folksy keyboards and guitar with shamisen music and taiko drums." I took a stubby pencil and a receipt from my fanny pack and wrote down the address. I was about to turn away when the smaller print caught my eye. "Introducing an original song by band leader Finn O'Riley, 'Usui's Ghost.'"

I'D THOUGHT ABOUT Finn all week, dreamt him, daydreamed him, inhaled the smoke of him into my lungs. How the poetry of another can wend its way into you, can leave a footprint here, a harmony there. Musk, cock of head, angle of nose, twitch of brow. How they can fill you up, and it's both thrilling and terrifying.

"Ladies and gentlemen, The Emperor's New Clothes!" Finn screamed. I stood behind massive columns in the night club. The band was thrashing and clashing in chaotic orchestration. A Western guy on bass, a bleached Japanese girl, arms dancing as she pounded a massive taiko drum, a thin Japanese boy playing the shamisen, holding the stems of the stringed instrument like the neck of some exotic animal.

The place was filled with pubescent Japanese girls. They went into hopping paroxysm on the sunken dance floor. Finn bellowed nonsensical words, kicked skinny legs up at his sides like a vaudeville act, went into a coughing fit and incorporated it into the song. The babble clanked hard in my head, and I was about to clutch my hands to my ears when the music transformed. The chaos quieted. The shamisen player took over, the twang and clank like the sound of an Asian banjo, short, grassy, familiar. As the ancient strings lulled me to the edges of an epiphany, the shamisen stopped and the female taiko drummer screamed a battle cry, hit the massive wooden sides of the drums with sticks. She moved her body as she drummed like a wild

air

woman. The vibrations ran through the floor and traveled up my legs and joined my heart in a cavernous beat. Boom. Boom. Boom.

Finn's voice was rough, hoarse, often off-key. The number ended with everyone on stage playing wild, like bird dogs set free from their pens for a long day of duck hunting.

I didn't move. The clash of two cultures, Western and Eastern, the clutter, the splendor. I wished Yuriko was there. The music was the very vibrations of her. The entire room was an odd cross of East and West. The space was round, and the bar, doors and stage were constructed of heavy dark wood. Most rooms in Tokyo were fragile, light, small. This place was full of depth and heaviness. Tiny lights were strung on overhead wooden beams, fanning out across the ceiling, twittering like lightning bugs. The thick columns were painted with ornate Asian gods.

The shamisen player started. The three-stringed instrument jangled like clunky wind chimes. Finn spoke low into the microphone. "This is a song I wrote called *Usui's Ghost.*" He crooned about tiny folds of reality, about seeing only the past in the shadowed faces. As he sang, he drew the syllables out in a whine as if he were in pain, and I couldn't make out all the words. I could barely breathe. His voice became my voice. The very essence of Usui was in that song. How had Finn gotten that much out of his stay at the mission? How had he understood Usui when he hadn't even met him?

I had to get to Finn, talk to him. I'd felt the same thing for Usui, this compulsion to be near him, to *be* him. I didn't know if it was Finn himself, or the ghost he'd just channeled, but I needed Finn now as much as I'd needed Usui. I walked down to the dance floor, went to the side area where I knew the band would leave the stage. When they took a break, Finn would have to pass right by me.

I wore the black turtleneck Yuriko bought me, smoothed it over my figure. Yuriko made me sit at the kitchen table while she braided my hair. I'd never had anyone touch my hair. I couldn't remember Mother even brushing it when I was little. Yuriko's hands felt shockingly intimate. I sat stock still, afraid to move. She turned me around after she finished. "Oh, you're stunning," she said, a look of surprise on her face. I turned red, and she added, "Behind all that hair, you're really a stunner." I reached up to move a strand, to pull it free to cover my face, but she grabbed my fingers and stopped me.

Finally, Finn announced they were taking a break. There was a group of us now gathered near the stairs. The band members filed down, girls reaching and screaming. Finn was last. He headed my way. I wanted to launch myself at him. He stopped right in front of me to talk to a Japanese girl. She was a bit older than the rest, wore a fur coat, long leather boots. She smelled of sex and shadows.

He put his hand under her hair at the nape of her neck. I watched him bend down, far down, to kiss her lips. I watched as they kissed, an eternal moment, his energy and the girl's energy swirling up and around. I was pulled into them, kissing with them, the three of us tied together in breath. My eyes were half closed, entering Finn's lips as he entered hers, unable to stop myself from falling. Then it was over. I took a step back, confused. The girl moved into him and put her arm around his waist.

He had a girlfriend? How could he possibly have a girlfriend? I was his girlfriend.

"Hey, there you are, Queenie." He came up and chucked me on the shoulder. "Chuffed you could make it." He turned to the woman. I could see her face now, and she was something out of a dream—ivory skin, those exotic eyes, lips small and succulent. "Let me introduce you. This is Aikiko."

I smiled and nodded. And nodded. And nodded. I couldn't seem to form words. I felt like a small-town nobody who was nodding at sophistication and beauty.

"Okay, then. We'll see you around. Enjoy the show," Finn said. They walked arm in arm past me. Her thick hair flowed down and down until it touched the top of her boots. I put my hand up to my face; I never wore makeup. I watched them walk in perfect harmony toward the bar. I stood deep in the shadows at the back of the club for the rest of the gig. I couldn't stay, and I couldn't go home.

It wasn't a surprise when they promoted me at the *Daily Kaze*. I may not have been good at romance, but I was good at work. I'd always been good at work. They started me early. At the *Kaze*, I was already pulling five times my weight. The senior editor, Yoshimoto-*san*, told me he was impressed at how I could "do the work of three good men."

The other rewriters were not happy. I'd only been there six weeks. Most of them stopped talking to me. What they failed to understand was that I was little more than a mule, a horse, a donkey. I'd been bred for this.

Father used to strap me to the plow. I'd told people about it over the years, but nobody believed me. Jason thought it was a joke. I was eight. We couldn't afford a mule. The truth is true even if nobody believes it. A lie is a lie even if everybody believes it.

Father had been the one strapped to the plow up to that point, with Mother working the worn wooden handles. But then it was my turn. I used to think it was because they saw how strong I was, that the situation came about because I was sturdy, and therefore wasn't as bad as all that.

The stuttered leather tore at the hips and shoulders. I had to bend nearly in half to pull the rusty blade through the stubborn soil. We had a garden the size of a football field, ringed by forest. It was a lot of earth to plow. The summers were so stinking humid I would be slimed with sweat and grit.

Every summer, I was the mule. It didn't sit well with me. Somewhere in my gut, it felt disturbing and wrong, the way they had to strap me in, the pressure of all that pulling on my young body, the way Father held the plow and ordered me forward as if I were nothing but his dog.

Something was set up that would last a lifetime, a grunting and pulling, a dumping. It wasn't just about using the energy, but controlling it, overwhelming it. *We are not free, child, so you shall not be free.* A legacy passed down through generations.

I now started every day in meetings with the editors. All the top editors were Japanese. I learned quickly that because I was a woman, if I wanted to get approval for an idea for a story, I could not present it myself. If I did, it was met with cold dismissiveness; they spoke over me in the editorial meetings as if I hadn't spoken. I learned if I whispered the idea to Michael, and he presented it, there was a better chance for the idea to be approved. *The only thing lower than a woman here is her younger sister.*

I learned how to commission stories from the Japanese reporters, send photographers out into the city, wait for the copy from the reporters, get it to the rewriters, review the rewriters' work, find the top international news from the AP wires, and lay out six pages daily, write headlines and captions—all to viciously tight deadlines.

I was good at the job, faster than the others, able to sort trauma in a single bound, put pictures with text and headlines that made stories pop. It was exciting to be the first to hear the news, to be the gatekeeper, to read, sort, delegate, caption, headline, illustrate, to see my name under the masthead as editor, to feel important and useful and at the forefront of it all. Benazir Bhutto, the first Islamic woman prime minister in Pakistan; Pan-Am 747 exploding over Lockerbie; Iraq gassing the Kurds, an earthquake in Armenia killing sixty thousand.

I was somebody now.

One day, the only female Japanese reporter, Choko, stopped me in the hallway. She was usually deathly quiet, kept her head down, wrote her stories and rarely made small talk with anyone.

"May I speak?" Her voice was lilting.

air

"Of course."

She took my arm, led me down the hall through the door into a stairwell. We took breaks in this stairwell, and cigarette butts were piled in the corners. It smelled hard and scratchy, and the walls were streaked brown with tobacco smoke.

"I must speak to you because we are the same," Choko said. "Woman and woman." She pointed to me and then to her nose. "Both woman working hard job."

I nodded. She had a plain, chubby face and looked like a teenager. She was part of the Fast Track for Women, a government program where women were brought into the workforce, trained and promoted. Up until this point, women in the commercial sector mostly served tea. We still had some tea servers at the *Kaze*, shuffling, quiet, head bowed. The government was trying to improve its relationship with the Americans to compete more fully in the U.S. market. They were trying to prove they were progressive.

"The male reporters…they say things."

"What do you mean?"

"What color are your panties? They ask me every day. What kind of bra you wear?"

I was shocked. Choko was such a competent reporter. Her stories were always clean, the facts straight. "Does Shinji-*san* say this?" Shinji and I had become friends after that first day. "Is Shinji the one bothering you?"

"No, Shinji-*san* is kind man. It is others, two or maybe three." She had a look of such fear.

Again I thought of how sexist Missouri was. Girls married young, and the men owned them. I thought I was leaving all that sexism behind. The treatment of women here seemed to be blown up, painted on a massive canvas. *You didn't get the country you wanted. You got the country you needed.*

Choko looked as if she was about to cry. I couldn't think. "Japan is so sexist," I said.

She nodded, flopping her head forward. "I do college exchange in Minnesota." I always wondered when I heard a Japanese person talking about the exchanges they did why they went to mid-America. What a shock it must've been to them on so many levels. Or maybe after Tokyo, she found Minnesota beautiful in an otherworldly way. Textured and raw.

She took my elbow. She couldn't have known how hard she was squeezing it. "After I graduate in States, do I get job and stay and live in America, live with no family? Do I come home and must fit into old Japanese way? It was hard, so much hard." I took out a cigarette and lit it, offered her one. She shook her head. "Finally, I take job. Still no family. Work in U.S. five years. It is too hard. I come back. Now I am age twenty-six. Now, I am day-old Christmas cake."

Japanese women were marriageable at twenty-five, but of no use at twenty-six. You heard the Christmas cake comment a lot.

"So, this old Christmas cake decide to work. I have college degree. I work for newspaper in America. So, I know I can do good work. But now, every day, it is what color your panties."

Back home, I would have gone to the boss with Choko's complaint. But here? There was no way any one of the Japanese editors would do anything but make it more embarrassing for Choko.

Choko looked at me as if I had the answers. I was about her age, and I was the boss and I was supposed to know what to do.

"Somebody has to be the first person hacking through the underbrush," I said. I didn't know where the words came from. I pulled my elbow out of her grip, stood facing her, and spoke with an authority that wasn't me. "Every time the world needs to change, there has to be a first group of people who create the change." I took both her hands and squeezed them, looked her straight in the face. "It is very difficult, because you're coming up against centuries of tradition. There is no other way. Be strong, because you have been chosen for this task."

Choko started crying. I sat us both on one of the steps and waited. It was times like this that I really missed Usui; I wished I could find him and talk to him.

"It is my karma," she said, nodding. Was my life my karma? The thought of it made me sick to my stomach. I stood.

air

"I'd better get back," I said. "I have so many deadlines."

As we got back to the office, and Choko retreated to her desk, I looked around the newsroom at Michael, at Jameson, the managing editor, at the editors in the glass cages. I couldn't imagine a single one of the men helping with this. This helplessness reminded me of growing up, so many years with no one to turn to.

Something about being a woman with your own mind. Something about cutting through the underbrush. Something about the fear of being utterly, totally alone.

What happened to a person when they rejected what society had put into place? What happened when you were one of the first people to do this rejection? What happened to a girl who left her culture altogether and learned a new way of thinking? Could she ever go home again?

I didn't do anything for Choko. I didn't know how. I'd have had to change the whole culture before I could even report what was happening. I went to the lunchroom to have a cigarette, sat at one of the tables and smoked one after another.

"You don't look well, Queenie," Finn said. I was so lost I didn't see him enter.

I looked at him, thought of his music and wanted to tell him everything—he was like Usui, someone I wanted to tell everything to.

"It's just that," I stumbled through the telling. "Well, okay, in Missouri, women weren't exactly treated well…you know. It's so sexist. I grew up with this—"

"That's the joy of moving countries," Finn interrupted. He leaned in, his long hands held up beside his face to make his point. "You can be anybody you wish to be. A fresh start."

I shook my head. "No, it's not about me…"

He placed his long fingers on my forearm. "You, Queenie, can be anything you want to be. Do anything you want to do. One must leave the past behind." His eyes were bright with fire, and I wondered if he was talking about himself or me. *Wait, can that girlfriend of yours really be anything she wants to be? Can Choko? Can I? Really?* I didn't say anything out loud. I didn't want to break the spell. I didn't want him to move his hand off my arm.

"Look around you. You're in one of the greatest cities in the world. Anything is possible."

I stared into his bloodshot blue eyes. I wanted to believe him. Oh, how desperately I wanted to believe him.

A few nights later, after deadline, everyone had gone home. Shinji and I stood staring out the tar-stained window at the nightlife on the sidewalk below. We'd become good friends. He was gentle, helpful, soft-spoken. He had the soul of Usui. Sometimes I wondered if I was even *seeing* Shinji when we were together; perhaps Shinji was a stand-in, a substitute. I wondered how often everyone did that, had a friend who was a replacement for someone else, had a friend who was the past and not the present. Like Yuriko. Sometimes she reminded me so much of my sister, Meghan—dark-haired, wild Meghan. Lost, forgotten, whore Meghan. Meghan who I had no idea where she lived now and hadn't heard from for so many years.

Below us on the sidewalk, a Western man and a Japanese woman were in heated argument in the glow of a street lamp. He looked American. I'd gotten to the point where I could tell an American from a Brit or Aussie. His jacket and tennis shoes were too white, and he took up so much space on the sidewalk passersby had to move around him.

The two stood gesturing at each other. The woman wore a white flowing coat with wide kimono sleeves. Her arms fluttered. A wind licked at them; the air flushed hard as it funneled between the buildings on both sides of the street. The current lifted the bottom of the woman's coat as she raised her arms. She turned her face to the sky. She was crying. She had a white oval face and blood lips. Her

air

black hair ebbed in wind waves, long strands like dancing fingers. She was like a crane trying to take flight. She was breathtaking.

"It is unusual couple," Shinji said. I turned to him. He'd been so quiet I'd forgotten he was there. He'd studied journalism on an exchange program in Seattle and knew how to talk to American women, where other Japanese men would blush red with shyness.

"He is good looking and she…" He shrugged.

"You mean *she* is good looking." The Japanese often got their pronouns wrong.

"What? No. What do you say?"

"The guy's a dork." He was the sort of guy you knew in high school who could never get a date. He was plain, pale, with thin red hair balding on top, and a soft pasty body. They were kissing below us, a frantic kiss, and he held her awkwardly around the waist as if he didn't know what he was doing.

"What? What is dork?"

"Dork means not attractive, ugly, not classy."

"You think *she* pretty?"

"She's gorgeous!" I shook my head. "That guy would never get a woman like that in the States."

"This very confusing. To Japanese, she not attractive. Flat face. Narrow eyes. We see man with light hair, so tall. Eyes color of sky. We think, how does plain woman have luck to be with such man?"

Shinji and I stared at each other. So little understanding, so much confusion. I thought about the two painfully insecure people below us who thought the other was more special than they deserved. Were we all so confused all the time? I looked at Shinji and back out the window.

A janitor came in and emptied the trash. He left and didn't turn off the light. Now as we looked out the window, instead of seeing outside we saw reflections of ourselves. Shinji beside me was pale as a ghost, so thin, suit trousers, a white shirt, black tie. His reflection the ghost of Usui.

"We are twin," he said.

"What?"

He gestured a circle around us. "See, we like same person."

In the reflection, I wore a white button-down shirt, black trousers, had my wild hair pulled back. I was pale and thin, too. We did look alike.

Shinji and I turned toward each other. I leaned in, and he leaned in. We kissed in awkward jerky movements, the mismatched couple below us kissing in harmony with us, our reflections echoing along, the janitor wheeling his trash down the hall.

The next morning on the train, regret over Shinji set in. What had I done by kissing him? I didn't know the cultural significance. Technically, he was my subordinate. How was a woman supposed to act in these circumstances in Japan? I didn't even know how a woman was supposed to act in my own culture.

On the train, a salariman held the strap in front of me and stared at me. Japanese women were servants, and Western women were sluts. I could see it on his face. They watched TV shows like *Dallas* and thought every Western woman was a whore.

He got off the train and was replaced by a stooped elderly women. I stood and offered her my seat. From behind the old women emerged a boy of about twelve. He took the seat while the grandmother stood over him protectively. I'd seen this a dozen times before. Boys were honored more than girls, more than mothers or grandmothers. Certainly more than foreigners.

At the next stop, a group of Japanese girls in uniforms boarded. Two men pushed themselves against the girls as the train left the station. We'd written about it at the *Kaze*, the harassment school girls faced on the trains. All around me, the truth of how women were treated in exaggerated relief.

By the time the train reached Ohtemachi, I decided I had to keep the relationship with Shinji a secret in the newsroom. There was

air

just no telling what the cultural consequences would be, and I couldn't risk it.

I wondered if every woman went through this, wanting to end something with a guy, but being trained as a woman that it wasn't proper, it wasn't done, and then spending months or even years pretending. I wondered if some women didn't just spend their whole lives pretending.

Shinji and I strolled through Ohtemachi looking for an udon café. We'd been dating now for several weeks. Our affair had not gone unnoticed in the newsroom, smirks from the Westerners, leers from the Japanese. I told myself that somehow I'd created this and now I was responsible for him.

He'd only kissed me so far, as we parted ways at the train station after work. He never made any other kind of move. I didn't know the customs. He'd said something recently about me meeting his parents, and I nearly choked on my fried plantain.

Something brightly colored caught my eye at the side of the road. A skinny homeless man with dreadlocks was posing wildly dressed dolls on the railings of a traditional arched bridge. The bridge was crumbling. You saw bits of old Japan falling apart like this, thrust up against the new and modern and useful.

"Look at that, Shinji," I said, trying to lead him over. I'd stopped using the "*san*" after Shinji's name, thinking I didn't need to be so formal, although I wasn't sure of the rules.

"No, Purr!" He held my arm against his side and led me away. "Unclean," he whispered.

"Shinji." I sighed in exasperation and yanked my arm away. The homeless were not treated well in the U.S., but in Japan it was worse. Most Japanese preferred to believe homelessness didn't exist, and they ignored them. It was easy to do as the homeless never asked for handouts and mostly disappeared during the day.

I left Shinji on the sidewalk and went up to check out the dolls. More than a dozen were balanced on the railing, in vivid-colored outfits, legs and arms twisted up and out. Two of them were doing backbends. I picked up one of the dolls. She was wire thin, wore a red miniskirt, a halter top and a red scarf.

Underneath, she was made of wire hangers twisted into a torso, a head, arms, legs and fingers. He'd wrapped white cloth in strips over the wire, and over that, dressed the dolls in the hand-sewn outfits.

I assumed he'd gotten the materials out of the trash. *Gomi* day was trash day in Japan, a once-a-month event when Tokyoites threw away everything—electronics that worked, furniture, small refrigerators, household items. Every Westerner in Tokyo knew about *gomi* day. Yuriko and I had furnished our entire apartment with *gomi*.

I carried the skinny doll to the homeless man. Shinji eyed me warily from the sidewalk. I held the doll up to the man while fishing in my purse for money. There were holes in his shoes.

"She is you," he said in English.

I looked up. He had a grimy face and his skin was almost black. "Usui-*san*?" I whispered.

"Purr-*chan*."

I flung myself at him. Shinji yelled from the sidewalk.

"Purr, Purr," Usui said and tried to push me back, but I clung to him. He smelled like urine and rotten eggs.

He took the skinny doll from my hands. I'd forgotten I was holding it. I had so many questions. "She is you," he said, holding the doll up to me. She was a multidimensional version of his origami. You could feel spirit in every fold of her clothes. Not just Usui's spirit, a spirit that was all her own, and something even bigger than that.

"Beautiful," I said. I didn't say, *What are you doing acting like a homeless man?* I took the doll from his hand and handed him a wad of yen. He wouldn't take it.

air

"I do not sell. Only give."

I held the doll by the waist and touched one of his long dreadlocks. "Where have you been?"

"Away from the world of Ideko." He looked behind him at Shinji and then at me.

"Purr-*chan*, we must go," Shinji yelled.

I looked at my watch. "Can I come back and see you?"

Usui took my hands, his long fingernails encrusted with dirt. "Purr-*chan*," he began.

"Let us go!" Shinji yelled. I looked from Usui to Shinji. This was impossible. I was never going to be able to have a conversation with Usui with Shinji around.

"I'll come back tomorrow, okay?" I said, leaving the bridge. "Tomorrow, same time." I ran with the doll to Shinji. As we walked away, I looked back at Usui. He stood watching me, shoulders bent and arms hanging, like a helpless little boy.

The soul cries out. The spirit wraps around. Passions mingle. The spirit of another fills you. It reaches beyond time and space, defies practicalities. Money and society have no say in it. We can hope to love this person or that, but we cannot choose. We have no choice whatsoever in the matter.

As soon as the lunch bento boxes arrived, I grabbed two, avoided Shinji's stare and ran out. I'd bought a blue scarf to wear with my black coat. I wanted to show Usui a touch of color.

The bridge was empty.

Maybe it wasn't this bridge. How many such bridges could exist in the area? I walked around in a daze and kept coming back to the same spot. I climbed onto the bridge and found a scrap of colored cloth, the same cloth Usui had used for the dolls.

It wasn't possible. He wasn't there. I walked the high arch to the middle. I scanned the dozens of people walking by, the shops, the cars, the scooters. I let the cacophony of city sounds wash over me, hoping for some sound or scent that would tell me where Usui had gone.

I put the bento box down as if it were an offering. Usui had misunderstood me. Surely he just didn't get the day right. His English wasn't very good. I stood for an hour in the middle of the wooden bridge waiting, the blue scarf snapping in the wind like an angry bird.

The next day I wore a red scarf and brought a bag of oranges. The day after that a green scarf and a box of the pastries. The following afternoon, it was a yellow scarf and a cake. The gifts were ravaged each time I came back, either by animals or humans, but I left them anyway.

By the end of the week, I had several new scarves and no Usui. Then, one day, I forgot to wear a scarf. A few days later, I gave up on bringing an offering. I'd walk by the bridge and look over only to be disappointed, but I no longer stopped.

For the next month, I spent my lunches again in the newsroom. The black dog depression was coming back. It festered beneath the surface. I thought of Yuriko. She didn't deserve to have to deal with that from me again. I knew I didn't deserve it either, but it was easier to think I was doing it for Yuriko.

Instead of plunging, I'd have to go back and "speak" to Usui even if he wasn't there. I took the bento box and left the newsroom.

At the bridge, I took the rainbow scarf and a handful of incense I'd purchased on the way. I lit the incense and put in a ceramic bowl in the center of the bridge. I wanted to make an offering. I said a silent hello to Usui, an unspoken goodbye.

air

As I was leaving, I caught the flutter of something at the edge of the bridge. I went to the railing. Below, clinging to one of the support boards, was a doll. I had to lay flat on my stomach to reach it. It took a while to figure out what the doll was caught on. The hands were twisted around a post, like she was clinging to the strut of a plane. I released her and brought her up.

She was one of Usui's dolls all right, beaten up by the weather. She was big, twice the size of the skinny doll that sat on a shelf in my room. She was voluptuous, with large breasts and rounded hips, and she wore a multicolored robe, a broad black sash around her waist. The robe had a hood that went up over the head. She was heavy in the hand. She was substantial. Something dropped out of her dress. It was a note written in Usui's delicate script.

"She is really you." Just as I'd left an offering, this was Usui's offering to me.

I held the doll out in front of me and burst into tears.

S HADOWED CRANES PIROUETTED across the white snow. Dozens. Hundreds. From a distance, they had the soul of Usui's origami cranes, but these were real birds. Wings spread wide, hopping, thin black necks bobbing up, bobbing down. A second crane echoed the first. A third. A fourth. The land danced, quivered and pulsed with the cranes' movements. Here and there stick legs jigged up in sudden glee.

We were on a bus in Hokkaido. We were passing dancing cranes in a frozen landscape. Watching them, my heart ached for Usui.

"Pearl Elizabeth Swinton, this is *your* life." Yuriko's loud stage whisper dragged me back to the present, back into the bus. Every year, the *Kaze* sponsored a retreat. Yuriko was my plus one.

"In this corner, the boyfriend." She used air quotes around boyfriend and pointed to Shinji, who sat a few rows up. "Shinji Kurosawa. A man you could have simply had fun with, but no, the good old Catholic guilt took over and you actually *had* to start dating him."

I wanted to go back to the cranes. I wanted Yuriko to shut up. Shinji looked back at us, and I smiled at him reassuringly. "Shhh. Come on," I hissed, pinching Yuriko's arm.

"And in this corner," she continued, rubbing her arm, "we have the fellow editor, Michael Creepy. Yes, he has only dreamy eyes for you." She pointed to the back of his ponytailed head four seats up in

air

the next row. Ever since I'd started dating Shinji, Michael would stare at me with scary intense eyes. I'd told Yuriko this. I told Yuriko way too much.

Finn walked down the aisle, heading toward the bus bathroom. My heart leapt. He didn't look at me. He didn't look at anyone. He stared at the floor with red eyes. There was something wrong with his face; it was smashed into itself.

"But we've saved the best for last. Finnegan O'Riley. Musician. Man with a vortex," Yuriko said.

I shook my head, pinched Yuriko hard. Sometimes you had to slap Yuriko down, and sometimes you had to drop bombs on her head to shut her up. "You're going to make me regret bringing you along."

"Hey, at least I'm honest," she said, lifting her sleeve to rub the latest welt. "You need to do what I do. Love 'em and leave 'em. That way you don't have to put up with all the expectations. Before you know it, each one of those guys could make a good little wifey out of you."

I looked out the window and tried to ignore her. Sometimes Yuriko's "truth" left a dark sucking pool of mud in your head.

An unexpected storm the week before had torn up the land, and you could still see signs of it. The retreat had almost been cancelled. A pumpkin field had been submerged in early snow and the sudden orange looked like some disturbingly beautiful abstract painting, a child's pop-up book. The pumpkins were like bodies in orange life jackets. Yuriko leaned onto my lap to snap photo after photo.

Still, even with uprooted trees and blown-about limbs, the land was glorious, stretching in textured diversity. White fields became frozen lakes led to snow-tipped evergreens. Clouds wept into fog.

Ever since we disembarked from the train in Sapporo—it'd been an eighteen-hour journey from Tokyo—I'd felt an affinity with Hokkaido. It calmed me in a way that the earth back home could, but here there was no violence attached to it. Japan was a clean slate. Like the Midwest with its land-locked isolation, Hokkaido was so far north it was disconnected from the rest of the world, a place where the earth had a lot to say, where one could not ignore the seasons.

The bus passed another swollen lake draped in mist. So married to the landscape were the cranes I didn't see them at first. Then their dance began, and it was as if the snow were alive. Two took flight, massive white bodies, black necks, black stripes on iridescent wings, dark legs dangling. I felt a force in my chest, a desire to fly with them, a need to soar.

Usui's origami cranes. It hit me like a hot wind. Usui had grown up in Hokkaido. How could I have forgotten that? I sat up straight and looked around with renewed interest. I remembered they'd lived outside Sapporo. We passed tiled houses nestled hard against the rock as we twisted up a mountainside, and I searched frantically from side to side as if I'd see Usui or his father suddenly standing there.

We rounded a corner and veered hard to miss a horse-drawn buggy; Yuriko fell onto my lap. I tried to see over the heads of the others to get a glimpse of who was driving the buggy and could just make out an older Japanese farming couple. I tried to see Usui in them, but instead saw my mother and father back home on the farm. Most Westerners talked about how different Japan was from America or Britain or Australia, but in some ways it was the same. The rural and the urban. The stubbornness of the old ways, the hope of the new.

"It is redneck, two redneck!" a Japanese reporter in the next aisle yelled.

The bus erupted in laughter. I blew red with shame, as if they were laughing at me. Ever since I'd moved to the city, I'd noticed how the educated, the "civilized" made fun of all things rural, how they mocked the earth. If you came from the land, they treated you like a handicapped cousin, a demented halfwit. It wasn't just corporations killing the planet, maniacs murdering children. The average intellectual had a lot to answer for, too.

We turned onto a rocky dirt road, went a few hundred yards and came to the inn, a *ryokan*. The building was made of wood and paper, low, flat and nestled back against craggy rock, with woodland

air

on the side. Red paper lanterns and small flags flapped wildly in the wind. As I got off the bus, I heard a strange cacophony of music. On a nearby pagoda hung dozens of wind chimes of all shapes and sizes. I walked instinctively over, leaving Yuriko in midsentence.

The wind blew in schizophrenic circles, emerging from several directions at once. The chimes echoed the discordance. Clinking shells, glass balls painted with flowers, tubes of all shapes and sizes, curved strips of metal from which messages dangled in Kanji. It was a forest of clashing music. Teak. Ceramic. Tin. Bamboo. Discordant, absorbing, stirring.

On the other side of the chimes, someone stood with their back to me, as immersed as I was. He turned. It was Finn. On his face a sadness so desperate I caught my breath. I moved quietly away and left him to the sound of the dissenting wind.

A miniature woman in kimono and high wooden sandals showed Yuriko and me to our room. Even with the elevated shoes, the woman stood only four feet tall. She walked in tiny steps, and we followed at a crawl down a cold narrow hallway. Yuriko wore a spattered paint shirt and torn dungarees. She hissed, "No need to bind their feet, just give them ridiculous sandals they can't walk in."

I waved my hand to shush her. At the door, we took off our shoes. The room's walls were simple wood, the floors straw *tatami*. One of the windows was open, and bursts of snow blew in. Yuriko said, "Brrr," and went to close it. The woman gestured with her hand, "No, No. *Auto hoei*." She waved her arm around the room in arcs and blew air with her lips, a wind goddess clearing the room of evil.

After she left, Yuriko and I unpacked, bundled in our winter coats. We could see our breath. Again I was reminded of home, where the elements didn't necessarily stay out of doors.

"If we're going to be so frickin' cold, let's at least get some good out of it," Yuriko said. She took off her coat, started unbuttoning her shirt.

"What are you doing?"

"What does it look like I'm doing? I'm getting naked."

I backed up.

"Oh, don't flatter yourself," she said, whipping off her bra and exposing her full breasts. I turned around as she pulled off her underwear. "The *ryokan* has hot springs. Didn't you read the brochure?"

"I'd prefer to go check it out, see if anyone is already in there."

"Suit yourself. I'll be busy having fun."

"Okay. Okay, give me a second." I went to the corner of the room like a child put in time-out and tried to hide as I undressed. Yuriko laughed. She found *yukata* robes and sandals in the closet and handed me a set. I took it without turning around. The robes were paired with matching short woolen green vests with wide arms. In her *yukata*, Yuriko looked old-world Japanese. Sometimes I wished I was an artist, like Yuriko, like Jason, so I could paint people, could capture scenes like the cranes taking flight, like Yuriko looking so medieval.

We found a back door. As we stepped out onto a stone path, frigid winds climbed up my naked legs beneath the *yukata* and pimpled the flesh. In front of us stood a wild vista of distant white mountain peaks, which led to a snow-covered valley devoid of life. Yuriko breathed heavily as she took it in. As we maneuvered the icy path, we passed a mixed forest of evergreens and bamboo. The forest made music in the wind, swish and hollow conk. *Swish, conk. Swish, conk.* This world was gray, white, black-green. The temperature had plunged in the last half hour. Breathing hurt the lungs.

We turned a corner on the path and below us was one of the natural hot springs. It was ringed with boulders, and in the center of the steaming pool rose three giant rocks, like the stones in Usui's raked garden. A naked boy of about ten was climbing one of the boulders.

air

We slipped our way down the icy path. At the hot springs, we could see two more natural pools behind it, full of people. The boy in this spring was with his family, grandmother, mother, father, little sister. It was too cold to be shy, and we threw off our robes. The boy stared at Yuriko. She looked Japanese with her clothes on—admittedly a big-boned Japanese girl—but with her clothes off, her breasts and hips were like no other image of a Japanese girl or woman I was sure the boy had ever seen.

The water was too hot to fully submerge ourselves, and too cold to be in the open air. I went from sitting on rocks to submerging the lower half of my body, in and out again. We had small towels. I used mine to cover my breasts as I moved. Yuriko walked openly, brashly, as if her naked body had rights of ownership.

You didn't know how a city entered you until you left it. You didn't know how the clattering vibrated veins, quivered muscles, juddered intestines. You didn't know how the noxious smells floated into bloodstream, swam into lungs, sank into brains. You didn't know that too many buildings and sidewalks scratched the spirit until you bled. You didn't know until you touched earth, smelled the mud and listened to the roots. You didn't know until you let air steam up the face, freeze icicles into hair and prickle the flesh.

My head lolled on my shoulders. I could barely stay awake. Yuriko was quiet for once. She looked medieval, her hair fanning out in the water, glimpses of her body in and out of the steam. On her face glowed something so wise, exhausted but sagacious. Behind her, two trees grew, solitary in the landscape, the only ones as far as I could see that were not part of the forest. Someone had covered the base of both trunks with straw mats to protect them from the ice. They had been forced into odd shapes by winds coming off the valley, their tops slanted back in surprise, their twisted branches like pleading arms. They were haunting and beautiful in their isolated, poetic pose.

Yuriko rested her head against a rock, her breasts floating. I swam to her, put my head back against the rock next to hers. The two of us, floating.

Thirty minutes later, I just couldn't stay awake any longer. I told Yuriko I'd be in the room. My limbs were like Jell-o as I put on the *yukata* and then started back up the path, slow and wobbly like an old woman.

Halfway up, I noticed a flash of red in the forest. Someone was about thirty yards into the trees, leaning over, wearing a crimson scarf. The forest played its swish and conk. The hollow conk of the bamboo came loud and sudden, then soft and subtle, like a varied drum beat.

The man stood, sucked on a cigarette, and the smoke curved and wafted above his head. He had what looked like a camera in one hand. As I watched, he put the object on a rock, then put his hands to his face. His shoulders jerked. He was weeping. The evergreens in stark horizontal, the man's deep green flowing *yukata*, the red scarf, smoke like incense, wending. He took something out of his backpack and played with it, a stick or something. I couldn't tell. He turned toward me. It was Finn. He was so lost in his own pain, he didn't seem to see me.

Icicles formed in my hair, my breath made clouds in front of my face, the inside of my nose grew hard and scratchy. I began to tremble. Minutes went by and still I watched him. My body began to shake violently, but I didn't move. He bent and cried again. He stood, motionless, staring into the forest, twirling the stick. My trembling became violent. I started my labored crawl back up the path. I had to get back inside. As I reached the door of the *ryokan*, I heard flute music, soft tones like pleading fingers reaching out on the wind.

air

"Jesus, you sleep like a dead person. I've been sitting here vibing you for half an hour."

Yuriko sat on the *tatami*, staring at me. I tried to focus. "I'm exhausted. I think I'm exhausted."

"You don't have to tell me. Even in Japan you could win a prize for the work hours you put in." She paused, leaned forward. "I have white-boy goss."

One of the things Yuriko and I had in common was our insatiable interest in gossip. We could gossip about people we didn't even know. We loved the stories, gnawed on the details like bones.

I crawled out from beneath the cover. It was the most comfortable futon I'd ever slept on, the most comfortable bed I'd ever known in my life, even more comfortable than Usui's. It was like sleeping on a cloud. I wanted to stay in it forever, to live in it. I sat and leaned toward her. My body felt like a rag doll. I still couldn't seem to focus.

"I heard through the grapevine that Finn's geisha lost it," Yuriko said.

"Finn's geisha?"

"Finn?" She rolled her eyes. "His girlfriend?"

"Aikiko?" Finn sobbing in the woods, I couldn't remember if it was a dream.

"Finn comes home, and anyway, I'm not sure what happens next, he has to take her to the hospital, because she's just losing it, like epic madness. They've broken up. He apparently decided to come on this trip to get his mind off the whole thing."

"Who told you?"

"He confessed it to one of the reporters. Never tell a journalist anything."

I felt horrible. Poor Finn. I put my hand to my heart, to the ache for him that settled there.

"Come on. What's your take?"

"No take." I climbed back beneath the futon cover. I didn't want to pass on the information of Finn crying, didn't want to gossip with Yuriko about how deeply I felt for him, didn't want to rip him apart, to gut him, to read his intestines like tea leaves.

"No take? When do you not have a take? Anyway, I for one don't see why so many women fall for the guy. He's just a typical *gaijin*, scoring with the geishas."

I moaned and put the cover over my head.

"You're no fun," she said. "Come on. You should eat this up. This is your opportunity."

I peeked out at her. Something flashed in her eyes. "I have an idea," she said, popping up off the *tatami*.

"Where are you going?"

"Never you mind. You're tired. Rest."

"Yuriko, leave him alone."

She was at the door. "Don't worry. I won't steal him from you."

"Yuriko, leave him alone. Please, just leave him be." She was already out the door. I didn't have the energy to stop her.

Something else was niggling at me, something besides Finn and Yuriko. I couldn't put my finger on it. I stayed in the futon, unable to go back to sleep, unwilling to get up off this cloud, this niggling thing beneath the surface. Finally, I realized what it was. I was glad Yuriko wasn't there. I couldn't have explained what I was about to do, because I wasn't even sure.

I got up and dressed. I couldn't believe how exhausted I was. Brushing my hair was a colossal endeavor.

The woman at the front desk wouldn't give me Shinji's room number, but I turned to see him walking through the front door, talking animatedly to Choko.

"Shinji," I nearly yelled. Choko looked up at me with an almost frightened look.

"Hi, Choko-*san*." She waved but then took off down a hallway. Shinji's intense, sad eyes confused me, but he clicked back to normal as I approached.

air

"I want to find this guy, Usui-*san*. He lives around here somewhere. Mateo Usui-*san*. His son was a missionary in Tokyo, Genji. And he had a son who died named Ideko."

Shinji shook his head. "It is our retreat, Purr-*san*. I am, how do you say, off the clock." He pronounced it "crock."

"Please." I grabbed his arm, leaned up against him. He turned red.

"Okay, I will see, but I only do a little. I not promise."

He spoke to the clerk at the desk. She was a young woman and didn't seem to know anything about any of the nearby towns. She led us down a long hall, pointed to the door and explained something in Japanese.

"She say this woman know all people in Sapporo."

We went into the kitchen. It was like something out of medieval Japan, chopping blocks piled with raw tuna, eel, pickled cabbage, piles of tofu, vats of steaming miso soup. Aged knives hung from ceiling posts. The room was filled with vegetables, dirt-packed roots still attached, and even with the dirt, it was the cleanest kitchen I'd ever seen. The dirty, raw smells made me want to go back to my heavenly futon and sleep. I could've slept for days. I could've curled up on that kitchen floor and slept among the sensuous rubbish.

An old woman in an apron approached. Shinji spoke to her. She kept nodding. I had learned some Japanese, but her accent was so thick I couldn't make out even one word. Shinji turned to me and said she knew three or four Usui families.

"His son was a missionary in Tokyo. And the other son died from *karoshi*."

He explained this to the woman. Her face fell, and she nodded. She drew figures in the air. She traced their lives into the emptiness. Shinji nodded, his face soft toward her. I couldn't remember when he'd looked at me that softly. We were supposed to be dating. He bowed low to the woman several times. We headed toward the door.

I stopped, grabbed his arm. "I forgot. Ask her what he does for a living."

Shinji went back to her and returned. "Retired teacher."

As we walked back toward Shinji's room, he was talking, but I wasn't paying attention. I had to come up with a feasible reason for meeting up with Usui's father.

Shinji looked at me as if he was waiting for an answer.

"What?"

"I speak to you about our dating relationship. Will you not hear me?"

It was easy to keep Shinji at bay at the *Kaze*, because we were always so busy. Here, I didn't know what to do with him. "Sorry, Shinji. I promise we'll talk about all it later. But I need to meet this Usui. Listen, I need to set up an interview. Can you get his telephone number, set something up, and translate for me?"

"I am on holiday," he said.

"Do you want me to get someone else? I'd rather it be you."

"What kind of interview?"

"I'm starting a special for the *Kaze* on retired teachers across Japan."

"You did not know his work until just now. What are you doing, Purr-*san*? Who is Usui-*san*?"

"Please?" I leaned my body against him and kissed his cheek. I knew I had a strong physical effect on Shinji. We still hadn't slept together. I had no idea why. Every time I put my body close to his, he'd quiver and make an excuse to leave. I wondered if his reaction to me was because I was a foreigner, and the sheer taboo of it was too much.

"Your charm will only take you so far, Purr-*san*," he said. "You act like boss, not girlfriend." *I am your boss*, I didn't say.

"Please, pretty please." I put my hand flat on his chest.

I felt his body tremble. He backed up as if I were a snake about to strike. He shook his head, walked to the front desk, asked to use their phone, dialed a few numbers, and within minutes had set up the interview for ten a.m. the next day.

I went up and kissed him full on the mouth. He pulled hard away, shame-faced. I turned to see Japanese reporters watching us. Choko stood among them, her face doing all sorts of gymnastics.

That night the *Kaze* held a dinner. The dining hall was a low wood-beamed *tatami* room. We sat on floor cushions around gleaming cherry wood tables. Bowing women in kimonos served tiny portions presented whimsically on handmade pieces of imperfectly formed pottery—yellowtail teriyaki, deep fried tofu, stuffed crab, pickled vegetables, glazed salmon. Miso soup bowls when drained revealed delicate hand-painted flowers, a different flower at the bottom of each bowl. Chopsticks flew in from all sides toward the delicacies, the table a rich, gleaming piece of art, a strange orchestral movement.

The editors made toasts. Long sake bottles made the rounds. One of the Japanese editors toasted me, repeating the line that I did the work of three good men. Everyone laughed. Yuriko was wedged between Finn and Shinji. She had a way with men, especially with alcohol around, and both boys leaned in toward her as if by magnetic pull. She kept running long fingers around the small food plates, feeling the flowers and leaves etched into the pottery. I couldn't tell if she was being consciously sensual, but all the reporters followed her fingers. I also couldn't tell if she was planning on taking both Shinji and Finn for herself. The thought set me to drinking, and soon the night became a slow-motion whirl of laughing teeth, waves of clinks and clatters, swirls and flashes of rings and bracelets and wristwatches.

The after-party was in a separate conference room, a disco ball, a bar with free beer, wine, sake. Colored lights bounced off floors and walls and reminded me of my mother's Christmas. Every other day of the year was brutal hard work, but Christmas was a miracle, the only joy in that hard-packed life. The whole season was a glittering, a reflecting, a twinkling. I was so drunk, the disco lights blending and swirling. I danced with whomever asked, saw Yuriko dancing with Finn, drank some more, Yuriko with Shinji, drank some more. I saw Michael at the edge of the room, staring darkly. Everyone knew he was a recovering alcoholic, and he witnessed our drunkenness with difficult eyes.

Late into the night, I looked up and Yuriko was putting Finn into my arms. His long, thin arms wrapped around me. My head came onto to his chest. He smelled of cigarette smoke and marijuana. The brass button on his jacket pressed symbols into my cheek. I felt I was losing myself, losing my footing. I wove my head up to see if I could find Shinji in the crowd, to make sure Shinji was okay. I saw Yuriko waltz with him over to Choko, saw the two fold into each other. Then Yuriko was near Finn and me again. She pulled us to the edge of the floor, led us, still swaying to the music, down a hallway. Then she was gone, and Finn and I were in a storage room, still holding each other, then kissing, falling.

The kissing became desperate. I couldn't stop myself, would not stop myself, my need deep, too. We were two shipwreck victims, clinging to each other.

"Who do you remind me of?" he asked, looking at me at one point, his brow furrowed.

I was too drunk on sake, too drunk on him to answer. I leaned forward and kissed him hard. I didn't want to speak. Tongue on tongue, hands on breasts and thighs. I was sitting on a low refrigerator, and my ass was frigidly cold. The warmth of his breath, the sheer winter of my lower regions. I knew wrecked men. I knew gentle men gutted by this crazy world. I knew him.

I led him out the back. Sometime during the evening more snow had come. A thick white blanket glowed up the path. We slipped our way to the hot spring. I knew some of the others would think of this later, but it was early enough, and we had time. The moon glow went in and out from behind clouds.

I slipped and fell hard on my ass, got up and fell again. Finn tried to help me up and fell, too. At the spring, we turned our backs on each other, shyly, and took off our clothes. Our white bodies glowed like ghosts. Finn's torso was long, his legs stretched, his neck extended. He could've been a swan or a crane. Again, I wished I could paint, wished I could immortalize his glow.

air

Then, just our heads above the mirror-black pond, so hot it was hard to breathe, and meanwhile my black hair growing icicles. We kissed and floated. Steam fogged us. Finn pulled back and looked at me. He swam away and turned and looked at me.

"I wish I had my camera," he said. "You're like a black-and-white night painting." He came toward me. "White skin, black hair, white snow behind. Light and dark." He reached a sad hand to fondle one of the icicles in my curls. "I don't know if I have anything to give you, Queenie."

We kissed again. I ran my hand down his stomach, but he moved away. Such sadness in the curve of his back.

I floated belly up, staring at the stars. How the night clouds threw dark shadows over the bright moon. How easy it was to forget the universe of lights when the clouds came. How one could forget that the stars were there the whole time. How a person could be fooled by the darkness.

W E WERE NOT *of the highest geisha house. Our possessions were plain. But it was a good house. We were not abused. The mama-san kept us fed. We had clothes, a futon.*

From the second-story window, I could see that the roads had hardened as night fell and the temperature dipped. All day the byways had been a thick morass of mud. The houses were dark, except a single candle in one far-off window. I was so tired of waiting. It was cold. The walls were thin wood, and a bitter breeze seeped through the cracks. I tightened my yukata. There was no way to heat yourself this late at night. Anyway, I was expected to wait for him. I didn't have a choice but to wait.

My mother put me here when I was thirteen. I had a father. We adored each other. But he died suddenly. She needed the money. My brother needed schooling. I told myself that I would not have met Etsuko if she hadn't put me here. I relieved myself with that thought. If he would just come, the business would be over, and I could climb into my futon and warm up. I could rest, just have some rest.

Everyone else in the house was asleep. My visitor was the only one who came this late. In the corner, a plain screen. Behind the screen a bowl filled with water grown icy, for washing up. Afterward.

Finally, I saw him turn the corner. He came briskly toward the building. I was ready and didn't need to do any preparation. I was expected to be ready.

I heard him at the door, heard him speak to the mama-san, heard him climb the ladder. He opened the door to my room. He gruffly said hello, and I, in high-pitched voice, responded. "Good evening. How are you?"

air

"I am well, and you?" He sat on the tatami. He wore a male kimono. I helped him take his boots off. It was always this way.

He was on top me, my body a resignation. I tried not to whine. This was my profession, but still it caused me to fuss. They did not know me, just saw the young girl with long, black hair, wanted only the flesh, not the soul. I mixed the whines in with fake moans, but still I could hear my discontent; I worried he could hear it, too. Nothing, though, stopped them from coming back.

Afterward, I went behind the screen. I took a towel, dipped it in the chilly water, washed between my legs. The man dressed himself.

A sudden disturbance downstairs. An angry voice. Fear overcame me. I ran from around the screen. The man was crouched, staring at the door. The door burst open. A young man wielded a sword. He screamed. Below, the other girls were screaming. He was a new customer. I had been with him only twice. He was handsome, young, headstrong. Sometimes this happened. They thought they were in love. They knew only the flesh and fooled themselves that it was love.

My yukata hung open. The young man scanned my naked flesh with rage. It was too late. He lunged, grabbed my hair, pushed me to my knees. He swung his arm back, arched the sword expertly. He slit my throat. I fell, blood flowing, arm stretched in useless pleading.

I left the body. I floated above and saw myself dead. I could think only of a few of the other girls in the house. Etsuko especially. My friend. She knew me for who I was and loved me. I loved her, too. Love was all there was after death. No regrets or rage or fear. Just love.

I knew Etsuko would have a terrible time with my death and asked the spirits to help her, to pour love into her soul, to help her not to succumb to bitterness. The mama-san ran into the room, threw herself on top of me, wailed over my bleeding body. All I saw was the love.

"No need to thank me." It was Yuriko. I couldn't focus. Where was I? How long had my eyes been open? Was I awake now, or had I been awake then? Was the Japanese geisha I'd just witnessed a dream? A vision? Was she me?

"Truly, no need to shower me with gifts. All in a night's work." Yuriko spoke as if everything was normal. Half in the geisha reality, half in the normal reality, I kept blinking, hoping to right myself. "I knew there was no way you were going to extract yourself from Shinji and get with Finn, so I orchestrated the whole thing. Needed the boys to be eating out of my hand first. They're so much more pliable that way."

I stared at her blankly, looked around. I was obviously back in the *ryokan* room, on the futon. I couldn't shake the deep grief of the murdered geisha. My back ached, my neck. My toes were curled. Usually, that meant a vision. But the experience was so unusual, so attached to the intricate story of one person.

"So, where's my goss? I deserve that." Yuriko sat on the *tatami*. Her *yukata* hung open. One of her breasts hung lower than the other. I had a sickening flash of the man killing the geisha, killing me with the sword. The sun screamed through the window, and I put my hand to my throbbing head. I couldn't remember what had happened after the hot springs, but I did know that I was brutally hungover.

"Shit!" I bolted off the futon, and thrust my palm on the tatami to steady the dizziness. "What time is it?"

"Nine forty. Why?"

"Shit." I scrabbled up, nearly fell.

"You're still drunk."

I grabbed what I wore the night before, stumbled myself into it. "Why didn't Shinji come by?"

"Oh, he did. He did. And you can thank me for that, too. I sent him away." I ran toward the door. "Hey," Yuriko yelled. "When you get back, you're required to dish!"

I ran down the hall and knocked on Shinji's door. As he opened it, he wouldn't look me in the eye, and I thought shamefully that he already knew about Finn. I just needed to break up with Shinji; what we had wasn't really a relationship, anyway. What was I waiting for? Why was I dragging it out?

air

We walked in silence outside and got into the van. Shinji gave the driver the address. "It is not good to be late in Japan," he said.

"Sorry. Sorry."

As we wound our way down the mountainside, I searched my pockets for a hair band but found none. I hadn't looked in a mirror, and I couldn't imagine what my hair was doing. I spat repeatedly on my hands and tried to press it down. Shinji still wouldn't look at me.

The powerful grief of the geisha girl hung on me like a robe. It wasn't so much the death as the life, the way the men loved her with their ponderous weight, the way they pummeled her flesh. Or was it *my* flesh. Was she me? I felt her whine, her grief for not being seen. All my life, I'd whined like that, too. When I was a little girl, I whined because no one would listen to me when I spoke. No one would hear me. No one would see me. Mother used to call me the whiner. I understood that geisha girl, how everyone weighs you down with their needs.

I'd never had a vision that like before, never so real, never so personal. I had seen myself as a Civil War soldier in high school history class, but even that hadn't seemed so real. Most of the time, the visions were apocalyptic, as if I was seeing some world tragedy as a disembodied spirit. But was that true? Maybe I was seeing through someone's eyes. Maybe I was always entering other people's lives. The thought excited me, just as I'd been excited when Usui had given me a plausible understanding at the mission.

The van braked hard. We lurched forward. I felt last night's sake in my throat. I couldn't see any houses, but the driver opened the door, and we got out. The snow had hardened and the earth crunched. A sudden flush of memory of Finn sent warmth up my torso.

We stood at a wall of interwoven vines and bushes. Shinji pointed out the top beam of an oriental entryway engraved with Japanese symbols, like pictograms. He called a greeting in Japanese through the shrubbery. A woman called back. He pushed the gate, and the vines moved with it. We walked down a stone path. The house was made of dark wood and seemed to be partially built into the rocky side of the cliff. A woman waited at the front door, bowing repeatedly. Shinji introduced us, then told me the woman was Mateo Usui's wife, my Usui's mother. I knew I needed to think of my Usui as Genji, but just couldn't. He would always be Usui to me.

I looked at his mother, for what? Signs of Usui? All I could see was a normal older woman, no more than four-foot-nine, wearing a simple wool sweater and black trousers. She avoided our eyes as we took off our shoes in the entryway. Her shoulders were curved and her head lowered as she led us down a hall into the living room.

The house enveloped us. The architecture, the light, the dark wooden beams—it wasn't a normal Japanese home. Skylights in the living room ceiling rose to a triangular peak. Thick tapestries hung on the walls. Heavy overstuffed Western furniture and built-in dark wood shelving filled the room. Glass doors led to glimpses of an exotic garden, backed by the rocky side of the mountain. It seemed more like a person than a structure, a richly dressed, well-educated person. Like when I entered the house, I had entered this person's psyche. I felt like an older vibrant man, an exciting man.

Even in Tokyo this would be an unusual house, but here in the countryside it was a shock. I couldn't imagine a school teacher made enough money to own such a place. Shinji was having the same reaction, looking around saucer-eyed as if he was in a museum. Usui's mother excused herself and left the room.

We roamed around. Photos were perched on a polished log that served as a mantle over a stone fireplace. Two boys in blue school blazers and shorts were obviously Genji and Ideko. My Usui was looking whimsically past the camera while his brother stood ramrod straight. Another picture of two boys—it took me a while to understand that it wasn't my Usui, but the senior Usui, Mateo—when he was a child, standing next to his brother. And the photos went backward in time from there, three children in worn clothes in a worn landscape, and four children in elaborate Japanese kimonos before that.

As I roamed around, looking at the room, I would think I was a young teenage geisha and forget I was Pearl and this was 1988. I'd

air

found this with other visions, too, this inability to shake it off afterward.

"Pearl, come see," Shinji said. Through the glass doors, there was a rock garden hemmed by hand-built stone walls on one side, and backed onto the craggy side of the mountain behind the house. A humble stone deck led to a rock path that wound past craggy truncated trees. The rock mountain at the back of the garden gave it a harshness that was stark. The creator of this rock garden had manifested another world. I'd never seen anything like it.

I kept roaming, seeking Usui in the space. I went back inside, down a hallway, cold tiles beneath stocking feet. The mother was in the kitchen, her back still hunched. I sensed profound grief there. I thought again about how I was here on false pretenses. Why didn't I just tell them I'd seen their son? I assumed that Usui senior didn't know his son was homeless. Why didn't I just pass on the information about where I'd seen him last? What were my motives in being there? To see what Usui's father and mother were really like? To see where Usui had lived? Was that a fair motive? I wasn't sure.

As I felt the woman's grief, the story of her sons lodged in her bent shoulders, I felt ashamed for interfering in these people's lives. But the stigma against homelessness was so terrible in Japan, would it be better for them to know about their son? Maybe the right thing to do was *not* tell them. Or was I just trying to get myself off the hook?

When I came back into the living room, Usui senior was there. He wore a freshly pressed shirt and black trousers, nothing like the sweater, dungarees and boots he'd worn at the mission. He introduced himself, Shinji responded, and we all bowed. He looked at me closely, and I bowed again. He said something to Shinji.

"Usui-*san* says he think he recognize you. Have you met another time?" I shook my head. I hadn't thought this through. All I could hope was that he was too traumatized when I met him at the mission to remember me.

"No, I don't think so," I lied.

Usui senior sat in a thick rust-colored armchair, Shinji and I across from him on a deep green sofa. They talked for a while, general niceties and introductions. I understood some of it. Shinji told him we were doing a series on Japanese teachers. I lost the trail of conversation after that and looked wistfully out at the garden. After a while, Shinji turned to me. "Did you hear? This his house. What is word? Created it? Made it?"

"Do you mean *designed?*"

"Yes, designed. Architect. He is architect. He gave up to become school teacher."

I looked at Usui senior with new respect. I suddenly understood why I'd felt the place was familiar. The lines of the house reminded me of the folds of Usui's origami. He bowed his head toward me. He and Shinji spoke for a while longer.

"Let us begin interview," Shinji said.

"Oh yes, of course." I fished through my purse, hoping against hope there was a reporter's notebook in there. I often carried one. I found one, but dug around and couldn't find a pen. Shinji shook his head and offered his. I tried to shield the notebook so he couldn't see I hadn't prepared anything.

I groped around for basic questions about teaching, trying to find my footing. Shinji translated. Of course I wanted to ask about his son. What was he like as a little boy, a teenager? What made him laugh? What was the worst thing he'd ever done? Silly questions. I needed the mythology. I wanted Usui's legends.

As Usui senior spoke, he reminded me of a refined version of my own father. I got the distinct impression that he was brutally strict in the classroom. I couldn't understand how this clenched man could've been the same person who designed this house. The spirit of the place was so full of glory.

I looked up to see the two men staring at me, waiting. I shook myself. "How did you get into teaching?" I blurted.

Usui senior spread his arms toward the ceiling. Again, I morphed into the geisha girl and thought that the man talking in front of me was one of my johns. I thought I would have to lie on my back for him. I shook myself.

air

Something was upsetting the older Usui. As he spoke his arms constricted and his shoulders sagged as if a weight had fallen on them. Even the timber of his voice changed. As a geisha, I was trained to notice the slightest change in inflection and to keep the men charmed, to keep them happy.

His wife came in with a tray of tea and pastries. She knelt in front of a gleaming coffee table and served us without looking up. In her stooped shoulders she held the death of one son and the disappearance of the other. I almost reached out to touch her back, but stopped myself.

Shinji translated that the senior Usui had studied architecture in Germany. He'd built this house and others like it in Hokkaido and become famous locally for his craftsmanship, but then something had happened, and he gave it all up. He realized that children needed a better education, so he went back to college to become a teacher.

Shinji whispered to me, "I know you want to ask what makes him give up architecture, but it was tragedy, I can feel. In Japan, not done. We do not ask such things."

"It must've been something that happened long before his son died," I said to Shinji.

"Yes, my son die. How you know?" Usui senior said in English. I blushed. I kept forgetting that everyone in Japan learned English in primary school.

"I am so sorry, Mr. Usui. I am sorry for your loss. I heard about it from someone at the *ryokan*," I lied. Shinji bowed his head repeatedly and whispered condolences in Japanese.

"So you know he die from karoshi, sitting at desk in downtown Tokyo. Decent job. Very good company. Why my son not happy with work? Why he die?" He actually spoke good English. He pointed to his nose. "I fix! I can fix. I can teach." He stood and went to the corner, pointed to the intricate matching of beams above our heads, to the triangular glass skylight, to the origami of wood and crystal. "To make perfect. So to speak. To make fit." His mouth stretched to a thin line, his jaw taut.

I saw in Usui senior my father, and every father. He was thousands of fathers throughout time and history. He was millions of fathers. The status quo, the rigidity, the brutality. The load these fathers were made to carry, forced to transport the status quo forward. Refusal to fulfill the role meant being beaten down or ostracized or worse.

When I was little, my father would get up at four a.m. several days a week to go fishing. He'd drive the truck and fishing boat down narrow rutted lanes to brambly river edges. He'd back the boat in. At dawn, he'd be the only person on the molten water, here and there a croak, a plop, a caw. He'd come home several hours later. Mother and I in the kitchen, listening to farm reports on the radio. *Corn futures softened. Live cattle futures saw some gains. Traders are keeping a close eye on the weather.* He'd hold up a half-dozen crappie or catfish. He'd stink. He'd be slopped with mud. But he'd be happy. Within an hour that would change. He'd have to dress for his construction job. The cigarettes would come out, and the scowl.

The house itself was a witness to the older Usui's soul. But he gave up his spirit for what he thought was his duty. All these people thinking they were doing good, when in fact they were destroying themselves and hurting the rest of us.

"We die if we not strong. Whole nation must be strong." Usui senior raised his voice. "It is life or death. We begin with children."

The children would learn or he would beat it into them. We'd run enough stories in the *Kaze*. I couldn't understand the harsh stories of Japanese teachers, beatings and more beatings until Shinji gave me a history lesson. Schools in Japan prior to World War II were military recruiting grounds, often with military personnel as teachers. It gave some context to the brutality. Who was I to judge? I'd had my own brutality with the nuns at Holy Cross.

air

I guess I thought other cultures would be better than what I grew up with. I was the opposite of ethnocentric. What did they call it? Xenocentric? I thought every culture *had* to be better than Missouri. Apparently, it just wasn't true.

A white glow on the table beside me caught my eye. I reached for it. It was an origami crane. It was made by *my* Usui. I held it by the delicate wing, and my heart sang for him, for his spirit, for his desire to fly.

The elder Usui stood in front of me. I looked up. He said something hard and fast in Japanese. Shinji shook his head with grave disappointment. The mother rushed into the room.

Shinji said, "He know where he met you. He says from the mission. You know his son, Genji. He want to know real reason for you at his house." Shinji's shoulders slumped, as if someone had just dumped a bucket of shame on his head.

Usui senior towered above me. I scooted away and stood, still holding the paper bird. "Yes, I know Genji."

"Why you here?" Usui senior's face turned red. He had spittle on his chin.

"I'm friends with Genji. I'm sorry for the false pretenses. I just wanted to see…"

"Where he? You know where?"

The mother grabbed Shinji's arm, frantically speaking in Japanese. Shinji translated for her. "Where is my son? Where is my son?"

"I saw him in Ohtemachi in Tokyo several weeks ago," I said.

The mother ran toward the hallway, then ran back, as if she didn't know if she should run to get her son, or wait to hear more.

I hurriedly added, "He's not there anymore. He moved on. I went back several times."

"What you mean? What this mean *moved on?*"

I swallowed. "He's homeless."

"Homeless?" the father barked. Shinji translated for the mother, who held her stomach, moaned and sunk to the floor.

"Homeless?" Usui senior spun around the room, looking upward. "Homeless?" He continued to spin, holding up his arms to the ceiling. "Homeless? Homeless?" Then his shoulders sank. "I am no home for my son?" He sat on the chair, defeated. His wife rocked back and forth on her heels.

Shinji said something in Japanese, but they barely looked up to acknowledge him. He turned to me, took my arm. "We must leave. This much shame."

I started to apologize, but Shinji interrupted, bowing deeply, thanking them for their time, apologizing. He pulled me to the door.

Usui senior called in English, "Tell him, there is home. There is home." His voice wailed up, echoed off the skylight and shattered like shards of glass.

On the drive back, Shinji kept shaking his head. He turned to say something to me several times, then gave up. When the van pulled into the *ryokan*, I started to get out, but he put a hand on my arm.

"In Seattle, in mountains where we go hiking, I saw signs on trails. *Leave only footprints. Take only memories.* I thought, this is about life, about living good life, and not interfering or hurting. I thought, Americans know this. Americans good people."

He turned his head away from me. "You come Japan. You stir trouble." He pointed toward the ground. "You are visitor here." His face was flushed. "You must leave only footprints."

Maybe some people were supposed to stir things up. Did he ever think of that? Maybe some people were meant to tell the truth! Maybe it was time someone disturbed the peace! I sat hunched forward on the seat. I knew he wasn't just talking about the scene at the Usui house. I'd always been told I stirred things up, that I was trouble. I'd been beaten and shamed my whole life for my way of seeing. Shinji started to get out of the van. I reached to stop him, but he brushed me off.

air

He stood outside the van door. *"Domo arigato gozaimasu."* He bowed low, cold, formal. A distancing bow. A goodbye bow.

Yuriko and I were packing. She was badgering me for gossip. "And now you won't even tell me where you just snuck off to for three hours." I was trying not to talk to her. I needed to be left alone. I needed to think.

There was a knock at the door. We still had thirty minutes before the bus left. Yuriko answered. Shinji burst in.

"Pearl must come," he said, breathless. "Choko-*san*. Please. He pulled at my arm. Choko-*san*."

I was shocked Shinji was even talking to me. I'd never seen him like this. We ran down two hallways. Yuriko was behind us. I turned and gave her a hard stare. She said in a loud whisper, "Hey, if you're not going to tell me what's going on, I'm going to find out for myself."

When we came to a stop at a door, Shinji paused and took deep ragged breaths. He opened the door quietly. The three of us bent to take off our shoes. The energy was so fragile and thick, I felt as if I were entering a church or an emergency room. A girl was crouched, holding her head, in one corner. Choko was on a futon. Her face was red and enflamed, and she was shaking. I recognized the Japanese girl in the corner as one of the tea ladies from the *Kaze*.

"Is she sick?" I asked.

Shinji kneeled by Choko. I kneeled beside him. "She not speak. No speaking."

Her fingers clutched the futon cover. I put my hand on hers. She opened blood-red eyes, saw me, and grabbed for me, going for my shoulder, but instead grabbing my hair. She yanked until my face was inches from hers. She smelled of something yellowed, stained. She spoke in Japanese, and I couldn't understand.

"She want to speak to Pearl," Shinji said to Yuriko and the girl in the corner. "We leave." When Yuriko didn't move, he shouted, "Leave!"

She went out reluctantly. Shinji went to the girl in the corner and led her away.

With my hair in her fist, Choko mumbled something in English.

"Choko-*san*, what is it? I can't understand."

"What color are my panties? What color? What?"

Something sunk in my stomach. I knew that look. I was the whining thirteen-year-old geisha under the weight of too many men.

"Who did it?"

She shook her head. I put my hand on her pillow. It was sopping wet.

"Who?"

She opened her eyes wide, pulled my face hard down to hers. "I will never tell you. You understand? You will not do anything. Never. Not in Japan. Never."

A rage enveloped me. When people said they could never see themselves killing anyone, I always thought, *I could.* I could slit someone from crotch to throat and rip out their guts. I could throw their innards to the dogs. Some days I had so much violence in me, it took everything I had not to smash someone in the face.

Choko let go of my hair. She fell into something between despair and sleep. I sat with her a few more minutes, feeling horribly to blame. Why hadn't I done something earlier when she first told me the reporters were harassing her? What was wrong with me?

This was the way you kept a woman down. This was the way you kept her small and scared. This was the way you broke her spirit.

Choko obviously wasn't playing the necessary submissive role. Choko needed to be put in her place. *Who do you think you are, Choko-san?* The sickness went down so deep there was no bottom.

I went out to the hallway. Shinji was grilling the Japanese girl, who was cringing and crying. He turned to me. "I know what happened." He pointed to girl. "She say someone run out of room late last night when she come back. She too drunk to see who it was."

air

I looked at her, but she was so fraught. My face was too full of rage, and she backed up from me as if she were scared. Yuriko paced, hands on hips.

Shinji smacked himself in the forehead. "How stupid! I was drunk. I should walk her to room." He hit his forehead again. "Stupid. Stupid."

"It's not your fault, Shinji." My voice came out like black tar.

"It's my fault. I got Shinji drunk," Yuriko yelled, hysterical.

I didn't tell them it was all my fault. Choko had come to me for help, and I hadn't helped. I couldn't tell them because I couldn't bear their condemnation.

"Maybe it's best if we blame the guy who did this," I said.

"Okay. How do we get the police?" Yuriko said, in control now. "Shinji, we'll need you to translate. Pearl, you should go tell the company boss or something."

"No," I said. "Choko doesn't want to report it. It's her decision."

"Screw that." Yuriko charged down the hall. I ran and grabbed her arm.

"Yuriko, you don't have to live with the consequences of this. She does." She looked at me as if I'd killed her firstborn, as if I were the greatest disappointment for a woman she'd ever met. I held her gaze. I had no idea if I was right. I had no idea about this culture, about myself, about Choko. The only thing I knew for sure was that I didn't know anything.

Yuriko yanked herself from my touch, turned and stomped back toward our room.

On the bus, Choko sat between Yuriko and me. Shinji sat in front of us. When Finn got on, I caught his eye. He smiled. I smiled. His pain, mine, Choko's.

I needed time to think. It was snowing, and thick white flakes turned farm and field a headache white. As we drove, the earth glared. I rubbed my temples. I had to think. About Choko. About men. About violence. About fathers. About teaching children how to live. About who was raising all the children up, everywhere. About the why of it. When I was five, I knew I had to raise myself up. The people I was born to weren't going to do it right. Besides the brutality, they were forcing me into a box of who I was supposed to be instead of who I really was. I was beginning to see it wasn't just me who needed raising up, it was everyone, everywhere.

From Sapporo, the eighteen-hour journey back to Tokyo seemed never ending. We took turns sitting with Choko. Nobody spoke much. It was a lot of time to think.

By the time we pulled into Ueno Station, I knew what I had to do. I had some power, right, being an editor of a national newspaper? I did have that power, surely. I decided instead of letting all the Japanese editors dictate the stories, I'd run a few stories of my own. First, I wanted to get reporters on a series about *karoshi*, about all these people dying at their desks, about the when, the where, the who and the why of it. I wanted personal interviews, statistics, answers.

Then, I wanted to look at Japan's homelessness. Who was homeless? Why? How did they live? Where? And yes, there was the selfish desire to find Usui.

Finally, when Choko was ready, if she was ever ready (she was the only Japanese woman reporter at the *Kaze* so it had to be her) a series on women, on how the Fast Track was affecting them. And if she was ever ready, maybe just maybe we could run a series on rape, under-reported and unreported, and articles on how to deal with the aftermath.

Someone was holding my hand. I looked down. It was Choko. She had my thumb in her grip. Her lips were nearly blue, her face streaked with tears. I thought of Keiko, the girl with Down syndrome. And then for some reason, I thought of the doll Usui had given me, the second one, the big voluptuous doll, the woman he thought I was.

air

The woman who looked nothing whatsoever like me. The woman I so wished I could be.

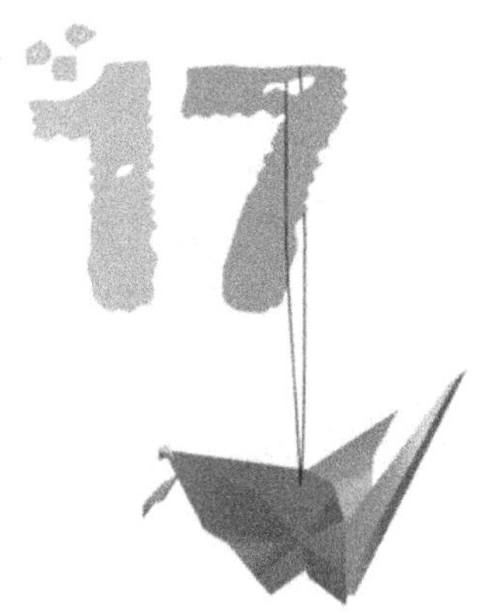

I CAME UPON Finn at dusk at Yoyogi Park. He stood with his back to a concrete stairwell. He was playing the sax. His old overcoat was weighed down by a heaviness in the pockets. Light echoed. Sound echoed. His music floated to meet the clicks and snaps of pedestrians on the overhead walkway above him. The tones bounced back from the birds that flitted among skinny trees. The melody was like candy thrown out at a parade.

Three times a week, we met here. A glow surrounded him. Spotlights of the setting sun peeked through the alleys of the buildings across the street, popped color and light. He was so tall, so thin, his white-blond hair even after months of dating him, still a surprise. He wore fingerless gloves, and the soprano sax was a toy in his long bony fingers. The scene glowed canary, electric lime, fern and magic mint, like a child's crayon drawing.

When he saw me, he lowered the sax and laughed. I laughed. Finn laughed a lot. Finn set the laughing world in motion.

We'd been inseparable over the past three months. Several nights a week, I rode the handle bars of his Schwinn as we tooled around the back streets; how he balanced with his sax case on his back and me on the front I couldn't figure out. I'd never been the passenger on someone else's bike. On these days, I missed my childhood bike, Miss Universe, riding her wild and free down gravel roads and across fields. Finn had a way of meandering, of being open. I'd learned to schedule things, control them. Growing up, with the

air

endless labor, the gutting, plucking, weeding, and hunting, you didn't meander. Not often. Hippies meandered. Hippies were useless on a farm.

We'd chat about silly things as we cantered down the narrow, winding lanes, veering around people on the sidewalk and in the streets, so many people. So many houses crammed together, hidden behind gates, a collection of disjointed monuments, wild nature climbing the walls and hanging like curious onlookers. Sometimes the branches bore fruit, and we'd grab persimmons, oranges, pears. Paper lanterns, oriental eaves. For whole hours, I was able to forget myself.

With Finn at the concrete stairwell, I held up a box of sashimi and a bottle of wine. He laughed again, almost a bark. I brought them every time. It was our dinner three nights a week. He took the sax from around his neck, opened a blue velvet-lined case and tucked the instrument into it. I went up to him. He kissed me on the mouth. An electric shock up the spine.

We meandered through the park. The light was dying, the wind grew bitter. My face and fingertips fell into numbness. Around us narrow trees and thinning grass. Branches crackled, popped.

I lived with Finn in a floating world. I was his musical instrument. He blew air into me and made music, a tune that was me, but with notes I sometimes didn't recognize. I was clear-headed enough to know he'd done the same thing for Aikiko and could do the same thing for any other woman at any other time. The thought made me cling hard to his arm as we walked.

We didn't talk. Hours would go by between us with few words. Other Japanese couples walked in just such a way, choreographed wandering with no soundtrack. I loved the silence. I wanted just silence and him playing me. Just those two things.

He pointed to a bench. We huddled on it against the bitter breeze. I spread out the sushi, looked through my bag and realized I'd forgotten the corkscrew. I was always forgetting it. I spread empty hands toward him. He burst in laughter, got up, rummaged beneath a tree, found a stick, put the bottle between his legs, pushed the cork down. I'd also forgotten cups. Finn shook his head, and took a swig from the thick-lipped bottle and handed it to me. We ate the sashimi—salmon, tuna, shrimp. Seaweed. Rice.

From the pocket of his oversized coat, he extracted his stash, the pouch the color of watermelon. Rolling papers, matches, a small metal rod, an envelope with a sticky square of hash. He'd done this a hundred times before, a thousand. His daily ritual. He took a notebook out of his bag, laid out a rolling paper, crumbled a cigarette into the paper. He lit a match, held it to the hash and crumbled it onto the tobacco. The wind threatened to blow the whole thing sky high, and he hunched farther until he was bent almost in half. Supplication. When he finished rolling, he used the rod as a reamer. From the book of matches, he tore a corner from the cardboard cover and inserted it into the end for a filter.

He handed the joint to me. His ritual had become our ritual. I'd never smoked hash or marijuana in my life before I met Finn. It was part of this new life of floating, of gliding, hovering, drifting, hanging.

He lit it for me; I took a deep hit and handed it back. He put it to his lips, inhaled, threw his head back, stretched his lips wide, and held his breath. Afterward, we gulped down the wine.

I got up. I always climbed a tree. There were only a few in the park that were big and healthy enough to hold the weight of an adult.

Before Finn, Shinji had brought me to this park. I'd been complaining of missing the earth. The loss of the land felt like a lost limb, and my need for it emerged in a whine. Shinji called my feelings for home *natsukashi*, sweet remembering.

He presented the Tokyo park to me, saying, *Such a beautiful nature, see? Look at the foliage. Look, trees!* I smiled wanly. I'd only known rugged terrain, skittering critters and twittering air, full of insects, birds, the night lit with fireflies. How could this compare? To me, the park looked like a worn-out old man. As I stood there with Shinji, I was filled with grief. It was anorexic. The park was starving, or I was or we both were.

But I'd gotten used to it. You can get used to almost anything.

There was one tree that had properly positioned branches for climbing, a husky fellow. I was a good climber, up into the top

air

branches quickly. Finn followed. I shimmied out for clearance and hung upside down by my knees. Finn climbed higher, to the top, sat in the crook of a branch. There was still enough light. He took a small camera out of his pocket and snapped pictures.

He was into birds. Tree sparrows, large-billed crows, rock doves, brown-eared bulbuls—he'd taught me all the names. He was a gifted photographer, as good as anyone at *National Geographic*, but he didn't see it. He'd traveled all over the world to capture the feather and tweet of birds. Boxes of audio tapes and portfolios of photos were stored in his closet. He'd climbed to tree canopies in New Zealand, maneuvered footbridges in forest canopies in Costa Rica, hiked hills in Nepal to capture the trill, tweet, cheep, caw, chirp, coo, squawk, shriek, cry, hoot, click, clatter. He'd been to an aviary in Malaysia where musicians met to jam with the birds. We'd listened to the tape, and it sounded like chaos to me, like jazz that was so improvisational it made you tense and jumpy, but it'd made him cry, right there on the *tatami*.

And in his photos, there was a love, a weighty grief, a tenderness, a haunting. Every time I saw one of his snapshots, I wondered how he survived loving like that in this world.

Finn set the upside-down world in motion, the buoyant, throaty, light-headed world, a place far from intestines, severed heads, emptied bowels, guts thrown to dogs.

I was floating from the tree. From the wine and the hash, my head floated down, so far down. The edges of the earth bled out, watercolors melting and combining. Without Finn there, I would not have felt safe.

"Queenie," he whispered, "Come have a look." When I didn't move, he said, "Seriously, come up here. You must see this."

I got myself right side up, dizzy, and climbed until I reached him. He pointed through the leaves. In the distance, fires were burning. I could only make out bits of it, campfires, people, a primordial scene.

"Come on," he said. I was lost in the mystery of whatever it was. Finn was already on the ground. "Queenie, hurry!"

I scrambled down, bark burning belly as I slipped down the trunk. We made our way through the park. Lying on the ground here and there, lovers huddled beneath coats and blankets, lying as close together on the cold earth as they could get. Piles of lovers in mounds of form and color, like crooked roots or bizarre hedges growing up from the earth. We wound around them and leapt over them.

Deeper into the park. A thick copse of trees that in the dark expanded until they became thick woods. I pulled back on Finn's hand, but he urged me forward. What a different notion men had about safety. What darkness they could fall into that was not open to women.

We went into the forest. In my stoned state, we were in the thick for seconds or hours, I could not tell. I did not like how hash played with time. It was too close to my visions. Minutes could go by, and it'd seem like hours. Or a day could go by in an hour. It disturbed me. When we came out into a field, I had no idea how long we'd been in the trees.

Fire. Here and there flames shot from barrels, the sparks like sudden epiphanies in the dark, lighting up the cheeks, chins and foreheads of dozens of men. It was some sort of homeless tent city. Makeshift structures lined the edge of the field. Finn and I stood in the shadows and watched.

Most of the men had dreadlocks, wore dark coats, dark trousers, dark shoes. Most of the men looked like Usui. They were eerily quiet. The scene bled black at the edges, with sudden flames of carrot and crimson, and deep blue ice. The subtle glow from the barrels turned the faces ancient like a Rembrandt.

Then I saw Usui. I couldn't be sure, it was so dark, but energy shot up my spine. He was staring at me, as if he could see me hidden in the forest shadows.

I heard a clank next to me, and Finn whispered, "Bloody hell."

Four men stood beside us, nearly on top of us. We hadn't seen or heard them. One of them inched closer to me, whispered something in low Japanese.

air

"Run, Queenie, run!" Finn yelled. He grabbed my hand and pulled. I was confused. I wanted to see Usui. I could smell the urine of the homeless men. One of them was reaching up to touch my hair. Finn yelled *run!* again. I felt a terror enter my groin and shoot up my back and broke into a sudden sweat. Every woman knew this threat. Whether you'd been raped or not, every woman knew the danger, had felt the panic in their throats.

I turned to run, but stumbled, falling hard on a root and popping my knee. The men argued drunkenly in Japanese. The one who touched my hair grabbed at me and caught my hair. Finn tried to pry the man's hands loose. Two men attached to my head.

Then I heard a slap, a scuffle, men cursing in Japanese. The man released his grip. Finn let go as well and yanked me up by the arm. We started to run. I turned to see a glimpse of Usui's face beneath dreadlocks as he held his body on top of the hair-touching man. The two other men pounded Usui's back. Finn was far ahead, running. I turned, ran back and kicked one of the men in the side with all the force I had in me.

"Purr-*san*, go. Now!" Usui screamed. I saw other homeless men running toward us, hoping they were coming to help Usui.

The man I kicked was coming at me. I knew I wouldn't win this one. He was twice my size. I knew Usui would only be hurt worse trying to help me. I turned and ran. Despite my knee, I ran hard and fast. I knew how to run. I knew how to press down on the pain, to bring the breath down into the belly, to set a pounding rhythm. Even terrified, even with a knee pulsing with pain, even stoned and drunk, even now that I was smoking again, I could run. The drunken man swore and stumbled behind me. I let the leaves slap my face, felt rocks and roots and grass beneath the soles of my shoes. I lifted my feet high, my head up. I ran like the wind. I ran as if I were not of this earth, as if I were a beast that floated just above the sopping wet flesh of the rumbling soil.

I overtook Finn. He said something, but I ignored him and kept running. I ran out of the woods, sprinted across the field, jumped over lovers, cleared hedges, wound around trees. I didn't stop until I had to, until I was at the edge of a street teeming with cars. I bent over, breathing hard. My knee pulsed with anger. Finn came up, rasping for breath. He put his hand on my back. "You all right, love?"

I shook off his hand, turned my back on him. I wanted to punch him in the face. It wasn't his fault, but I felt like blaming him. Men didn't protect you. Men put you in danger. I knew this from the time I was a little girl with my father, and I knew this from every man I'd ever known, barring Jason. *And what about Usui?* a voice asked in my ear. *What sort of danger was he?*

"Look, I'm sorry, okay," Finn said. "I should've never led you into that mess." I ignored him, pacing and trying to get my breath back. I had to quit smoking.

"Who was that homeless bloke helping us? Did you know him?" I looked around for a police kiosk. I walked down the busy sidewalk, looking, with Finn following.

The patrol centers were all over the city, small shacks with windows. Would the police even do anything? I knew how the Japanese viewed the homeless. As invisible. Expendable.

I finally found a kiosk two blocks away. The officer looked younger than me. Steam was coming off a Styrofoam bowl on a table behind him. I told Finn to translate that a homeless man was being beaten up in the park. The officer shrugged. He wrote something down. He told Finn he'd look into it. He blew on his noodles. I wanted to scream at him, grab him by the hair and drag him through the park to the scene. After standing there for several minutes and being ignored, Finn and I gave up.

On the train, my knee throbbed, my scalp hurt. When we came close to Finn's stop, I turned and looked at him. I just wanted to go home, just wanted to hang out with Yuriko. How long had it been since I'd hung out with Yuriko? He took my hand. I let him lead me off the train at his stop. I couldn't seem to say what I wanted. I lost my voice. This happened often. I wasn't allowed to speak when I was little and didn't think I had any right to speak as a grown-up, especially when love was involved. Especially then.

air

Finn's basement flat was dark and heavy. When I saw it in the light of day, the filth shocked me, a grime so thick and engrained the place would never come clean. The entire apartment was just one *tatami* room and a kitchenette. The windows toward the ceiling revealed a torrent of shoes—flats, stilettos, business shoes, sneakers, an occasional old woman in ancient wooden sandals and the edge of a kimono.

We were getting stoned. When you grew up with violence, you didn't learn an appropriate reaction. You forgot about it too soon. You pushed it down deep and pretended it was normal. The thing could be forgotten, but the energy of it went underground and titillated the flesh, for days, for years. Finn and I got stoned and pretended that it had been a normal night, and we were going to do our normal rituals.

In the corner, his canary, Siddhartha, was singing. I got up to feed him. He was bright orange, with a head full of mangy-looking feathers. Siddhartha was one of the gentlest, most fragile creatures I had ever met. Finn had used a chopstick to show me how to entice the bird out and onto your finger, but this night, I knew I could not manage it, so I left him in his cage. They said dogs were like their owners. I didn't know what Siddhartha had to say about Finn. The cage bothered me, though. Growing up wild, you didn't see birds in cages.

I went over to where Finn kept his Buddhas and lit a candle and incense for Usui. How badly had they beaten him? I was forgetting about what'd happened to me, but I could never forget when something happened to someone else. It was like glue in the heart. It was the not knowing that ate at the stomach.

Finn's Buddha collection came from all over Asia, carved in cherry wood, stone, jade—laughing, sitting, stretching. Incense swirled protectively around the small figurines. I rubbed each one of their bellies. For luck. For Usui.

Finn handed me a glass of beer. I held it up to the soft light of the paper lamp. The glass was filthy.

"Let's have a look then," he said. He lifted my trouser leg, and there was a scrape and a bruise. He put his hand in my hair. I cringed.

He refilled the pipe, toked on it, handed it to me. I took a long hit, handed it back. I was floating around the room. Siddhartha was humming a tune Finn had taught him using his flute. The song sounded like tings at a *pachinko* parlor, but sometimes swung low and high like a British ambulance siren.

"So who was the homeless bloke?" Finn asked, his voice disembodied.

"That was Usui."

"*The* Usui? The fellow who'd gone missing at the mission, the one whose father we met?"

"Yes, that Usui."

"Odd that he was there just when you needed him."

I pondered Finn's face. He had such smooth skin. I didn't say, *It's not odd at all. That's what happens to me. That's what has always happened to me. These serendipities.*

Finn took my chin and looked me in the face. "Queenie, there's more to you than meets the eye. I didn't know you could run like that."

People often said that to me. *There's more to you than meets the eye.* Surely that was true of everyone. Surely we were all more than met the eye. If not, then this world was in a whole lot of trouble.

Finn opened the closet doors and took out a single futon and a cover, spread it out on the floor. He came to me and put his body up against mine. He was so tall, my face came only to his tattered T-shirt.

Even upset, I was strongly affected by Finn. I was like a stray dog in heat. I wanted to get on all fours and present my backside to him.

"Queenie, what a crazy night." His voice was muffled against my hair, the pressure painful, but I didn't want to pull away. "Outrageous."

He was kissing me, and I was falling. He took my wrists and forced me backward onto the futon. There was an edge to him, an echo of the park. He held my wrists above my head, trapped me with his angular weight, drove into me. He bit my shoulder. The writhing, the grunts, the high-pitched whimpers like a lonely composition for wind instruments. Siddhartha's siren song. I watched it all from the corner of the ceiling. Finn on top. Nothing but the pouch around my neck to protect me.

All night, I dreamed of the park. The images morphed into mythological proportions, speckled fire, shadowed faces, mounds of lovers. The drunken men swelled to the size of Fujin, storms blew from their massive bellies, the field transformed into a dark temple, and in the shadowed distance, Usui like the Fujin in my vision, opened his mouth and screamed.

As soon as the sun rose, I left Finn sleeping and took the train to the park. It was so different early morning, people rushing to work, a class doing tai chi, punked-out teenagers playing a boom box. It was as if nothing sinister at all had happened the night before. My knee throbbed. I found the tree I'd climbed, took the same walk I'd taken the night before. The going was slow because of the knee.

In the daylight, what I'd thought were woods were barely even a smattering of trees. The quiverings of the flesh didn't stop me from entering the trees and walking through them to the field. I was used to having to revisit places where violence had happened, used to having to live in the very place of the violence. Maybe somebody else wouldn't have come back here, daylight or not, but I was used to this. This was my story.

I hobbled across the field. It was quiet, like a rural campsite in the morning. The barrel fires had burned down, the rotting, rusted barrels still generating heat.

More than a dozen structures were built behind the barrels. The area was surprisingly clean. I wasn't that familiar with tent cities in the States, but I just knew there was something going on here. The structures were constructed of wood scraps, nailed together in quixotic puzzles. Each was covered with a blue tarp. They had windows and doors. They were built in a protective circle. One person had painted his door red. In the center were office chairs on wheels, four of them in brand new condition, circled around a fire pit.

Someone had hung a string of scarves like prayer flags from one structure to another. I was studying a purple one rimmed in gold sequins when someone opened the door next to me. I stepped back and screamed.

You think you've got a handle on the fear, but it comes out in the voice.

The man screamed back at me. "Ahhhhh!" He clutched his chest, his voice high like a girl's. "*Nan desu ka?*" he cried.

I should not have called him a he. He was a she. She wore purple eye shadow, false lashes, blood-red lipstick, and a floral scarf around her forehead, thick dreadlocks spilling down. Her face was pockmarked and the whites of her eyes shot through with broken blood vessels. Her skin was so pale, and blue-black whiskers grew below thick pancake makeup. She wore large hoop earrings that threw reflections from the sun.

"*Gomennasai,*" I said, *excuse me.* "Usui-*san?*" I waved my arm in an arc around the tent city. "Usui-*san onegaishimasu.*" *Usui, please.*

air

She wiped her tears. She stayed half in the shadows in her doorway, spoke in soft Japanese I could not understand and wove long languid hands in front of her face.

I wished Yuriko could paint her. There was something epic about her, epic and broken.

She pointed to her nose. "Akina-*san*," she said. "*Watashi wa* Akina-*san desu*." *My name is Akina.*

"Pearl," I bowed slightly.

"Purr-*san*."

She spoke in rapid Japanese, and I could not follow. She went to one of the other doors and called a greeting, opened it and spoke. A Japanese woman with no teeth looked around her at me with open aggression.

A man came around the corner from the park, and Akina spoke to him. From his reply and Akina's reaction, I knew we'd found Usui. Akina motioned for me to follow, and we set out across the field in the opposite direction.

A brightly flowered robe peeked from beneath Akina's black threadbare coat. She wore a pair of large ruby ballet slippers. I felt safe with Akina, and at home. I rarely felt at home. She was my mythical escort through the woods for a meeting with the king.

What was Akina's story? How could you possibly figure out a person if you didn't know the who, what, where and why of their evolution? It was like that with Father. So little information about his childhood, a handful of phrases. Runt of the litter, chip on his shoulder, needed to prove what a man he was. How could a daughter build a story out of that? I needed details, stories of teeth pulled, and missing shoelaces, of pet dogs that his father shot between the eyes. I had no context for his sudden rages, for the cruelty, nowhere to put the slap that landed hard across the side of the head.

Akina's story seemed to be lodged in one thigh, seemed to pulse from the left side of her face.

We entered a row of trees and came out the other side. In front of us was a slope leading up to a tall rail bridge. A train rumbled far overhead, the vibrations twittering my bones. On the bridge's supporting beams, vines with white flowers had grown and dangled down like a curtain. A soft wind blew the vines apart, giving us a view of what lay behind them. There he was, Usui.

I ran up, through the dangling flowers. They weren't flower vines, but strands of origami cranes. There must have been five hundred. I stood above Usui. He looked up. He had a black eye and a fat lip. He sat on a rectangular piece of cardboard and folded origami birds. No sign of the dolls. What had happened to the dolls? Akina bowed and moved to the side, as if waiting to escort me back.

"It is foolish to be here after last evening," Usui said, returning his gaze to the crane in his hand.

"I had to make sure you were okay."

"I am okay. And you?" he asked.

"Yes. I'm fine. Are you badly hurt?"

He shook his head, focused on the crane between his long fingers. He smelled like soap. His hands were clean. His dreads and coat were the same from when I'd seen him on the bridge with the dolls. He'd lost weight. I wanted to go back across the park and find a store that sold ice packs and come back and take care of his face. I didn't know if I should. I didn't know if he'd freak out and disappear again.

He finished the bird, stood and held his stomach as if in pain, took down a strand of cranes and added the new one to the string.

"I'm sorry," I blurted. "For last night, and for…" I blushed, "…the stuff at the mission."

He sat, took up a sheet of origami paper and began folding it. "Do you know why we keep meeting?" he asked.

"No."

"No, I do not know either."

I lowered myself gingerly to the cardboard. "Can I just ask one thing? At the mission, when you were…so upset…you know, on the futon. What was wrong? What was going on? I mean before I climbed in there with you. I know why you were upset with that." Off to the right, I noticed Akina sit on a patch of grass.

air

Usui bobbed his head as his fingers worked the paper. "I must understand why Father Dennis sent you to me."

"Usui-*san*," I said, putting my hand on his coat. "What was wrong?"

He was quiet for a while, and I thought he wouldn't answer. He finished the crane, put it to the side and started another. "For long time, I have desperation. For years, I seek to understand it. After despair, something bad always happen. When child, on futon with bad grief, later grandfather die. Ojisan. He was only person who understood me. This time after despair, brother dies."

"Wow." I hadn't thought of depression in this way before. "So your despair is like a premonition."

He nodded. "But no information. Just bad feeling. Sometimes continues for day, sometimes week."

"Sort of like another version of my visions."

He looked at me. The bruise around his eye was bright purple in the sun. "Perhaps."

"So, why this?" I pointed around me at the rail beams, the cardboard. "Why did you run away? Why make yourself homeless?"

"You make yourself homeless, Purr-*chan*. True? You leave Misery, your home. Why? To see life differently. True?"

"I just wanted to get the hell out of there."

"I believe it is more. I believe Father Dennis send you for reason. For both of us."

He was on his third crane now. He folded the cranes like I smoked cigarettes, obsessively. "I must understand why so much darkness in world. I do not speak only of me, Purr. I speak of so many with darkness."

"You have to make yourself homeless to figure that out?"

"Did you?"

I stood and hobbled over to his string of cranes. The question made me anxious. I worried one of the hanging birds between finger and thumb.

"It is Legend of the Thousand Cranes," Usui said. "Ancient legend promises if person folds one thousand cranes he will be given wish by a crane."

"Have you made your wish?"

"No. I do not yet know wish."

I looked around the site. In a nearby ditch was a stream of trash, soda bottles, cans, fast-food wrappers. I'd never really thought about the practicalities of homelessness. How did Usui shower? Where did he go to the bathroom? How did he brush his teeth? How did he get enough food? I went over and looked down at his bowed head. "Can I help you in some way?"

"I need no more help than you do, Purr-*chan*." I wasn't sure what he meant. I figured I needed a *lot* of help.

"Can I bring you something? Do something for you?"

"Remember, pity is violence."

Did I pity him? "I'm just trying to help."

He didn't answer.

"Can I at least come back and see you?"

He'd finished another crane and stood with the pile of birds.

"Will you promise not to run away?"

With his back to me, he hung bird after bird in silence.

Akina and I hurried back across the field. I'd lost track of time and was going to be late for work.

Usui had so filled my senses I didn't see it coming. It hit me just as we came to the edge of the tent city. As my body flung upward, I grabbed Akina's arm and cried out Usui's name.

I was this bird with a powerful wingspan. Wherever I flew, people below me were bent in supplication toward their gods. I was a primordial, mythic bird, swooping across nations, coasting over oceans to foreign lands, heady with the power of the wind.

On every continent, every island, every village in every hemisphere, people were begging. Pleading. Praying. Everywhere they were seeking.

A global wave of supplication. Everywhere, everyone implored for some relief, beseeched for some meaning, besought some answer to the pain.

I flew into dark clouds and everything went blank.

I awoke in a shadowed place and blinked to adjust my eyes. It was one of the structures in the tent city. Akina came and squatted in front of me. She cooed to me in child-like Japanese as she placed a damp cloth on my forehead. I was on top of layers of blankets, what I assumed was Akina's bed. As I tried to get up, she put a soft hand on my shoulder.

I was late for work. I was never late for work. I had to get to a phone. Akina again pushed me down. I let myself lie back. My head was spinning, my stomach churning.

A children's song played from a boom box in the corner. A Japanese lullaby. Akina sang with it.

Her lilting child-like voice, the wet cloth on my forehead, Akina's eyes outlined with eyeliner, fake lashes, her lipstick smudged. She smelled of green incense and filth. She looked at me with such care as she bent with the water bottle to give me a drink. As a child I'd never been cared for like this.

She went to restart the lullaby. "I wish I could talk to you, Akina. I wish I could know your story," I said to her curved back.

"I am Hokkaido," she said. She stood and came to me. "My English no good." She pointed toward the ceiling, "Hokkaido." I assumed she meant north.

"You speak English?"

She shook her head. I asked, "Did you know Usui-*san* in Hokkaido?"

"No. No, Usui-*san*. I come Tokyo ten before."

"Why did you come to Tokyo?"

Her face turned red as she tried to figure out the words. "To school for wind," she said and spun her arm like a fan, blew air from her lips. "Wind."

She made a triangle with her fingers. "Mountain. Hokkaido. Wind." She moved her hand back and forth. "Strong wind. Hokkaido sacred wind. Dashi." She put her hand up to her mouth, made a tube and blew into it.

"The mountains funnel air?"

"Funnel," she said, but it came out like "funny." She said in perfect English, "Turning winds into an asset." I guessed it was their English-language motto.

"Oh, you studied wind energy to go back to Hokkaido to work for a wind-energy company?"

"Yes, turning winds into an asset," she said again. She screwed up her face and tried to say something. The words seemed ripped from her throat. "For me not outside wind. Inside. Inside wind."

I didn't know what she meant and looked at her blankly.

"You," she pointed at me. "I," at herself. "Funny wind. Great power."

"I funnel wind?"

"Yes, you funny." She took two chopsticks from a nearby crate. "You," she held up a chopstick. "Usui-*san*," she held up another chopstick next to it. She took the two chopsticks and pretended to stab herself in the heart. "You. Usui-*san*. You. Usui-*san*. You funny wind. Here. Usui-*san*, funny wind." She pointed a chopstick at my heart, then went about stabbing and stabbing herself in the heart. "Great power. I see."

I wasn't sure what she was saying. "And you, great power?" I asked, pointing toward her heart.

air

"Me, different power. You, Usui-*san*, great power. Me, different power." She struggled for a word. "Unusual power. Not so happy for other Japanese."

I closed my eyes and listened to the lullabies. Akina opened the door and window, a light breeze blew in. It was surprisingly peaceful.

"This tent city seems so unusual, Akina-*san*. So different from other places for the homeless."

"Yes," Akina said excitedly. "Usui make. I help."

Suddenly, it all clicked into place. The tent city was like one complex piece of origami. Of course Usui had created it. I thought of Usui's father's house in Hokkaido. Like father, like son.

"Usui-*san* no live here," Akina said.

"Why?"

"Too much people. He wants alone."

Everyone was bending forward at their desks as if in devotion. It was the next day. I was at the *Kaze*, standing in the doorway. I thought I was having another vision. The rewriters were curved over their work, the editors bowed over sheets of paper, the Japanese reporters arched toward their computers. I grew dizzy and confused as I stood clinging to the doorframe.

Maybe these people were seeking. Maybe this was a form of invocation, a searching for something more than this mundane world. Maybe every one of us in the newsroom was searching for some answer, looking for a way out of the mess the world had become. Maybe this was praying, too. I held on to the doorframe and waited for the churning to stop, begged myself not to go into another vision.

The day before, when I was finally well enough to leave Akina's, it was too late to go to work. I went back to Gyotoku. Luckily, Yuriko was out for the evening. I called and told the executive editors I'd been attacked and I had been too traumatized that morning to call in sick for work. I held the phone and bowed and apologized. I'd seen Japanese people do this, bow while they were on the phone and now I was doing it. In Japan, everyone was always apologizing. Shinji had told me there were at least twenty ways to say you're sorry in Japanese.

At the *Kaze*, Michael came over. I was still holding on to the doorframe. "Are you all right?" He put a dank palm on my shoulder, and it took everything in me not to swat it off. "I heard what happened. You okay?" He squeezed my shoulder. I grimaced as if it hurt, and he removed his hand.

"I'm getting better." I was good at lying. I'd grown up with liars and secret keepers.

"We'll take it easy on you today." He tried to take my hand, but I pulled it away just in time.

But it wasn't an easy day. Things were getting worse. Piles and piles on my desk of traumatic stories that had to be sorted, edited, polished, paired with pictures and captions, fit into the appropriate column inches.

The earth was getting worse and the violence was getting worse. More mudslides. More murders. More hurricanes. More war. More drought. More domestic violence. The newsroom, too, was worse, cigarette smoke so thick it was like smog, tar up the nostrils that

air

turned snot black, Westerners screaming foul words that bullied the air.

I went into the hall to breathe. I bent over trying to breathe. I was gasping for breath. Was it the vision? Was it some delayed reaction to the attack, some post-traumatic stress? Was it the trauma of the world infecting me? Or was it all three?

Choko came toward me, stood with her hands in fists. She burst into sobs. "Why they attack us?" she cried. She cried like her heart was breaking. I made soothing baby noises as I tried to catch my breath.

I led her to the lady's restroom. She washed her face while crying. "*Gomennasai. Sumimasen.*" *Excuse me. Sorry,* she said. "What they want from us? They take and take. What they want?" She kept bowing and sobbing. "*Gomennasai. Sumimasen.* I am too upset about myself. You just have attack, and I think of myself."

My attack was nothing compared to hers. I didn't know how to explain this to her. I thought maybe she needed me to have experienced what she had so I said nothing, just sat in the corner on the floor tile. Her face in the mirror was swollen, her eyes and mouth like blood slits made with a sharp knife. We stayed for thirty minutes, me curling up in the corner, Choko crying. I had no answers. I had no answers for anyone.

Who, what, when, where, why—these were the questions we were taught in journalism school. But there were other whys that we were never taught to ask.

Why so much violence? Why were women beaten down? Why was the earth crumbling? Why so much grief and despair. Why?

YURIKO WAS PAINTING the melting faces of women. All around were studies of dissolving female faces—tacked to the walls, taped to the closet doors, stuck to the windows. Yuriko's hair was held up by a chip clip. She was chain smoking. "I'm calling the series 'Losing Face,'" she said.

I'd been living with Finn and hadn't seen her in months. She wouldn't look at me. I chattered as if things were normal. I told her about finding Usui, how he was homeless. I talked about Finn's serenading of the birds at Yoyogi Park. She stared daggers at the canvas. "I'm going back to Missouri at the end of the week. Just for a visit." She didn't say anything. "I'll be back," I said.

"You know you abandoned me, right?" she said.

"No," I said, but then I went quiet with guilt. She was right. I'd dumped her for Finn. Perhaps I'd learned it from my mother, this letting go of people without a thank you, this switching off. This notion that women were expendable if there was a man in the picture. This shutting down all emotions, better to feel nothing at all than to open the door to the heart and all the pain stored there.

"The problem is, deep down, you don't think anyone really loves you, Pearl."

Yuriko's truth felt like a slap. She went to the closet and grabbed a painting, handed it to me absently and went back to her half-painted mother.

The painting was a portrait of me. The left half of my face had melted into black. The eye popped out of the right side as if I were in perpetual shock.

Abandonment. Mother and Father had taught me how. Then Mother and Jack. Big abandonments and small ones. I'd learned well. I'd learned from the masters. But it was more than my personal story, right? It was always more than a single person's story. We'd abandoned the earth before that. And for years at school, we were taught to abandon ourselves.

I held the painting. I wanted to grovel at Yuriko's feet. I wanted to say a little girl *sorry*, but the word stuck in my throat. Yuriko stood hard-edged and angry, slashing red across her mother's face.

Later, I took the painting back to Finn's and put it in the closet. I couldn't bear to look at it.

I awoke with a jolt. Turbulence. A woman was leaning over me, asking me something. Did I want chicken or fish? I was on an airplane, on my way to St. Louis. I felt a desperate need to go back. I was losing myself. I needed to go backward to go forward. I needed to see who I was, or who I used to be. I needed some semblance of roots. I had to go back in time and see if any part of the past was worth keeping.

I told the *Kaze* I had to go back for a funeral. They required that I prep everything for the days I would be gone. I'd taken over so much responsibility in the newsroom, it was no small feat. I could see how people could die at their desks. I could see that happening.

We were flying above a blanket of clouds, the sky so unobstructed. You forgot how clear it was above the clouds, how different from being trapped beneath them when on the ground.

When you left one culture for another, there was a two-year mark, a rite of passage. All the expats talked about it. You started losing yourself, your mind, your connection to your roots. It sparked a flailing, a fear of falling. Should you go back? Go forward? You had to find out for yourself.

The captain announced our descent into St. Louis; the window suddenly fogged as we entered the cloud cover. I'd lived between the two worlds of matter and visions all my life, and now, I had two more disparate worlds, the Asian and the Midwestern, the American and the Japanese.

Japan was causing me to question everything, a place where individuals did not hold the power, but the group did. The old Japan where the ghosts of ancestors and the spirits of animals were the real religion. It made me question how I was raised. It made me question my core. It made me question God.

The view snapped out like a windblown quilt, the exhaling sky, the tops of rough-chested trees, the familiar patchwork of forest and farm. As we descended, both sides of the landing strip churned with mud. Spring was always like this there, thick, wet, grimy. I felt the familiar tug in my gut, the Missouri loam an umbilical cord that wrenched the belly.

I met a lot of Americans in Tokyo who'd left their homeland, searching for something. When I talked about home, which was not often, what surprised them most was not that I'd left. They'd sneer at Missouri, such a backward place, such a backwater. No, what surprised them was how much I loved the flesh of it, the soil, the expansive sky, the stench and texture. *If you're sophisticated,* their faces sneered, *if you're cool, you would never love a place like that.* But what are you to do when the earth where you were born is the same color and texture as your very body?

In the causeway, the air had the pong of spring. It brushed cheek and hair, a sweet, filthy presence. It riveted me in memory. It felt familiar and alien—both. *Natsukashi.*

Jason stood at a column behind the waiting area. I waved. He didn't seem to see me. He wore a worn-out Cardinals baseball hat, his red hair longer now. He'd grown crazy handsome. Girls and women turned for a second look. I stood almost on top of him before he recognized me.

"Pearl?" He reached down and touched my hair, moved in to hug me, hesitantly, because he knew the old me often recoiled from touch. I let myself fall against him. He wrapped his arms around my back, and I put my hands inside his jacket, held him over his plaid shirt. He smelled like pig and hay. I didn't know if he'd grown, or if I'd shrunk, but my face pressed against the plastic buttons at his chest. He said into my hair, "Pearl Elizabeth Swinton." He was the only person who knew me from root to toe.

He wore Father's boots. On top of the bloodstains from the farm were smudges of ultramarine blue and naphtha green. He pulled back, looked me up and down. "Are you okay? Are you sick?"

"No." I took a few steps back. "What do you mean?" I ran my hand through my hair, trying to tame it. "I just lost weight is all."

"You just look really pale." He took the bag from my hand.

"What a thing to say to a person you haven't seen in two years," I said. "I've been traveling for twenty-four hours straight." He tried to smile, but it came out as a scowl. I mumbled under my breath, "Why don't you try doing something different with your life and see how it affects you." He must've heard, because he walked away briskly with my bag, and I had to hurry to catch up.

It was a two-and-a-half-hour drive to Jason's house. We were in the orange truck, my old truck, a '59 Chevy with a stripe down the bed, and three on the tree. It was weird. I was a passenger on the trains in Japan and now a passenger in my old life. Still, the torn fabric of bench seat felt familiar and warm, as if I were finding something I'd lost, something I'd left behind.

Through the windshield, the sky stretched out in immense blue, with wisps of spring clouds. I put my head out the window and let the gust mess my hair. The overwhelming breadth and width of the sky—Tokyo had only the barest sliver. Air, so much air.

When we got to Jason's, we sat in his scrubby backyard and drank Budweiser. He talked about art school. He was having art shows up at the college. Of course his life was continuing on without me there, but it was hard to come to terms with. I wanted him to be the same old Jason. A broken bike had weeds growing through the spokes. Jason's old bike. The memories. They'd choke you if you weren't careful.

He barbequed store-bought beef and brought out ketchup, mustard, a bag of buns and potato chips. He burned the burgers, but we ate them anyway. Dusk came on, and we were serenaded by the croak and chirp of a Midwest evening. The jet lag, the memories, the beer.

We'd buried Lady Luck in the back corner of the yard. The handmade cross was still there. I got up, got another Bud from the cooler, and went to look at the grave. Jason joined me.

Lady Luck was a boy—his name was Father's sense of humor. He was a mutt. All his life he was tied to a chain next to a dilapidated dog house in the back yard. Father must've seen himself in that mongrel because he beat the dog up regularly. It made you want to vomit, thinking about it. When I left home at seventeen, I hauled the poor beast into my arms and got him out of there.

We'd had hunting dogs for a while, blue tics in a pen. Their only human contact outside hunting season was me throwing entrails over

air

the top of their cage. If one got on Father's nerves, he'd take him out to a field and put a bullet between his eyes. Every day I waited for Father to haul Lady Luck into his truck, take him to the woods and shoot him between the eyes.

When we got Lady Luck to Jason's house, we bathed him and found out he was white, not brown. You'd think years chained up and Father's kickings and beatings would make him distrust people, but it was as if the old Lady Luck died and a new one took his place—a happy, waddling, slobbering goofball. I thought he'd stick to me, but he attached himself to Jason's mom. When Mrs. Paulson was sober and painting, Lady Luck would be at her feet. Mrs. Paulson would dribble paint from the easel and it'd land on the dog, and for days he'd have ultramarine speckles, lemon dots, sage smears. Lady Luck died after a year. He was old. He was lucky to make it a year.

Mrs. Paulson came in crying. She couldn't get him to wake up. We went in and stood over him on Mrs. Paulson's bed. He looked deflated. The spirit was gone and all that was left was an empty body.

As Jason and I looked down at his grave, the screen door opened and Mrs. Paulson came out, wine bottle dangling. She'd aged. I'd seen it with my relatives. They could hold the booze for a while, then they hit a certain age and their bodies took revenge.

"How you doin', Mrs. Paulson?" I'd lived with her and Jason for four years. She was like a crazy aunt to me, not like a mother. But she wasn't even like a mother to Jason.

"Pearl, you're a sight for sore eyes," she said, tears springing. She was a sensitive soul, had a bottomless pit inside her that nothing could seem to fill. She hacked a smoker's cough, turned and went back inside.

"Wait here," Jason said. He ran inside and came back with a folded sheet of paper. "I saved this." He handed it to me.

It was the eulogy I'd written for Lady Luck. As we stood over the dog's grave, I read it in a whisper, the night critters like a backup orchestra, remembering when he died.

"I always felt so guilty I didn't do anything for you, Lady Luck. I didn't know that I could do anything. I think about that almost once a week. Why didn't I do anything? I want to apologize for that."

"But you did do something," Jason said. "You saved him."

"I think maybe your mom saved him," I said.

I continued reading. "I'm glad you had a year of happiness. I thank Jason and his mom for that. That you still had the love to give her, that was a miracle."

I had a realization as we stood there, Jason's work boots and my city boots spattered with mud. It hit me like a shock. Lady Luck had come into my life to take some of the beatings for me.

I said a silent prayer: *Whoever is out there, if there was such a thing as other lives, if people and animals are born again, maybe Lady Luck can come back and be loved from the beginning. Please let him be around someone who gives a shit about him from the beginning. Please.*

We went inside. Jason grabbed a couple beers and popped the tops. I walked to the corner of the living room where he had his studio. The easel was facing away; I picked my way over a paint-spattered tarp and tubes of oil to turn it.

I thought it was jet lag and too many beers and that I was seeing things that weren't there. He was painting a self-portrait, and the edges of his face and neck melted away at the sides as if the flesh had no boundaries. The face itself was smeared like a big burst of wind had blown the nose and eyes sideways. It was so close to Yuriko's paintings it was astonishing.

"You don't like it," Jason said.

"No, I like it," I said. He crossed his arms. "I like it," I repeated. How did I tell him, *It's that two people thousands of miles away could both be melting the edges of their faces. It opens my soul up so wide my innards become soup.*

Jason often mistook people's reactions to his art for dislike. When we were growing up, boys bullied Jason. The burly boys

air

thought he was a wimp. Low self-esteem was his quicksand. Now he was tall and muscular, but even the slightest wind could knock him down. *Oh, Jason, there are places in the world where men are different, where you wouldn't be judged for your gentleness.*

Jason said as if to himself, "Sometimes it's like I have no edges. I get close to knowing myself, but something blows me into confusion, and I feel chunks of me get blown on the wind. Like something out there doesn't want me to get to know myself." He took a long, deep swig of his beer.

When we'd lived together, I would come back from journalism school, swarming with the day's news, with local or global trauma, and his canvases would rip my chest open. I'd become aglow with the thing he was painting. I'd dream liquid, light, color. If he painted sky, I became the essence of sky, like some ancient god full of mythology and rancor. After my sky dreams, I'd be falling and floating, unable to get any ground purchase, any rootedness, for days or weeks. I swore his art gave me more visions.

"You really hate it, don't you?"

"Jason!" I turned to him. "What I'm thinking is I can't believe how powerful you are." The essence of his work swarmed the soul. I needed to say this to him, but I couldn't seem to figure out how.

He moved toward the sofa, shoulders slumped. "Jason, I like it." He didn't turn around. "Listen, you can't let one person decide if your art's good or not." He always did that. Put all his self-belief at other people's feet. "Maybe it's not about being good at all, but about just doing it." He slouched onto the sofa. "I'm not explaining it right."

I sat next to him. He wouldn't look at me. I didn't say anything else. Sometimes words just made things worse. We sat for a few minutes in silence.

"You going to go see your mom?" he asked. I finished my beer and got up to get another one. He said, "I see her and the twins around town sometimes."

"Yeah?" When I was seventeen, Mother had me committed. It was more complicated than that one sentence. Maybe I was out of control. I'd had a brutal father, an accomplice mother, a prostitute sister, visions of the apocalypse—and I was a teenager. It was a lethal combination.

In the end, I ran away from the psych ward, convinced Mother to let me go, to let me live my own life. That was when I moved in with Jason.

"I ran into your mother right after you left," Jason said. "We were both pumping gas. I said something about Japan, and she looked confused. I couldn't believe you didn't tell her you were leaving the country." He looked at me. I lit a cigarette. "When I told her, she looked like she was about to pass out."

I had tried to go see her before I moved. I'd parked a few houses down at the cul-de-sac where she'd moved with Jack. I watched her bundle the twins into the car. When she drove past me, I hunkered down so she wouldn't see, but she was already distracted by the kids.

"Does she ask about me?" I asked.

"She used to."

Later, we went to the corner gas station and bought another twelve pack. We sat on the sofa, told stories about Lady Luck, gossiped about Bonnie and some of the other kids from school, and drank. We drank and drank.

On the mattress in the corner of the living room the next morning, up early because of the jet lag, I stared up at the cracked ceiling. I'd slept beneath those cracks for five years.

Memories flooded. Maybe when you moved away, it was easier to remember the good things. Maybe with some distance, you got a better perspective. The painful stories sucked you in, but when you moved away, it let back in some of the delight.

air

I could taste Father's barbeque chicken. After the butchering, Mother would take three or four chickens, slice them up. Father would cook the meat for hours over charcoal in the barrel barbecue out back, basting it with butter. The charred meat, the burst of butter in the mouth, the smoky tenderness. Mother or I would make German potato salad and green beans, picked or dug up from the garden. We'd sit outside at the picnic table and feast. Later, Father would get his fiddle out. The depth of woe he could evoke with those strings.

I let the good memories wash over me as I lay counting the ceiling cracks. The smell of blackberries boiling on the stove in the summer as Mother put up jars of jam. The homemade bread rising on the hearth next to the fireplace before Mother switched to Wonder Bread. The time she helped me draw Native American designs in crayon on paper bags—an Osage shirt and headband for Halloween.

And the fireflies. Meghan, with her lanky teenage gait and my little girl self so full of spit, running through the darkened fields, chasing the sporadic flashes. We'd fling the open mouths of our canning jars upward, cupping each firefly, trapping it. I'd stand still and let one crawl up my arm, its head red and winged body black and thin, such light coming from something so fragile.

You thought the bad memories were hard, but it was the good memories that could trap you.

Jason walked into the room in sweats and a T-shirt. He had to work early. I got up, forced my lagged body into the shower. We drove to the farm where Jason worked slopping pig pens and bailing hay. I dropped him off and got behind the wheel.

My arm hanging out the window, the mucky smells of cow shit from nearby farms, and a sky so big you had to turn 360 degrees to take it in. I used to drive my truck for miles, just meandering, down rutted dirt roads, along flat highways, on back roads, pacing myself like a runner, losing myself like a runner.

I drove to IHOP and gorged myself on eggs, bacon, biscuits and a side order of pancakes. In Japan, for breakfast, Finn and I ate pickled vegetables, miso and rice. I thought I missed the big

American breakfast, but already the grease wasn't sitting well in my stomach.

I wore one of the tight-fitting tops Yuriko had bought for me, and it was getting way too much attention from the truckers and other dark-whiskered men. As I walked out, I could tell it was taking the old guys all they had not to reach out and pinch my ass. Here, if you wore tight clothes that showed your curves, you were asking for it.

I drove downtown to buy more appropriate clothes, something blousy with a bow, something polyester. There was a mall miles away, but I hated malls. When I walked into one, I couldn't breathe.

The downtown was a ghost town. Buildings boarded up. There were a few shops, a bridal shop, a shoe store, but nobody was on the sidewalk, nobody was shopping. I kept wondering where all the people were. Was it a holiday? Then I realized that this *was* all the people. It was the rural Midwest. There weren't any more people than this.

When I saw the shoe store, I realized maybe I hadn't come here to shop. I parked, found a couple quarters for the meter and went to the door beside the shoe store. The hall was so dark I had to feel my way with a hand on the wall. At the top, I took a deep breath, knocked. I heard rustling, a woman yell, "Just a moment, I gotta put some clothes on!" I could feel her press her body against the door to look through the keyhole. The door opened.

"Can I help you?" she asked, squinting.

"Bonnie?" She leaned farther into the hall. It was two in the afternoon, and she wore a white nightgown. She'd gained at least a hundred pounds and hadn't been skinny before that.

"Lord Jesus Christ, Pearl?" Her face opened, then shut hard and fast. "You're so pale. And so skinny. I thought you were a ghost." She laughed. "Well…come in. Come on in. I wish you'da called first."

Bonnie was my best friend. I guess I had no right to call her that. Even before I left, I hadn't seen her in years, except vaguely in the distance, towing a kid on her hip.

"I'm a mess. You shoulda called."

air

"I didn't know I was coming."

Guiding Light played on the television in the corner. Bonnie and I had spent our summers with the soaps, *As the World Turns*, *The Young and Restless*.

"Jackson's at school." Jackson was her son. She'd gotten pregnant in high school and was eight months along at graduation.

"He's a baby," I said whimsically.

"He's seven." She turned to me annoyed. "He ain't been a baby for years."

I'd met the kid only a couple times. After Bonnie got pregnant, I just couldn't take seeing her. Her bringing another life into the storyline like that, when we were only teenagers and didn't know who the hell we were. It confused me. It upset me, like Mother's new set of twins.

I sat on an orange sofa. The shag carpet was orange and the walls were orange. Against the far wall was the kitchen, and the fridge and stove were orange, too. Bonnie fussed around in the cupboards, brought over a bag of sour cream and onion potato chips and two cans of Diet Coke.

"I didn't know it was possible for you to get any skinnier."

"I'm not that skinny."

"You're a skeleton." She took a mouthful of chips and handed me the bag. "When was the last time I saw you?"

"That time at church." I'd seen her sitting a few pews up, her kid fidgeting beside her. She'd turned and caught my eye. The kid kept turning, kept staring at me with dark eyes and darker mouth. Afterward, out in front of the church, I told her I was moving to Japan. "Get as far away from this hellhole as I can get." It came out more shaky and bitter than I intended.

She had winced. "Well, that's about as far away as you can get." The kid stared up at me. We stood there awkward and quiet for a while. "Well, Jackson and me better be getting back. You take care of yourself over there in Japan."

She turned and walked off toward the parking lot, her kid a mini-human with his tiny footsteps freaking me out.

I knew it was the last time I'd see her for a long while. I also knew she would turn back, knew we needed one final moment. She did. We said goodbye without words. We were animals that shared the same pen for a while.

Bonnie went and got some napkins from the cupboard. "So, you got yourself a boyfriend over there?" she asked.

"Yes," I said. On the TV, Beth and Philip were fighting. I wished we could just watch the TV and not talk, live inside the fictitious lives for a while, pretend we were kids again.

"You should have someone to love. Everybody needs somebody."

"How's Byron?" I took a sip of Diet Coke and the burn of it going down reminded me of being a teenager.

"Still stocking at the shoe store. He come home last week with a pair of defective high heels. Let me get 'em."

She went into a back room and came out wobbly on spiked red stilettos. She still wore her white nightgown. She was so big, I couldn't imagine the weight per square millimeter on those tiny heels.

She laughed as she walked.

"You can't see no defects on 'em," I said. I couldn't believe how quickly I'd reverted to my twang.

"Don't know where I'd wear them."

"I know where Byron wants you to wear them," I said. She laughed, snorted, sat heavy on the sofa and wedged them off her chubby feet.

"How're you doin', really?" she asked, looking at me only briefly, then focusing on the chips. Bonnie had emotional intelligence. You could mistake her for stupid, but she wasn't.

"Can't seem to stay in my body." I hadn't meant to tell her the truth. "At work. Well, everywhere now."

"Like with the visions?" She talked with her mouth full, a mash of soggy chips.

"Yeah."

"I guess that's something that hasn't changed, huh?"

air

I sat hunched forward.

"Well, I don't know about being outside your body, but God must've given the visions to you, right? They're a God-given gift. They're for a purpose. None of it would be happening if it didn't have *some* meaning." She ate some more chips. "When you told me you was going to Japan, I thought won't it be a lot harder being around so much that's different? It's like you're poking the bear. What is she gonna do when she's outside and has a vision in Japan? Find some rickshaw to take her home?"

"I guess I was hoping someday they'd go away, like I'd grow out of them."

"Yeah, right." Bonnie laughed. My face fell. "Get over here and eat some of these." She wiped her greasy hand on her nightgown. When I didn't move, she said, "Seriously, Pearl, a strong wind is going to come and blow you off the planet if you don't eat something."

I took the bag. Bonnie gossiped about people we knew. Most of our classmates had kids now. I let her voice roll over me like a stream over rocks. It was nice, like watching a soap opera. After an hour, she said she had to go get dressed so she could pick up Jackson. I stood and headed toward the door.

"You can stay. Meet Jackson. He's a real big boy now."

"I'm going to see my mother."

"Oh," Bonnie said. "How's she doin'?"

I shrugged.

As I opened the door, she reached over and hugged me. At first, I resisted, but then I fell into her softness. She was like an overstuffed sofa that was hard to get out of.

"I'm glad you got yourself someone to love, Pearl. Real glad. Every one of us needs somebody to love."

I PULLED INTO the cul-de-sac and parked on the edge of the playground. It was one of those new developments, the houses all alike, three stories with siding and three floors rising above a two-car garage. Somebody's cookie-cutter fantasy of what a home should be.

I sat and sat and sat. Frozen. An hour went by before I was able to get out of the truck. I was shaking as I walked down the street and up to the two-story forest-green house. It looked like all the other houses, the only difference the street number on the mailbox. I pushed the doorbell and waited. The door opened. Jack stood behind the screen.

"Yeah, what?"

"Hi."

"Can I help you with something? I'm working…" He stopped, opened the screen door, and looked me up and down. His scrunched his face backward. "Pearl?"

He opened and closed his mouth like a fish in the bottom of a boat. He'd grown thinner, leaner. His hair was almost fully silver now, still cropped in a flat-top. He could've been in an ad for JCPenney.

"Your mother's not here." He leaned in closer. "Are you unwell?"

"What? No. I just came for a visit." I fidgeted on the small slab of concrete that was the front porch. His energy had always rattled

air

me. If we were animals in a pen, we would have used whatever we had to tear each other to shreds.

He stood holding the door, blocking the entry with his body. "I heard you moved to Japan."

"Yes." A car pulled into the driveway. I turned. Mother looked at me through the windshield. Her face went white.

"Sarah, look who's come for a visit," Jack screamed. The twins jumped out of the car. They must've been around eight years old.

"Hello. Who are you?" the boy asked, running up to me. I looked down at him in shock. I saw myself in his eyes. The instant connection I felt to him was a surprise.

"That's your Aunt Pearl," Mother said, coming up behind them with a bag of groceries. *Sister Pearl*, I didn't say, *not aunt, sister. I'm their half-sister, Mother.*

"We don't have an Aunt Pearl!" the girl said. They were dressed in matching blue-and-white polyester shirts and pants. They had our black hair and wan skin, Jack's small wiry body. All I knew about them was they were named Matthew and Katherine, Matt and Kat.

"I've met you before," the boy said.

"No," Mother said. "This is the first time."

"I met her before!" he screamed.

I smiled at him. I knew what he meant. I felt as if I knew him, too. He leaned against my arm.

"Jack, take the kids and get them cleaned up," Mother said, pulling the boy off me.

"I've got work—"

"Jack…" Mother's voice had a hysterical edge.

He opened the door and started pushing the twins from behind. "Left, right, left, right. Soldiers to your barracks."

The boy started whining, lifting his legs as if it pained or bored him or both, but the girl ran in, laughing. Jack screamed at her to take off her muddy shoes, but she pirouetted in the foyer. I followed Mother through a fancy living room full of heavy wood furniture to the kitchen.

"Pearl, you should've called." She put the groceries on the counter.

"I'm just in town for a few days." I hadn't even visited when I lived there. The truth of that hung in the air like smoke. She unpacked the groceries.

"You frying chicken?" I asked.

"Chicken and mashed potatoes and beans." She held two fryers wrapped in suction plastic. Father would've given her a hard time for buying that chicken from the grocery store. He used to say, *If you can't kill it, you got no business eatin' it.* He used to think city folks wanted all their food sanitized so they could live in a fantasy.

"I heard you were living in Japan." She reached to get a bowl out of the cabinet. Her long hair was rolled behind her head. She wore a powder blue leisure suit. She'd gotten fatter. On the farm, she did physical work and her muscles used to be twisted, hard and rubbery.

"Still am," I said.

She turned and looked at me. She looked me up and down, really looked at me. I realized this was why I was here, to get somebody to look at me, somebody who'd known me all my life. I didn't ask for much else from my mother. I was never allowed to ask for much else. I'd learned not to expect, not to ask. I was searching for one person to look at me so I could use it as a post in the ground to tie a rope to.

"Listen, you got to eat. Don't let yourself slip backward, Pearl. You're letting yourself slip backward." She looked helpless as she stared at me, hunched forward, her back curved and her arms useless. When I was little, after Father died, I'd lost so much weight I nearly disappeared.

Mother squared her shoulders, turned back to the counter. "You staying for dinner?"

"Sure." I cleared my throat. "Okay."

I had a vision once, when I was a kid, where Mother was Native American. She rode a horse to a clearing, and she was handing her baby over to another group of people also on horses. They weren't in

air

Missouri. It looked more like the American Southwest, with cliffs and scrubby trees.

She handed the kid over and was sobbing horribly as she turned the horse away, the wrench of it. She had to give the baby away. It was the only way to keep the child safe. She rode away on her horse, fast and hard.

I was the baby in the vision. As Mother heated lard in the skillet, I thought maybe this had all happened before. Maybe she'd had to leave me before. Maybe this relationship between us happened hundreds of times, and we'd lived this lesson over and over. "Has anybody heard from Meghan?" I asked. Another abandoned daughter.

"No," Mother said, turning to avoid the conversation. "Your Aunt May died." She pointed to a newspaper clipping on the fridge.

I wanted to ask more about Meghan, but knew it was useless. I went up to the clipping. May was mother's sister. It listed the survivors, so many names. Mother had twelve siblings. They were rough, toothless, full of past memories Mother wanted to forget.

We'd never visited anyone, except Aunt May. About the rest of them, I only knew tiny snippets, single snapshots, a couple lines of verse. I was used to it, this silence. The knife tip of our stories were buried deep in belly and bone.

Aunt May had a pig farm in Versailles, pronounced "Ver-sails." In her living room, she had hundreds of copies of *True Stories*, magazines about the size of *Reader's Digest*. I'd sneak six at a time, go find a place to hide and read. Father hated when I had my head in books. The stories were sordid, like the one about a handicapped girl whose brother brought teenage friends home, and the friends gave her candy to have sex with her. She didn't know what was going on. She ended up pregnant. We had no books in the house at home, no magazines, no stories. I filled myself with dozens of these morbid tales when I was at Aunt May's, hundreds.

We were in Versailles when a major tornado hit, hunkered down in the mud room. The house had a tin roof and the rain sounded like horses stampeding. We were surrounded by the smell of musty potatoes. Outside, the wind threw an old tire swing up into the air, breaking the rope. We all thought we were going to die.

"What'd she die of?" I asked, fingering the clipping.

"Cancer." Mother angled the tip of the knife into the hip of the bald chicken to slice off its thigh and leg. Many of Mother's relatives died of serious illnesses at relatively young ages. That was what untold stories did to you.

"I didn't know."

"No, you wouldn't know, would you?"

I turned to her, ready to burst. What was I supposed to do? Act all family-like when she and Jack had thrown me out, had started a new family and discarded me? Become Aunt Pearl to her kids so she wouldn't have to explain? It'd always been this unfair, and sometimes I was near to bursting with it, the pressure like a starved dog.

Jack came into the kitchen. "So, what happened over there? You run out of money?" he asked.

It took me a second to realize he was asking me about living in Japan. "No." I wanted to punch him in the face. I always wanted to punch Jack in the face.

"You're awful skinny. They don't feed you over there?"

"I don't…" I took a breath. "Mother, can we go somewhere and talk?"

"Pearl, you should've called. I've got to get dinner."

Jack put his hand on my shoulder. I winced. "Why don't you stay for dinner? Right, Sarah? That's the right thing to do."

The last time I saw both of them, we'd struck a deal. I'd go live somewhere else and let them have their normal life away from me and my visions, and they wouldn't commit me to Fulton State Hospital, home of the truly insane. How long had it been? Eight years?

I sat at the table, and Mother put a glass of sweating iced tea in front of me. She went back to the counter and covered the chicken thighs, breasts and legs in raw egg, rolled them in flour and put them in the skillet to fry. She peeled potatoes, chopped them and put them in boiling water. She'd been doing this ritual of cooking for decades and centuries, as far back as time. In the farmhouse, she used to stand

air

at the window and watch the bird feeder while she washed dishes. I used to love her expression when a bird hovered and fluttered, her eyes light and face calm, their wings the pulse of her heart.

Jack came up to where I sat and crossed his arms. "So, what've you been up to?" He was always so fit, so lean and angular. If there had been just even the smallest crack. He worked as an Army recruiter down at Fort Leonard Wood.

"I'm a journalist. I work in a newsroom." I said it loud enough for Mother to hear over the sizzling.

"Money in that?"

I rolled my eyes. Mother said, "Jack, I need you to go check on the kids."

I wanted to talk more about what I was doing. I wanted Mother to know what a good job I had, what an important person I was.

Jack left, and Mother took a head of iceberg from the refrigerator, chopped it with a big knife. She put the bowl of lettuce on the table along with a plastic bottle of ranch dressing. She put the chicken on a platter, mashed the potatoes and plopped it into a bowl.

A silence settled. I watched Mother make the food, start to fill the dishwasher, finish setting the table. I was supposed to be helping. In Missouri, if you were a girl, you helped in the kitchen or else.

"It's time to eat," Mother called after a while to the other room.

Matt and Kat ran in, and Jack followed. The kids talked excitedly, scraping the heavy wooden dining chairs as they lugged them out and climbed up. When I was growing up, no one was allowed to talk at the dinner table. Dinner was always just the smacking of lips and the clink of silverware. The kids chattered on even after we started eating, and I looked at Mother, expecting her to yell for quiet, but she didn't.

The girl had a green bean on the end of what seemed like a pitchfork in her tiny hands. She wiggled it around. "Aunt Pearl," she said, "where do you live?"

"Japan," I said. I realized I had to be careful, since the kids thought I was an aunt, not to call my mother *Mother*.

"Where's Japan?"

"Stupid. The teacher showed us in school. It's across the ocean." The boy smiled at me.

"Can we come visit you?" the girl asked. She made a hole in her mashed potatoes with her spoon and began fighting with Matt over the gravy so she could create a gravy lake.

"Quit playing with your food," Mother snapped. "Eat your dinners now."

Mother looked at me, tears in her eyes. No, they would never come visit me. I was the only one who knew Mother's old life, knew the first man she'd married. Nothing around her now existed to remind her of that old life, and here in one day was her long-lost daughter. She never did anything to stop Father from beating Lady Luck. She never did anything to stop Father from beating me. He was a mean sonofabitch. His rage transferred to my flesh. He'd beat me with a belt and smash me down with his words. She never did anything about that.

Jack said too loud, "We just got back from Disneyland, right kids?"

The kids started screaming. "I met Goofy!" Then, "We rode Magic Mountain!" They leaned their faces into each other and screamed in competition over who'd had the most fun at Disneyland. Mother stared at her plate. I willed her to look up but she didn't.

Who was I to judge her for this new life? I was in Japan now, shutting the door on my past. I'd learned real good. I'd learned from the master. Toughen up, right, Mom?

Dinner was over. The kids went to the living room to watch a video. Jack disappeared. As Mother cleared up, I looked at some of the pictures on the wall. I knew there wouldn't be pictures of me, or Matt and Kat would've recognized me as soon as they saw me. None of Father. Certainly none of Meghan. It shouldn't have surprised me.

She had a new husband now, and memories of the old one had to go. Father brought the smell of the outdoors into the house, the grit and shit. He traipsed in the woods, he tracked in the feral, and brought the stench of the wild inside. My childhood was about stench. But this new house had no sign of the detritus of the wild

air

earth, only the bottled scent of air freshener. No sign of the trauma either. Mother had always wanted a clean life. Finally she'd gotten it.

When she was happy, Mother used to stand in the doorway between the kitchen and living room in the farmhouse, potatoes boiling on the stove behind her, and she would face us and laugh and lift her leg and jig it back and forth at the knee. Her little happy dance, Father and me as her audience. How the good memories floated up.

She used to be impressed with my accomplishments, the trophies I won at school, the good grades, how I taught myself guitar. I'd overhear her talking to somebody like Aunt May on the phone. *Pearl can do anything.* She'd say it with real delight. *Pearl can do anything she puts her mind to.*

The pride and the subjugation. Both realities were true. One held in the palm of each hand. I didn't know how to hold these two truths in my soul. I had no idea where the center was between these two points that would create some balance.

I sat watching cartoons with the kids. Mother came in, and said, "Pearl, why don't you spend the night? We got a spare room." I didn't like this new house. It smelled like fake perfume. It purred with too many appliances. It was wrapped in suction plastic.

"I think I've got to get the truck back to Jason."

"It'd sure be nice if you could stay."

"Okay." I grew confused. "Okay."

I called Jason, and he said I could keep the truck as long as I needed it. There was something soft in his voice. When eight o'clock came and Mother told the twins it was bedtime, I was happy to go, too. Sitting there like everything was normal took it right out of me, tired me to the bone. There was something about the boy, the way he looked at me with expectation.

The next morning the alarm said six a.m. I slept in a Disneyland sweatshirt with the tag attached that Mother gave me. As I changed into my clothes, I could hear the little girl downstairs in the kitchen. I walked out, and when I passed the kids' room, I noticed the door was partially open. The boy stood at a desk.

"Hi, Matt," I said. He jumped. I went in. "What're you doing?"

An ant farm sat on the desk. Dozens of ants climbed hills. I looked at it and looked at Matt. He seemed scared. "What's wrong? Is something wrong with the ants?"

He shook his head. "Dad doesn't like it."

A rage grew in me. *Why're you afraid of your dad?*

"I was talking to the ants," he whispered.

"Oh, I talk to ants, too. Every time I see an ant hill, I kneel down and have a conversation. What are yours telling you?"

"Shhh," Matt said, looking at the open door. "I told Dad they talked, and he got real mad."

He turned and put his face up to the plastic ant farm. I saw a sheet of paper peering from the desk drawer and pulled it out. It was a crayon drawing. I couldn't tell what it was, maybe a flower. There was something shocking about it, something so open in it, truthful. I felt a physical pain in my gut looking at it.

"Did you draw this?"

He nodded, but kept looking wide-eyed at the ants. He seemed to be trying to speak to them telepathically.

I had a sudden memory. I'd been just a toddler, four maybe, sitting on the kitchen floor, coloring a picture. I'd forgotten how

air

much I adored doing art, how much the colors entered my soul, how the process of opening to the textures felt like my visions. Father had come in from doing yard work. Something triggered him. Some small thing brought up the fear and rage in him. He started screaming. His body writhed with fury. I was so open, coloring the glory of the world, and his screaming started me shaking. I held the crayon while I quivered and trembled. I couldn't even run away from him. Just sat at his feet and quaked.

The boy turned and grabbed the drawing. "No," he said, "I can't talk to flowers either." He stuffed the drawing in the drawer. "Dad doesn't like it."

"What does Dad not like?" Jack stood at the open door. Matt's face fell. I put my arm around his small shoulders. "Matt, go on down to breakfast now, the pancakes are getting cold," Jack said. The boy gave me a pleading look and ran out the door. Jack came in and looked at me. He put his hand on the ant farm, and I held my breath, thinking he was going to take it or smash it.

"Don't," Jack said in a low voice. "Just don't."

He'd missed a spot shaving near his earlobe.

"Sarah is already more upset than I've seen her in years. Go back to where you came from. You and your crazy sister need to leave well enough alone."

The mention of Meghan was like a fist to the side of my head. I held the chair for support. Where was she? Did anyone know? How disposable the girls of this family were.

"I will not allow any of this in my house." His knuckles were white as he held the ant farm. "If this house were a country, do you think it could defend itself with citizens like you running around, half out of their minds? I will protect this family."

I wanted to keep my cool, but I couldn't. "Why don't you try traveling sometime, and I don't mean in some military box. Why don't you try opening your little tiny mind just one inch?" I turned to leave. He grabbed my arm.

"No, you listen. You almost destroyed my marriage. You're not going to mess with this family."

"I almost destroyed your marriage?" I asked incredulously. "Mother was ready to kick me to the curb the second she met you."

"What are you talking about?" He looked at me confused.

"What are *you* talking about?" I looked at him confused.

I had to get out of that house. Something deep was threatening to overwhelm. I'd lost my whole family. I'd lost the very earth beneath my feet. "You got everything. Everything!" I shoved around him and headed toward the door.

"Poor Pearl. Poor little Pearl," he said behind me. "Everybody feels sorry for you. Give me a break. You know exactly what you're doing. You know exactly how destructive you are. Anything that's normal, anything civilized, you make sure you somehow, someway, figure out how to tear it down." I turned to him. Right then I could've destroyed his face, beat it to a pulp. We faced off, both of us muscle-taut and ready. I would've fought him. I'd done it before, when I was a teenager, thrown myself at assholes bigger than him, gotten myself beaten up, but still gotten a few punches of my own in. Made a few guys bleed.

"Jack? Pearl? What's going on?" Mother looked in at us from the crack at the door. She wore a housecoat and slippers.

"Nothing," Jack said. "We'll be right there. Pearl and I are just having a little…discussion."

"I'm leaving," I said. I went by Mother into the hall.

"You don't want any breakfast?" she asked.

I rushed down the hall. I felt a rage welling in the belly. As I opened the front door, Mother ran up behind me.

"Hold on, just a second." When I kept moving out the door, she clicked her tongue. "Just hold on one second, Pearl. For God's sake, one second!" Again that hysteria in her voice. I stood stock still on the porch with my back to the door. She disappeared into the house.

It was so quiet in the cul-de-sac, so deathly quiet, everything so manicured the wild had nowhere to hide, nowhere to make its noise. I heard Mother behind me and turned. "I just wanted you to have something to take with you." I grabbed the paper bag from her hand.

air

"Come back whenever you want, Pearl. You're welcome. Come back anytime."

I opened the bag while driving. It was a sandwich, a fried chicken sandwich with a thick slab of Velveeta. I couldn't take the furor building in me. All my life I was thrown out. First, it was Father with his rage, making it impossible to have any kind of life. Now it was Jack and his control. Always these people like angry dogs barking at the gate, refusing to let me in, refusing to let me be.

I rolled down the window and held the sandwich over the road as I drove. What was worse? Thinking my mother didn't love me, or thinking that she did? Yuriko's words came back to me. *You don't think anybody can love you, Pearl.* Where did Yuriko think I learned about love?

I let the sandwich slip from my fingers.

RANDOM BACK ROADS. Farm and forest, barbed wire, the pong of cow shit. Hours and empty miles of it. I drove and drove. I did this as a teenager, too, meandering down gravel roads, passing farm and forest, thinking. It was like long-distance running, but a person could smoke.

There'd been a spate of tornadoes. They always came in spring, but they seemed to be getting worse. Here and there wreckage. Trees uprooted. Barns tattered like fallen Legos. Engorged winds. Like the floating pumpkins in Hokkaido, the twisted barbed wire looked almost like art.

How could you find yourself when the very earth beneath your feet was unstable? How could you figure out how you were or what you wanted, or how you wanted to grow up, if you couldn't even trust the air or the water? What did that do to your psyche? What did that do to your soul?

My head lolled toward oblivion. I couldn't seem to stop myself from falling into sleep. It happened sometimes, not really sleep but mini-comas like unconscious visions. I'd be pondering something, and my body would just shut down. I cranked down the window, let the air snap my hair, turned the country station up and lit a Marlboro Light. Dolly Pardon's twang.

How had everything gone so wrong with my family? Even Bonnie had a mother who visited her. Even Jason's alcoholic mother didn't abandon him. Mine was so broken. The last time I saw

air

Meghan, she was taking off in a beat-up blue truck for California. Now, nobody knew where she was. My head bobbed like a dashboard dog's.

It went back generations. As soon as my mother married, she cut off most her family. She thought she'd married above her station, but she hadn't. Every time my train of thought went this way, I grew confused and left my body. Mother wanted off the land, away from her people. And now here I was living as far away as I could get. I turned up the radio and blared Hank Williams.

Floating above my body, I looked down at myself driving the orange truck, the sharp profile, the crazy black hair like a nest, the cigarette burning. Still the beauty, even with the land raped by the winds, could catch me in the throat, juxtaposition of red barn, broken-down farmhouse, field of thick farm beasts—like a poet's dream. But I didn't belong here anymore, and I'd never belong in Tokyo.

I lived in the space in between. Every step I took forward was movement with no ground, a leap onto air. Living in Tokyo was like spending my life floating. I'd chosen it, this floating life. Did it make it easier to know I'd chosen it? It had its consequences—no traditions, not even language to comfort you. But it had its benefits, too. I was beginning to see so much.

I passed the Current River, a body of water that ebbed in the veins of my memories. When I was at journalism school, a *National Geographic* photographer came for a photo shoot of the rivers of middle America. He'd contacted the university, seeking a guide. They put me in charge of showing him around. Theodore was short and balding and had bad teeth. We drove around in his rented Impala. I took him to the Current. I took him to the cliff where Meghan and I once smashed a box of thrift store dishes. I took him to where Father used to fish on the Missouri. I drove him to the Osage and the Meramec. In the end, he let me position the tripod and set up about half the shots, heaping praise on my "vision" and my "eye." I melted. Praise was hard to come here. I told him about my plans to move to

Japan. He took shots of the Mississippi. We were on the scabby shore.

"When you go abroad, your whole life will blow up like a balloon. When you do something big like that, your life will just keep expanding." He stood with his camera on his hip, talking to me like a real person. Dragonflies buzzed low over a stagnant pool. I remembered it as if it were yesterday. "You'll have to keep broadening your horizons to keep the balloon full. You'll have to keep it from deflating."

But did freedom carry a price? Would this new floating life mean I'd never fit anywhere ever again? I often felt as if I'd climbed out to the end of a branch and at any moment it could break off.

Town. I forced myself back into my body. I drove past the high school, past the outdoor track. As a sophomore, I ran long-distance. Competed and won. I could go miles. The coach said he'd never seen such stamina. He'd spit his chew and say I had real potential. I had this way of dealing with pain when I was running. When it started to hurt, I'd study the ache. What was pain? A sensation, a pressure, nothing more. It didn't have to control you.

But then, Meghan showed up. Some things could control you. After that I got drunk a lot, pulled men off her, smoked pack after pack, wrecked my car. I shouldn't blame Meghan. Everybody blamed Meghan. Some people were easy to blame, like the earth.

I didn't know why I was taking this trip down memory lane. No good could come of it. I drove past Holy Cross, the fenced complex of church, primary school, rectory, housing for the nuns. Next to Holy Cross, the graveyard where Father was buried. I had never been back to Father's grave after the funeral. I could revisit a dog's grave, but a Father's was too much to bear.

air

"Look in the truck bed." Jason was driving now. I was a passenger again. I'd somehow made it back to Jason's house and passed out on the corner mattress. I had no idea how long I'd been sleeping when Jason woke me up. In the truck, I looked through the murky back window and could just make out two sleeping bags and a brown grocery sack.

"That's part of the surprise," he said. We drove for about thirty-five minutes, talking about small things. When he turned down the familiar gravel road, I knew the other part of the surprise.

"I'm not doing it," I said to his profile. I lit another cigarette. "You can't make me do it."

"Don't worry. That's not what we're here for."

We pulled up to the hangar. In the field next to us a young woman was landing beneath a tricolored parachute.

When you come in for a landing, you're taught to wait until you're close to the ground, then pull both toggles down to a V at your crotch. That way, the chute lifts you up and deposits you on tiptoe. Pull too soon, and the wind whips you up and lets you go and you hit the ground hard. Only a few feet marked the difference between a soft landing and a good bruising.

That first time I skydived, as I was coming in for a landing, I'd pulled the toggles and hit the scrub grass on tiptoe, like a ballerina.

But then I'd fallen on my back and the wind took my chute. I was dragged across the knotty landing strip. I scrambled for foot purchase, clawed for hand purchase, grabbed for chute purchase. I was thumped and tugged and bounced along the gnarly field.

The drop zone staff stood back, watched and laughed. They laughed and laughed.

Jason was leading the way into the hangar. A jump master and a half-dozen students were sitting in chairs in the cavernous room, eating lunch. The girl who'd just landed came in hauling her parachute in her arms.

"Mack!" Jason yelled. The jump master looked up. It was the same guy who'd been with me on that first flight when I'd freaked out. I'd almost died. Mack had risked his life, leaning out of the plane, grabbing me and hauling me back in by my parachute. I could've died. He could've died.

Mack did a double take when he saw me. He stood and turned to the group of students. "That's her. That's the one I've been telling you about."

Mack and the others stood. They started applauding. I was getting a standing ovation. I spread my arms, put one foot in front of the other and curtsied. I turned this way and that and curtsied and bowed. They clapped and clapped.

Jason and I helped ourselves to the ham sandwiches and bean salad. We stayed for a few hours, watching the students taxi off in the single-engine Cessna, waiting until they came floating to the ground. A few of them asked me about my legendary first skydive, but they all already knew the story. I avoided Mack. When he'd gotten me back into the plane on that fateful first jump, he'd turned to the pilot and screamed at him to fly around and get the plane back in position. He'd hollered at me, "I've never had anyone die on me, and you're not going to be the first. Now get your ass up and get out." And I had. I'd climbed the strut. I'd arched. I'd flown. I owed him a lot, and I couldn't talk to him.

Late afternoon Jason said we had to go. He rushed me back to the truck. "Now for the second part of your surprise."

"I thought we were spending the night here."

"No, not here."

As we entered the highway back toward home, he said, "I just wanted to show you how you're quite the legend around the drop zone."

"Legend of the fool," I replied.

"It's not just that."

I snorted.

air

"Okay, it is that, but it's more than that. How many times did you skydive after that first time? Ten?"

"Eleven."

"Not many people who are that scared keep putting themselves out there like that. I mean, come on. You're scared shitless, but you just keep throwing yourself out of the plane. Who does that?"

I lit a cigarette.

"You should've talked to Mack. He actually has a lot of respect for you."

When Jason drove through town and kept going east, before he even turned down Powwow, I knew where we were heading. He pulled up to the house where I grew up and idled. It was two stories and made of wood from the forest. Father had built it with his own hands. A big oak took up half the front yard. The upstairs had dormer windows. The new owners had added red shutters, and the front lawn was thicker and greener, but the house was pretty much the same. My whole self had been defined by this place. I wasn't sure I wanted to be here. Memories of the past already threatened to take me over, and here I was staring it in the face. I wasn't sure it was helping.

"Seen enough?" Jason asked. He turned left onto a road next to the house. We rattled two miles over uneven dirt and deep potholes. The barns and fields opened up like a painting. This was my first love, this earth, that field for the cows, those oaks and elms, that parcel we used to garden. The pulse of it made my heart beat faster.

It was a different place now. The barn had been fixed up, painted firehouse red, and the x-shaped slats on the doors were now a pure white. This acreage had sold separately from the house. When we owned it, the barn doors were rotting, the paint flaking. Outside were wrought-iron tables and chairs. They'd hung metal sculptures of chickens. They'd mowed. They'd landscaped. It was like something you'd see in a magazine.

"Your mom told me the owners are only here a couple months in late summer."

I opened the truck door. The smell was of dirt and sap. I could have curled up right there by the truck and slept. Jason grabbed the sleeping bags. I carried the grocery sack. We both knew where we were going as we headed for the forest line. Crisp bite to the air, the kind of air where you just see the edges of your breath. Winter lingered. Underfoot, a blanket of new wet growth. Branches stood in silhouette against a blue sky. We went deeper and deeper. Trees and shrubs were overgrown. We tore our way through thick brush.

Jason parted some branches and there it was. The clearing. It glowed silver. I'd spent my childhood here. If you kept walking through the forest another quarter mile, you'd come to the back of the house.

He led me to a flat rock. "I brought the rock in. The log is all mulch now, and you can barely sit on it."

The sassafras, the grass that leaned sideways like long hair, the copse of alders, the stinky stagnant pond, the crunch underfoot of forest debris. When I was little, I felt no separation with this forest. My whole childhood I was no different from a tree. I saw my flesh as bark, my hair as leaves. My blood and the sap inside the tree were the same.

I understood little Matt perfectly—ants were people, too, and so were twigs, squirrels, conkers, granddaddy longlegs. Now, as I sat there, I felt only separation. They beat separation into you. Some long ago plan. I knew this truth in my bones, and I didn't know how to resist it or what to do about it.

I went over to the sassafras and put my palm flat against the knobby bark. I never could understand how someone could *own* a tree. How could a person own a piece of earth? Wasn't it a given that at the very least the earth itself was free to all who were born to it? People, plants, animals, rocks and rivers?

"You know, you look like a totally different person," Jason said. I put my hand up to my hair, smoothed down my wrinkly clothes.

"I don't mean your clothes." He handed me an apple. I took out a Marlboro Light, lit it. He bit wide-mouthed into the flesh of his apple.

"What do you mean I'm different?"

"You're just…" He hesitated. "Different."

air

"So, I look bad. That's what you're saying, right? Ever since I got here everybody says I look bad." I stood above him and crossed my arms. It was dusk, and the light glowed his face orange, his red hair, blue eyes, the orange tint of his skin. His face was a sunset.

"You do look worn out, like the world is sucking you dry. But that's not what I'm talking about."

"Thanks."

"Something's different. I'll let you know when I figure it out."

"Thanks again."

"The good news is you look ten years younger out here. You're still wearing the pouch. That's a good sign."

"I feel younger." I felt grief seep out of me into the soil.

"At least the new owners didn't cut the forest down and sell it to Walmart."

Jason stood and kissed me. His lips felt like pond water, sassafras bark, like the sounds of the tree frogs. I felt an insatiable hunger, for him, for these woods. I wanted to eat his flesh and devour his innards. He kissed me deeper, and then we were on the ground.

"Jason," I said, trying halfheartedly to push him away. "I…" We'd had sex once before, in the airplane hangar at the drop zone, the night before my first skydive. After that, we'd just been friends. When I was in college, I couldn't live with him and sleep with him. It would've meant we would end up married. It would've ruined my life.

"Don't talk," Jason begged, body pressed against body. "Please for once, just please shut up."

Thighs, hands, sweat, grunts. Hair twigs, belly dirt, shoulder rocks. I felt myself enter my body. I felt myself fully as flesh again. All the floating disappeared. I'd been missing for a long time. With the re-entry, a crazy surge of physical pain. My body was seared by a storehouse of memories. An excruciating throbbing in the gut, deep aches in the shoulders, a darkness in the womb. I thrashed with the pain. I took Jason on the wild ride of my pain.

Jason had his own demons. Inside he was all mush, something to do with his alcoholic mother. I'd noticed it the first time we'd made love. I couldn't find traction. You couldn't find a place to put your feet inside Jason. He was hollowed out. Being with him made me feel as if I was falling, falling.

Afterward, we lay naked on the leaves. It was cold, the bitter breeze on thighs and breasts. The sun was setting. The flesh pimpled.

"Listen, I'm going to ask you something and don't say no right away. Think about it." I moved uncomfortably in his arms, but he tightened his grip and put his face in my hair, and I could barely hear him. "Stay. Don't go back."

I turned and looked into his face. He looked so young, like a little boy.

"I have a life there."

"A life that's sucking you dry. You need to be near this." He took a damp clod of earth and crumbled it along my thigh, rubbed it in.

"Jason, I have a career." I shoved the dirt away, tried to stand. He held me tight.

"Let go." He loosened his arms, and I stood. "Nobody's asked me anything about Japan since I got back. No one's asked me a single goddamn question about my job as an editor of a newspaper! I spend my whole life with no one ever asking, like I don't even exist if I don't live in this shithole."

"You could have a career here."

"Give me a break. Work for the *Eagle Tribune*?" I panted with rage and paced. "I hate how women turn out here. Their greatest pride and joy is how clean they can keep their fucking house."

"Pearl, you can count every one of your ribs."

I gave him an annoyed look. "Don't change the subject."

"I'm not saying you don't look fantastic."

"Stop with my body. This has nothing to do with my body."

"It has everything…" Jason bolted upright and pointed at me. "I'm not saying in some heroin chic way you don't look fucking fantastic. But your body is telling its own story, and it *ain't* pretty. Obviously, something *isn't* working in your new life. Nobody can be that skinny!"

air

"Get off my body! What is this about my body?"

Jason said, "You go on about cutting down forests to build a Walmart, about how precious the earth is, and you're doing the same fucking thing to your body. You're treating your body the way people throw garbage out their car windows."

I wanted to smack him. I yanked my blouse off the ground and put it on, misaligning the buttons and having to do it again while Jason watched. It was thin material and I had no bra on, and it still left my crotch showing. Jason wouldn't stop staring, so I leaned down and put my face in his.

"It's like I'm a balloon, okay? Going to Japan has expanded the balloon. It's not just about the career. How am I ever going to figure myself out if I stay here? I have to expand. If I move back now, I'll lose the air and the balloon will deflate."

Jason quickly kissed me, a peck, then pulled himself to his feet. I looked at his body. It was shocking, beautiful, like a healthy lean pure-bred dog. I felt fragile and breakable next to him. I'd only been around wan and small city men for more than two years. Finn was British and so pale, so painfully thin. Thinking about Finn surged me with guilt.

Jason put on his trousers. "I'm worried about your balloon exploding. You think nobody here in Missouri gives a damn about you." His voice lowered to a whisper. "But I do. I care about you." The buzzing started at the base of my skull. My toes curled hard over sharp twigs. Jason leaned down, picked up my trousers and started to hand them to me. "Meanwhile, could you please put on some pants? You're driving me…"

I entered my father's body, became my father, felt the darkness of his psyche as my darkness, the gloom, the terrifying shadows. I flushed backward with him until he was a little boy, watched him being beaten with a belt, saw other boys chasing him through the woods, throwing rocks, heard his father insulting him, saw him running and running, such cruelty on such a tiny child's head. No stories were ever told about Father before he died or afterward, so I'd never known his life as a child. I saw tiny moments of solace, Father as a boy, hiding in hollowed-out trees in the woods, or by himself in a boat on the river, the only times he knew any peace.

I went further back still, became the embryo, further still entering the bloodstream of his father. Back and back, witnessing violence, hatred, madness. I saw an ancestor murder his wife, striking the back of her head with a hoe. How it was kept within the family, never spoken about afterward. Still backward, down generations.

Behind the ignorance and blindness, I could feel a pulse of love that no one dared to explore. I felt the love back generations. They had this belief that it wasn't the hurt that broke you, but the love. They were scared of the love.

I woke up half-naked, twisted in the dirt.

"Oh, Pearl." Jason lifted me. It had grown dark, and the forest was in silhouette. His hands were shaking, his eyes hooded. He looked about to say something, but then sighed and shook his head. "We need to get your pants on. Let's get your pants back on you."

As he tried to get the trousers around my feet, my mother's voice from childhood, *You can't live like this and survive in the real world, Pearl. You need to toughen up.*

Toughen up, Pearl. Toughen. Up.

ETAL STAIRS. SYRINGES. A steaming mound of dog shit. Candy wrappers. Up and up. So many stairs. Swirling ground beneath steel grid. So boring, this climb. Endless. Below us a bald courtyard with a bench blown in half as if someone had thrown a bomb, goo on the butt of my palm from the railing. The walls were concrete block. You could bloody your knuckles with one swift punch. You could break your hand if you pummeled the wall hard enough.

We were in the rough part of Tokyo at a housing development. Yuriko had brought me. It was a surprise.

"One more flight," she panted.

I wanted to go home. I wanted to get wasted. I wanted to get out of my mind. I'd been back from the Midwest for about two months. The clouds were thick and black. I hadn't been spending much time with Finn. He was upset. I told myself that any day now the darkness would lift, and I would get back to normal. I would be with Finn and we would live happily ever after. Any day now.

"Come on. I know you like adventure." Yuriko turned and smiled. For the past two months, she'd been way too nice. "You know you're not alone, right? I've been through this. You miss home. I know it feels horrible. Home is nowhere you really want to be, but you can't really call this place home either, right? I've had my moments about Seattle. It's gut-wrenching. I don't think anyone who

air

hasn't left their country behind could possibly understand how hard it is."

I couldn't stop seeing Jason at the St. Louis airport. He was bent sideways like an alder in the wind, in ripped jeans and Father's boots, his flesh begging. He looked shell shocked. I knew he thought I'd stay after the vision in the clearing. Didn't he see I'd be sucked back into the muck of that old twisted life? Didn't he see I would barely survive?

I forced myself to get on that plane. I couldn't stop sobbing; my body was racked with it. The woman next to me had asked, "Did someone die, dear?" I nodded. Nodded and nodded, squeezing my face. "Yes, someone is dying." I picked furiously at my thumb. "Someone is dying."

Yuriko turned onto one of the landings. Gray walls and gray doors and gray railings. We walked down an outside walkway. She knocked on one of the doors.

A small woman who looked Indian answered. The smell was curry and cigarettes. The living room walls were made of warped clapboard, and the carpet was matted and pulling up at the corners. The furniture was heavy and floral and overwhelmed the room.

Yuriko introduced us, but I missed the woman's name. She pushed me forward. "She's going first."

To the back of the house and into a tiny kitchen. She was so small. I stood a full head above her. She pointed to a folding chair. The box that heated the water for the sink was right behind my head and I was forced to lean forward. The tablecloth had pictures of toasters. Gnats flitted around my face.

The woman's hair had slipped from its clip and wisps poked out like antennae. She turned to a side table and lit incense. The smell was chalky, earthy. She took a lime velvet bag out of a drawer, pulled the drawstring and extracted a deck of cards.

I should've known she was a psychic. What else could she have been? I despised psychics. In the newsroom, we made brutal fun of them. Psychics lived in trailer parks, drank tall-neck Millers and had Lucky Strikes dangling from cracked lips.

"Please give me your hands." Despite myself I reached forward. She had dirt beneath the fingernails. A gnat landed on my nose.

She closed her eyes, chanted under her breath, swayed in the metal chair. I felt my body swaying with her. When she opened her eyes, her pupils were dilated. She pulled her hands back and shuffled the cards, keeping up a low tone in her throat. She turned ten cards over onto the table.

She reminded me of a fake version of the priests at Holy Cross, with their chanting and swinging of the engraved censer full of frankincense. She reminded me of a sillier version of Usui's rituals at his closet altar. I'd been reading about different religions, inspired by Usui, Buddhism, Shintoism, Hinduism, Islam. She reminded me of fake version of these, too.

"You do not trust magic." She floated her outstretched hands over the cards. "This is why they will keep talking to you the way they do, because you have no trust for mystery. They will scream loudly at you until you pay attention. Is it nightmares you have? So many nightmares. There is a message the gods want to convey, but you will not listen. So the gods give you these nightmares so you have to listen." She used air quotes around the word "nightmares."

"These nightmares are all over the place. Different themes. Different messages. Sometimes there is no connection between any of them. They do not make sense to you because there is no one theme. When you are ready to listen, they will calm down. When you are ready, they will make sense."

I crossed my arms over my chest.

"This comes from your family, a long line of it in the family. But you have the chance to hold this gift in a powerful way. Before not so powerful. Before many could not handle the ghosts speaking to them, and they decided it was better to die than to have to understand.

"You are a powerful soul who could help many in this world." I snorted. "The magic isn't wrong. It's the not listening that causes so many problems." She stopped and breathed heavily. "Many in the family. So many. Many in the past, and many will come in the future."

air

I felt sweaty. It wasn't hot, but trickles of sweat traveled down my spine. I hadn't been feeling well since I'd gotten back.

"When you wear yourself down, there will be trouble. Not just small trouble, but very big trouble. You must be careful with this physical body that your soul has chosen to enter. It can take only so much. Too much and it will crack. It is like the earth, yes? If you pollute the earth, it falls apart. The same for the body. I am sure you understand this."

I lifted my eyes to the ceiling. She was just a mind reader. She was just repeating what Jason said to me. I tried to clear my mind. She reached forward, rested her forearms on the cards and took my hands again.

"But it is not just how you treat your body. There are other darknesses of the world. Someone who is sensitive must be very careful with the ugliness." She started to cry, and I pulled back at my hands, but she held on.

"I am sorry. I am sorry. You are such a beautiful, powerful soul. So beautiful, so gentle. I know that many have beaten you down. I am sorry for this. They fear such power, such beauty, for it shows them their own lost beauty. Can you understand?"

I sighed.

"When they see the light in you, when they see this love you have for the world, they must wipe it out. They must wipe it out." She slammed her fist down onto the table. "It has been wiped out of them. It must now be wiped out of you! How dare you hold on to it! How dare you!" I felt sick to my stomach.

"There is much darkness to come for you. I am so sorry." She sniffed, wiped her face on the tablecloth. "You are in a place of manifesting negatively. When you're not aligned with spirit, you'll bring into your life what you do not want. Then you must violently extract yourself."

I yanked back so fast I hit my head on the corner of the water heater. I put my hand to my hair and came back with blood. She kept talking as if she didn't notice.

"You are not alone," she went on. "Many, many people manifest in such a negative way, then react to it violently. It is the way of the world. It is an old-fashioned way. We are stubborn. Many will not listen. The gods have already started to yell very, very loudly. Everyone will be forced to listen. Or we will all die."

Again, the sweat. I worried for a second I might lose consciousness, or worse, have a vision. I started to get up. She leaned forward and gripped my hands again.

"Listen to me. You and I." She had tears in her eyes. "You and I, we are the most derided, the most disliked of women. With our gifts, we have been much misunderstood for many thousands of years." I wanted to yank my hands back and slap her. We were nothing alike. I was nothing like her. She nodded with her eyes half closed. "So derided. In some places, but not everywhere. There are new places where there is more understanding. You will find a place for yourself."

She had tears in her eyes. "Your gifts are so much needed in this world. It will get worse, and you will be even more needed. No, you cannot see it now," she said. "You will understand later what is asked of you. You have such power. A gift. But to have a light to shine, first you must burn."

I took my hands back and tried to steady them. I hated that this woman was having such a strong effect on me, and didn't want her to see my shaking fingers. I tried to look both annoyed and bored. She looked at me openly, and when I wouldn't meet her eye, or smile or engage her in any way, her shoulders sagged as if she was disappointed.

She spoke in a shallow and happy tone. "Perhaps you'd like to ask about your love life? Most young women end up asking about their love lives. Perhaps love life would make you more happy?"

The sweat pooled beneath my breasts. I was so hot. I was on fire. My belly raged with heat. "No, I'm perfectly fine. I'm good. How much?" I stood and scraped my back on the heater.

She took her time collecting the cards. I noticed them then, an old Indian design I'd seen somewhere before, tiny figures on tapestry,

air

ringed around with red dots that glowed up like rubies. The edges of the cards were worn as if they'd seen a hundred, a thousand, readings. Moghul art, was that what it was called? They glowed up from the table. "How much?" I said again, louder than I meant to.

"Two thousand yen," she said. It was fifteen dollars. No wonder she was poor. I handed her the money. "Please send in Yuriko," she said, not looking up at me.

I waited for more than an hour while Yuriko had her reading. I couldn't stop sweating. The smell of curry made me nauseous. My hands were clammy, my armpits wet. I was getting sick. That was just what I needed. What the psychic had said to me swirled around me like a haunting.

Yuriko came out of the kitchen, laughing, the woman like a pygmy beside her. Yuriko bent down and took her in a bear hug. Their love for each other was overwhelming in that overcrowded room. I couldn't believe Yuriko *liked* her.

The woman showed us out.

"*Namaste*, Yuriko," she said, bowing and bringing her hands in prayer to her face. To me she said, "Please take care of yourself." I hated when people said that to me. I'd been taking care of myself my whole damned life, with no help from anybody.

Outside the apartment, on the walkway, Yuriko said, "How'd it go?" Before I could answer, she said, "I've got to go to Seattle, to see my mother. Man, oh man! I guess I've got to. I just hope it's not as horrible coming back for me as it has been for you."

"She should charge more," I said.

"What? You mean Sakina?" She looked at me, confused. "Well, I think she feels like it's a gift and she should give it as a gift to others. Are you okay? You don't look so hot. So, how'd your reading go? You're not going to clam up on me now, are you? Dish. Dish."

Sweat rose from the depths of my belly. I ran to the edge of the walkway, leaned over the rickety railing, and vomited to the bald courtyard below. A deep, heavy retching. I vomited once, twice, three times. Yuriko gathered up my hair. I heard the door open and saw the edges of the Indian woman's skirt. I vomited until there was nothing but bile. When I finished, I plopped down against the concrete wall, knees up, and wiped the slimy sweat and bits of puke off my face with my sleeve.

Yuriko leaned down. "Shit, Pearl. Why didn't you tell me you were sick? I would've never dragged you out here. Let's get you into a taxi." She helped me stand.

The Indian woman asked, "You are pregnant?"

"What?"

"What?" Yuriko screamed.

The little woman stood in front of me, smoothed back my sweaty hair. "You are pregnant, my dear. You are with child."

Yuriko's gentleness petrified me. Her solicitousness unarmed me. We were back at the Gyotoku apartment. I wanted the old Yuriko back. The sarcastic, angry, horny Yuriko. She poured green tea while I smoked cigarette after cigarette. Never once did she offer advice. She barely spoke at all. It was a show of restraint for her that I'd never seen before. The way she was acting made me understand that something was really, tragically wrong.

I hadn't told her a thing about my trip home. I didn't have the words for it. How do you tell someone casually about not having a family? How do you explain a broken life? At the table now, I told her about sleeping with Jason. I was on the pill, but it wasn't a hundred percent effective, and I came from a long line of fertile women, a fecundity that went back generations. I could've let Finn think the baby was his. It would've been easiest. Of course it could've been Jason's or Finn's, but with all Finn's dope smoking, I was pretty sure who the father was.

Yuriko sat quietly while I called Finn, told him I needed a break, a whole month to myself. I told him not to worry. I could tell he was worried.

air

Yuriko sat with me late into the night, listening. She sat with me through an entire pack of cigarettes. She sat with me through four large cans of Sapporo. She tried to get me to talk about what the psychic had told me, but I didn't have the words for it. I wasn't able to speak about that.

Finally, when I went to bed, I could not sleep, my head full of swirling thoughts. When I was eight, I made a vow not to have children. I'd stood on the hill overlooking the house, wind whipping hair. A storm was coming. Father was nearby mending a fence. I looked out over the land, the earth filling me to bursting, and I vowed, *I will not get married. I will not have children.* Even then I knew. Someone had to say stop. If I grew up and had a child, even then I understood I'd be continuing the pain.

I believed in God then, the Catholic God of virgin births, angry nuns and stained glass. I made a promise to God that I would grow up and be a healthy person. *Whatever it takes*, I told the stormy winds, *I will be healthy.* And then I thought, watching Father struggle with a fist full of barbed wire, *One day, the whole world will grieve this. The whole world will help us heal this.*

I fell into fitful sleep and dreamt I was pregnant, but it wasn't Jason's child. I dreamt the fetus was made by the dirt of that clearing. A fist fashioned of soil extended up, reached into my vagina, deep into my womb and latched on to me. The soil itself put its seed into me. The earth invaded me, grabbed on and wouldn't let go. I reached between my legs and yanked at the root. I tugged and wrenched.

For the next two weeks, I was frozen, unable to make a decision, unable to think about anything practical. I'd get up and go to work as normal, come home and smoke at the kitchen table. Smoke and smoke and smoke. And drink.

Yuriko put off flying back to Seattle to see her mother. She set up an appointment with a doctor and forced me to go. She sat with me through the diagnosis. Just over ten weeks. I leaned against her as we left the doctor's office. The muscle and bone of her were like a rock, like ballast.

The night of the diagnosis, I was on the futon. It was maybe seven. I stared at a tiny spot of light in the otherwise dark room, a reflection from the outside street light.

Yuriko knocked and slid the door open. She knelt beside me on the *tatami*. She wore a painter's shirt and held a fat paintbrush that had wet blue bristles. "We've got to stop meeting like this," she said and laughed. I rolled over and put my back to her.

"Okay, look," she said. "I'm just going to brain dump here. Take it. Leave it. It doesn't matter, but I feel like I've got to say what's on my mind."

She paused. I said nothing.

"First off, I'm here. Okay? Right here."

I had abandoned her for Finn. I had no right to expect anything from her.

"Okay, so you can imagine, right, that I might've been in this same position myself before?" She laughed, but it turned into a cough. "I'm not going to give you all the gory personal details. You do what you need to do."

She touched my shoulder, and I had a visceral memory of Meghan's finger dancing over my back, drawing pictures into my flesh, images that I'd have to guess. Bike or dog, sun or moon.

"And I'm not going to go into what a feminist I am about this. How one in three women gets abortions. You know all that stuff, right?"

"What I am going to tell you is what Sakina, the psychic, told me when I had my abortion."

She took a deep breath.

"The soul will enter elsewhere. Nothing is killed. The soul of the child will just find another person to be born to."

I turned and looked at her. She held my gaze.

air

The next afternoon I got off work early, came home and told Yuriko my decision. She helped me make the call. We drank wine into the evening.

"I have an idea," she said. "Come with me. A surprise outing." I blinked at her.

"You'll feel better. I promise. Come on."

We walked the narrow streets. It was a cold May night. A nearly full moon threw shadows of puckered cherry blossom branches onto the garden walls and elongated them onto the streets and sidewalks.

We came to a low building with a wooden trestle that hid a heavy wooden door. People were exiting, carrying towels—sons and fathers, groups of women.

"I passed this place the other day," Yuriko said, opening the door. "And I was dying to check it out."

An old man with missing teeth stood behind a counter. Men came and went from a door on the right. Women from a door on the left.

"It's a *sento*, a public bath," Yuriko said. She took out some change and paid the man. He handed us small white towels, bars of soap and tiny bottles of shampoo. We sat together on a nearby bench, and she handed me half the supplies.

"Okay, so I have this guide book with the rules of the *sento*." I was glad she'd brought it. There were so many restrictions in Japan. Rules for men. Rules for women. You couldn't walk across the room without tripping over a rule.

"Number one," she read from the book. "Take off your clothes and put them on a shelf in the anteroom. You'll find plastic stools and buckets in the anteroom. In the bath are lines of spigots with mirrors. Place a stool in front of one of the spigots. Fill the bucket and douse yourself. Sitting on the stool, scrub with soap. Shampoo your hair." She stopped, and read the rest to herself, and then looked over the top of the book. "It says you have to scrub yourself like your life depends on it, otherwise the Japanese will think you're a dirty foreigner." She went back to reading. "Rinse with the bucket. Repeat. Then you can get into the group bathtub."

I stared at her.

"Don't worry, just follow my lead."

We stood naked at the cusp of the bath. I'd been naked with Yuriko more than with anyone else in my life. In my family, nudity just wasn't done. I held a small hand towel over my lower area.

It was like a whiteout on the side of the mountain in the bath, steam afforded only glimpses, subtle hints of shimmering blue-black hair, of elbows and thigh. The flesh of the Japanese was even toned, and the breasts of even the forty-year-olds small and tight. If you didn't see the women's faces, if you just followed the long ebony hair down the center of their backs, you could imagine they were teenagers, you could imagine they were girls who never grew up.

The steam cleared. In the center of the room, a large woman roosted. All of the other women were thin no matter what their age, but this woman was rotund, fleshy. A bevy of younger women fussed around her, seeming to argue over who got to scrub her shoulders.

The clearing of steam also gave a clear view of Yuriko and me to everyone in the room. Yuriko with her big American body, her Japanese face. Me an obvious foreigner. There were no other foreigners in the bath as far as I could see. Many faces, variously hidden by steam, turned at once to stare at us. I put a hand to my steam-frizzled hair, worried I looked like a wild animal or a homeless person. They stared at Yuriko's ample hips and my large breasts.

Yuriko handed me a plastic stool, a bucket, and another hand towel. There were rows of knee-high spigots, each with a mirror. In

air

the corner were two huge bath tubs that looked as if they each could hold six to ten women.

I watched Yuriko and echoed her, took my blue stool, put it in front of the spigot and squatted on it, my knees up around my shoulders. We used the spigots to fill the blue bucket. Still the other women stared. I doused myself with water and scrubbed vigorously with the towel and the tiny square of soap. The other women scrubbed themselves raw, soaping themselves in epic proportions.

A girl of about five appeared in my peripheral vision. I turned to her. The girl's lips were pursed, and she stared fixedly at my breasts. Trickling strands of blue hair stuck to her shoulders and forearms. She was small and bone thin, her ribs etching shadows at her torso. Her black eyes took up most of her face. She pointed at my breasts and said something in Japanese.

"*Konbanwa*," I said, *good evening*. The child kept rambling on, pointing at my breasts.

"*Konbanwa*," I whispered again. I bowed my shoulders in quick forward movements. I wanted to get her on my side, get her to lower her voice. I didn't want to attract the attention of the women around us. She kept speaking in high-pitched rapid Japanese.

"What is your name?" I whispered in my pigeon Japanese. "What do you want?" The girl stared and didn't speak. I stole glances behind me.

She yelled, "*Okaasan!*" *Mother!* "*Okaasan!*" She pumped her arms and slapped her thighs like a little bird fidgeting in its nest.

I put my hand out to shoo her away, too many women were paying too much attention. I turned to Yuriko for help, but she was over near the bath.

The mama-*san* I'd seen earlier was suddenly standing behind me. The bulge of flesh at her belly dripped with beads of sweat. Her breasts were loose flaps, her nipples hanging toward the floor. Under her arms hung folds of flesh. She talked to the girl in Japanese. The little girl did not move. The posse of younger Japanese women appeared. The mama-*san* said something, and the posse laughed. She pulled up a small stool next to mine and squatted on it.

I felt the brush of her arm before I saw it. She was going for my hand and I pulled back and kicked over the bucket of water. She laughed and her posse laughed. Japanese women usually laughed behind their hands, but not there. In the confines of the bath, these women bared their teeth, their hair in wild strands about their faces. They barked, snorted, guffawed, like creatures in a fairy tale.

The mama-*san* snatched the towel out of my hand. She held it over her head like a trophy, and the women laughed louder. I smiled uncertainly. The mama-*san* took the towel and started scrubbing my back.

All my life, I never knew where I fit with other women. Growing up, the women would be in the kitchen and the men outside, and all I wanted was to be outdoors, but it wasn't allowed. I'd pace around the house, as if I were in a trap or cage. Mother taught me all the womanly arts, knitting, sewing, cooking, baking. When I was twelve, she gave me a hope chest for my birthday, filled it with table linens, cutlery she got with green stamps, a set of plastic mixing bowls. It wasn't the sort of hope I had in my chest.

The mama-*san* wasn't just scrubbing my back, she was pummeling it. She pushed so hard, I was thrust forward into an awkward slump, hands flat against the smaller mirror. She scraped until my back felt raw.

The little girl came around and stood on the other side of me. She watched the mama-*san* scrubbing my back, called again for her mother and ran away into the steam, the tiny slap of wet feet on tile as her voice faded. I didn't know why the child was so obsessed by me. Her presence seemed like an omen, like a message, but I didn't know its meaning.

The mama-*san* scrubbed. She pushed the towel along my back over and over. I knew the Japanese thought foreigners were dirty, and it was true our bathing habits were not so nearly as thorough. Still, I didn't know if this was normal scrubbing or if the old woman was trying to prove something. I clung to the mirror. My arms grew tired, and I was forced to lean my forehead against the glass.

air

The little girl ran out of the steam. Behind her was a woman in her twenties I assumed to be her mother. The child pointed at me, turned in circles, pumped her arms as if she were trying to take flight. She pointed. "*Okaasan, o mite. O mite.*" Look, Mom. Look.

Just as suddenly as she had started, the mama-*san* stopped. I was still holding the mirror, my hair hanging in loose clumps. I turned to look at her. She smiled and handed me the towel. The posse was eerily quiet. The mama-*san* watched me. There was something I was supposed to do, an etiquette. I was supposed to say something to the mama-*san*. Do something. But I didn't know what. I didn't know the rules for fitting with women back in the Midwest, and I didn't know them here. I bowed repeatedly toward the mirror. "*Domo arigato,*" I repeated. "*Domo arigato.*" I just wanted them all to go away.

Yuriko and I left the *sento*. I reached up and felt a glob of shampoo in my wet hair. Escaping had become more important than rinsing.

I didn't understand exactly what had happened in the bath. I knew it had something to do with me being a foreigner entering a sacred Japanese space. It had something to do with coming to a country where I'd never fit, a place where my not fitting was being painted upon a massive canvas.

As Yuriko and I walked home, steam rose off our bodies, and our moon shadows on the street looked as if we were people on fire.

I T WAS STICKY hot. Summer. Sun diffused beneath layers of smog. Sticky beneath armpits, between legs. The trees in the park were dried up, brittle and brown. The grass was brown, too. The land looked burned.

Since I'd gotten back, I was trying to notice the weather. I kept telling myself if I could stay with the seasons, I'd be okay. I'd know where I stood.

I carried sushi and wine and a plastic bag full of gifts. Usui sat on his cardboard. He was folding origami birds. He looked up and his face was pallid.

"Are you unwell?" I asked.

"Please to sit down, Purr-*san*."

More strands of origami cranes on strings hung from the rail beams like hair, cascading like the branches of a willow. I felt better at the sight of them, and of Usui.

"I brought you a couple gifts," I said. He coughed, hard and rattling. His eyes were glassy. I handed him the plastic bag. He reached in and pulled out a new pair of trousers. I'd noticed last time that his pants were threadbare at the knees. His face flushed red.

"Are they okay?" I asked. "Are they your size?"

"Please, Purr-*san*, I do not want from that world." He went into a coughing fit. He handed the trousers back to me.

"I'm just trying to help."

air

"You don't understand. It is separation that I want."

"Usui-*san*, you're sick." He wouldn't look at me. "Does it really have to go this far?'

He held his nostrils and blew snot from his nose into the dirt. I'd seen other people do this, but each time it shocked me. When he kept folding origami and wouldn't respond, I said, "There's another gift in the bag. I know you don't want gifts, but…"

He reached into the bag. He swayed as he sat, and I wanted to feel his forehead to see if he had a fever. He took a box from the bag, lifted the lid, and extracted a deformed green cast-iron teapot with a twisted spout. I'd gone back to the potter to the shelves of misshapen pots. Usui laughed, hard from his belly, and it degenerated into a cough.

"It's all twisted," I said. "I fell in love with it. It's probably even a dumber gift since you can't really boil water up here."

"No, not dumb gift," he replied, holding the teapot on his lap and petting it as if it were a child or a puppy. He reached under his cardboard and held a book out to me. "A gift for you, Purr-*chan*."

I wasn't sure if he'd bought the book as a gift for me, or if it was his, if he'd found it somewhere, and he was just giving it to me because I'd given him something.

It was a battered book of poetry by Basho. It was hot where Usui's hands had touched it. I should've refused it, but it was only the second book I'd ever been given and I loved it, valued it higher than any jewel anyone could ever give me. I rubbed my palm over and over the beaten-up cover, tracing the cover image, a black-and-white photo of two hands holding a bird's nest. I read the back, flipped through it and read several of the poems like a starving child. It was food, and I was starving.

I pulled the wine and sushi out of the other bag. I'd remembered a corkscrew and opened the bottle. I knew he was sick and shouldn't be drinking, but I took the teapot and poured half the bottle inside. Inside the box were four squat, deformed cups. I gave one to Usui, tipped the pot sideways to compensate for the twisted spout and poured wine into the cup as he held it. He took the teapot and poured for me as I held my cup.

"To being homeless," I said, holding out my wine. Usui clinked the cup.

"To us who look for home elsewhere," he said.

We drank for a while in silence. Above us, the commuter train ran every fifteen minutes, the regular rumble of it comforting in an odd way. Dust and specks floated down from the overhead rail like black rain.

Usui lay back on the cardboard. He cleared his throat and coughed up phlegm. "Purr-*chan*, tell me story. I am very tired."

I told him about my trip to Missouri, leaving out certain parts, but giving him a surprising amount of information about my mother and her new family, about Jason wanting me to stay.

I didn't tell him about the pregnancy. I didn't tell him about the trip to the clinic, the waiting room like a school bus, women and girls sitting in blue cushioned chairs lined up in two rows. I didn't speak about how they gave us each a blue pill and how everyone kept falling asleep sitting up, and rolling off their chairs.

I didn't tell him about how they called my name and took me back to a small room. How I stared at the heavy lights and tried not to think. How a young doctor came in with the nurse. How he didn't speak, repositioned my legs, turned on a device that made a suction noise. How I grabbed the nurse's hand, squeezed it until she had to extract it and give me her other because I was hurting her.

How even after the doctor left, I was gripping her hand and couldn't stop. How she tried to pull away, but my whole body pulled with her. How she cooed to me in Japanese. How I felt her concern, felt the hole this work left inside her.

I didn't tell him how on the train home later, Yuriko's mouth was set hard. Her eyes were fierce, her body coiled. How she looked as if she could kill every man we saw. How she looked as if she would punch any man in the face if he looked at us funny.

How for two days I lay on my futon and stared at the dolls he had given me, the skinny one and the large one, well rounded and

air

substantial. The one that was me now, and the one that I was supposed to become.

I didn't tell him what the psychic had said to me, about manifesting negatively, about bringing into my life what I didn't want and then having to violently extract it. How so much of the world lived this way, in violent extraction of what they did not want.

All the stories I did not speak out loud, all the stories that were not spoken by my family. The legends the world didn't tell, the difficult heart-wrenching tales, the stories hidden like a woman beneath a burka, only her eyes showing. What happened to the world's untold narrative? The vocabulary rumbling beneath the surface of the planet, trapped air ready to burst. What would it be like if everyone told their version of things? Would the world break right open?

I didn't tell him how deflated I felt, as if someone had popped my balloon. Or how Yuriko came into my room, pulled me off the futon. How she'd set up a small table in the corner of her room and on it put a can of paintbrushes, a box of child's watercolors, a pad of paper and a cup of water. She put a brush in my hand. She went back to her easel. I dipped the brush. I painted swirl after swirl in black and blue.

"Purr-*chan*," Usui said in a weakened voice from the cardboard. "Where you go? Come back. You go so far away."

He sat up, swayed, leaned into me and looked into my eyes. "I see," he said. "It is death."

I jumped.

"When leave home, must go through stages of death. It is death of Misery. I can see in eyes. It is depression." When I didn't say anything for a long time, he said. "Why you come here again and again, Purr-*chan*?" He lay back down.

"I guess I come here looking for comfort."

He laughed and coughed. "Comfort on a piece of cardboard under railroad bridge on day of much boiling heat."

"Are we the only people in the world who don't fit?" *And there's Yuriko, too*, I thought.

Usui coughed. "Yes, just you and me." He laughed and coughed.

I blushed.

"No, Purr-*san*," he said. Even from far way, I could smell the sickly sweat of him. "The truth is many people not fit." He slurred his words. "Ideko fit, no. Akina-*san*? No. All the Idekos in Tokyo—they are paid to fit."

"Japanese say you have three faces," he said. "First face, you show world. Second face, you show family, friends. Third face, you never show. That is real you."

"What if you yourself have never seen your third face?"

He didn't answer.

I'd picked my thumb bloody, noticed and put it into my mouth.

"What plans for life do you have?" Usui asked.

"I don't know. To find someplace where I fit."

He laughed.

"You're laughing a lot lately."

"Maybe it is all funny. Maybe everything is funny."

"What are your plans?" I asked.

On his back, he put up his arms and motioned around him.

"Surely there's a way to make a life that is not homelessness and not an Ideko life," I said. "Like the work you did with the handicapped kids. That kind of life is worthwhile, right?"

"I separate myself like you to understand who I am."

"But come on. I've asked you this before. Do you have to go this far?"

"Maybe some people, Purr-*chan*, have to go more far than others."

I lit a cigarette. Usui was right. This was a death, and not just the death of the unborn child, but the death of my past. The separation felt as if someone was skinning me, tearing off my outer layer. It felt like being flayed alive. A nick from crotch to throat, a rending of the skin. Missouri was being sliced out of my core, a gutting, a hollowing out.

air

The work in the newsroom did not help. It was as if the darkest part of human nature was invading my flesh. The world was shameful and worthless. I stamped out the cigarette, lit another. It seemed to be getting worse. Hurricanes. Mudslides. Ozone layers.

"Separation or no, I'm not sure any of it is worth it sometimes, Usui-*san*."

"Why you think I leave everything? It is drastic. We must be drastic!" He almost screamed the words. He was Usui on the futon when we were at the mission, the rancid, depressed, disappearing Usui. "Whole world becoming homeless!"

I didn't like this Usui. He scared me. The origami papers sat between us on the cardboard. I fished one out and handed it to him. He took it and groaned as he sat up. I could feel the heat of his fever pulse off him. He started folding a crane.

Soon the white paper took him over. His fingers reminded me of Finn's, working the paper as if he was practicing a tune, as if he were blowing soul into the bird. He handed me the finished crane, and I put it on the string. He took another sheet of paper and started folding. Handed it to me when he was finished. And another. And another.

When I'd strung a dozen, I took the strand of edgy birds to the beam and hung it there.

I N THE FLOATING world, there was no one to define us. In the life of the hovering, rules of the past, rules in the present, had nothing to do with us. As winged ones, we flitted here. We fluttered there. We ascended like wisps of smoke, farther and farther from the earth. Higher and higher. We could be anyone we wanted. We could do anything we wanted. And there was no one at all to stop us.

Finn and I were stoned. Ecstasy, speed, and behind it all, hash. There was always hash. I sat in a salon chair in Harajuku. Finn was telling the stylist in Japanese what to do to me.

I said in a bad cockney accent, "You're going to teach me to walk and talk and act like a real lady."

The Japanese stylist was in her early twenties, tiny with thick hair. She kept bowing, and saying, "*Hai. Hai.* Yes. Yes," to Finn. She was too pretty, and Finn was too close to her.

"Off with the hair," I shouted. The stylist jumped. Finn gave me a look.

She kept my back to the mirror so I couldn't see. I wasn't one of those women who spent time on her looks. Finn was in a chair with his long legs stretched out. That languid way he had of relaxing. I wanted to slither up to him and coil on his lap. He stared at what the stylist was doing with difficult eyes. I had never had a vision in front of Finn. I knew the day was coming. I watched him watching the

air

stylist. I didn't want to lose him. In this new floating world, he was all that I had left.

During the crisis after I got back from Missouri, I didn't see Finn for more than a month. Finally, he came looking for me in the *Kaze* newsroom. He asked if we could talk. I met him at his flat after work, but we didn't talk. We fucked. Got stoned and got laid, and then we were dating again.

In the chair, my head kept spinning. I wasn't used to so many drugs. Anybody at that point could've taken my hand, led me anywhere they wanted. The stylist sprayed, combed, cut and ironed. I wasn't good at being touched and just wanted her claws away from my scalp.

She finished with the hair and knelt in front of me with a makeup tray. She smelled like peaches, had a tiny mole next to her crimson mouth. Her eyes had eyeliner at the edges. I could hardly breathe looking at her so close.

"*Sugoi*," she said in a whisper. *Wow*. She turned and spoke to Finn, words I couldn't understand. Finn's mouth stretched over crooked teeth, his sexiest feature. He pulled his lips into a wide smile for the pretty Japanese girl. He laughed, and she laughed back. I picked my thumbs until they bled, scratched them raw under cover of the smock.

Sometimes in his basement flat when I was feeling blue, Finn would sing a song to me. "Nobody likes me. Everybody hates me. I guess I'm gonna eat some worms." It was his way to make me see how ridiculous my sadness could be.

The stylist turned my chair to the mirror. My hair hung in straight sheets by my face. I had straight hair. I'd never had straight hair. You could see my face. She'd trimmed the bangs, and with eyeliner, my eyes glowed, lime green and haunted.

Finn whistled, came up and whistled again. He kissed my cheek. "Now, that's a new Queenie for a new era."

The stylist said, "So beauty. Hiding the beauty." Others at the salon stared. I blushed.

Finn purchased a flat curling iron, and the stylist showed me how to use it. I was exhausted just listening. I had always jumped out of bed, thrown on clothes and was out the door in less than five minutes. I was proud of that side of myself. It was wild, low-maintenance like a field where even the weeds were beautiful.

Finn led me down to street to a boutique. I wasn't a shopper. I'd never liked it. Jason used to say it didn't matter that I didn't like clothes, that I could wear a potato sack and still look hot, but that was the old me. That was in Missouri, where most people bought their clothes from a Montgomery Ward catalogue.

Boots, trousers, turtle necks, blouses, skirts—everything in black. I stopped counting after the equivalent of a thousand dollars. I'd never had a man purchase clothes for me. Even my mother had rarely shopped. We were too poor. She sewed for me a few shirts and pants, but mostly I wore Meghan's hand-me-downs. I didn't know what to think of Finn's attention to my appearance. Didn't know if it was freedom from the old life or something different.

I tried on a pair of thigh boots. Finn had me walk toward a full-length mirror. I saw a woman there, not a girl, a woman I didn't recognize. She was me, but not me. It reminded me of Usui's garden. I was being manicured.

I reached up and untied the pouch from around my neck. Finn said, "No," took the pouch from me and tried to put it back around my neck. I took hold of the worn leather and pulled it from him. "No, Finn. A new Queenie for a new era, remember?" I put the leather pouch into my purse. The surprise was how white my neck was, how pallid and soft.

I floated above myself and watched as we walked toward the subway. From above, I watched men turn to stare. I watched the new me smile nervously. I watched Finn watching the men and liking it.

air

We ate dinner at a low-lit restaurant, and I changed in the bathroom—miniskirt, sleeveless turtleneck, thigh-high boots. The clothes clung to my body. The top fit snug around my breasts. I'd never shown this much of my figure. The restaurant men turned and stared.

"Queenie, by God, you're bloody beautiful." Finn shook his head as I sat. "You're so hard and angular, and then the curves." He looked down, like a shy little boy. "No more hiding behind a mop of hair and loose hobo clothing. You deserve to be beautiful. You deserve it." He took my hand.

"I don't know what happened in Missouri," he said. "But you can leave all that behind. Don't go backward. Be anything you want to be. That's the point of all this, right?" He waved his arm, and I assumed he meant Tokyo, living abroad. "We can choose to be anything we want." He lifted his beer glass. My hand shook as I lifted mine.

Yuriko looked me over, the new hair, the fancy duds. "You don't need me to tell you how gorgeous you are," she said. We were in her room. She went back to her painting. "Straight hair, frizzy, you're a babe."

I didn't say, Yes, I do need you to tell me, Yuriko. I've had so few compliments in my life, so many insults, I can live on one kind word for months. For decades.

"It's your inner light, though, more than your looks. You know that, right? That's where you're really knock-down, drop-dead gorgeous." I felt the syllables swirl around me. I would hold on to those words for years.

Yuriko had just gotten back from visiting her parents in Seattle. The room smelled like sperm and oil paint, but mostly sperm. She went on sex benders when she was stressed. I took a seat on her sperm-addled futon. I was stoned. Stoned was my new normal.

The women's faces were shattered into pieces, like a fresco after an earthquake, a corner of an eye here, the upper lip there. Faces blown apart. Yuriko's new series. She told me she was calling it "Lost Fragments." Something boiled beneath the surface; I had to keep my face turned away as she talked.

She told me about her visit. Her mother was in the midst of a full-blown depression. She didn't get out of bed for the entirety of Yuriko's visit. Yuriko sat by her bedside. She'd never seen her this bad before. It was as if her mother's body was filled with sludge. Yuriko must've picked up some of the darkness, because she was heavy and frowning at the canvas.

I told Yuriko about the aviary. Finn and I had found a bird sanctuary in Gyotoku. Yuriko and I had lived there how many years and we didn't even know about the aviary. Finn and I had gone on a tour. Herons, egrets, cormorants and such. Lotus pond, reeds and paddy fields. Such a profound relief after all the concrete. Finn had taken out his flute, played a few notes, and the birds responded.

"He jammed with birds!"

Yuriko was looking at me darkly. "Where's your pouch?"

"I put it away. It was old."

"Hmm." She turned back to the canvas.

"There's a letter for you on the table," she said. I went into the kitchen. It was from Jason. Yuriko came in behind me, rubbing the bristles of her paintbrush with a towel. I slipped the letter into my purse.

"You're not going to read it?"

I wobbled my head. I was coming down off the weed. I needed another hit. I fished in my bag for a cigarette.

"He deserves to know what happened, Pearl. If I know anything after visiting my mother, it's that secrets will eat you up and spit you out. And they'll spew all over anyone who has the sad fortune to be close to you."

air

"It's the past. I have a right to let go of the past. Don't people say let the past go, live in the present?" I rubbed sweat off my brow. I felt claustrophobic. I needed out of there. I headed toward the door.

Yuriko reached out and stopped me. She turned me around and took my chin in her hand, her fingertips blue, a dark torture in her eyes.

"Be careful, okay," she said. I'd never seen Yuriko so upset. I knew it was about her mother. I knew Yuriko was not doing well. I knew I needed to stay and be with her as she had been there for me, but I couldn't breathe. "Don't float away on me, Pearl. Okay?"

I pulled myself away, slipped on my shoes and left. I walked until I was well away from the apartment. I bent over and gasped for breath. Something was threatening to break open in me. I couldn't seem to get enough air. I gasped and gasped, trying to get air.

The *Kaze* was getting crazier. I was at the editor's desk, the surface piled high with white sheets of paper, each one a chronicle of the sorry state of our world. I wanted to collect them up, take them to Usui and have him fold each one into a bird, add them to his string.

The Australian rewriter handed me a story she'd just reworked. I looked up at her. She was a physical powerhouse. I felt like a meek mouse next to her. The new clothes and haircut were getting me a lot of attention from the men in the newsroom, especially from creepy Michael. It wasn't making me very popular with the intelligent women in the office.

As I added the paper to the pile, the headline caught my eye. "Homeless Man Set on Fire at Park."

I grabbed the paper, scanned the document. *Four teenage boys. Lighter fluid. Homeless man sleeping. Woke up on fire. Died in the ER. No name given.*

I saw that Shinji was the original reporter. I knocked over my coffee in my scramble to get to him, choked out his name as I ran to his desk.

"Do you have any more information? Was there a name?"

He looked at me confused.

"The homeless man who was burned."

"No. No name."

"Where is the body now?"

"At the morgue."

I ran to Michael and told him to take over the editor's desk. I went back and grabbed Shinji. "Come with me." He resisted. "Now."

We ran out of the newsroom, down the stairs and through the streets to the subway. The only way I would know it wasn't Usui was to go to the park myself.

Shinji had a hard time keeping up with me. I was running across the park. I kept having to slow down. Mothers played with their children. Kids threw large red and blue balls. There must've been someone selling the balls, because the same balls were everywhere, huge, bouncing, and rolling. The things a person focuses on during trauma. Sweat roiled my armpits as I ran. I had to keep slowing down so Shinji could keep up with me.

As we passed the tent city, I saw Akina. "Akina-*san*," I called. "Usui-*san*?"

Akina picked up my fear. She yelled, "No. No." I wasn't sure what she meant. I took off across the field, Akina behind me, Shinji following Akina.

We found Usui in the fetal position on his cardboard. I almost laughed outright when I saw that he was alive. He was curled up into himself. His face beneath his dreadlocks was covered in a film of sweat. I knelt beside him. "What is it? What's wrong?"

Akina said, "I found last night. I can do nothing."

I put my palm on his forehead. His flesh was hot, like fire, but with none of the clamminess of the flu. "How long have you been this way?" I knew he was having one of his depressions.

air

His voice came out as a croak. "Leave me." I ran my hands along his chest and arms. He was horrifically thin. His face was so pale, he looked like a ghost.

"Akina-*san*, can you get a doctor?" I had no idea if a doctor would do house calls to a piece of cardboard beneath a rail bridge.

Usui groaned. "It is not a sickness. Doctor cannot help."

I took a wad of yen from my purse. "Shinji, can you go with Akina-*san* to get some water, some paper towels and something for Usui-*san* to eat?"

They went off together. I could see Shinji reacting strongly to Akina. I remembered how he acted when I first saw Usui with the dolls on the bridge. I watched as he did his best not to recoil from Akina.

Was Usui's depression a premonition? Was his depression a barometer for the world? Overhead, trains barreled across the rail bridge like sudden storms.

Dozens more strands of cranes hung from the beam. He must've been working furiously to make so many. I did a quick estimate. He now had enough for two wishes, more than enough— more than two thousand birds hanging from strings. They hung from the beam like thick white hair.

I knew it was no use to try to talk to Usui, so I just sat with him, one hand on his wrist. Soon, Shinji and Akina came back with a plastic grocery bag. I gave Usui water, tried to get him to eat an orange.

Shinji said he had to get back to the newsroom. He took me aside and handed me a wad of yen. "Purr-*san*, be careful. Please be careful. This is not safe place." I didn't ask him, *Where is safe? Where, Shinji? Tell me.*

I took over for Akina, who was holding a damp cloth to Usui's brow. Akina told me in stilted English that Shinji had told her about the homeless man who'd been attacked, and she had to leave. She had to find out who it was.

The sun began to set. It was autumn and cool, but with Usui next to me, it was as if I wore a thick down coat. This depression was worse than the last one. With this one, he was flat, unmoving, not talking. It was as if he were lost, as if he were not there.

I wedged my hand between the cardboard and his back, palm flat between his wings. It started to rain, a soft mist. Train rattle, rain patter, in the distance flickering barrel fires. I leaned over him, such grief in the eyes. I held my hands, just waiting. I felt the faint flicker of an urge toward movement in his body.

I moved in conjunction with the urge, a small movement of hand and Usui's flesh. I arched him two inches. Another intuition of energy, and I moved his head sideways. Minutes passed. Slowly, I began moving one arm, dancing it upward, then the other. I felt his urge to sit up, and I sat him up.

Then we were kneeling, and then awkwardly standing, like two broken marionettes. I circled his wrist, pulled his arm up, and floated it in wide arcs.

Now his body was in my arms, flesh and bone like a rag doll. But still I was following his lead, watching for his urge to move.

Rickety, wobbly, we arched in miniscule movements. I held the weight of him. Fragile. I started a song. "Amazing Grace." My favorite. He sang with me. His accent, and my little girl voice. Echoes of Holy Cross. Oh, how I used to sing high and mighty. Oh, how I used to believe.

The dancing at first tentative, but with each breath, the spirit reanimated the flesh. Greater and greater movement. Eddying, lyrical, languid. Usui and I beneath the rail bridge with no audience, spinning, singing. The awkward dance, the spit of fire in the distance, the methodic train rumble overhead.

"I know why Father Dennis sent me to you, Usui-*san*," I whispered to him. "To help me believe."

The breath rising, then falling, then calming, then lying down. As I fell asleep next to him, I heard him say—or it was the breath of the wind, I couldn't be sure—"You are the one, Purr, helping me."

I WAS IN the dark and musty basement of the *Kaze*. I was alone in the belly of the beast. The *Kaze* published special supplements every six months. I was putting together the Top 25 events of the second half of the year. The world's worst traumas, those sure to affect the planet, not just in the moment, but for the next seven generations. A celebration of horror.

It was a punishment. The *Kaze* editors were not happy with me. How could I have just left the newsroom like that? It wasn't done. There had been too many days, too, when I was tardy, too many vacations, too many times I'd called in sick. It wasn't done. I wasn't keeping up. At night, I dreamed the papers piled on the editor's desk grew so high they avalanched and smothered me.

The only other person who came into the basement was the archivist, a bent old guy who shuffled between the shelves. The room was full of heavy wooden tables crowded together, a host of filing cabinets of different shapes and sizes, and massive shelves of newspaper-sized binders. Every surface was covered in a fine dust.

I chain-smoked. I took the binders down one by one, read each headline, each story, article by article, month by month. My fingers became blackened, smudged by the newsprint.

Every article confirmed to me what savages we were. What feral hordes. What desperately handicapped people. Dizzy, I made out a crazy list, one that in no way captured the essence of it. Instead I was attracted to side stories. A Japanese mother abandoned her children

air

for nine months in Sonomo, an Ethiopian student beaten to death by neo-Nazis in Portland, a prototype of a new stealth bomber with the word Spirit in its name. I knew I should've been compiling a list about major events, the global wars, the plagues of viruses, world starvation, mudslides burying whole towns, but I kept getting pulled sideways into individual brutalities. It was like trying to organize a box of old photographs. You kept getting pulled down into the memories.

When I was a girl and had my paper route, my hands would get grubby with ink like this. I'd get home from school, roll dozens of the *Eagle Tribunes* and squeeze them into baskets on the side of my bike. I rode wild for six miles on unpaved and paved roads, throwing newspapers, delivering "stories" to peoples' doors. It was my first love for journalism, my first dedication to storytelling. Now, as I compiled stories about suffering, I thought about that little girl on her bike, about how I'd gotten from there to here, from wild abandon to this.

Surely there was another way to tell a story. Surely all this rage and violence wasn't the only narrative. Who'd decided that these words and paragraphs were the way to tell the truth? Who'd decided the subject matter? The content? The manner in which the tale was recounted?

Even as a little girl, I knew the way a person told a story saved their lives, demonized them, or killed them outright. I knew how Mother told her tale, how she extracted the parts she didn't like, threw them like gutted innards into the dog pen. I knew how Father described Meghan and me. How he demonized us. How he convinced the world and himself that we were evil.

You could set the whole world to one way of thinking about you or about life in general if you told a story in a certain way. You could set the whole world against a person or against life by the way you talked. Or you could bring them up with the beauty of the tale. There was that, too. The Basho poetry, the lyrical syllables, the tales that heightened the soul.

In journalism school, objectivity was beaten into us. But I didn't believe it. It depended on who was doing the telling. It always depended on who was telling the story. We were not objective. As a student body, we were white; most of my peers were middle class, well-educated, liberal. How objective was that?

Who came up with this concept of lead, nut graph and facts in descending order of importance? Even those parameters made me question objectivity. Besides, I was in my twenties. What experience did I have of the world to be making these choices? Which event outweighed the other? Which trauma was worse?

I'd had a terrible argument at the *izakaya* right before I left for my trip back to the Midwest. I'd met Yuriko and some people she knew. They were talking about something in the news. They kept arguing the story as if what they'd read was set in stone. I'd had too many glasses of Sapporo, and said, "Don't believe everything you read."

"What do you mean?" a young lawyer asked. "You're supposed to be a journalist. We're supposed to be able to believe the basics of a story in the newspaper, right?"

"Please," I spat. "Do you know who's writing that news? People in their twenties! People like me who haven't a clue about this culture." I waved my arms around the smoky pub. "Let alone about Iran or Kenya or Kathmandu. We're misquoting people left, right and center. Please. You cannot read the newspaper and think it's the truth. It's not truth."

The young lawyer screamed at me for twenty minutes, hollered and berated and used his brain to beat me down, to render me to pulp. "How dare you tell us that the stories you're printing aren't the truth? Where are your professional ethics?" He could not abide what I had said. It blew his face red and sent spittle across the table. Finally, I had to get up and leave. I learned from the event not to talk about what goes on in the newsroom, not to tell the truth, to keep my mouth shut.

As I sat in the archives, typing the half-year's trauma into an old computer, I knew I had to watch it. I was questioning everything, even my career. I had to get myself under control. Bonnie used to say to me when we were kids, *You always have to question everything, Pearl.*

air

You can't just let things be. Nobody can live like that, questioning every single little thing.

My career was the only thing that separated me from my illiterate upbringing, the only thing that got me out of middle America, the one thing that had saved my life. Without this career, I was nothing.

By the end of the day, I'd compiled a list I knew the *Kaze* could not use, small sudden madnesses from around the globe. I'd have to come in tomorrow and do the real list. I was just making more work for myself.

The door opened. Finn walked in. He smiled when he saw me, and said, "Time for happy hour, love."

I stood abruptly. My chair knocked over with a crash. It was out of my control. I slammed the keyboard off the table with an errant arm. I knew as it was happening that this was horrible, that Finn shouldn't see this, that I could do nothing whatsoever to stop it.

People were on fire, and they were flying. They fell like fiery angels through the sky. The wind was blowing hard, and buildings kept falling down. The people flew, their wings ablaze. I wanted to fly, too. I stood on the ground, watching the flying people. I lifted my arms to fly. I was lifted from this earth. It was good, I wanted to leave it all behind, to spread my arms and ascend. The ground shook. Quaked and shuddered. People tumbled. Houses crumbled. Around us, the fiery people flew.

Finn had his shirt off. I could see his skeleton. Sometimes post-vision, I could see people's skeletal structures, as if I had x-ray vision. He dabbed at something at my temple. I reached up and touched my head and my hand came back with blood.

"Pearl, you hit your head when you fell over." I closed my eyes. "What *was* that?" he asked. I didn't answer. "As soon as you can stand, we'll get you to a doctor."

He didn't call me Queenie. It was the first time he didn't call me Queenie. "No. I don't need a doctor." I'd fallen on the keyboard and it was digging into my hip. How did I tell him, *Oh, you see, I have these visions. Ha. Ha. Let's go get that happy hour drink and laugh about it.*

"You passed out. When people pass out, love, they require a doctor."

I'd never told him about the visions; how did I start now? "No. It's not... I'm not sick. It's just...sometimes when I'm really stressed..." I couldn't find the words. He rearranged his shirt to find a clean spot. "I don't know how to explain it."

"Try me."

I told him, sort of. "I have a kind of fit sometimes when my stress levels are high." I didn't explain that I had visions. "I've been to doctors for years. I promise you, there's nothing a doctor can do for it."

"I'm not a bloody idiot. You're not telling me the whole truth, are you?"

I didn't want to lose Finn. I'd lost too many people. "No, I swear. I'm telling you everything."

He shook his head. "I don't know how much I can take, Queenie. There's something else going on here." I saw the fear in his face, and post-vision, I could read his mind. He was thinking of Akiko, of women who go crazy, of women he has to throw out, of women who lead him to an edge he can barely come back from. There was more to the story, too. Something about his mother. There was a crevasse, a dark hole, where memories of his mother should've been.

"Sorry," I said. I tried to scramble to my feet. "Sorry. Sorry."

USUI WAS MISSING. I went to his cardboard four days in a row to talk to him, but he wasn't there. Akina was worried, too. I wasn't doing well. I was losing it at work, losing it with Finn. I had to hold on. I had nowhere else to go.

I had Shinji call the mission. Yes, Usui had been there. They wouldn't tell him more than that. The relief. At least he was still alive. I took the train out. When a young man, no more than a boy, answered the door and heard Usui's name, he let me in. I roamed around as if I owned the place. Usui was not there. I went back to the rail bridge day after day, but still no Usui.

Finn was a different beast. On stage. Vibrations held together by loose breath. Off-pitch and imperfect. Stunted sounds, tightly wound. Crazy grace. Crashing and thrashing. Small tremors in the soul.

The Emperor's New Clothes was taking off. Night after night a new venue, a new gig. We ran a story about them in the entertainment section of the *Kaze*. Other magazines did articles, too.

Most nights I sat on massive speakers as the band set up. Drugs, beer, tequila. Gin and tonics. Young screaming Japanese girls

air

in short plaid skirts and knee socks. Trips into alleys to take more drugs.

One night I invited Yuriko. It was late, and she still wasn't there. At break, I followed the band into the alley behind the club. We smoked pot. My head slipped sideways. With Usui missing, I was feeling a growing neediness, a terror of loss. I was a balloon tethered by a frayed rope, and at any moment it would break and I'd float off into the universe. I went to the wall where Finn was leaning, smoking a cigarette, and clung to his arm.

Inside, too many Japanese girls in tiny skirts reaching out to touch Finn. Often, he stared at the female taiko drummer as she pounded her drum. She stared at him, too. My shoulders knotted into anxiety.

When Yuriko walked in, she was gigantic, like a statue of some goddess. Besides dungarees and boots, she wore a red silk oriental shirt that buttoned at the shoulder. I'd never seen her in Japanese clothing. The red glowed up her face, turned her black hair to fire. I waved her over to the table. I was so happy she was there.

The band took a break, and Finn came down and kissed my cheek, and said, "How's my Queenie? All right there, love?" I smiled and kissed him back. "How's it going, Yuriko."

She said, "Fine," but gave him a look. He backed away. There had always been some animal dislike between the two. He went back to the stage.

I went to the bar and got a drink for Yuriko. She liked Long Island iced teas.

"You're coming to my art show next week, right?" she asked as I put the drink in front of her. She handed me a flyer. I took it, even though she'd already given me three. A fringe gallery was showing her "Losing Face" series. She was giving some of the proceeds to a fund for survivors of the Nagasaki and Hiroshima bombings.

"I promised I'd be there and I will be there."

"I just want to make sure. I haven't seen much of you lately."

"Sorry," I said.

We gossiped about Mrs. Reinkemeyer, Jerry and the teachers at the school. "They'll all be at the show. A lot of people miss you." She gave me a look. "Including me."

The band started playing, and we couldn't hear each other unless we screamed. Yuriko stayed for most of the set, but then leaned over and yelled that she had to leave. I followed her out to the sidewalk, lit a cigarette to stall her. I just wanted her to stay.

"Seriously, Pearl, how can you abide all that masturbating on stage," she said.

"Why do you dislike Finn so much?" Despair crept into my voice. I didn't want to lose her, too. "He's not a bad guy."

She leaned toward me, touched my arm. Her fingers were huge, like a giant's. She said too kindly, "Where the hell are you in all of this, Pearl?"

"I'm right here, Yuriko. Right in front of you."

"Are you?" She shook her head. "You know it's Feminism 101 that you need to know yourself before giving yourself to someone else. And especially you, with your sensitivity. Don't hide yourself to make him happy. You could so easily get completely absorbed into any guy…"

I shot smoke out through my lips. I didn't mean to blow it into her face. Really. "Give me a break. I'm a newspaper editor. I have my own life. How many women here do you know are editors? Give me some fucking credit here."

She held up her hands. "Don't kill the messenger."

I turned away, annoyed, and pulled hard on my Marlboro. Who was she to tell me how to live? If it were anyone other than Yuriko, I would've told her to go to hell. What she said had a way of getting under my skin until I didn't know what to believe.

Something moved in the alley beside the club. I peered into the darkness. Usui. He was in the shadows, behind a stack of empty crates. He was watching me, watching out for me.

"Usui-*san*?" He stood and turned away. "Usui-*san*?" I threw my cigarette to the sidewalk and started after him. The faster I came

air

toward him, the faster he hobbled away. He was limping. Something was horribly wrong with one of his legs.

"Pearl, what are you doing? It's not safe…" Yuriko said, following me. "For God's sake."

"It's okay, Usui-*san*," I yelled. The alley grew darker the farther we went.

He tripped and fell. I caught up to him as he lay on the ground. His face was turned away, and I reached down and turned him over. He had an open sore running down his cheek. "My God, what's happened?"

His hand came up and clung to my wrist. Liver spots, long filthy fingernails. He reeked of sake.

Yuriko was behind me. "This is Usui? This is the guy you were telling me about? The homeless guru?"

I came out of the fog. Below me was an elderly homeless man with open sores on his face, neck, arms. He was not Usui. "No, it's not Usui," I said. I let him go, but he wouldn't let me go. I was bent over with the man clinging to my wrist.

"I'm sorry," I said to the man. "*Sumimasen. Gomennasai.*" Sorry. *Excuse me.* Still he wouldn't let me go.

Yuriko took his bony wrist and started shaking it. "No. No. Don't. Let…her…go." She pried at his fingers until he released me.

She tried to pull me out of the alley. "Pearl, come on!" I held back. "Come on." I felt fear for Usui in my gut. I knew this man wasn't Usui, but the fear for Usui was deep and strong.

The man was following us, he was speaking in a low whine. I reached into my pocket, thrust money at him. I bowed. I was sorry to have chased him when he was so obviously ill.

Yuriko got behind me, put both arms around me, picked me off my feet and carried me out of the alley. She put me down on the sidewalk. Finn was there, smoking. His left eye twitched when he saw us. "What's going on?" he asked.

"Are you losing your mind?" Yuriko yelled at me. "Seriously, are you losing it? Do you need some kind of help?"

"Queenie?" Finn said, coming toward me.

"Look, dude. She's not…You've got to fucking pay attention…I mean, really be present with her…" She shook her head. "Forget it. This isn't my business. Forget it." She looked at both of us, sighed heavily and turned and walked quickly away.

"We'll start as always with open discussion," the man said. "I find if people are able to speak, get it all out in the open, it's much easier to meditate."

It was a week or so later. Finn and I were at an introductory Buddhist meditation class. It was Finn's idea. He was trying to help me, or himself, or both of us. I'd become untethered. I kept seeing things that were not there. Eighty percent of the time I was okay. It was the remaining twenty percent that scared me.

Rain hit the small windows. Outside sounds dragged into a slur. Sloppy sloshing of sudden feet, slapping and slipping and sounding, like children clapping, the smear of hundreds of tires.

A dozen people sat on the floor. A mandala hung at the front. The teacher was bald and skinny. I could count his ribs at the V of his shirt. He leaned sideways and lit incense. It was musky and smelled of sex. He had a New Zealand accent. I'd learned to tell an Aussie, from a Brit, from a Kiwi. The things Tokyo was teaching me. "Anyone want to share?" He made circles of his thumb and forefinger, rested his hands on his knees, closed his eyes.

It wasn't just Usui going missing. It wasn't just the onslaught of bad news at the *Kaze*. It wasn't just the visions.

It was all the noise, all the people. It was the concrete. It was the rain coming down and not meeting earth. It was the sky seen only in the narrowest of slivers.

A middle-aged man spoke rapidly as if he were speed reading his own mind. "Okay, okay, I'll go first. This Japanese guy, I'm like looking at the frickin' rail map, 'Can you get to Ochanomizu on the

Shinjuku line?' That's all I'm asking, 'Ochanomizu, Shinjuku?' I keep repeating it like a jackass, and the dude takes my arm and goes on the train with me all the way to Ueno, on the Maranouchi Line, not the Shinjuku! So I'm not so bloody angry today because of this crazy fellow, but some days I'm so stressed out I want the city to just blow up. I'm not going to blow it up. Maybe with my bleeding brain. Then there's my mama-*san* landlady, sweeping outside my door at five a.m., waking me up, will not cease and desist no matter how desperately I beg." He stopped talking as abruptly as he's started, like a squeal of tires making a sudden stop at an unexpected red light.

A woman raised her hand. "I've got something to bitch about." She was American. "What the fuck is the deal with these asshole Japanese men?"

"Elisa, come on," her friend whispered.

"What do you mean, come on? The guy said I could talk. So I'm talking." She had bleached frizzy hair and so many lines on her face they looked painted on. She put her hand out in front of her and counted on her fingers. "Number one, I'm not fucking good enough because I'm a woman." The people in the room grew visibly agitated. Someone started fake coughing, and she had to talk louder to be heard. "*Numero dos*, keep your mouth shut, girlie, be a good little subservient girlie…"

I choked a laugh. Finn shot me a look. I gave him a look back. I couldn't help it; I liked her. I thought difficult women were the best women, the honest ones. They were not like the rest of us, trying to squelch down who we were lest we offend somebody's sensibilities. Besides, she reminded me of Yuriko.

"Number three," the woman continued. "No fucking Western guy is going to date you with all the oriental meat around…"

I barked a laugh. It wasn't just Yuriko she reminded me of, but Meghan. I worried that I kept forgetting about my half-sister. Someday I would have to find her again. Or she'd find me. The thought sent a chill down both my arms.

"Okay, okay," the leader said. "Let's move on to the meditation." He spoke in a faux soothing voice. The ranting woman whispered in the same mock voice, "We're moving on to the meditation now." I had to stop myself from laughing again.

"Close your eyes. We're going to relax our whole body. At the top of your head, feel the scalp loosen up." Again that voice. "Move down to the eyes, the cheekbones, the lips and mouth. Your neck and shoulders are letting go of tension. Feel the relaxation travel down your arms to your fingers. Then relax your stomach. Let all the tension go in your legs and feel it leave your body and go into the floor through your feet.

"Now focus on your breath. Watch it from a distance as it travels into your body and fills your lungs and how it travels out. Don't try to control it. Just observe. The idea here is to let go."

I couldn't quite connect to this concept of letting go. I'd been required to let go of everything I loved all my life. How could that be spiritual?

"Let the thoughts come and go, but always come back to the breath. Notice the breath."

Why was my breath so shallow? I breathed into the top of my shoulders. I lived my life panting. I didn't know if it was the cigarette smoke, the smog or what, but I couldn't seem to breathe. It was the first time I'd noticed how little I breathed.

I started panting, puffing, gagging. Finn moved over so his knee touched mine. It calmed me, but still my breath didn't go much lower than my breast bone.

I had trouble with the fact that they all were men. The Buddhist masters, the Hindu gurus, the Shinto authors, the Catholic priests. As a kid, I went to Mass twice a week for school, and once more on Sundays, until I was eighteen. I loved the robes and the ritual, the incense, the stained glass, but I was bothered by how men set the rules, dominated the thought, commanded the room, and then how the nuns ran after them, cleaning up their messes. It seemed to be the same in every religion I studied.

"Okay, let's take air all the way down to the base of our spines. Inhale deeply into your lowest chakra."

air

I gasped in a big mouth of air and coughed. I never knew how difficult breathing really was. The air triggered a fear as yawning as an abyss. The visions, the dreams, my father, my mother, Meghan, every memory was locked inside my belly, and the breathing threatened to explode it all outward. Fear welled up and surrounded me. I took ragged breaths. I felt as if I were going to die. Finn put a hand on my knee. How could breathing be so terrifying? If anything was going to make me lose my mind, it was breathing. Breathing was going to send me right over the edge.

Behind us, a strangling noise. The ranting American woman had her forehead on the floor. "I'm going to vomit," she cried. Her friend leaned over her. The strangling noise from her throat grew until she sounded like a distressed chicken, croaking, cawing, spewing. She went into a coughing fit, and her friend took her arm, lifted her to her feet and helped her pick her way over the bodies to the door. Her coughing a death rattle.

"Okay, okay, let's remain calm. Everyone, let's not get distracted. Let's start our mantra. Try to keep breathing deeply as we chant. Ohm." Everyone repeated the word "Ohm."

"Let's say our mantra together twenty times and then go back to the quiet noticing of the breathing."

The voices humming that one word sounded like old church bells echoing between stone walls. Ancient. My hands became claws on my knees. I could've killed for a cigarette.

"Now we're coming to an end. Slowly open your eyes. Don't move or talk for a few moments. Just sit and observe the body."

My body felt dry, used up. I wanted to curl into the fetal position and suck my thumb. I didn't know meditation could make you feel like shit. I could see why people never meditated, just kept going and going until they had a breakdown. Stopping was terrifying.

People were standing. It was over. I pulled my body off the floor. "Let's go home," Finn said, taking my hand. I looked into his face. He looked as if he was going to break into sobs. You got so caught up in your own issues, you didn't see someone else's.

He led me into the hallway, down the corridor and around a corner away from the others. He turned to me, took both my shoulders, his tall lanky body bent over mine.

"I love you," he said. Again that hysterical sadness on his face. He shook me. "I really, really love you." He bent and swallowed me with his skinny arms.

You don't think anyone can love you, Pearl.

He pulled back, his eyes watery. "I want to leave Japan. Let's just go, okay? Chuck it all and travel. Let's spend a year away from everything." He held my hand, looked at the back of it as if it were the saddest sight in the world. "Just think about it, okay?"

I nodded.

"Let's go home," he said.

On the train to Ebisu, he clung to my hand, studied the veins on the back as if it were a map. His bent blond head, bags dark beneath the eyes, he seemed so troubled. I knew so little about this man. He'd left his home country, too, and he must've had his reasons. He was homeless, too.

Home, he'd said. What was home? First, it was a cackling, crackling and buzzing. Home was dirt-covered radishes and insects buzzing up the face. Home was popping beans on the porch, chopping wood, picking gooseberries. Home was a violence, a shotgun pointed at your temple, a threatening fist.

Four years in the corner of Jason's living room on a mattress, weeks in Usui's basement, a couple years in a tiny apartment with Yuriko, Finn's dark basement flat. Home had become a series of flimsy replacements. Home was a place they threw you out of and never let you back in. Home was homelessness.

Now Finn wanted to replace one state of homelessness with another. A year with no place of our own. I felt the rope holding my balloon unravel, come one step closer to snapping.

"EMPEROR BLEEDS FROM Rectum." "Jaundiced Emperor Sleeps through Night." "Doctors Distraught over Rectal Infection." "New Bleed Found in Lower Intestines."

The emperor was dying of pancreatic cancer, and the newsroom and country was turned upside down. Finn and I had to put our plans on hold. We'd already tacked a map to the wall of his flat beneath the window of streaming feet. We'd marked our future with push pins. We were going to spend a year backpacking across Asia. The Philippines, Indonesia, Nepal, Malaysia, Thailand, India.

At the *Kaze*, we wrote about the emperor's innards, about his pus, his bowels, his urine. No detail was too intimate. Banner headlines describing his most private parts splashed black and heavy across the *Kaze's* front page. Shinji told me it'd started with Emperor Hirohito's father, that reporting mucus and bowel movements had begun a generation ago, and now the public expected it.

I ran between editor, reporter, the paste-up team, back and forth, hither and thither, spinning. The top editors told us what to do, what to write, how to write it, tried to micromanage every period and comma. We were puppets. This was too important to leave to foreigners.

Still, I was able to commission a few stories. The editors were so crazed I figured they wouldn't notice until it was too late. I wanted to know the man behind the emperor. What was it like to be a symbol

air

of an entire country? What happened to the human being behind it? I wanted stories on the emperor as a mortal.

It wasn't done. You could invade the emperor's flesh, you could analyze his bowels, but his psyche was off limits. Still, I persisted, cajoled, sent the reporters out. Got Choko and Shinji to work as a team.

They came back with articles on his life as a marine biologist, on the books he wrote on the subject, his rambling collection of bonsai trees set on an ascending rock staircase, like a miniature kingdom. This reminded me of Usui's bonsai and my heart thickened with his continued absence. They reported on how painfully awkward he was around people, his profound reserve and need for privacy. They discovered he'd asked to be buried with his microscope and a Mickey Mouse watch.

More officially, we covered how MacArthur argued with Truman after the end of the war to keep the emperor in power to appease the Japanese. How the American-imposed Japanese constitution plunged the emperor from his divine role. Hirohito made a formal statement about this fall from the skies, saying how the ties between him and the Japanese people did not depend upon mere legends and myths.

Still, the legend lived on. After the war, Hirohito tried to humanize himself by traveling amongst the masses, unheard of before his time. But still his mythology persisted. His visits only served to blow the legend deeper into the souls of the Japanese people.

With his illness, the nation walked on eggshells. On the trains, on the sidewalks, in the newsroom, everywhere a quiet descended, as if the sick emperor was in the other room and they didn't want to wake him. People stopped laughing. Some openly wept.

I was working seven days a week now, sixteen-hour days. Hirohito's illness stretched on, days turned into weeks, weeks into months.

One night I worked past midnight as usual, but I could barely function, exhausted by the last-minute headline changes, the sudden copy shifts, the barely controlled hysteria. I could barely walk in a straight line, let alone make it to Finn's. In the upstairs gym, I lay down on one of the workout benches. It wasn't the first time I'd done this. Around me were six snoring Japanese men. Mostly the guys used the space to sleep during the day. Only a few slept up there all night. It was strange how these men accepted me, a Western woman sleeping next to them on a workout bench. It was strange how safe I felt. Perhaps, like me, they were too exhausted to care.

I dreamt of a flying emperor in black kimono. His shadow covered the archipelago, arms outstretched, kimono flapping in high wind. Below, the Japanese people curled into each other in poetic choreography, danced their lives as if the emperor were their conductor or their cozy blanket.

The wind took his cloak, blew it off him. The people cried because they did not know what to do. A voice said, "What will they do without their god? What will we all do without our gods?"

I jerked awake. Light flaked through the smudged windows. I felt horrible. I rubbed drool from my mouth, turned to see Finn sitting at the break table, staring at me. I thought I was still dreaming, rubbed my eyes, but there he was, a slight beard, a wrinkled jacket.

"Hey." I tried to straighten my shirt and trousers. I'd lost more weight and the pants had twisted almost backward on my hip bones.

"Are you okay?" he asked, coming over and offering me a hand.

"What do you mean?" I sat up with a groan, put my hand to my hair and tried to pat down the wiry mess. I'd stopped straightening it since Hirohito's illness. I got a whiff of my underarms and cringed. "Sorry. It's just with the emperor dying…"

"Can I do anything? What can I do?" He spoke loudly to me as if I were hard of hearing.

I started laughing. "Call the emperor. Tell him to die already."

"Seriously," he said. He sat on the bench next to me. His blue eyes were cracked, like ice.

"What are you trying to say? I'm fine." I stood and cinched my belt tighter, took a rubber band out of my pocket, and twisted it into my hair.

air

"Listen." He looked as if he was about to cry. "I'm no good at this, Queenie. I wasn't good at it with Aikiko, and I wasn't good at it with…" Again the tears. I knew so little about this man I lived with. He so rarely talked about his past. "Be really careful, okay? It's not worth it. None of this is worth it. You have to take care of yourself." I didn't understand the tears. He backed up, looked me over, shook his head. He seemed about to say something else, but instead turned and walked toward the exit. "I have to get to work."

Rage clicked inside me. I wanted to scream at his back, *I've been taking care of myself my whole goddamned life. No one has ever taken care of me. I've been working nonstop. And every free moment I'm at one of your gigs! Where's my goddamned support?*

I stormed to the bathroom and rubbed liquid soap beneath my pits. I looked in the mirror. It wasn't a pretty sight, the black under-eye circles, a sneer around the mouth, my stringy, oily hair. I seemed to be unable to straighten up, stood with a permanent hunch. Grudgingly, I thought about what Finn had said. Why *was* I letting these people suck me dry? I thought of Jason, about forest clearing and Walmart. My body was a clear-cut forest, and they were building big box stores on top me. My only question was, if I said that's enough and took care of myself, who was going to take care of the world?

Pandemonium in the *Kaze* office, reporters running, people yelling, four languages screamed at once. The tower of Babel. Somebody had spilled an entire pot of coffee, and people were jumping over it. Cigarette smoke hung like low clouds, the room as foggy as a Japanese public bath.

Shinji ran up. "Hirohito has died now," he cried. "The emperor is dead."

He looked shattered, as if a bomb had gone off in his body; something deep was traumatized there. I thought of my dream. All the Japanese staff looked broken, walked with their arms pressed to their sides as if they were holding themselves together. I thought of Yuriko's paintings, about how much this nation had gone through with the war, Hiroshima and Nagasaki. How the past was the present was the future.

Reporters, photographers, and members of the layout team descended at once, all calling for some urgent task. Shinji's shattered face receded into the crowd.

By the time I'd assigned all of the articles to the reporters, talked to the photographers about getting archival photos of the emperor as a child, of his father, Emperor Yoshihito, and grandfather, Emperor Meiji, as well as photos of the incoming emperor, Akihito, the trash can overflowed with stained Styrofoam coffee cups and cigarette butts. I had almost finished a pack of cigarettes and it wasn't even noon. And I couldn't find Michael. Where the hell was Michael?

I was up to my elbows, editing stories as they came in, matching them to photos, writing captions, printing the pieces on the layout printer, running back to make sure the paste-up was going smoothly. I had five pages to finish by the end of the day, did not have time for lunch, so lit another cigarette and poured another cup of coffee. The managing editor whispered in my ear that Yoshimoto wanted to see me. Yoshimoto was the executive editor. I got up nervously. I'd never been called to Yoshimoto's office before.

He paced. He had a fat face and his neck spilled over his collar. His suit was too small for him. He moved in tight motions as if he were trapped. Newspapers were stacked in two areas of the room, and the only clean surface was his desk, which sat low and looked like a coffin.

He spoke to me in Japanese, or to himself, I couldn't tell. He brusquely handed me a white sheet of paper. It was a list of headlines. "Emperor Succumbs." "Goodbye to Emperor." "Emperor Finally Meets Peace."

air

He began speaking English, roughly and tentatively. He kept his back to me. "My father died in war. When war ended, I was ten. Many uncles dead. Fathers of my friends…so many dead. We put on radio to hear Hirohito tell nation of surrender. Until that day, it was not thinkable for ordinary person to hear his voice. He tell people endure and surrender, but we already endure. We endure too much. Government told us Japan winning war. All neighbors around radio, my mother and me. We were bitter."

I'd never seen a Japanese person talk so openly. He paced the small room.

"After war, emperor traveled around Japan to give hope. It was God coming to meet us. His car passed through my city. I waved flag when I saw car."

He turned, stood in front of me, stared into my face. The Japanese rarely stared so boldly; usually they avoided eye contact. His eyes were hooded, but behind them burned a boiling passion.

"I am seeing articles you commission. The ones we not tell you to commission. I am seeing something. I am seeing that you have understanding." He nodded at me. Not knowing what else to do, I nodded back.

"Now, we have his death. I am seeing finished pages. They are small. Not big. We cannot see big picture. My question, how to translate this? How to show English speakers in world bigger meaning?"

His proximity made me fidget. He had what I noticed in everyone else, a traumatized energy in his body, as if the emperor's death were an earthquake. He smelled more virile than I'd expected, as if he were a handsome, exciting person and not this chubby middle-aged man.

"You, Pearl, you see different way. I ask you for this. It is big asking. We need to translate him."

I nodded. I took the sheet of headlines and held it at the corners in both hands and bowed. I felt unfamiliar respect, both *for* this man, and *from* this man. I usually despised older men.

The first man I'd ever met in my life despised me, and I spent my life reciprocating. This respect was something new to me.

I learned very quickly this could not be a solo pursuit. Every story had to be rewritten. Each needed a fleshing out, an elevation in the verbs, musical tones added to the facts. I held a rewriter's meeting. We had to up the game, be translators from one culture to another, not a translator of language, but of culture. We had to build a bridge.

Yoshimoto was right. I did get it, intrinsically. One culture wasn't better than another, just different. I could hold the two realities, one in each hand. This culture in the right, this in the left. Missouri in the right, Japan in the left. This world in the right, that other world in the left.

The pride I felt in how the rewriters stepped up to the plate filled my chest to bursting. I already had the reporters to thank for the personal stories of the emperor's life. I had to get the paste-up guys involved, design the pages with a greater air of dignity. I held a meeting and had Shinji translate.

They were in a union, the paste-up guys, older men in their fifties. They listened intently as I talked and Shinji translated. I waved my arms, paced the room, spoke to them about the epic nature of our task. The pages had to be operatic. They reminded me of the men at Mrs. Reinkemeyer's school.

When we finally had the inside pages ready, when finally the front page was pasted up, I asked Yoshimoto to join us. In the paste-up area, he put on his glasses, leaned in and read the stories. Each had an intrinsic beauty, but we'd also arranged the articles on the pages so they choreographed to tell an ongoing story, like the bonsai plants I'd seen in Usui's garden, the architecture of a miniature kingdom. Page to page, the story deepened. The massive headline across the front page read simply, "The Mourning of an Emperor."

Yoshimoto took off his glasses and bowed. *"Domo arigato." Thank you.* He had tears he tried to hide. *"Domo arigato gozaimasu." Thank you very much.*

air

I swung my arm in an arc toward the paste-up guys. I bowed to the team and then led Yoshimoto to the rewriters' desks. We moved over to the Japanese reporters. Everyone stood as we passed. They bowed. We bowed.

I understood then the Japanese respect for group dynamics. This furious need for individuality was American. I understood how important the group was. A lesson I'd come to Japan for, an expansion of my balloon. As I looked at a teary-eyed Yoshimoto, when he'd asked me individually to take on this task, was he beginning to understand American individuality? Had we taught each other?

Now that it was finally over, I felt my body falling. I could've gone to my desk right then and put down my head and left my body for good.

I KNOCKED, FRANTICALLY pounded. Nobody was answering. *Please answer. Please.* Next door, a tired-looking man in T-shirt and boxers opened his door and spoke in what I thought was Korean. He waved his hand toward the bombed-out courtyard, but I didn't know what he was saying. I went back to pounding on the door.

"What is going on here?" A woman's voice beside me. Sakina. She was weighted down with plastic grocery bags. Oh, the relief. I wanted to throw myself at her, kneel at her feet.

"I need to talk to you. Please." I'd had another vision in front of Finn. I was so shattered from the emperor's death, I had no defenses against it. I couldn't push it down or run from the room fast enough.

It wasn't even a bad one. I'd floated over this field of people. They were all lying down, sleeping. One woke up, stood, and this joy flooded through her as she awoke, and she was surrounded by a rainbow light. Then another person woke up, a man this time. And another. Through every awakening, this crazy joy, and this splash of rainbows. And I came out of the vision for the first time in a long time with something like hope.

But there was no way to soft sell the theatrics in front of Finn. He demanded an explanation. I hesitated at first, but then ended up telling him everything, starting with this first vision and ending with this last one.

air

It didn't go well. I was losing him. I could tell he was getting close to an edge.

"I do not do readings, my friend, without an appointment." Sakina unlocked her apartment door.

I grabbed two of the grocery bags out of her left hand. "Let me help you with those," I said. She gave me a look, but let me follow her into the apartment.

It must've been the vestiges of this morning's vision, because she was also surrounded by rainbow light. I put the bags on the counter. She was prettier than I'd remembered. She also must've done something to her apartment, because it wasn't nearly as ugly as it had been the first time.

"Frankly," she said, filling the kettle. "I am quite surprised to see you. I didn't think you much liked our first encounter."

"Look, I have money." I took out six thousand yen from my purse. "Three times what you charge. Please."

"I've already decided I will give you a reading. But never again. I don't allow this. My reasoning is that something must have sent you to me, and that it must be my duty to comply. But not again. Do we understand that? If you want a reading you set an appointment. I am not a circus monkey."

"Of course, yes." I sat at her table and put out my hands, ready for her to hold them, ready for her to tell me how to fully stop the visions. I was ready to listen.

She took her time preparing tea and putting away the groceries. I kept my palms up on the tabletop. She fussed with lighting incense and getting out the cards. Finally, she sighed and sat. "I do not like to be on demand like this."

She shuffled the cards. "Before I start, please tell me what you have come for. What people come for and what they receive may be two different things."

I told her about that morning's vision, and about all the others. I reminded her about her last reading, that she said something about how they were screaming to get my attention. "All I want to know is how to stop them from screaming at me." I didn't say, *I don't want to lose my boyfriend. Help me keep my boyfriend.* After her remarks last time about how most women asked for readings about their boyfriends, I didn't want her to know it was about Finn. Anyway, I hated that I was just there to keep my boyfriend. It was bigger than that. Wasn't it?

She took my hands, swayed and hummed as before. She let go, picked up the cards, threw a spread. The cards, too, glowed with rainbow colors. She studied them. She looked up at me.

"I'm sorry I've forgotten your name."

I didn't say, *Aren't you psychic? Shouldn't you know it?* "Pearl."

"Pearl." She looked at the cards. "Why is she so resistant to who she is?" She spoke to the cards. "Why is she so closed down?" She kept nodding and seemed to be listening to voices I could not hear.

"Okay, Pearl. The cards cannot provide a simple answer for you. They have suggested something else. Are you willing to try it?"

"Anything."

"Well then, I need you to close your eyes."

I did so. She said she was going to lead me on a guided meditation. Her speech was lyrical. Why hadn't I noticed her voice before? She talked to me about a path in the woods.

"We're going to walk up this path. It will be steep. I am going to lead you. We are going to meet someone at the end of the path. And you will engage him. If you are willing to work with this person, and you are willing to listen, you will be provided with answers."

To the sound of her voice, I hiked up the path. It was a temperate rainforest. I passed alder trees, a massive redwood, forests on both side full of mossy evergreens. Up and up, over rocks and roots. Branches dripped with rain. The forest was full of mist and fog. Finally, we came to the top. I stood next to a clearing. It was easy to visualize it all. It was as if I were right there in the woods.

"Do you see someone in the middle of the clearing?"

I nodded. "He has a beard and is wearing a brown robe, like some kind of old-world traveling minstrel."

"You are very good at visualization," Sakina said. "Very, very good. Many people find this difficult the first time they try it." I didn't

air

say,*Oh, Sakina, believe me, I have no problem whatsoever seeing things that are not there.* "Now I want you to go meet the man, and after you have greeted him, I want you to step into his body."

"Step into his body?"

"Yes, you will see. It will be easy."

I went up and shook his callused hand. I stepped toward him. I entered into his body, became him.

Confusion. Panic. I felt as if I were falling. I flailed my arms, started hyperventilating, gasping. "Stop it. Make it stop. Stop!" It was like the meditation. I couldn't breathe. I was going to die.

"Pearl, come!" Sakina's voice. "Back down the path. Now. Now!" I thrust myself out of the old man, ran out of the clearing, fell headlong down the path. "Open your eyes only when you have reached the start of the path."

I opened my eyes. I was clinging to the chair. My teacup was on the floor, tea spilled across the linoleum. Sakina stood beside me with her hand on my back.

"Now I see why it is you are so closed. It will be a long path for you, my friend. The gargoyles at your gates are particularly frightening. They are guarding the light. One's light is as light as their dark is dark.

"This is your calling," she said. "It will be difficult, but the only way through is to work through this fear. It is the only way."

"Oh joy," I said, speaking more to myself than to Sakina. "Great. That's just what I need, more work." I reached down to the floor and picked up the tea cup.

Usui was back! Someone had dropped off a string of cranes at the *Kaze's* reception desk along with a simple note. "Usui-*san* here now." I asked the girl, and she made a face, said it was a man dressed as a woman. Akina! I wore the cranes like a necklace of flowers, ran to the station, jogged through the park. He was back. He was back.

He sat on his cardboard behind the strands of origami hair. He'd cut his dreadlocks. He was clean-shaven. He wore different clothes, not new, but clean. I wanted to grab him and smooch him.

"Where have you been?" I sounded like a mother. I sat. He handed me a tea cup full of wine. He seemed excited, renewed, rejuvenated. He told me the story.

"After we do crane dance, something say in my ear, *Go back to old life.* I must go back!"

I laughed. It was just so great to sit there and watch him talk.

"At mission, of course, new missionary. He tell me go to head office to get job back. I go. Speak with Jesuit leader. We talk long time. Long, long time. I have some understanding. I must go see Mother and Father."

He'd borrowed money, went to Hokkaido to his childhood home. He gave me a sideways look.

"Oh," I said. I realized what the look meant. I'd never told him I'd gone to see his father and mother in Hokkaido. "I guess I should've told you I stopped by your house."

"My father tell me very interesting story about a girl journalist who come to him."

I nodded sheepishly.

He shook his head. "So, we talk long time. Long time. It is not such good talk as with Jesuit leader." Usui's shoulder's sagged. "How do Americans say? Don't rock boat? Well, if you *rock* boat, Purr-*chan*, they will not let you *on* boat.

"What is most important is finally I understand. I understand." I took a sip of wine. "Everywhere wrong thinking. Jesuits, Catholics, salariman." He put his right hand up, his left below it. "Up, down. High, low. Top, bottom. It is not way. God not *over* us. People not *high,* animals not *low,* men not *up* and women *down.* I not shepherd. People not sheep."

His eyes were on fire. "When I leave mission and become homeless, you ask me why. Why radical? I did not know. Only that I

air

could not do it anymore. Now I understand. Homeless time was break for me to be able to understand.

"Like you, Purr-*chan*. Time outside Misery. It will help you understand."

Usui continued. "I cannot have security of Jesuit life, or father's life. I cannot have its money or safety. It is lie. I must leave it. It is only myself now. I must see what it is I really think, what I really want to do."

The dark Usui was gone. He was so light, as if he could float up and away.

"So what will you do?" I asked.

"This is what I must meditate on. I come back because mind is clear here. No distractions. I stay without home until I decide, then I move on." He took my hands, turned the palms upward. "You have much in hands. Crane dance saved my life. What will you do with your gift, Purr-*chan*?"

My hands still in his, I felt myself floating into his soul. In less than six weeks, I was leaving. I couldn't bear to tell him. I couldn't bear to lose him again, even if I was doing the leaving this time. "You're the one with magic. You're the one who saves *my* life."

Usui slowly pulled his hands away. "Purr-*chan*, you understand between us, we must only be friends."

I blushed. Yes, I knew it, but maybe somewhere deep down I hoped otherwise. I didn't tell him this.

"Sometimes person is made not just for one other person. Sometimes person is made for world. Same with Jesuit missionary or Catholic priest. We keep free to be available to world."

We didn't talk for a while. He took a small square of paper and began folding.

"You have enough for more than two wishes you know, Usui-*san*." I gestured to the strands of cranes blowing in the wind.

"Yes, and already one wish true, my new understanding."

"Why do you keep making the things?"

"The world is in need of much wishes, Purr-*san*."

I took out a sheet of white paper. I watched his hands. He did one fold. I echoed him. Another. I matched him fold for fold. When we were finished his crane was alive, and mine was crooked.

"It is beginning," he said.

He handed me his crane. On the beam, I took down a strand that was half full. I added our two cranes and strung it back up.

INN'S THIRTIETH BIRTHDAY. Disco balls, lights dangling from exposed pipes, candles with tiny shots of fire, disposable cameras. We were at the Swing Bar in Ohtemachi, not far from the *Kaze*. It was called the Swing Bar because wooden swings hung from the ceiling by thick ropes.

Something wasn't right. I'd been off all day. Something was wrong, but I couldn't figure out what. I'd stopped to see Usui and some of the darkness had returned for him, too. By the time I'd left him, we were both worried he was having another premonition.

The party wasn't a surprise. Finn's band was setting up on a tiny stage. I'd snuck a cake with Finn's name on it behind the bar. I had his gift in my purse, tickets to see Dizzy Gillespie at the Blue Note. I wore Finn's favorite black miniskirt, leather thigh boots. My hair was flat, straight, glistening black, my face a mask of makeup, darkness circling eyes, red shadows beneath cheek bones, ruby lipstick.

Yuriko walked through the door. She looked more Japanese than I'd ever seen her, curves tugging at the seams of a silk oriental dress. Two jeweled chopsticks held up her hair. Her face glowed white in the darkened room, her lipstick bright red. Someone was with her, a woman. It looked like the Indian psychic, Sakina.

I walked up to them and realized it wasn't the psychic. This woman was younger. She wore a sari, necklaces, and her bangles made music as she walked. She was large, with rounded breasts and thick calves. Everyone in Tokyo wore black, and the color and

air

reflection of the two of them was like a jolt. Next to them, I felt as skinny as a scarecrow.

"This is Asha. Asha, Pearl," Yuriko said. I saw they were holding hands and stared at Yuriko's white fingers entwined with Asha's brown ones. I knew it was awkward, my staring, but I couldn't stop myself.

"Yes, it *is* what it looks like." Yuriko brought both their hands up and kissed Asha's knuckles. I could tell Asha wasn't Indian. You couldn't fit her features or coloring into one culture. She was like Yuriko, a mixture.

"Excellent," I said, smiling and nodding, in short jerky bows. "Perfect." I didn't know what to say. I looked up into Yuriko's eyes. She seemed happy. Deep down happy. I wanted to cry. Not because I wasn't happy for her, but because I knew I was losing her.

"Sometime, when you have a chance, Pearl, I'd like to tell you the whole story. It started when I went to see my mom in Seattle." Yuriko laughed. "No, I guess it started on the plane. Funny. Remember when I met you? I said I was going to Japan to find my roots. Well, I think I found them." She kissed Asha's knuckles again.

Others showed up. Yuriko and Asha drifted off. When Yuriko was sleeping with men, she was frantic and hysterical. With Asha, she emanated quiet, calm. I turned to greet Shinji and Choko. Choko had started work on a series of articles on Japanese women in the workplace. After the emperor's death, I was able to push the idea through with the editors. We got the big Australian rewriter to help her. It was funny watching the two across the office, Choko so tiny, a third of the size of the Australian.

Mrs. Reinkemeyer arrived next, waved to me and went and sat with Yuriko and Asha. Other rewriters showed up. Even Mr. Jameson. There were only swings left now to sit on, and Mr. Jameson sat awkwardly on one. A stream of people came in—Finn's workmates and other musicians he'd met along the way.

"Ladies and gentleman," Finn yelled into the mic. "The Emperor's New Clothes!" The sound came from a half-dozen speakers placed around the room. Taiko, saxophone, keyboards, shamisen. I watched the female taiko drummer warily. She moved the sticks and her body as if she were having sex with the drum. I watched Finn watching her. People got up to dance. Choko and Shinji. Asha and Yuriko. Mrs. Reinkemeyer was surprisingly light on her feet, dancing with Mr. Jameson.

The band played a full set. When I knew they were on the last song, I snuck behind the bar and got the cake ready, hid it behind one of the side speakers, lit the candles. As soon as Finn's voice faded, I jumped on stage and took the microphone.

"The Emperor's New Clothes!" I yelled, motioning to them. People hollered and clapped. I put up my hand for quiet. Somebody wolf whistled. Finn looked out from under his hand into the audience. "She's mine, you bloody bastard," he screamed. The wolf whistle again. "Behave yourself," Finn yelled.

"You all know why we're here," I said into the microphone. The taiko drummer did a "kacha boom." Applause. "Finn, happy thirtieth birthday!" I yelled. He dipped me dramatically and kissed me. When he released me, I ran to the side of the stage and came back with the cake. The band played a soft rendition of happy birthday as the crowd sang.

The buzzing was well underway before I noticed it, a frantic jabbing at the base of my skull. The clash in my head was like sudden movements of underground rock. The gods were shaking me like a rag doll. Wake up, they were screaming. Wake up! I almost fell over, but righted myself and saved the cake. *Oh, dear God, not now. Not now.* I tried to bear down on it.

A music stand fell over. The stage started to shake. Dogs barked in the distance. A siren. I heard a scream. Someone in the audience yelled, *"Jishin! Jishin!"* And someone else screamed, "Earthquake!"

It wasn't a vision at all. It was an earthquake. The cake slid from my hands. Chunks of the ceiling rained down. I looked around frantically to find a place to hide, a doorway, a table, but it was no use. I couldn't move without falling. The building shook. Beer glasses rolled and shattered. The stage lights were blinding. Finn was trying

air

but couldn't stand. The lights went off. We were thrown into darkness.

Blinded, I barely made out the outline of Finn as he rolled and fell off the stage. Something fell from the ceiling and hit my shoulder before shattering on the stage. I fell flat to the floor and knew I had to move before something else fell. I started to crawl. Everywhere the sounds of shattering glass, people screaming, car alarms, a crunching and tearing, a falling apart.

It was as if a bull were bucking me. I tried to make it to where Finn had fallen, but was tossed up and off the stage at the other end. I fell on my already hurt shoulder, and the pain was piercing. The taiko drum rolled from the stage, fell and landed on my legs. I ducked my head just as a light plunged from the ceiling. A woman screamed louder and more piercing than the others.

How many minutes did the earth shake? How many cries, screams for help? How long would we live in this place of chaos?

Finally, a calm. It was pitch black. Whimpers and moans. Sobbing. "Finn, where are you?" I whispered.

"Here! Bloody hell!" he said from a few feet away. Others screamed out names. "Makiko…Juishi…Martha…Genji…Kyle…Cahol." Names peppered the uneven darkness. A man cried like a child in some far off distance. Smoke came in through the shattered windows.

I heard Yuriko calling, "Pearl! Pearl!"

"Yuriko, I'm here. Are you okay?"

"We're okay."

The lights over the bar came on, an emergency generator. A glow permeated the trashed room. All the swings had fallen. Ropes and broken seats littered the floor. Broken glass was everywhere, sticky liquid on everything. People were sprawled on benches, floors, tables. A Japanese man had a cut on his forehead and had taken off his white business shirt to stem the flow of blood. Groups of squatting, huddled people started to stand. An American girl, a friend of one of the band members, cried and held out a twisted arm that was clearly broken. Debris had fallen from the roof and lay shattered on the floor. Several people were unconscious.

I felt a sudden spiky pain in my gut, a deep sharp burning. My shoulder hurt and my leg, but I didn't think I'd gotten any wounds to my torso. There it was again, a sharp deep pain. I reached down, felt my stomach. No wound. Ugh, it seared like a lead pipe. Then a voice in my head said so clearly it was as if someone was speaking into my ear. *Usui is hurt. This is Usui's pain.* I had to get to him. I stood, wobbled, ran willy nilly over the wreckage to the door.

Finn hollered, "Queenie, what the fuck?"

Yuriko yelled, "Where are you going? Pearl, for God's sake."

I just kept moving. I had to shove a beam from in front of the door to get out, jarring my shoulder even further. The stairs were dotted with rubble, and I picked my way as fast as I could to the street.

I started running. It was an obstacle course. I had to work to find a foot purchase, veering down the middle of the road, leaping over debris on the sidewalk. An aftershock sent me falling, and I stumbled sideways, more on the ground than on my feet. Fires everywhere. Severed electrical lines uncoiled like snakes, throwing sparks. Cars had smashed into each other and littered the streets. Car alarms, sirens, honking. An overhead neon sign was on its side in the street, the *kanji* lettering like confused hieroglyphics.

An unconscious woman hunched over the steering wheel of a white Toyota. Trees had been uprooted along with chunks of sidewalk. People huddled together in groups by the side of the road. Here and there, someone hysterical, someone bleeding, someone lying in a doorway. I had to dodge an electricity pole; it swayed, then fell right in front of me, falling and demolishing a moped.

I ran by the *Kaze*. It was on fire. The smoke grew thick. I put my face in the crook of my good arm.

Even on a normal day, the *Kaze* building was bombarded by wind. It stood at the end of a street, the end of a wind tunnel. The rushing air whipped the flames into a frenzy. It was tribal. Primal. The

air

burning turned everything around it red, the buildings, the pavement, the metal bodies of dented cars.

The flames were mesmerizing. My body filled with the heat, the utter destruction of it. All the work I'd done, all the life I had given to that place, all the office equipment, printing equipment, the very walls and floors, everything was burning to ashes. What did it all mean when everything you broke your back doing was destroyed like that? I wanted to stay with it, to live with those flames, but I heard Yuriko and Finn behind me. I turned. Yuriko looked around like a mad woman; I could tell she was seeing it all through her artist lens. She would be painting this for years to come. I saw Asha a block behind, trying to keep up.

"Pearl!" Finn yelled. "You're bleeding horribly! You need to see a doctor. Bloody hell, stop goddamnit!"

I kept running. I put my hand to my shoulder and realized Finn was right. I had an open wound and the running had torn it farther. But there was no time. The running was growing harder with the smoke, the debris, the blood. Match the feet with the breath, slap, inhale, slap, exhale. The pavement was shattered. Inhale *yah*, exhale, *weh. Yah*, slap, *weh*, slap. *Yah*, a boy with a leg twisted backward, *weh*, sitting up next to a garbage bin. *Yah*, a woman leaning over him, crying, *weh*.

In the park now, jumping over uprooted trees, around people putting down blankets, others hobbling, or carrying the wounded.

"Just slow bloody down and let us catch up," Finn yelled behind me. I didn't slow. Tree branches had broken off. A pedestrian walkway had collapsed. It was most difficult running through the trees because it was pitch black and there were so many limbs and branches.

In the field of homeless men, the barrels had overturned and started small fires. Men were trying to put out the flames with their coats. I went through the second set of trees. Usui was on his cardboard, grasping his stomach. A girder from the rail bridge lay next to him. I looked up. A train had stopped right above us. The metal bridge creaked ominously. People on the train screamed horror out the windows.

Yuriko and Finn ran panting out of the trees. Asha trailed behind. I leaned over Usui. "Oh, Usui-*san*." I ran my hands over his body. "Where's the pain? What can I do?" He held his lower abdomen. I ran in circles looking for something to ease his pain. What could possibly help him? There was nothing and no way he could be moved.

Moving his hands away, I lifted his shirt. He screamed, but I had to do something. So much blood. I tried to swipe it away with my palm and realized that the blood was mine. I'd gotten it all over my hands and was now rubbing it on Usui.

A bruise spread out across his stomach; something was broken inside him. Again a strange eerie quiet. The moon glowed Usui's face silver.

Yuriko, Asha and Finn gathered around. Finn whispered, "Queenie, there's blood all the way down your side. You're losing too much blood."

I screamed, "Everyone back up. Just back up!"

I moved Usui's hands away from his stomach. He groaned, his face sickly white, his lips purple. He was trying to speak. I put my ear close to his lips. "I can't hear you, Usui-*san*," I cried.

He sputtered out the words. "I figured it out."

"Yes," I said, crying. "Yes, you did."

"No," he grunted. "More. There is more."

I put my hands on his stomach. Willed them to do something to heal him.

He said, "This homelessness. I understand. We have separation from spirit; that is the homelessness. No home in our own body. Do you understand? You must understand."

I pushed on his stomach. "Listen." He screamed in pain. "You must not be this homelessness! Find yourself inside. I am no longer Ideko. You must not be Ideko."

"Okay," I said. "It's okay. Just calm down."

"No, you must listen. You must."

air

He was dying. I could feel it. I put my hands on his side, my head on his upper belly, careful not to put any pressure on his lower abdomen. I needed some kind of power. I needed it now. I felt myself pulled into him, and vice versa, felt the essence of Usui in marrow and veins. I breathed him in.

I looked at Finn and Yuriko and felt them, too, all of us as if we were one. Just like on the farm when I was growing up, when every sassafras tree was me, every twisted root. I was Yuriko in her torn oriental dress, in the crazed wildness in her eyes. Finn made fists, and I saw myself in his clenched fingers. I saw something extraordinary in Finn at that moment, something I hadn't seen before. He was exquisite, unusual, extraordinary. He was so bruised. So terribly, painfully delicate.

"Aye. Aye. Aye," Usui screamed and arched. A sigh blew long, low and slow from his lips. He was dying. Beneath my cheek on his chest, beneath my palms, he was dying.

He turned his head, and his eyes were clear. "My soul and yours are the same. You appear in me. I in you. We hide in each other." The English was too perfect; it was a quote, a poetic reference I did not know. He grabbed my shirt. I gasped with the pain to my shoulder. His eyes burned with fire. "Where is home, Purr-*chan*? It is Misery? Is it mission? Is it cardboard? Is it flesh? Where?"

His chest deflated and he grew calm for several minutes. He seemed to be out of pain, even getting better.

"Do you hear the voices, Purr-*chan*?" His eyes glowed as he stared upward.

"I know you hear."

I kissed his cold cheek. I did hear them. They weren't human. They were the voices of the air.

"This is voice we must listen for." He jerked his head sideways. "You understand. You must understand. To this voice that so many ignore, you must listen." He grabbed my shirt and pulled my face to him. I panted from the pain in my shoulder. "Do you see? The world has lost magic. You have magic. The Ideko world, no one can survive. World cannot survive without magic."

His body arched, and all the air left him moved from his toes through his legs up his torso and out of his mouth. With all my spirit, I put myself into him. Myself inside him would save him. I felt his soul leave his body with this last exhale. I felt his whole being rise onto the air.

I lifted with him. I left my body. I was flying up, too. "Usui-*san*?" I said, my voice nothing more now than the wind.

I looked down and saw my body. The bloody shoulder, how I'd smeared blood all over the side of my face, my hair fanning out over Usui's pale skin. We soared upward. I felt so free, free of that body, of that restraint, of the crushing inner pain.

"No," Usui said, his words like a wind chime. "You must go back. You will die, too. If you follow me, you will die. You must go back." He tried to push me off.

"No. I will not."

"Go back. You think I am one with power. You give me your power. Dying is my power. It is not yours." He tried to throw me off.

"Come back with me."

"No," the word fading on the wind.

I looked down at that bruised and pock-marked earth. Die and live in that air place forever, or fall back to earth. It was my decision. I knew it. I felt it. Free will.

I let go. I fell. I hit the earth with a soul thud. Coming into my body, the pain in my shoulder was excruciating.

Finn was prying me off Usui. "Queenie, we have to do something about your shoulder. You're losing a lot of blood. Queenie. Goddamnit, don't lose consciousness. Goddamnit. Can you hear me? Queenie, wake the fuck up!"

There are things that happen that sear the soul. Images that embed themselves for a lifetime. Events that change forever the way you view the world. At first, we didn't understand what was happening. I was in the gravel. Finn had his shirt off and was pressing it into my shoulder.

Asha screamed. Her scream brought us all into the terror until we were all one, all screaming. It had started to rain. Human bodies.

air

The bodies were on fire. The people flew with flames shooting out from behind them. It was my vision.

On the railway bridge above us, the train that was stuck was on fire. The rail bridge was broken. There was no way out. The first body hit about thirty feet from Usui. And then another. Another. One woman was still alive and was whimpering in a heap. It was raining humans. People were jumping from the train doors and windows, their clothes aflame.

Yuriko ran up, pulled Usui's body down the incline and away from the falling people. I watched it all sideways, from the ground. Flames licked the paper cranes still hanging from the beam. The strings burned first like a wick. One by one, each bird caught fire. The wind took the paper birds, flew them upward. Dozens of tiny cranes, then hundreds, flaming up into the air. Burning bodies falling downward, fiery cranes streaming upward. Finn was still holding his shirt against my shoulder. I looked up at him, and his eyes were sunken as he watched. Yuriko was trying to venture forward to help the moaning woman, but each time a body fell near her and she was forced back. The trees behind us started to burn.

"We have to get out of here," Yuriko said. She and Asha lifted Usui's body. He was so thin it didn't take much effort. Everything and everyone went in slow motion. Finn held the shirt against my wound and helped me up. As bodies burned behind us, we limped our way through the trees.

Above, the rail bridge creaked ominously.

THE LAPPING WATER of the bay was a kingdom for birds, long-legged herons, egrets, kingfishers, cormorants, cranes. Wetlands, marshes, foxglove, pickerel weed, bamboo, the aviary was just outside the wreckage of Tokyo, a sudden watery patch of Eden. Around us, birds took flight and landed, bellies and wings using the wind, glorying in the wind.

It was dusk. An early autumn breeze blew the bamboo—the bird calls, the bamboo conk, an organic chorus. In Tokyo Bay, birds perched on posts, first the real bird above and then the watery reflection below. At an airport in the distance, planes descended and ascended.

It was Finn's idea. A benefit to raise money for the people made homeless by the earthquake. We thought about using the Gyotoku aviary, but he did some research and found this bigger bird sanctuary in Tokyo Bay. Such a relief to be near the earth. I couldn't believe this wild patch of nature could even exist this close to Tokyo.

The band set up near the bamboo blind. A long line of people streamed down the scrubby pathway and into the park. They carried paper lanterns. At the door, they donated what they could—money, cans of food, blankets, clothing. They wove in, found a place in the wet grass, put down blankets, set up picnics. More than nine thousand people had died in the 7.5 magnitude earthquake. Another four thousand were injured. Many were made homeless. The fire that took the *Kaze* took most of the financial district with it.

air

My shoulder went into a spasm, and I bent forward to ease it. Among the dead were two people at the Swing Bar, Mrs. Reinkemeyer and Mr. Jameson. An air conditioning unit had fallen through the roof onto them.

Finn and I had been to too many funerals over the past few weeks. The grief on some days made me feel old and broken. A falling beam had broken both of Shinji's legs. I went to the hospital to see him. He was crammed into a ward with hundreds of others. The wound in my shoulder was healing, but the story of that night had lodged into my flesh and left a memory embedded there.

The *Kaze* had set up a makeshift newsroom in the warehouse of one of its printers. Several journalists had died in the fire. No one could locate Michael—he'd gone missing when the emperor was dying and never showed up again. I knew in my gut he wasn't dead. I imagined the emperor's death and the earthquake triggered his post-traumatic stress. I imagined him hiding in his darkened apartment, waiting for the monsters to subside. Those of us journalists who were left, bandaged and shell-shocked, sat at long tables in the warehouse and fought over the use of two telephones.

Beside us, Yuriko and Asha ran a food bank from the printer's loading dock. Choko had helped them set it up. It didn't take long before they attracted a horde of expat volunteers. Yuriko and Asha and the volunteers would arrive at five a.m., haul crates of donated food out of the warehouse, take donations and give out food and water all day, and late at night haul the crates back inside.

We did not expect this many people at the bird sanctuary. The ones already on the grass with their picnics were forced to put everything away and stand to make room for the newcomers. A stern-looking elderly woman took off her coat and put it around the shoulders of a teenage punk girl with red highlights. The quake was renewing my faith in humanity. Everywhere since that day, sudden unexpected kindnesses. One day, Finn and I were on the subway, and a middle-aged man holding on to a pole started sobbing, and the entire train car broke into sobs with him—a communal grieving.

Finn and I were leaving in a week for our Asia backpacking trip. He wasn't doing so well. Siddhartha had died in the quake. The tremor had scared him and he'd flapped like crazy and got his wing trapped in the metal door of the cage. By the time Finn and I got home, it was too late.

Siddhartha's death, the image of the burning falling people, I wasn't sure which haunted Finn more. Something was cracked. He was already fragile. Perhaps more delicate even than me. I had had my visions for so long, and with the newsroom trauma, my childhood memories, images of disaster were nothing new to me.

I had Finn call Usui's father the day after the quake. It wasn't easy telling parents their final surviving son had died. It seemed fated now that Usui went to see his father before the quake.

We attended the Shinto funeral. The senior Usui kindly held it in Tokyo for his son's many Jesuit friends. I had Choko talk me through the Shinto etiquette. We filled an envelope with yen, nothing divisible by four because four meant death. I couldn't decide on a sum. How did you put a price on a life? Shinji suggested the amount. We wrapped the envelope in cloth. When we entered the building, we handed the envelope to two women sitting at a front table.

Inside the main room, besides the dozens of Jesuit priests, a band of homeless men from the tent city gathered. I saw Akina. I went up and put my forehead against her faux fur jacket. She had a black eye and a bandaged wrist. I was just so happy she was alive. She petted my hair and spoke to me in childish English.

Two lines of relatives stood on either side of a photo of Usui. Finn and I went up to it, as Choko had instructed. A bowl of holy water sat in front of the picture. I hardly recognized the photo of Usui; it must've been taken before he became a missionary. His hair was short, the hint of a smile. He looked so clean, so vigorous, so innocent. We bowed to each of the relatives in turn. From the father, such grief, such a wail rising from the throat. The mother gave me a quick return bow.

The open casket sat in another room. Only men were allowed. I caught glimpses as the door swung open. The men sat around the

air

coffin in a semicircle, drinking sake and talking. I wanted desperately to go in, but it just wasn't done. It didn't matter. I knew Usui wasn't in that body anymore. I knew that flesh wasn't his home. I'd felt him in the air the moment I'd entered the room, his spirit floating down.

Back at his picture, I took up beads, draped them across my palm and prayed. *Thank you*, I said to Usui's ghost. *Thank you. Thank you.*

The sun was setting on Tokyo Bay. Finn made an announcement from the bandstand. It was time. People swarmed to the bay's edge, sending birds into wild flight.

Each person lit their candle, leaned and set the lantern on the water. *Toro nagashi*—"lantern flow." The light would guide the spirits of the departed back to the other world. *Toro nagashi* was a tradition that went back centuries. It was a ritual used on the anniversaries of the Nagasaki and Hiroshima bombings.

I was next to group of elderly women. We lit our lanterns and set them afloat. The crowd had to go in turns because there wasn't enough room for everyone at the shore. The band came down at the end and sent their lanterns off, too.

Thousands of tiny spots of light like fireflies across the bay. The current took them, floated them outward. The band started to play a subdued tune. It was Finn's song, *Usui's Ghost*. The haunting sounds blew upon the wind, stretched over the rippling water. I wanted to pretend every one of the lanterns was for Usui. I wanted to imagine all the lights were there to guide only him. He was a good man. I'd grown up with a damaged man, and the goodness of Usui had wound itself inside me. *Please do not be Ideko, Purr*-chan. His voice in my ear as if he were there next to me.

Dancing lights on the water. I'd finally read Jason's letter. He'd gotten another dog, named it Lady. He wrote that he'd take good care of her from a pup, so she wouldn't need the "luck." At the end he added, "I finally realized what was different about you. In the clearing. I was seeing that you'd made up your mind. That you weren't coming back. Ever. Even if you didn't know it yet, I saw that you were moving on. I saw how much courage that took. I saw how brave you are. I saw how that would change you, had already changed you."

Yuriko was right. It was time I wrote him back. He deserved to know. Yuriko. By God, I would miss Yuriko when Finn and I left Tokyo. Another death. Another prayer sent out with the receding lights on the bay.

Something was happening with the band. People stared at the bandstand, then out to sea. Cries went up from the crowd. I strained to see. Finn was center stage. He seemed to be the only one playing. He blew short sharp notes on the sax. From out in the water, there was a staccato reply. The notes from Finn, the reply from the water. Back and forth.

I worked my way through the crowd to get to the water's edge to see what was going on. Profiled in the darkening sky, perched on one of the posts, was a crane. With every note Finn played, the crane responded. Call. Response. Call. Response.

Relief or grief or joy hit the crowd in waves.

Usui-san? I knelt on the shore. *Usui*-san, *is that you?*

I understood then why he had folded two thousand cranes, why he had worked so hard to create enough for two wishes. The second thousand were for me. He was granting me a wish.

To the clank of the sax and the crane's stuttered rejoinder, to the specks of radiance fading on the horizon, I leaned my forehead down to the ground in supplication. Instead of a wish, these were the words that came to me.

I'm ready.

PEARL'S JOURNEY BEGINS in the prequel, Earth, the first book in the Elemental Journey Series.

Pearl is 13 on the day of her awakening. In the garden with her mother, an Osage woman appears in a sudden vision that transform's Pearl's world. More visions follow and Pearl tries to understand what is happening to her. She learns her Aunt Nadine has a similar "gift", and bicycles across the state to find her, a journey that will lead her to her run-away sister. Pearl's visions, her parents' fear, and society's judgment will take the girl down a slippery slope. She will have to figure out how to survive in a world that wants to brand her as crazy.

Read Earth, the first book in the
series. Available at your favorite
online booksellers, and
at _carolineallen.com_.

THE FOLLOWING QUESTIONS are designed to spark discussion around plot, characters, setting and themes in *Air* for book groups and individual readers.

To investigate further, readers can find an Enhanced Book Group Guide, including additional discussion questions and writing exercises, as well as recommended reading on subjects like mysticism and visual art at www.carolineallen.com.

1. Pearl left Missouri to find a place where she could float above the culture, a place "where even language could not interfere." What does the book say about distancing oneself from a place, or from the past? What are the benefits of such distance for Pearl's life? What are the negative consequences?

2. Distancing appears in other ways, including distancing oneself from the earth. "Toughen up. They taught me well, leathered my soul and callused the spirit. Growing up, everybody's vision of the earth was so mean. Each day of my life, each year, was a study in distancing." How does Pearl's experience of being distanced from the earth as a child reflect in her own distancing now, from Missouri? From Jason? Bonnie? Her mother? What are the continued consequences of such distancing?

3. Another aspect of distancing is Pearl's desire to create distance from herself. What are some examples of how Pearl attempts to pull back from herself? Is she successful in doing this? She says she learns that you can't outrun yourself. "That was the problem. I couldn't get distance from myself." Can a person create distance from themselves, in your opinion? If so, what are the consequences of backing away from ourselves?

4. Breathing and breath play a big role in the book. Father Dennis tells Pearl, "Do you know that the word *yahweh* stands for breathing? *Yah* is the sound of inhaling. *Weh* is the sound of breathing out." In what other ways does breath play a role in the book (characters, situations)? Why is this an important theme?

5. Pearl finds Usui living as a homeless person. Why has he made himself homeless? He says that Pearl, too, is homeless, that by leaving Missouri she has made herself so. Do you agree with this? How does Usui's homelessness reflect Pearl's?

    He says toward the end of the book, "Where is home, Purr-chan? Is it Misery? Is it mission? Is it cardboard? Is it flesh? Where?" What is the book saying about homelessness and finding home on a bigger level than just Pearl and Usui? How does Usui equate homelessness to people like Ideko, to the world? Do you agree with his assessment?

6. The book talks a great deal about magic. Pearl sees a psychic who says, "You do not trust magic. This is why they will keep talking to you the way they do, because you have no trust for mystery." Usui says, "Do you see? The world has lost magic. You have magic. The Ideko world, no one can survive.

World cannot survive without magic." What does the word "magic" mean to Usui? To Pearl?

7. Pearl finds herself juggling realities several times in the book. "All my life I'd lived between worlds. This physical world with tray tables and seat cushions, and that other world, that other reality that I did everything in my power to avoid, ignore. Smash down.

She also must juggle two cultures, the American and the Japanese. What are the benefits of maneuvering different cultures? The difficulties?

Yuriko, with her Japanese-American heritage, must come to terms with two realities, as well. How is the challenge of being part of two nations reflected in Yuriko's life?

What other elements are the characters attempting to balance in the book?

8. When Pearl starts dating Shinji but really doesn't want to, she wonders if some women didn't just spend their whole lives pretending. Why does Pearl pretend that she wants to date Shinji? What other types of pretending occur in the book? Why and in what capacity do people pretend in their lives? How do you think pretending affects a person's ability to grow?

9. Serendipity abounds in *Air*. Pearl shows up at her new apartment and realizes she'll be sharing it with Yuriko, the woman she met on the plane. They "were always laughing about the serendipity of meeting each other again."

Pearl notices that Jason's paintings are similar to Yuriko's. "I thought it was jet lag and too many beers, and that I was seeing things that weren't there. He was painting a self-portrait, and the edges of his face and neck melted away at the sides as if the flesh had no boundaries. The face itself was smeared as if a big burst of wind had blown the nose and eyes sideways. It was so close to Yuriko's paintings it was astonishing." The two artists are thousands of miles apart.

How could it be that Yuriko and Jason are painting a similar theme? How is it possible that Yuriko and Pearl meet again and share an apartment? Do you believe in such serendipity?

What other instances of serendipity exist in the novel? What do you think the author is trying to say about serendipitous events?

10. Pearl has chosen not to take the traditional female route of marriage and children like her childhood friend Bonnie, who has a son and husband. "Her bringing another life into the storyline like that, when we were only seventeen and didn't know who the hell we were. It confused me. It upset me." We know what Pearl thinks of Bonnie's life choices—what does Bonnie think of Pearl's? What do you think of these two different life trajectories?

11. The psychic tells Pearl, "You are in a place of manifesting negatively. When you're not aligned with spirit, you'll bring into your life what you do not want. Then you must violently extract yourself."

In what ways does Pearl have to violently extract herself? In what other ways does this violent extraction show itself in the book?

12. As Pearl works in the *Kaze* newsroom, she notices, "The earth was getting worse and the violence was getting worse.

More mudslides. More murders. More hurricanes. More war. More drought. More domestic violence." Do you think world violence and global climate change go hand in hand, as Pearl seems to suggest?

13. Pearl says, "How could you find yourself when the very earth beneath your feet was unstable? How could you figure out how you were or what you wanted, or how you wanted to grow up, if you couldn't even trust the air or the water? What did that do to your psyche? What did that do to your soul?" How do you think climate change affects a person as they are growing into adulthood?

14. "When you go abroad, your whole life will blow up like a balloon. When you do something big like that, your life will just keep expanding," a *National Geographic* photographer says to Pearl on a photo shoot of Missouri rivers. "You'll have to keep broadening your horizons to keep the balloon full. You'll have to keep it from deflating." How does Pearl's "balloon" expand in Tokyo? With Usui, Yuriko, Finn, in the newsroom? Jason is worried she's under so much stress her balloon might pop. In what ways do you see this playing out in the book?

15. As he obsessively folds cranes, Usui discusses the Legend of a Thousand Cranes. If one folds a thousand cranes he will be granted a wish. He ends up creating more than two thousand, enough for two wishes. At the end of the book, Pearl bends down to make her wish, the wish that Usui gave her, and these words come to her: *I'm ready*. What do you think this means?

Print layout and design by E-BookBuilders;
digital division of The Book Connection